The Devil on Her Tongue

Also by Linda Holeman

The

DEVIL ON HER TONGUE

TONGUE

A Novel of Eighteenth-Century Portugal

LINDA
HOLEMAN

RANDOM HOUSE CANADA

PUBLISHED BY RANDOM HOUSE CANADA

Copyright © 2014 Linda Holeman

This book is a work of fiction. Names, characters, places and incidents either are the product
of the author's imagination or are used fictitiously. Any resemblance to actual persons,
living or dead, events or locales is entirely coincidental.

Interior image credits: p. 1, From W.H. Koebel's *Madeira: Old and New*, illus. Mildred Cossart.
(London: Francis Griffiths, 1909); p. 9, Credit: DEA Picture Library/De Agostini/Getty Images;
p. 151, © British Library Board/Robana; p. 261, *Vue De L'Ile De Madère Prise De La Rade*, drawn by
E. Goury, engraved by Alès (1841); p. 469, *Vista y prospettiva del palacio del Rey de Portugal en Lisbona*,
G.G Winckler (1750), courtesy of the National Library of Portugal; borders © Nadezda Kostina/Dreamstime.com

Library and Archives Canada Cataloguing in Publication

Holeman, Linda,
The devil on her tongue / Linda Holeman.

Issued in print and electronic formats.

ISBN 978-0-307-36162-2
eBook ISBN 978-0-307-36164-6

I. Title.

PS8565.O6225D478 2014   C813'.54   C2013-906397-8

Cover and text design by Terri Nimmo

Cover images: (woman) © Yolande De Kort / Trevillion Images;
(beach) © Luisafonso, (border) © Nadezda Kostina, both Dreamstime.com

Printed and bound in the United States of America

2 4 6 8 9 7 5 3 1

For Martin

PROLOGUE

ISLE DE MADERE

OCEAN

I MADERE

I.es PORT SAINCT

S.te Croix

Funchol

I. DESERTE

Marasylo

Leon

OCCIDENTAL

MADEIRA ARCHIPELAGO PORTUGAL

1730

ESTRA WALKED THE DESERTED STRIP OF CALHETA BEACH EVERY
morning as the sun rose, searching for limpets and treasures. The
curve of fine yellow sand was protected by the rocky islet of Baixo,
creating a small natural bay that collected what the sea spewed up
during the night. The stretch of Atlantic between the Madeira
archipelago and North Africa regularly washed up the salvage from
ships. During the worst of the storms, caravels and galleons,
brigantines, doggers and corvettes went down as they attempted to
sail west to the colony of Brazil or east, around the Horn of Africa,
and the remnants ended up here, on the beach of the small island of
Porto Santo.

Under a sky washed with pink streaks, Estra poked her stout pole
into the hard, wet sand between the algae-covered stones that
emerged as the tide went out. She had already been beyond the
wind-buffeted rocks above the dunes to collect vegetation for her
potions, and now she adjusted the sling, brimming with kelp and sea
rocket, knotweed, purge and milk thistle, across her chest.

She didn't see Arie until she was almost upon him. He was lying
on his stomach in the surf, foamy water swirling around him. His
face rested on one bent arm, and his hair, caked with sand, was
almost white, but not the white of an old man. It was white-gold.
A knotted piece of leather was around his neck. Estra pushed back
her crown—the circle of tough seagrass wound with bits of glass
and shot she had fashioned for herself—and poked his back with
her pole. He didn't move.

She leaned over, thinking him a dead pirate. It wouldn't be the first time she had found a dead man, usually a bloated mound with trailing strips of cloth and fingers stiffened into claws. She always left them where they lay, and eventually the fishermen of the beach tied stones around them and disposed of them far out to sea.

A tiny sea crab scurried through that odd-coloured hair, dropping onto the sand below. The man was attached to a swollen wooden cask stamped with the letters *VOC* by a chain looped around his narrow hips. Ragged rope encircled both wrists. The barefoot body, in loose black trousers and a torn shirt of coarse bleached cotton, held no secrets. There was no salvage near him, nothing but long knotted seaweed and stinking kelp, so he wasn't from a caravel that had gone down. No, he must have fallen overboard. She knew it happened: young men, new to the rise and fall of the ship's rhythm, sometimes fell from the crow's nest or the high riggings. She touched the barrel with her foot; it rolled, watertight and empty. But why was he attached to an empty barrel?

She knelt beside him and bent to get a glimpse of the side of his face. There was a small oblong piece of silver attached to the leather thong around his neck. She picked it up and tugged, hoping to tear it free. With unexpected, shocking swiftness, the man's hand grabbed her wrist. She cried out as she yanked free and leapt back, holding her pole in front of her.

The man slowly rolled over. His straw-coloured eyelashes fluttered as he looked up at her, blinking sand. His face was burned and flaking, crusted with salt, his lips puffy and cracked. He croaked out a sentence—it sounded like a question—but she couldn't understand. As he painfully sat up, Estra backed farther away.

She had never seen hair like this, nor eyes such a clear, pale blue. She drew a deep breath.

It was him. He was here.

⁊

Arie ten Brink thought Estra was an apparition, perhaps the Black Madonna he had heard about, whose plaster image could be viewed at the monastery of Montserrat near Barcelona. Or maybe a dusky angel with her nimbus askew, the sun glinting off it and casting prisms onto her face.

The last face he had looked into had belonged to Broos, his executioner. Broos had led Arie to the prow of the Indiaman *Slot ter Hooge*, his hands tied in front of him with thick, tar-smeared rope. Broos was instructed to run Arie through with a sword—no point in wasting ammunition—and throw him overboard. But Broos was from Arie's home of Middelburg in Zeeland; they had been childhood friends and had joined the Dutch East India Company at the same time. They had crewed together before, and on this voyage, aboard the ship bound for the strongholds of the Dutch East India Company in Batavia, Broos had the bunk below Arie's. They often passed the dark hour before sleep sharing memories of their lives in Middelburg. On their steady sea diet of maggoty salt pork and weevil-ridden hard tack, fusty water and warm, sour beer, they fantasized about their mothers' spring vegetable soup with meatballs, or the pots of cooked red cabbage and apples always on the stove, or Sunday breakfasts of *stroopwafels*, syrup waffles so sweet they gave toothache. They compared the girls they remembered, and talked of the autumn air, cool and fresh, blowing in off the Zuider Zee.

But less than a month into the eight-month voyage, Arie had killed the bosun Falco, a heartless, meat-handed man who found pleasure in taking the youngest cabin boys in the most bestial of ways. When Arie came upon Falco brutalizing little Jansie, ten years old and on his first sea voyage, he tried to pull Falco away. Falco, laughing, wouldn't be stopped. Arie saw Jansie's face with its panic and pain, and suddenly the years fell away and it was his own face he saw. He picked up the nearest object—the heavy breech lock of a broken cannon—and struck Falco. Meaning only to stop the child's torture, he broke Falco's neck.

While the commander did not approve of the coarser pastimes of some of his sailors, he could not let the rest of the crew think he condoned killing. Falco had already been wrapped in a winding sheet and tipped over the ship's edge with small formality; now it was Arie's turn.

While they had all hated Falco, Arie was a friend to many of them. Fearing mutiny over the condemning of Arie, the commander kept the crew below deck, pouring extra rations of kill-devil, a foul-tasting, fermented sugar-cane concoction that passed as rum. He allowed no one to follow Broos as he led Arie away.

Alone on the deck, Broos asked Arie why he had been so foolhardy as to try to protect Jansie. Jansie would have survived. Broos said, "Arie, we survived."

Arie said nothing. In that moment of picking up the breech lock, he'd thought of Jansie growing into a man with memories that still woke him at night, sweating, the taste of fear in his mouth. A man like him. He didn't wish that on the child.

Before Broos lifted the sword, he apologized, and Arie closed his eyes and took a deep breath as the blade whistled through the air. But Broos only sliced through the ropes around Arie's wrists, and said, "I can't kill you, old friend. But . . . what am I to do?"

"Tell my parents I died an honourable death," Arie said, then climbed over the side and dropped into the water. As he bobbed to the surface, Broos threw an empty water cask, wrapped with a chain, into the waves. Holding on to the barrel, Arie watched the ship until it disappeared into the heavy swells.

He managed to wrap the chain around his waist and attach himself to the barrel. He pulled the cork from it, but there was only the stink of the algae that spoiled so much of the stored water. He banged the cork back in and held on, floating with the cask, through darkness and light and darkness again. By the time he felt the hard push of sand under him, he was incapable of forming a rational thought. As his body scraped in and out against the shelf of sand with each push of the water, he imagined himself a piece of glass, his rough edges smoothing in the tumble of sand and salt and sea.

And then he knew nothing more until he was awakened by a pull on the thong around his neck.

He met the girl's unblinking green eyes under thick, arched black eyebrows. "Am I in Heaven?" he asked in Dutch.

The apparition reached up and scratched her cheek. He saw the dirt under her broken fingernails, and with that knew she wasn't an angel. He looked from her face to her white blouse, patched and yellowing, to the ragged brown skirt and finally to her bare ankles, delicate yet strong. A cloth sling across her chest was stuffed with kelp and plant life. He couldn't imagine how long he'd been in the water, nor how far the tides had carried him. He only knew he was alive. He silently thanked the God of his Calvinist beliefs, the God who arbitrarily chose to damn some men and allowed others to live.

He brought his silver amulet containing the fragment of his own birth caul to his lips and kissed it. His mother had been right to keep it, and give him the sailor's talisman when he first went to sea. With God's hand, it had saved him from drowning.

"Azores?" he asked.

"Porto Santo," the young woman replied.

It was another miracle. Had he been carried farther south, he might have been dashed to death against the rocky shoreline of the neighbouring island of Madeira. More luck had been with him that the current hadn't pulled him to the tiny chain of Ilhas Desertas, with no fresh water or flora, the only inhabitants monk seals and bird colonies. He would have perished, with no hope of rescue.

He slowly got to his feet, leaning heavily on the barrel for support, but his legs felt filled with sea water. He fell. The girl, whose face had changed from suspicious to something else, something almost welcoming, handed him her pole. He took it, grateful, and was able to haul himself up. The trembling in his legs abated, and he took one hesitant step. She tipped her head, gesturing for him to follow her. Arie leaned heavily on the pole as he followed, dragging the barrel, over a berm of seagrass and flat cacti to a rough shelter in a hollow of rocks. A dented, blackened pot sat on a pile of glowing embers in the sand.

She pointed to a broad, flat stone. He lowered himself onto it and the girl handed him a wooden bowl of warm broth filled with chunks of fish and pungent greens.

"*Obrigata*," he said, fighting tears of exhaustion and gratitude, and then drank, his hands shaking. "Excuse me," he said when the bowl was empty. For all he was a sailor, and had for the last seven years lived at sea in the roughest of conditions, he still had the manners his mother had instilled in him. The young woman took his bowl and filled it again, and this time, his hands a little steadier and his stomach calmed, he was able to sip.

When he had finished the second bowl, she produced a small earthen pot of ointment, cool and musty-smelling. She lightly brushed the sand and salt from his burns and smoothed the ointment, with barely discernible strokes, over his skin and lips.

When she stepped away, he stood and said, in halting, clear Portuguese, "I am a Dutchman. I was employed by the Dutch East India Trading Company, on a merchant ship run by the Verenighde Oostindische Compangnie."

The girl lifted a section of his chain, tugging lightly on two of the links as if to test them.

He bowed slightly. "My name, senhorita," he said, straightening his torn shirt, "is Arie ten Brink." He watched her hands on the chain. "And if you can help me unburden myself of this barrel and direct me to the nearest town, I will not trouble you again."

PART I

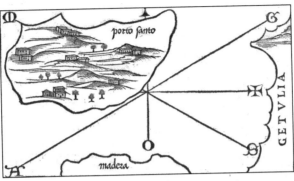

CALHETA BEACH, PORTO SANTO

Fifteen Years Later

1745

CHAPTER ONE

My father woke me as the sun was rising. He didn't speak, but something about the way he looked at me in the dim light of our hut filled me with a prickly foreboding. He took my hand, pulling me out of bed, and led me into the morning air, pink-tinted with the rising sun. In his other hand he was carrying a canvas sack.

My mother called our names in a voice high and breathless, threaded with fear. We both looked back at the hut as she ran from it, her thick black hair loose. She was crying; that alone was strange and frightening. I had never seen her weep.

"You're not taking her, you're not, Arie. She's mine. You can't leave with her," she shouted.

"Stop. Stop it, Estra. Listen to what I have to say." My father had raised his voice to be heard over Mama's. He dropped his sack.

My mother stopped abruptly, tears running from her eyes. The pipits nesting in the long grass in the dunes were stirring, softly worrying and calling.

"*Vader,*" I said. "What does she mean? Where are you going?" I was confused and frightened at my mother's words, spat out with such venom. The part about him leaving couldn't be true. My father, so tall, with his yellow hair almost white from the sun and his eyes the colour of bleached blue porcelain, wouldn't do such a thing. He was only going to walk up the length of the golden beach into Vila Baleira, as always.

"He's going back to the sea," my mother railed now, still weeping. "I always knew it. I saw it the moment he washed up on the beach.

He would betray me and leave. I saw it, and yet I paid no heed."

I looked from her to him. I was past thirteen, and for the last few years had heard so many shouted words between them. In that moment I understood my father really was going away, going farther than town. But all I could manage was, "Don't go, *Vader*."

He put his hand on my arm, but Mama stepped between us, pushing me aside as she slapped his face and ears. "Go then, go to your diamond dreams, Dutchman," she shouted. "Go and leave us to starve."

My father took her slaps until finally she stopped, exhausted, her hands hanging at her sides.

"Estra. We've spoken of this for too long. I have tried to make you understand—"

"I understand," my mother said. "You're a bastard, and a deserter. First the ships, and then your family. Is that what you want *her* to understand?" Mama's voice caught in her throat as she waved in my direction.

And then there were only the cries of the gulls. My hands turned into fists, and I brought them to my mouth. My father held my shoulders and looked at me. His face became close and too large, and then small and far away, like the white face of the moon. My stomach hurt.

"*Meijn klein vos,*" he said. "My little fox. I will take you if you want to come. I have waited until you were old enough. I'm going to the New World, to the city of São Paulo in the colony of Brazil. You can come with me or stay with your mother. Your choice."

I squeezed my eyes shut. Then I opened them and looked at my mother, her face wet with tears.

"Don't leave me, Diamantina. Don't go," she said. "You're all I have." Surely her unfamiliar tears meant she loved me. She'd never told me she loved me, unlike my father, who whispered it to me every night as he blew out the candle beside my pallet. Now my mother fell to her knees. "Don't leave me, Diamantina," she said again. "It's not written in the smoke that you leave yet. You know the smoke tells the truth."

The gulls were closer, screaming as my mother had moments earlier.

"What will you choose, daughter?" my father asked quietly, against the soft, steady rush rush rush of each tiny wave to the shore. "Will you come with me, or stay with your mother?"

A rottenness rose in my throat, the taste like fish that had sat in the grease of the pan too long. "I don't know what to do," I finally whispered.

"You know what to do, Diamantina. Indecision is for the lazy."

I lifted my chin. "I want to go with you, but how can I leave Mama?"

He stared at me, his lips tightening. Then he said, "Yes, she needs you more than I. It's right. It's right, Diamantina."

Was my decision made by my question? I couldn't think. I swallowed and swallowed, and when I was finally able to speak, I said, "You'll come back, won't you? You'll come back."

I saw my father's throat move. "I will see you again, Diamantina," he said, in a voice that was not his own. "I give you my promise that we will see each other again. I will write to you when I arrive in São Paulo." He looked at my mother. "Go to the church when you are in need," he said. "Father da Chagos will help you. I have already spoken to him. I will send word and money through him to you."

My mother made a sound as though she were drowning. The rising sun was behind her, and I could no longer see her face.

My father held me then. I put my arms around him and wept against his chest, my cries similar to those of the circling gulls. I smelled his familiar scent, salt and tobacco. Then he pulled away from me and took off his talisman and put it over my head.

I closed my hand around the soldered piece of silver. "No, *Vader*. If you're going back to sea, you need this."

He almost smiled. "The caul saved me. It only works once for its wearer. Now you will be protected from the sea."

He slung his canvas sack over his shoulder and turned, walking briskly away from me on the hard, wet morning sand.

I ran after him, something cutting into the bottom of my foot. *"Vader,"* I called, and he turned. "No, no. I want to come. I said the wrong thing—take me with you."

"You chose, Diamantina. Once you make a choice, you cannot go back. Stay with your mother."

I was crying, standing on one foot and pressing the big toe of the injured one into the sand for balance. "Please, *Vader*. Please."

He turned again and kept walking, farther and farther from me, until he became one of the stick figures I had drawn in the sand when I was a small child: two long thin legs, two long thin arms, a circle in the middle, and a smaller oval above.

Turn and wave to me, I thought. *Turn and wave, and then I'll know you're coming back.*

The leg holding my weight trembled violently, and then wouldn't support me any longer. As I fell, it was as if the beach had opened its big, sandy mouth and swallowed my father whole.

He was gone. He hadn't waved.

CHAPTER TWO

I didn't remember making my way back to the hut, but now I lay with my mother in her bed, both of us crying. The early morning light flickered through the cracks of the shuttered window, creating a dancing light that hurt my eyes.

And then I must have slept, for when I next opened my eyes I was damp from the heat of my mother's body, but she no longer held me trapped against her. As I sat up, she moaned and spoke in her secret language, and then turned to face the wall.

I limped outside and sat on the flat rock outside our hut. I looked at the bottom of my foot, and seeing the thick smear of dried blood across the pad of flesh just under my toes, went into the warm, lapping waves. The cut burned with the salt. I shaded my eyes and stared towards Vila Baleira; I would go there and find my father before he sailed away. I had made a mistake: I didn't want to stay with my mother.

Vila Baleira was too far to walk with my throbbing foot, so I went to my boat. On the bottom lay two packages, wrapped in stained canvas and tied with hairy twine. My name was written in charcoal on one of the packages, and my mother's on the other. I pushed my boat into the water and climbed in.

We had our fishing boat, with its woven bait basket floating behind. But this was my own boat, the one my father had made for me when I was six years old. It was shorter and narrow, with a set of oars a child could manage.

When he finished the last of the tarring late one summer evening, we lay on the sand, looking up at the sky. He told me about wanting to sail to the land called Brazil to search for the diamonds in great abundance there. "A diamond is like a star, hard and bright, sparkling and beautiful, but small enough to hold in your hand. Unlike stars, which are of the air, diamonds are of the earth. They grow in the dark, under the soil, waiting for someone to uncover them, so that they can show their beauty. That's how I came to choose your name. You are my own diamond. My Diamantina."

He flexed his hands, black and sticky, showing me the patterns of the stars. He explained how he had once weighed the sun with an astrolabe, and had guided a caravel through the night by measuring the height of the stars with a cross-staff and pointing his quadrant at the North Star and the Great Dog.

"Let's name my boat *Dog Star*," I said.

"All boats are female, Diamantina. You should choose a female name for your boat."

"No. I want it to be *Dog Star*," I argued, and he laughed and said, "All right, my girl."

The next day, as he stitched the sail from the heavy cloth he called *zeildoek*, he told me that with a sail *Dog Star* could go much faster, farther out into the ocean, and it would feel as though I were running with the wind. When he spoke of the snap and billow of the sail filling with air, and the freedom of being on the sea, something like regret was on his face. "The sea contains both terrors and marvels," he said. "I love the sea, and I know you do too, Diamantina," he told me, holding up his cutting knife so I could see my reflection. "But you also love the land—look at your eyes. They're the colour of both. Not green like your mother's, and not blue like mine, some days your eyes are the slate of the basalt of the island, and other days the silver of the fish."

I stared into my distorted image in the wide, glinting blade: my eyes framed by dark lashes, the tangle of my white-blond hair, my skin darkened further by the sun and wind. "With the sail, Mama and you and I can sail to Brazil, and find beautiful diamonds."

He put down the knife and smiled, pushing the heavy needle in and out of the thick cloth. "I will be a fine gentleman in a waistcoat with a watch chain, Diamantina, and you and your mother will wear shoes that click and clack along the paving stones of the city. And you shall also have hats with feathers and strings of diamonds around your necks."

I was too young to understand the distance between the islands of the Madeira archipelago and the New World. It was a fanciful tale about my little boat out on the open water, and it was our story, and I loved it.

But the sail had long ago fallen into tatters; it hadn't seemed important to make another. As I grew older, my father had made longer oars for me. Now I struggled to slice through the waves with them, as a difficult wind had blown up. The gulls and terns overhead seemed motionless, their wings spread as they battled to stay in place. I was one of them; as hard as I rowed, I made no progress. The wind was telling me I couldn't follow my father. Finally I dropped the oars and let *Dog Star* rock on the waves. Surely a caravel or brigantine would pass. I saw them regularly, passing Porto Santo, coming from far-off places like Nederland or England, setting their compasses to pass through our archipelago to the Canary Islands. After that, they would call in at Cape Verde and from there set a course, southeasterly, around the tip of Africa to Macao or Goa or all the way to Batavia, or southwesterly to Brazil. My father spoke of his many sea voyages, all easterly, saying that Brazil still awaited him.

My father would be on a ship that would sail by if I waited long enough. When it was within view, I would stand in *Dog Star* and wave my arms over my head. My father would see me, and know he didn't want to leave me. He would jump over the side and swim back to me, his arms making great arcs as he sliced through the water. *I will see you again,* he had said. He would see me now.

I sat in *Dog Star* a long time, clutching my father's amulet, looking at the packages he'd left us. The boat, rocking, drifted back to the beach. The wind and the water grew calmer. Nothing sailed by, either far out at sea or closer to shore. My foot hurt and I was hungry. I rowed the short distance home and tied the boat to its rock. I took the packages and went inside our hut.

My mother sat at the table in the centre of the room in a shaft of sunlight that fell through the open doorway, her earthenware bowl on the table in front of her. Smoke swirled around her and then rose in a fine, straight line towards the low, blackened ceiling. The scent of wormwood was light and comforting, and yet there was a darker undertone, an odour I didn't recognize. I thought I knew all the herbs and roots my mother burned.

In spite of the unknown smell, seeing her reassured me. "Are you making a potion to bring him back?" I asked, and she looked up. The sun cut her face in two, and she bared her teeth. The woman at the table was no longer my mother, but the witch everyone called her. Her thick black hair writhed around her head like snakes, and her green eyes, narrow and slanted, glinted and sparked. Startled, I drew a deep breath, and it was as if I'd called the unknown dark smoke into me. I dropped the packages and clapped my hand over my nose and mouth to prevent it from entering me. I stepped backwards and blocked the sun, and the light on her face changed, and she was my mother again.

"No," she said. "There is no such potion."

The image of the witch was too fresh. Not looking at her, I picked up the packages and went to my pallet. I untied the twine on mine. "*Vader* left us something."

My mother came and took the opened package from me. "It's the least he could do. Hopefully enough *réis* to support us for a while."

Books and passage charts fell to the floor. I knelt beside them: volumes in Portuguese and in Dutch, an atlas of the Iberian Peninsula, a map of Portugal, a bound collection of sea charts, vellum diagrams of the coast, written instructions for navigation and the location of ports.

"Books? Books and maps?" my mother said, her voice flat.

"That one's for you." I pointed at the second package on my pallet.

She opened it. There were the réis she hoped for. To me it appeared to be all the money in the world, a big pile of silver and copper coins. And there was also a pair of shoes such as the ladies of Vila Baleira wore when they went to church on Sunday: black leather with a silver buckle and low, solid heels. Neither my mother nor I owned shoes. Nor did we go to Nossa Senhora da Piedade, the church in the town square.

There was a scrap of paper tucked into one of the shoes. I pulled it out. My mother couldn't read, so I read it aloud to her.

Estra, I remember you once telling me that you had never worn shoes.

"Shoes," she finally said. "Shoes," she repeated, then hurled them into the cold fireplace. They hit the rectangle of stones and ash flew into the air, and I heard my father's voice saying that my mother and I would one day be fine ladies, our shoes tapping across city streets. She picked up my books and rolled maps and charts, holding them against her chest as she went towards the door.

"Mama, please. They're mine." I ran after her, pulling at the back of her blouse.

Gripping everything firmly, she strode from the house towards the sea, the afternoon sun glinting on the water. "This is what I think of what he left," she said, wading into the water up to her calves and tossing a book into the slight swell. "This and this," she said, throwing all of them into the sea before I could stop her.

Furious, I waded past her. I picked up the closest floating book and unfurling map, pushing against the water to get to the next book. I managed to retrieve three of them as well as the biggest vellum chart as others floated away. I waded back and dumped the books and map and chart into *Dog Star* and pushed the boat out as my mother went back to the hut.

I rowed towards one of the open, floating maps and used the oar to bring it closer. When it was within reach, I hung over the side as far as I could and closed my fingers around it. In this way I managed to retrieve two more books. Another small book kept floating just out of reach. I slid over the side of the boat and swam to it, putting it between my teeth and swimming back. I thought of my father taking me out into the warm, shallow water when I was small, my skirt floating up around me as he held me safe. I kicked my legs and put my face in and out of the water and moved my arms in the arcs he showed me.

By the time I hauled myself into the boat, the last book had gone. As my boat drifted to sea, I lay on the bottom, shivering in my wet skirt and blouse. I gathered the books to me and closed my burning eyes, the sun warming me. I thought of my father teaching me to read and write, first in Dutch and then in Portuguese, using a sharpened stick to write on the wet sand near the water. Every day when I went with him to bring in the nets or search for seabird eggs, I spent a long time using the pointed stick to write the words I had learned the day before.

Then, as I watched, the words were washed away by the tireless sea.

CHAPTER THREE

When I heard my name, I blinked and sat up, realizing I'd been asleep, dreaming that my father had come back to me. But it was Marco Perez, our neighbour from down the beach. He held *Dog Star*'s gunnel, his own small boat gently rocking against it. His son Abílio was with him.

Marco had a broad chest and thick neck, and was known for his violence. His wife, Lía, had sometimes come to my mother for help with her injuries. She had died the year before. Abílio, older than me by four years, was as fine-featured and slender as his mother had been. He moved with a confident grace, his hands quick and restless, his laugh easy. Today he had a bloodshot eye and a slightly swollen bruise on his left cheekbone. His father had broken his nose when he was a boy, and it had a slight lean to the right.

"What are you doing, Diamantina?" Abílio asked. "We saw your boat drifting so far out, and thought it had come loose."

I got up onto the seat and picked up the oars. My teeth were chattering, and I clenched my jaw, but that only made it worse.

"Come on," Marco said to his son. "She can get back to shore on her own." He started to push away from *Dog Star*, but Abílio grabbed my boat again.

"The wind is coming up," he said, and in one swift movement he climbed into my boat. He sat beside me on the bench and, taking the oars, said, "I'll row you back."

His father pushed away from us. Abílio effortlessly turned the boat towards the shore.

"I could have rowed myself," I said, sitting on the floor again and picking up the saturated books and charts.

He kept rowing. As we approached the beach, he jumped out and pulled the boat up on the sand and secured *Dog Star*'s rope to a rock.

I clambered out with my arms full.

"What have you got there?" he asked, coming closer and taking one of the small wet books from me.

"My father left them for me," I said. "*Gave* them to me," I corrected, not wanting Abílio—not wanting anyone—to know that my father was gone.

Abílio tried to turn the pages, but they were stuck together.

I stepped up to him. "Give it back."

He moved away from me, smiling, holding the book over his head with one hand as if I were a small child.

"Give it to me, or—"

"Or what?"

I narrowed my eyes and hissed some of my mother's words—words that had no meaning to me but that I knew carried weight.

He still smiled. "You think I'm afraid of your curses, little *bruxa*?" Nevertheless, he made the sign of the cross.

"Don't call me a witch," I said.

"Then don't act like one." He tossed the book onto the sand. He stared at me, and I stared back. He wasn't afraid of me like some of the island people, whom I frightened with my fair hair and odd eyes that changed from silver to slate with the reflection of the sky or the sea. My father had said that in his homeland my hair and my height—I was taller than every other girl my age on the island—would not be strange. Here people had seen little of the world, and to them we were an odd pair, with skin darkened by the sun, our light eyes and bleached hair. He also told me I should not upset anyone by staring at them for too long: the superstitious already believed I was of another world, like my mother.

I picked up the book and turned my back on Abílio. Inside the hut, I ignored my mother, who again sat at the table with the smoking bowl. I spread the books and maps on the floor in a patch of sunlight, pinning them open to dry with some of my mother's heavy bowls and earthenware containers. The calfskin and morocco covers were warped and I knew the pages would always be wrinkled, smelling of salt and mildew.

I went to the mantel and took my father's pipe and the box of dominoes he'd made and put them on my pallet. "The books and charts, and these things of *Vader*'s, are mine now," I told my mother. "You can't take them away from me." I was still angry with her because I had chosen to stay with her.

"Come here," she said. The bowl no longer smoked, but a heavy, unfamiliar odour permeated the air. It was a sad smell, a smell of disappointment and decay, of the mealy fungi that grows under the ground. She dipped two fingers into the dark black-red mixture and rubbed it across her forehead, down the bridge of her nose and across her lips.

"Now I will do the same to you," she said, picking up the bowl. "Come."

"No," I said, and brusquely shoved away her hand. The bowl crashed onto the floor, breaking into shards.

My mother cried out. I thought she was upset about the bowl, her favourite, used to burn all her mixtures, but she was staring at my feet. The dark substance was spattered over them.

She dropped to her knees. "Diamantina," she said, her voice low, trembling. "Not the feet. The spell is for the head." Her hands were shaking as well as her voice. "You've changed it. It's all changed now."

Frightened anew by her reaction, I took a step back. "Changed what?"

She slowly pushed herself up, then sat at the table, her face in her hands. "Your future," she whispered. "You've changed your future." She looked up then, and there was a hollowness in her eyes I recognized as grief. "The spell was to free you of your father's hold on you. But now . . . on your feet . . . now you will never be free of him. He will hold you down. He will haunt you forever."

I stood as if made of wood. "Your spell isn't powerful enough to drive my father from me anyway. I will always be the Dutchman's daughter. Always." I went to the fireplace and took out the shoes my mother had thrown there. I put them on, smearing the paste on my feet into my flesh. The shoes were too loose and hurt the bottom of my cut foot. I clomped around the hut nonetheless, staring at my mother until she rose and came to me.

She slapped my face. She had never before struck me. Although my cheek stung, I didn't move or make a sound. I simply stared back at her. She turned and went outside.

After a while, I removed the uncomfortable shoes; the pressure of the leather on the black paste had stained my skin with whorls and prints like the little plovers made as they ran along the sand. I took a rag and scrubbed at the marks, but they remained. I smelled the rag, and realized that she'd burned the sticky red blood from the dragon tree with the rest of her ingredients. She normally didn't use the dragon tree; she said it contained its own power, and needed to be treated with great care and respect.

She didn't return that night. In the past she had regularly left the hut for days, searching the island for herbs and roots and berries. I had never cared; I had my father then.

This night I was alone for the first time. Our small hut was like others on the beach: the walls and even the roof were made of the clay and sand and soil of Porto Santo, with a tiny wash house and *latrina* to one side. From a distance it became part of the island, undetectable where it backed into the dunes. It was at the very end of Porto Santo's southern beach, Ponta da Calheta. Here the sand came to an abrupt halt in a semicircle of craggy rocks and crashing, white-crested waves. It was close to where my mother had found my father. And it was here, in the past, that pirates from Algiers had landed and taken many inhabitants of Porto Santo to sell as slaves. From there, on a clear day, I could see the misty outline of Madeira, the biggest island of our archipelago.

My home was bright and hot when the door and shutters were open, dim and cool when shut against that light and heat. My mother gathered baskets of needles from the pines and tamarisks on the hills and sprinkled them over the dirt floor, replacing them every few weeks so that there was always a fresh earthy smell, mingled with the bitter and yet fragrant aroma of wormwood and the fainter scents of the herbs hanging from the ceiling on lengths of rope. On a long table against one wall she kept her collection of bowls and glass jars and vials filled with knobby brown roots and bright pods and petals and tiny seeds waiting to be crushed in her stone mortar. There were dried twists of kelp, holding ground powders that couldn't abide the light. And rosemary, always sweet rosemary. My mother made herself a perfume of it, and anointed her hair and neck.

I breathed in the fragrances my mother brought to our home as I fell asleep each night. It was like sleeping in a forest, on a beach, in a meadow: all of these sensations usually combined to bring me a sense of peace. But tonight there was no peace. I cried for my father, but I had made my choice, and as he had told me, once a decision is made, you cannot go back. Just before the flame sputtered out in its dish of tallow, I stared again at the marks on my feet.

If you do not come home to me, I will go to you, Vader. I will find you. I had never known a prayer, but this was to become the last thing I whispered to myself every night for a long, long time.

CHAPTER FOUR

I woke frequently through the night, staring at my parents' empty pallet, willing them both to be there, willing yesterday to have been a terrible dream. Before day broke, I got out of bed, angry with both my mother and my father. I took my wracking pole and started up the beach, jabbing my stick between the rocks where the curling foam broke on the beach. It felt good to thrust and stab.

As soon as I was old enough to walk, my mother had tied a long piece of braided twine around my waist and attached it to her own, so I wouldn't stray into the sea while her attention was turned to the shore. She encouraged me to dig with a short stick. When I was small, it was only a game. As I grew old enough to wander the beach alone, I found rusted cauldrons and broken belt buckles, barnacle-encrusted brass pins, the bases of thick, broken green goblets, tin pans, and misshapen lead shot. I ran my fingers over their surfaces, trying to imagine where they'd come from. I made necklaces of strange, wonderful coins with holes in their centres, stringing them on tough seagrass, and wove broken bits of colourful glass and the tear-shaped, dimpled lead shot into more seagrass to create my own crown. I always wore my flowered shawl around my waist. I had found it tangled in a nest of seaweed; the colours brightened my dull brown skirt, and I loved watching the fringes dance in the warm breeze.

The waves and tide tossed up the detritus of sea life: twirled whelks, fish skeletons, dead sea urchins smelling of rot, whorled tritons, carcasses of monk seals from the Ilhas Desertas, and graceful lengths of seaweed and kelp fanned out on the sand like a mermaid's hair. Occasionally I found something of value, and gave it to my father to sell in Vila Baleira. I always accompanied him as he set my found objects on the counter of the shop. He told me that gold or silver artifacts not too corroded by time in the salt water—a bracelet or necklace, an urn, a goblet, a jewel box—would be purchased by the few wealthier families living in Vila Baleira, or by sailors stopping in port looking for a gift for a sweetheart. Occasionally a merchant from Madeira came to buy items to sell to the wealthy English who had settled in the capital, Funchal Town, to prosper in the growing wine trade. The English, he said, loved unique old artifacts and collectibles from foreign pirate ships to decorate the fancy quintas they had built on the verdant hills around Funchal.

Today I went farther down the beach than usual, passing other huts, limping slightly on my sore foot. I saw Marco patching his roof with Abílio. Abílio had two older brothers, but they had left the island to escape their father's fists when they were only a little older than I was now. As Abílio climbed down the ladder with his bucket, he waved to me, and at the same time my pole hit something under the sand. The next small wave exposed a gleaming corner. I knelt and dug with my hands, then pulled the object out of the sucking sand and wiped it with my skirt. It was a small gold snuff box. Clearly, it hadn't been in the water long, as it hadn't been ruined by salt or dulled and scratched by lengthy tossing against sand and rocks. There were no barnacles. It would bring in more réis than anything I had ever found.

"Can I see it?" Abílio had come to me. He stepped closer and held out his hand. "Please?" He smiled.

I put it in his hand. He opened the lid of the snuff box, let it close, opened it and let it close. He brushed off more of the wet sand, then smiled at me again. "A good find, little *bruxa*."

I made a sound in my throat. "I told you not to call me that." I held out my hand for the box.

"It was in front of my hut," he said, still smiling.

"I found it. Give it to me."

His smile hadn't changed. "Of course." He put it into my hand but still held on to it. "If you want me to, I could sell it and give you the réis. The shopkeepers will give me more for it than they would you. You know that. They'll try to cheat you. They won't cheat me. Nobody cheats me. Or maybe I'll trade it for you, and get you something pretty. Something pretty for a pretty girl."

I hesitated, both of us holding the box.

"I'll take it into town right now and bring you something special later. Come on, pretty girl." He was relaxed, his hold on the snuff box loose. I wanted him to keep saying I was pretty.

"Abílio! Get back here," his father shouted, and as Abílio turned to look at him, I pulled the snuff box from his hand.

"I'll sell it and buy myself something special," I said.

He looked back at me, shrugging. "As you like."

I walked back towards my own hut, my pole in one hand and the snuff box firmly gripped in the other.

⁂

When I went into Vila Baleira with the snuff box later that day, it was clear by the way everyone studied me that the whole town knew of my father's departure.

It was the only town on Porto Santo, a quiet port where news of the outside world came in snatches and rumours. On three sides of the main square were fish and meat shops, with their dark smells of blood and bone. There were also the shops selling everything from cloth and thread to tin dishes and pots and pans, twine, spices, and presses for olive oil. The market, where the local women sold eggs, cheese, fruits and vegetables and all manner of seasonal items, was set up on sagging wooden tables and blankets under the shade of the palms and dragon trees that formed a canopy over the square. Nossa Senhora da Piedade, with its *piscina* for holy water at the entrance, dominated the fourth side of the square.

On scattered benches under the trees, farmers in their wide straw hats who crossed the island to bring their grain to market met with fishermen for wine and idle talk. As the shadows lengthened and the day progressed, more men came. In the evening they played quoits or games of *sueca* with thick cards.

A wide street ran from the square down to the long, narrow wharf that led into the sea. Skiffs were used locally around the island or to row out to the ships dropping anchor in the deeper waters of the Atlantic, a safe distance from the shallows near the beach. There were always packet ships from Madeira, carrying mail and the *Gazeta de Lisboa* and foodstuffs and wine and an occasional passenger, as well as the bigger caravels and brigantines from afar. The sailors who came to Vila Baleira might have been at sea a few weeks or a few months. They always went to Rooi's, the inn closest to the wharf.

The rest of the islanders lived scattered between the high cliffs and pebbly beaches of the north and my own flat southern beach. Although Porto Santo had a history of violence, attacked by the French, the Moors and Algerian pirates, the last major invasion had been long before I was born, and the island had relaxed into a sleepy routine, with only local gossip to stir the imagination.

As I crossed the square, Hermínia, the wife of a shopkeeper, took a loaf of bread from her basket and held it towards me. "Take it, dear," she said, but in the next instant her friend Maria grabbed her arm.

"Don't give her any charity," she said, looking at me. "They're heathens, the witch and the Dutchman living in sin, and this odd girl a creation of that immoral life."

My father told me that he had his own God, and that it was not the same one those on Porto Santo worshipped. My mother believed in no god, and refused to enter a church for fear of diluting her powers. Since it had been impossible for Father da Chagos to marry them, the islanders considered that I was born of an unholy union. Did I care? No. When I was small, I had sometimes peeked through the doorway of the church. It was always dark, with a few candles burning here and there, and usually one or two old women on their knees, praying. I'd told myself it didn't look like a place I would like to be on a brilliantly sunny day anyway. The only thing I liked about the church was its smell of incense, spicy and strong.

I narrowed my eyes at Maria and leaned closer, sniffing. She smelled of a rotting tooth, and I knew she was in pain. I could have told her to boil the bark of the ironwood tree and drink the resulting tea, but I had no intention of helping her. "You call my mother a witch, but you use her as a healer," I said. "Didn't you send your servant to our door for a remedy for the itch under your skirt?"

Maria had the decency to flush and look away from me. She made the sign of the cross and pulled on Hermínia's arm.

"How is that nasty itch, Maria?" I called after them, but they didn't turn back.

⚬⚬⚬

My mother knew about the powers of everything that grew under and above the earth, and how roots and seeds and bark and leaves and flower petals could be pounded and ground or cooked and mashed to heal the body and to influence the mind. Her potions gave off a rich, feral smell, like the fur of an animal, or the earth when upturned.

We had a garden, partially shaded by the outcropping of a cliff and protected from the sea wind that coated everything with salt; my father had carted soil down from the highland pastures. My mother grew herbs procured from Madeira: caraway and licorice root, camomile and rue, cardoon and rosemary, sweet yarrow and stock. She had me trudge daily with two goatskins to fetch fresh water to keep the garden moist in the heat of summer.

She taught me about the smells emitting from the body through the skin itself, and what those odours predicted. I learned how to tell what a person had last eaten, or if they had an upset stomach or a fever, but also if they were angry or upset, hiding it with a smile.

You're like a little animal, my father had told me, *a fox, always sniffing the air.* There were no foxes on Porto Santo, but my father described them to me. Little fox, he called me, patting my cheek. *Klein vos.*

My earliest memories were of watching my mother make her medicines, and of seeing her pull babies—pink, blue, chalky, bloody—from the hidden part of a woman's body. She taught me how to bring down the swelling of sprains and relieve the pain of bruises, how to set a broken bone, soothe a fever, or rid the body of the venom from a spider bite. She also studied the smoke of the wormwood and the small blaze of candles she dipped into a powder she made from sea water and herbs so that their flames flickered blue and green. She spoke Portuguese with a heavy tongue, but the secret language she chanted while the fragrant smoke whirled about our heads flowed from her lips in a beautiful, lilting melody. I learned these chants even though I didn't understand what they meant. Sometimes she would stop in mid-sentence, gazing at something I could never see, and I knew she was having a vision, or listening to the voices that surrounded her. The smoke and the visions and voices told her the future.

While other girls were playing with bits of yarn and little wooden figures made by their grandfathers, I was learning my mother's secrets. I felt her recipes and spells sewing themselves under my skin with tiny, careful stitches.

CHAPTER FIVE

I sold the snuff box and bought myself a square hand mirror edged in bone, and a little book of poetry. I knew I should have used the réis for food, but I still burned from Maria's insult. I stared into the glass, willing myself to be the pretty girl Abílio had seen.

I hoped my mother would scold me for spending the money recklessly, so that I could fight back. I would berate her for not being an ordinary woman like the others on Porto Santo. Maybe then my father would have stayed.

But before I went back to my hut on the beach, I went to Rooi's inn. Rooi Eikenboom was Dutch, like my father, and also like my father, he had once had a life at sea. Now he served sailors the local rum made with sugar cane, or wine delivered from Funchal every week during the good weather. In the storm season, when wild, howling winds blew the ships off course, away from the Madeira archipelago, Rooi closed his inn and went to the Canary Islands, returning when the winds calmed. My father said he had a family there, but I didn't understand why they didn't come live with him in Vila Baleira.

The inn was empty, but Rooi had already drunk a number of cups of wine. I could smell the sourness on his breath as soon as I drew near him. He looked at me sadly, holding his cup towards me.

"What am I drinking, Diamantina?" he asked. "Where on Madeira do these grapes grow?"

I didn't have the heart for our game today. "Did my father say anything to you about coming back?"

"Poor *meisje*," he murmured—"little girl" in Dutch—which made me miss my father all the more. "Ach, it's a hard life for us all," he said, setting his cup on the table. "Your father stayed on Porto Santo because he couldn't show his face at the docks in Madeira or Lisboa. He was supposed to be dead." His florid face, surrounded by long, thick white hair, was wide and flat. "I was the one who cut him from his chains after your mother found him. She came to me because she recognized that Arie and I shared a language. He stayed with me at first, waiting, he said, until it was safe for him to go to the ships again. But before that time came, he found that he was pulled by your mother's beauty, and her spells. And so he stayed."

"I know all this," I said. My father had many times told me what had happened aboard the *Slot ter Hooge*, and how the barrel had saved his life. That my mother had found him washed ashore. Rooi often told me his part in the story. I had heard the same story so many times it bored me, and I had no patience for it today. "But he's gone now. He did leave."

Rooi stared deep into his cup, as if searching for answers. He gave me one more sorrowing look, his eyes stopping on the talisman around my neck, then left me sitting alone on the splintered bench.

For as long as I could remember, I would sit beside Rooi on the bench and he would hold his cup of wine under my nose and tell me to breathe it in deeply with my eyes closed. Then he would ask me what grape it was made from; he had told me many times about the different grapes grown on Madeira. I learned to identify the wines, from the sweetest, Malvasia, with its pungent aroma of prunes and soft richness of burned sugar, and the Boal, with its full flavour of raisins, both grown in the lower regions of Madeira, to those thriving at higher elevations. Verdelho was rich and golden with the scent of almonds, while the driest, Sercial, had the slight tart-ness of burnt coffee from being scorched by the sea air and southern sun. I would smell deeply and then, when I guessed correctly— because I usually did—Rooi would nod, and I would take a sip. He instructed me to hold the wine in my mouth and let it soak into my tongue and cheeks, and feel its texture as it slid down my throat. The wine sometimes burned, but I did as Rooi asked to please him, and to see my father smile.

Rooi drank two cups of wine to every one of my father's. While my father grew happier when he drank, Rooi grew sad, sometimes weeping as he spoke of faraway people and places he said he would never see again. At other times he had me read to him from the *Gazeta de Lisboa*. Although he had never learned to read, I had seen him cipher the inn's expenditures and earnings in his head with astounding speed.

On our slow walks home along the beach after my father had spent all his réis at Rooi's, he would hold my shoulder for balance, and tell me my favourite stories. They were all of his life in the far-off land he had come from, the province of Zeeland in Nederland. He spoke of the air growing so cold the water in the canals and rivers froze into ice. I couldn't imagine it. He described how he glided along on runners carved from animal bone strapped to his boots. He used long, thin poles to help him move more quickly down the frozen canals linking the villages; this was skating, he said. The wealthy of Zeeland had skates made of iron; he had always dreamed of owning such a pair. I tried to think what it would feel like to have bones or iron encasing my feet. Sometimes we pretended we were skating, pushing our feet along in the sand as we swung our arms. My father often fell in our make-believe skating, laughing, and I had to help him up.

He told me of *sneeuwen*—snow, rain so cold it became solid. Surely it would hurt, hitting like stones. He told me he would one day take me back to his land, where I would play in the snow and skate on the ice and eat *honingkoek* his mother made.

It was so easy for him to talk about his life before he was washed up on Porto Santo. But my mother's past remained a mystery. I scoffed at her story of coming from the earth of Porto Santo, growing like a plant or a tree, knowing fully, from a young age, about the beginnings and birthing of all human and animal life.

And my father wouldn't answer my questions about my mother

either, although once, just once, he said, "Your mother was brought here by the sea, like me." His words were slow, tangling with each other because of the many cups of wine. "And her real name isn't Estra. She's just called that here. It's shortened from *estrangeira*: what the islanders called her when she came."

"Stranger? But what's her real name? And where did she come from?"

He stopped, shaking his head as if annoyed with himself. "I've said too much. It's your mother's story, and not mine to tell. She will tell you when you're ready."

On the second full moon after my father left, my woman's time came. I had been sitting in the clear, shallow water at the edge of the beach, reading one of the books my father had left me, when the water around me bloomed pink and murky.

My mother only nodded when I told her, but there was an expression on her face I didn't recognize. I didn't know whether she was sad or angry or simply surprised, even though I knew it was past due; I would turn fourteen at the time of the island's fall harvest.

That same night, I awakened in the dark, the flickering of flames drawing me to the open door. My mother, outlined by the light from a raging bonfire of laurel and tamarisk, was drawing in the hard sand with a stick. Sparks shot over her and ash fell on her hair. I walked out to her, and saw a pattern of symbols she was repeating in the sand.

"Here, Diamantina. Here is your future," she said. "I have been reading the smoke for many hours, and seen all of this for you. Trees for long life because of the roots—the leaves are knowledge. Look at the linked circles, like the chain that your father wore when I found him. I thought they were showing me his hold on you, because of the spilled potion, but now I believe they mean the strength you will always find. Here are eyes, to deflect evil back to the one sending it; you must never allow this evil in. These lines are water, and these are vines. Vines and more vines. Vines are important to your life."

"What's that one? The starry sun with a cross inside?"

My mother held her stick over the final symbol. "That one I don't understand, but it will come to you when you need it. It is in my vision with persistence," she said, "and so it must be part of your story. I will make the marks on you, so you will never forget your path."

"Marks?"

"On your skin." She held out a bowl, painting my face with dye made from lichens and berries with her index finger. Then she led me around the snapping, sweet-smelling blaze until I was dizzy. She gave me a potion, something tangy and unfamiliar, and my lips and fingertips tingled as I drank it down.

"Sit with your back to the fire," she said, and as I did, she sat behind me. She unlaced my blouse and smoothed her hands over my shoulders and then down my spine. Her palms were hard and calloused, but her touch was so rare. I closed my eyes with the pleasure of it. My whole body was slightly numb now, and I liked the feeling.

"I will mark you now," she said.

I opened my eyes with effort, looking over my shoulder, and saw another bowl, not the berry juice. It held something dark and sticky-looking. Beside it was my mother's knife with its narrow, whetted blade, and a long sharp needle of bone, its duller end stuck into a small piece of wood. As I watched, she held both knife and needle over a flame.

"Didn't you already mark my face with the symbols?"

"Those will wash away. I must mark you forever," she said, lifting the knife. "Don't move. It will hurt, but you are brave, and the potion takes away some of the pain."

The potion also made me loose and uncaring, for in spite of the knife and needle I didn't feel any apprehension.

I was aware of pressure against my skin, and then pain, even though my body was heavy and limp. My mother murmured as she worked, and each time I thought I would cry out, she stopped cutting, dabbing at the stinging with something damp and cool.

And then she was blowing on my back, blowing with long, steady breaths. "Take in my breath. Take it in—I come into you," she said, and I breathed deeply as she exhaled.

She gently laced up my blouse, and I got to my feet.

"You did well," she said, standing in front of me. "Try not to sleep on your back, and don't go into the sea for the next few days. The scabs need to form fully before they're washed away."

The cloth she held was coloured by the dye and my blood. She went to the edge of the water and washed it out, stepping back each time a wave threatened to wash over her feet.

I usually went in and out of the water all day to cool myself during the blistering tropical heat of summer, my wet clothing drying on me within half an hour, but my mother only went to the very edge of the sea to bathe, and regardless of the heat she wore many layers of clothing. Her neck and arms were ever more laden with the jewellery she fashioned from what she found. I had never seen my mother unclothed; like everyone on the beach, we slept in our clothing.

And yet in spite of her aversion to water, her skin—dusky and darker than the other women of the island—was clear and smooth. She brushed the ashes of burned laurel branches through her hair daily, and always gave off the light fragrance of smoke and sweet rosemary. I knew she was close by her scent even when I didn't hear her coming.

I watched her walk back to me with the wet cloth. She was beautiful at that moment, staring at me with such a strange, sad and yet pleased expression. She held my face in her hands and said, "I have passed my power to you, Diamantina. It is time for me to free myself of it. Part of what I give you is your free will, the will that can deflect evil and choose the good. Hold on to this power—never let it be taken—so that one day you can pass it, whole, on to your own daughter, as I do to you today."

I looked into her eyes, and in the glow of the fire saw my tiny reflection. But my image changed, and suddenly there was too much light, too much colour, and I was gone, lost. A surge of panic rose in me as she held my face more tightly and whispered unknown words.

She blinked, and in her eyes I was myself again. "Where did you come from, Mama?" I asked, my speech slow because of the potion.

"I will tell you one day," she said, and now it was not me but she who had changed. There was a new softness in her face. And as we faced each other, I realized that I was taller than she. How long had this been so?

CHAPTER SIX

After that, my mother spent more time sitting quietly, watching me as I took over the preparing of the remedies and potions. It seemed she had grown older after our night around the fire: as if passing her power to me had diminished her.

The women who came to our hut searching for cures for themselves or their children when their men were out on the water sometimes spoke of their problems in loud, annoyed tones. At other times they wept as they whispered why they had come. My mother stood beside me, her hand on my shoulder as she told each woman that I had taken on the healing.

They all looked surprised. I was too young, how could I know enough?

"My knowledge was passed on to her as she lay curled inside me," my mother said. "When she became a woman and her blood quickened, my knowledge was awakened in her." She still listened, nodding or softly adding information as I instructed the youngest of the good wives on ways to stop a child before it started with a bit of sea sponge soaked in vinegar. If the woman knew a child had already begun, and wanted to rid herself of it, I gave her a potion of rue to bring on cramping and her bleeding. I understood how desperately the poor yet pious women of Porto Santo struggled to view each child as a blessing from God, even though they could not feed those they had. I saw the tearing and destruction of back-to-back pregnancies: the lost teeth, legs covered with veins thick as ropes, ruined bladders and wombs so dropped they emerged from the body. I'd witnessed the pain and sometimes death that childbed brought.

If one had contracted a painful discharge or a miserable irritation from her husband's philandering, I cured her with herbal infusions and soothing poultices. I lanced boils with a small, sharp knife I held over a flame, and made mixtures of powdered milk thistle for the worms that created wretchedness. My hands perpetually burned and itched from washing with lye soap before and after attending to the women and children.

Sometimes I tied a strip of linen around my nose and mouth and went to visit one woman, thin and hollow-eyed, who was dying of the bloody cough. I took a tea of nettle and eucalyptus to hold back the cough and balls of poppy seed, which I fed her to send her into a dark sleep and ease the worst of her pain. For illnesses such as this and certain hard growths there was no potion or spell for cure, my mother told me; they always ended in death. We could only make the waiting less painful.

The women were grateful. They gave whatever they could, a few eggs or a plate of fish cakes, announcing they would pray for us at Mass for the next month. But these same women, when I encountered them in the company of their husbands, ignored me. Sometimes they made the sign of the cross when I came into view. I knew they did this to protect themselves from the wrath of their husbands. Their men didn't care who helped deliver their sons or daughters, or cured their children of worms, but for woman problems they told their wives that it was God who would help them, and that they should spend more time on their knees, praying for relief.

I was glad I had no one to tell me to go on my knees. I was glad I had a mother who taught me to help myself. Some days when she was outside, I took off my blouse and picked up my mirror. I positioned it over one shoulder and then the other, and admired the images across my shoulder blades and down my spine. I especially loved the woven gracefulness of the vines with their dots for fruit, and thought them beautiful. I wished for someone to gaze upon them, and trace them with gentle fingers.

I thought of Abílio Perez touching them.

The shopkeepers wouldn't let me put any food or supplies on what was once my father's *rol*. They would accept nothing from me but coins, and after four months the réis my father had left were gone. But I was able to keep us from going hungry.

As well as the food I was given by the women I helped, I could throw a net and gather the creatures from the sea, and I could trap. Long ago I had learned to walk as silently as my mother. I could sit without moving for an endless time, even slowing my breath so that my chest did not rise and fall as I inhaled or exhaled, and in this way I became invisible to the creatures of Porto Santo.

I knew where the seabirds built their nests in the pebbles and scrub at the base of the cliffs and sat, patiently, for hours. I become a gnarled tree, a rock, a petrified sand sculpture. Sometimes my hair was ruffled by the beat of wings as a bird descended to her nest. And then in one deft movement I threw my net over her just as she was settling, and picked up the fluttering, panicked creature, holding her wings through the netting, my thumbs against her warm head, calming her. I stroked that small knob of skull and then broke the neck with one quick twist.

I sat beside the aromatic shrubs and brambles on Pico do Facho where rabbits hid from the circling buzzards and kestrels. When I detected one of the creatures, I reached through the thorns with a single quick movement. Pulling out the wriggling animal, holding it tightly with one hand, I sliced the slender beating throat with my gutting knife so quickly the rabbit had little time for fear.

I always felt sorrow for the death of the innocent creature and, holding the limp body of the bird or rabbit aloft, I thanked it for feeding my mother and me.

I also sometimes crept along the high dunes and settled myself into the grasses and sand, wearing my invisibility, and watched Abílio help his father with their nets or cutting up the catch.

One afternoon as I searched along the bottom of a high, towering cliff for nests, looking to snare a bird for our supper, I heard plaintive cries from above. I shaded my eyes and squinted into the brilliant sun, but could see nothing. I climbed up on my hands and knees to find a nanny goat stranded on a narrow ledge. She must have slipped down from the rocks above. On my knees, I was able to tie my sling around her neck and tug and coax her down the slippery rock. My own bare feet slid in the scree as I pulled her, her front hooves wide apart, her head up, bleating in fear. When we were at the bottom, I recognized the marking on her back: she belonged to the Fontinhas, who lived at the far northeast end of the island, Pico Branco. They were a prosperous family with a large herd of goats, and Senhora Fontinha sold her milk and butter and cream in the market every Tuesday. This nanny must have broken from the pen and come all the way across the island. I reasoned that one goat would not make a difference to the Fontinhas, but she would to my mother and to me. I cut away the painted fur with my gutting knife and then, using my sling as a halter, led her down to the beach. Abílio rose from the bench outside his hut, putting down the net he was repairing to walk with me.

"You've bought a goat, Diamantina? Where did you get that much money?"

I said nothing.

He ran his hand over the newly cut patch on her back. "Did you steal her?"

"I don't steal."

"Really? But you couldn't have bought her," he repeated.

I tugged harder on the sling, and the goat's feet scrambled in the sand.

"You do what you like, don't you, Diamantina?" He crossed his arms over his chest and tipped his head to one side. "Being a heathen, and with no fear of either the confessional or God's wrath, it appears you have no sense of right and wrong."

I stopped, looking into his face. "I know the difference between right and wrong. Do you, Abílio?" He both angered and intrigued me. "Keep your thoughts to yourself."

"Enjoy your fresh milk, then," he called after me as I broke into a run, pulling the goat behind me, bleating and complaining.

At our hut, I tied her securely to a rock with a length of tarred rope. My mother came out of the hut and held the goat's head in her hands.

"I found her," I said.

My mother stared into the goat's face as it tossed its head, trying to pull away from her grip. But after a few moments it grew very still, and finally the wide-set, ochre eyes closed. "She tells me she called you to her," she said, raising her eyes to mine. "As you were a blessing to her, now she will be a blessing to us." She stroked the goat's nose, and the yellow eyes opened again.

"Then we will call her Benedita," I said.

I still talked to my father as I wandered the hills or the beach, telling him whatever was on my mind, thinking of small stories that would amuse him. Grief sat heavily in me. Although my mother was not unkind, it was not her nature to speak of frivolous matters, or smile fondly at me, as my father had.

I knew there would not be a letter from him for a long time. It could take five to six months for a ship to sail from Funchal to Brazil, longer if storms blew the ship off course. By the time he was settled and his letter made the return trip, it would be a year and more.

And yet, like a miracle, Father da Chagos stopped me as I crossed the square one afternoon only five months after my father had left. "I have something for you." He held out a folded square.

My breath caught in my throat. "A letter from my father? But how could it come already?" I smiled at him as I took it, but my smile faded at the broken wax seal. "You opened it?"

"I cannot read your father's language," he said, then turned.

I watched the priest walk away, trying to feel angry with him for attempting to read what my father had written to me. I stared at the paper and told myself to wait, to take it home and read it aloud with my mother. But I was too excited. Standing in the middle of the square, I unfolded it.

"*My dearest Diamantina,*" I read, and at the sight of his familiar hand a small cry escaped my lips. I heard his voice, and the extent to which I missed him struck me, fresh and painful.

I'm sorry no money accompanies this letter, and can only pray that you and your mother are not suffering. I am depending on the goodness of Father da Chagos and the church to help you for the next while.

When I left Porto Santo, I went to Lisboa, and I worked on the docks for these past months. I have received barely enough to pay for my food and shelter, and because of my shame in having no réis to send you, I have not written while there. I have finally been hired on by a carrack sailing to Brazil, and it is at this day of departure that I send this letter.

My next letter will come from São Paulo, and in it I will send you my address, so that you can write to me and assure me that you and your mother are well. I will also send as much money as I can. Within another year, I believe my position will be such that I will be able to send you the required sum for you both to come to Brazil, even though I do not believe your mother will ever be persuaded to leave the island. And if you are still unwilling to leave her, I understand, and further commend you, dear daughter. Although I will live with great heartache, I hold you in highest esteem for your loyalty.

Please think of me every day, as I do you and your mother, and know my thoughts come across the ocean to you.

Your loving father.

❧

I ran all the way down the beach to read the letter to my mother. She listened, burning wormwood and watching the smoke. "You will not leave here with your father's help," she finally said, and I slammed my hands onto the table.

"Why can't you let me be happy about the letter?"

She put a cover over the smoking bowl. "It's your choice to be happy or not. And you will leave Porto Santo. But you shouldn't wait for Arie to make it possible."

I made an angry sound in my throat, turning from her. Before I put the letter between the pages of one of the bound collections of sea charts my father had left for me, I kissed it.

⁂

Because my woman's time had coincided closely with my father's departure, it was as though my girlhood had disappeared with him. When I was little, the other girls had stared at me when I walked through town with him. Now I watched them walking with their arms linked, chirping and twittering like flocks of busy birds, accompanied by their mothers or aunts or grandmothers. They had dowries and would marry, their partners chosen by their parents from among the island boys. The girls and their husbands would make homes and have children. Sometimes I stood at the edge of a celebrating crowd outside the church and studied the young brides, knowing I would never be such a one.

And yet I liked my differences. Being taller than all of the other girls gave me the feeling that I was also more capable. I liked that I did not wear my skirt so tightly cinched at the waist or hide the fair sheen of my hair so carefully under a kerchief. I was glad the jewellery I made for myself from what I found washed up on the beach was so much more abundant and eye-catching than the simple crosses the girls wore around their necks. I was glad I did not have to cover my head with a piece of lace and put on shoes and spend a sunny morning kneeling for Mass. I walked with long, sure strides, swinging my arms, telling myself I had more freedom than the other girls would ever know.

But without my father to share my thoughts, I sometimes could not convince myself of the benefits of my freedom. At times a blackness came over me. That summer, as was usual on the nights of the religious festivals, the square was filled with flowers and strung with fluttering white flags bearing the red Order of Christ. The good ladies of the parish prepared huge feasts, and the men brought out their stringed instruments and tambourines. And on these nights I allowed myself moments of disappointment and sorrow. My father had taken me to these *arraiais*, and even though we were not accepted in the church community, after the Mass and procession we were allowed to partake in the festivities.

My mother never accompanied us. She cared little about being part of the larger picture of the island.

I didn't want to go to a festival by myself, so on those nights I stayed in the hut, helping my mother with her pounding and grinding. We didn't comment on the muted music and laughter carrying down the beach. Surely I couldn't really smell the beef slowly cooking on lava stones over a fire of sweet laurel, and yet just imagining that meat, dusted heavily with salt and accompanied with fragrant, doughy rounds of fresh *bolo do caco*, filled my mouth with saliva.

I glanced often at my mother as we worked. I wished I could be more like her, wanting nothing more than what I had.

CHAPTER SEVEN

That first summer of my father's absence was long and hot. Even though the rains were sparse in the hottest months, we could usually count on sudden showers blowing in from the ocean, causing the parched hills to turn into carpets of green. But that year the sky paled with heat of an unusual intensity, and the stones were too hot to step on. Leaves on the trees withered and curled and the birds seemed to hang, motionless, in the white sky, and then they disappeared. Even my wracking brought little of worth. We needed supplies: oil and candles, flour and grain, and a new cooking pot. My mother told me to go to Father da Chagos, as my father had instructed.

Father da Chagos had regularly hired my father to climb to the top of the bell tower and clean out the birds' nests and scrub the bells of the sea mist that threatened to tarnish them green. My father's years spent climbing the rigging had made him quick and unafraid as he scrambled up the rickety, narrow steps of the high bell tower. He would sit on the ledge of each of the four openings, his legs dangling, and work on the bells, whistling. Sometimes I sat in the square and watched him, so high in the air, fearless and capable. The daily pealing from Nossa Senhora da Piedade reminded me of him.

Father da Chagos had also called upon my mother for aid. He had come to our hut in the dark of night the year before my father left. Refusing to come inside, he spoke in a whisper to my father.

My father closed the door and grinned at my mother. "He wants something for stomach discomfort," he said.

"What kind of discomfort?"

"For the last few weeks he's been suffering with an undue amount of wind. He can't control it, even when he's performing the Mass."

I put my hand over my mouth so Father da Chagos couldn't hear my laugh through the shuttered window. My father winked at me, but my mother only lifted her eyebrows as she went to her table of herbs and medicines and picked up a small pot of ground wormwood.

"He asks that you don't speak of this to anyone," my father added.

My mother's hands stopped tapping the powder onto a small square of cotton. It was clear she was annoyed by the Father's insinuation. Porto Santo's *curandeira*, Teresa Trovão, was not called a witch, even though she performed the same duties as my mother in providing healing cures and delivering babies. She was a stalwart member of the parish, faithfully attending Mass and putting more coins into the collection box than most of the islanders. But she had a loose tongue, and those who came to her for help could never be sure their ailments wouldn't become the latest gossip. We all knew Father da Chagos had come to my mother because he was worried that Teresa would speak freely of his flatulence.

My mother finished filling the cotton and twisted it closed, holding it out to my father. "Tell him to mix the wormwood into a bit of warm liquid before meals. He can come back for more if he needs it."

Now I waited outside the chapel until an old woman slowly hobbled past me on her way inside. I asked her to please fetch Father da Chagos for me.

The priest soon came to the doorway. He was stout in his heavy black robe, his face and bald head glistening with sweat. Pearly beads ran down from his temples, settling into the creases of his broad cheeks. His eyes went to my blouse, and I looked down at my father's silver amulet strung on its leather thong, and the other necklaces I had made with shell and bone. I had also caught four dragonflies, which still clung to the fabric of my blouse with their tiny feet, their translucent wings trembling. They would stay there, resting, before flying off.

"What do you want, Diamantina?"

"Father da Chagos," I said, "my father said that you would help my mother and me. I know there will be no letter and money from him for a long time yet, but . . . we are in need." I was ashamed to say the words aloud.

"In need? What do you mean?" he asked. There was a sesame seed caught in the priest's front teeth, and I knew he had just finished his noon meal. I smelled the strong odour of octopus, and the buttery sweetness of olive oil, and I had to swallow the saliva that rushed to my mouth.

In the next instant a flash of discomfort crossed the priest's face, and an unpleasant odour wafted towards me. The richness of the octopus was already giving him wind; he hadn't come back to my mother for more wormwood, although it was clear it was a chronic problem. The priest frowned at me, as if I were the one guilty of the odour.

"I fish, and we have a goat. I find seabird eggs and use whatever the island offers. But we have no more money to buy flour for bread. We have no more oil, and no candles. I need réis to go to the shops."

"So you can feed yourself, yet you've come asking for charity?"

I stood straight. I knew the church gave bread and cast-off clothing donated by the wealthier families to the most destitute of the island, but I did not like to think this included my mother and me. "I am here for a job," I said. "My father worked for you. Now I will."

"Cleaning the bells is a man's job."

"I didn't mean the bells. Anything else."

I waited as he appeared to be thinking. Another bead of sweat ran to the end of his nose, and he swiped at it. He looked at me intently, leaning a bit closer. "Let me see your hands."

I wouldn't hold out my hands like a wayward child. I clenched them at my sides, angry, and yet at the same time afraid they might be dirty.

He studied my face, then said, "All right. The women of the parish volunteer their time to clean the church. But no one comes on Monday mornings—the women are too concerned with their weekly washing—and after Sunday's three Masses the church is in need of a thorough cleaning. I cannot always rely on the Sister who is my housekeeper to keep up with all her duties. You can have the holy task of cleaning the church on Mondays, and helping the Sister in the kitchen a few times a week, as she needs you. For this I will pay you a few réis, and give you anything left from my meals."

"I'm sure we will not need your leftovers, Father da Chagos, but I will accept the job of cleaning and kitchen work."

"Pride is not becoming, Diamantina." When I didn't respond, he added, "Don't come to the church with insects on your clothes, or that heathen frippery."

I nodded, guessing by his glance at my neck and wrists that frippery meant my necklaces and bracelets.

"Start this Monday."

"What day is today?"

He shook his head and made an annoyed sound. "Friday." He turned then, walking back into the dark fragrance of the chapel.

"Father da Chagos," I called, and he stopped, although he didn't turn around. "We've had no bread for many weeks now." I hadn't planned to say anything more, but he had angered me. "I will take some today, please."

He turned to me. I couldn't see his features in the shadows, but a ray of sunlight fell from the open door onto his feet. He wore straw sandals; his toenails were thick and yellow, the big toes scattered with wiry black hairs. He came back towards me, his hands kneading his stomach. He stared at me, and then said, "Come." I followed him around the church to a back door with a heavy grille over its top half. "Never again come to the front of the church. This is the door you will enter," he said, then called, "Sister Amélia."

A shadow immediately darkened the grille.

"This young woman will be helping you starting on Monday. Please give her a charity basket today."

The shadow moved from the grille, and in a moment the door opened a crack and a slim white hand held out a little basket, a cross woven into each side. I peered in at the round loaf of bread with a cross baked into the top, the piece of dried cod, the small vial of oil. The pomegranate. "Thank you," I said, taking it, and the hand began to retreat.

"She's Diamantina, the Dutchman's daughter," Father da Chagos said, and the hand stopped for a second, and then pulled the door closed. At the clang, one of the dragonflies flew from my blouse, fluttering high into the air.

"Return the basket when you come on Monday," the priest said, and walked away.

I called, "I'll bring you more powdered wormwood as well."

By the stiffness of his back I knew he was angry at my forwardness, and I was glad I had let him know his smell offended me.

⌒

"I don't want you going into the church," my mother said when I told her how I would earn the réis we needed.

"It's just a building, Mama. It can't hurt me. Besides, I'll stay only until we get the money from *Vader*."

She turned away. "I'll make a potion to protect you."

CHAPTER EIGHT

Early Monday morning, I stood outside the kitchen door of the church, in a plain skirt and blouse. I had tightly braided my hair and tied a scarf around my head. I wore no jewellery except the fragment of caul encased in silver, hidden inside my blouse.

As I peered through the grille, I could discern a slight movement, dark and light. I knocked, and the door opened.

Sister Amélia wore the same heavy robe as Father da Chagos, although hers was brown, and a long black rosary was tied around her waist. Her head was covered in two layers: a tight white wrap that formed a band across her forehead and was caught up under her chin then fell in folds onto her shoulders, as well as a looser black veil that obscured her vision on either side. Her feet were bare, like mine.

Sister Amélia's hands were covered in flour; a thin gold band glinted on one finger. There was a round of dough in a deep wooden oblong bowl on the table behind her.

I stepped in and handed her the empty charity basket. I was immediately too hot in the small kitchen, with the fire roaring and steam rising from a big pot.

"Are you useful with a knife?" Sister Amélia asked. Her voice was soft.

I put my hand on my waistband, where my blouse covered my gutting knife. I suddenly wondered if I should have brought it into the church kitchen. "Yes."

"Good," she said, and smiled. I realized she was young, much younger than my mother. "You can chop those onions and peel the sweet potatoes." She pointed to a thick board and a big knife, and returned to kneading the dough.

We worked in silence. My stomach rumbled, and I slipped a piece of sweet potato into my mouth and tried to chew it without making a sound, glancing sideways at Sister Amélia. She was watching me. I stopped chewing, but she said nothing.

By the time she had set the dough to rise, I had finished with the vegetables. She filled a wooden bucket with boiling water from the pot over the fire and took a basket with rags and some small jars with stoppers from a cupboard. She held out a long white garment with loose sleeves. "Please wear this surplice."

I put it on over my blouse and skirt. Sister Amélia then handed me the bucket of hot water and led me down a narrow, dim hallway to the church. The bucket was heavy, and I didn't want to slop water onto the floor, so I walked carefully and slowly. Sister Amélia stopped at a wooden door, richly carved. "You enter the church through here. You're to wash the floor, especially in the nave, all the way to the apse. Then, with a cloth dampened with a little olive oil," she said, pointing to one of the jars, "wipe all the woodwork of the sanctuary and the sacristy. You must be careful when you polish the silver candle holders and chalices—use this." She opened another jar and held it towards me. I smelled soda ash and salt. "Rub gently, to avoid scoring the silver. And you're never to touch the monstrance or tabernacle."

I set down the bucket before the closed door. "I don't know what any of those things you talk about are, except for the candle holders."

She looked at me for a long moment as I felt the steam from the bucket soft against my bare leg. Finally she said, "Is anyone in the church?"

I pulled open the heavy door and looked in. "No."

"All right. I'll come in with you and show you what you need to do. But I can't be seen."

I wanted to ask her why, but the hush of the empty church stopped me. For the next half-hour the nun explained it all. Then, as we stood looking up at the statues of the saints in their niches, the church was flooded with light as the front door opened to admit a parishioner.

In a whisper of cloth, Sister Amélia was gone.

I stood looking around me after she left, the bucket and mop at my feet. Ignoring the woman kneeling in prayer, I walked around the church, staring at the ceiling, which I now knew symbolized charity. The floor, Sister Amélia had said, represented the foundation of faith and the humility of the poor. I ran my hands over the columns, representing the Apostles. I studied the saints, imagining them whispering to each other from their niches in the empty church as I whispered to my absent father on the beach or on the cliffs.

I was happy to be surrounded by such beauty, and as I mopped and polished I hummed my father's sailing tunes under my breath.

When I came into the kitchen a few days later, it was empty, and the fire out. I quietly called Sister Amélia's name, and at her murmur, I went to the doorway beside the fireplace. Her room was tiny and steamy, little more than a closet, with a slit of a window covered with a wooden grille. Sister Amélia was curled on her side on a pallet on the floor. A large, rough wooden cross hung on the whitewashed wall over her.

"Are you ill, Sister?"

She slowly sat up. She wore a plain white dress with long sleeves and a high neckline. Her head was still covered by the white cap, but without the black veil. Her dark eyes glistened, perhaps from sadness or perhaps because they weren't shadowed by the veil. By the way the wimple fit snugly on her head, I could tell that her hair was cut short; only a few dark wisps showed at the hairline. Her heavy crucifix hung on her chest, and I tried not to stare at the high mound of her breasts, which were unnoticeable under her robe. I hadn't really thought of her as a woman before, with a woman's body and a woman's miseries.

"Is it your monthly time?" I asked. "I can run home and bring you back some dried chasteberries. They will ease your cramping."

"No. It's not that. I have a melancholia that comes some days. It will pass. It always does." She tilted her head. "Why do you stare so, Diamantina?"

I smiled at her, wanting to heal her, to make her feel better. "You're pretty, Sister Amélia," I said.

She frowned as if my compliment had upset her further instead of pleasing her. "You mustn't say that. I must not know any pride." She rose and smoothed down the white dress.

"Where is your habit?"

"This is my sleeping gown."

"Are sleeping gowns only for nuns?"

"No."

It struck me as strange that someone would wear different clothing to sleep. "Does Father da Chagos wear a different gown for sleeping?" I asked.

Sister Amélia's cheeks coloured. "Really, Diamantina. That is an unspiritual thought."

"I'm sorry," I said, but not sorry about my unspiritual thoughts about the fat priest. I *was* sorry for Sister Amélia's state of mind.

"Please go to the kitchen and start preparing the fish you'll find in the basket by the door," she said, "while I rouse myself from my bout of self-pity. And later we'll make banana flan. It's Father da Chagos's favourite."

As I turned, she added, "Take a banana for yourself before you start." I smiled at her again, grateful for her kindness.

When she came out a few minutes later, dressed in her habit, I said, "I delivered a baby to Ana de Mendonça yesterday." I wanted to cheer Sister Amélia with an interesting story. "It was an easy birth—her ninth, so the little girl almost slid out. She's a sweet baby, pink and healthy. Ana thanked God that she didn't have the split upper lip, like two of her others." Again I smiled at Sister Amélia as I filleted the long black scabbardfish, but she was silent, her lips trembling.

I had said the wrong thing. "I'm sorry, Sister Amélia. I shouldn't have spoken."

She took a deep breath and her lips grew firm. "No," she said, swallowing and then briskly rubbing her eyes, as if annoyed by her own tears. "I must be thankful for the path God has chosen for me. There are two paths for a woman: wife or nun. I am a nun."

I was silent for a moment. "I will never be a wife either, Sister Amélia."

She frowned. "Why not?"

"Who would marry me? I'm an outcast, looked down on as my mother is."

"But . . . Father da Chagos said your mother was a healer. And that you carry on her role."

"Teresa Trovão is the island's *curandeira*. We perform the same duties as her, but we're called witches, because we're heathen."

She shook her head and made a sound with her lips. "People are afraid of what they don't understand. You strike me as a clever and resourceful girl," she said. This was the first compliment I had heard since my father had left, and it filled me with a soaring pride. "I'm sure your future will unfold in ways you never imagined." She put her head to one side. "It appears to me that a young woman like you will not be without a man."

I wasn't sure how she meant this. The glow I felt from her earlier comment faded.

⁂

The few réis Father da Chagos gave me every week were enough to survive on. I always looked into the shops as I walked home, imagining the pleasure of cloth for a new skirt or blouse, or a new book, or even the smallest of sugar loaves, but I had no means for anything more.

I came to clean early on Mondays, before Mass, so later I could listen to the service at the opening in the carved doors. I also peeked at the congregation in the pale light falling through the windows, at the altar boys with their candles, and at the pious saints in their niches, looking down on the kneeling figures. I breathed in the fragrance of the incense from the censer and waited for the chime of the Sanctus bell. From my position I couldn't see Father da Chagos, but I felt as though the Latin words intoned by him were like my mother's magical incantations. As I'd memorized hers, I memorized what the small congregation repeated after him. I wondered if the words themselves contained some healing power, something to help the women who wept as they prayed, poor things.

Sister Amélia and I slowly learned about each other. She had never seen my father, but she knew of his work on the bells. I told her about his leaving, and about the life my mother and I now lived.

She had come from the convent of Catarina of the Cross in Funchal Town, and was a discalced Carmelite, meaning she was barefoot; part of the penance of her order was to be unshod. The Carmelites, she said, were enclosed nuns, freed of all attachments by separation from the world. "My order dictates that we do not see anyone from the outside world, and speak only for specific purposes. That's why I can't be seen by anyone, or have any communication, apart from Father da Chagos. And he only speaks to me once a day, to give me instruction. I'm not allowed to speak to him, except when he hears my confession."

She was beating eggs, her habit tied out of the way by a piece of twine. I tried to imagine never seeing or speaking to anyone. I said, after a moment, my hands in a tub of water as I scrubbed the dirt off whiskery carrots, "But you can see and speak to me."

She looked at me for a long moment. "It's because . . . Father da Chagos thought . . . as you are . . ."

"An unholy bastard?" I offered helpfully.

Her face flushed. "It's very sad that you're not a child of God. But I sense that Father da Chagos, in spite of his gruff demeanour, has allowed you in the kitchen to help me as well as you." She stopped beating and took a deep breath. "I miss the cloisters in Funchal," she said, "and the other Sisters. Once a year I was allowed to see my family through the grille." She stared down at the eggs. "But I will never see them again. I have been affected by sadness, and my work suffers. I think the Father saw your presence as a way to . . . to perhaps encourage me. To remind me of my purpose."

The carrots were clean, but I kept my hands in the cool water. I tried to think of a potion my mother used to treat melancholia. "Why are you here, if you were expected to remain cloistered for life?"

"I was sent to Porto Santo as punishment." She set aside the bowl and untied the twine from her waist. As had become her custom, she put a few *pastels de nata* in the charity basket she gave me each week. They were special convent pastries, filled with heavy cream, sugar and egg yolks, with more sugar caramelized on top. She had told me the pastries originated when nuns searched for a way to make use of all the egg yolks left after the whites were used to starch their wimples. I could smell the warm, fragrant pastry with its rich filling. The tarts were kept only for Father da Chagos and any special guests he might have—definitely not for the charity baskets. She also put a few altar candles in the basket today. From the furtive way she always hid the small extras, I knew she did not want the priest to find out.

"What did you do?" I thought of broken plates and burned bread, perhaps falling asleep during prayers.

"I used to have a daily struggle with obedience and humility. I found it difficult not to question," she replied, still looking down into the basket. "Perhaps in that way—needing to question what we hear, and see—we are a little alike, Diamantina." She finally looked up at me. "I tried to help a novice escape from the convent to run away to the man she loved."

I didn't move.

"I knew what she felt like. I wasn't brave enough to do it myself, but I helped her. She was caught, as was I."

"You were in love with someone?"

She waited a moment before speaking. "I was much younger when I imagined myself in love. I didn't fully understand what was best for me. I wasn't able to see the dangers, and wasn't ready, then, to accept the path God had chosen for me."

"And now you do?"

"And now I do," she said firmly, once more busying herself with arranging the contents of the basket. "And I will be here, serving out my penance, for the rest of my life."

CHAPTER NINE

Marco Perez died just after harvest that year.

It was said that Abílio had witnessed his father falling from his boat and cracking open his head on a rock. Few cared for Marco while he was alive, and even fewer mourned his death. I watched from under a dragon tree as his coffin was taken from the church to the graveyard. Abílio and his uncle, Marco's brother Rodrigo, walked behind the coffin, and I followed the handful of mourners. I had never been told I wasn't allowed in the graveyard.

On my way to work at the church the next day, I saw Abílio sitting on the bench outside his hut. He just sat with his hands on his knees. I had rarely seen him so still. He looked up at me as I passed, and I went to him. "I'm sorry about your father," I said.

He made a sound in his throat. "Are you really?"

I swallowed.

"I'm not. I should have . . ." He stopped, and lifted his hand to push his hair from his forehead, and I saw that all his knuckles were bruised and scabbed. I had a vision of Abílio refusing to take any more of his father's beatings.

"You should have what?" I asked. No. He couldn't have killed him, no matter what misery his father had brought upon him.

"He should have died a long time ago," Abílio said. "And I should have left a long time ago, like my brothers. But I couldn't leave my mother." He stood, and his jaw clenched. "Not that it did any good. I wasn't able to help her." He turned from me. "I'm not like him, Diamantina. And I'm not like my brothers, willing to take whatever work they can just to feed themselves."

"Where are your brothers?"

He shrugged. "I don't know. We never heard from them after they left."

"So they don't even know your mother died." I felt a sudden shiver, imagining someone you loved dying, while all the while you thought them alive and well.

"Do you believe that I'm not like them, Diamantina?" he asked.

"I always thought you were like your mother," I said with sincerity.

"I learned to read, and will do more than work with my hands all my life. I'm not going to live the way my father did." His voice was hard, angry. "I hated him."

Coughing and throat clearing came through the open door of the hut, then the sounds of spitting. Abílio frowned. "My uncle Rodrigo. He's staying a few more days, and then he'll go back to Madeira."

I didn't know what else to say. I turned to leave.

"I've heard you're cleaning the church now," Abílio said, and I looked back at him. "It must be hard for you to dress that way. You almost look like the other girls of Vila Baleira. Almost." He still had that strange, rough tone, which maybe was grief, masquerading as anger.

I ran my hands down my skirt.

"You like being paid to go to your knees to clean the church you're not allowed to attend?"

My cheeks were hot. "It's a way for us to eat, Abílio."

"I saw you, filing into the graveyard at the end of the procession. Will you always accept that you stand behind everyone else on Porto Santo? That you're considered of little significance? Do you like it? Why don't you have Father da Chagos baptize you and be done with being treated like an outsider in the community?"

His uncle came to the open door to lean against the frame, watching us as he dug in one ear with a piece of wet flannel.

"I don't believe a few words uttered by Father da Chagos will change anything for me. And I don't care. I am who I am," I said, and turned and left.

"Diamantina," Abílio called after me. "I'm sorry."

That was the last time I saw Abílio for the next few months. His fishing boat remained on the beach, and the door and windows of the hut were tightly closed. I heard in town that he had gone to Madeira with his uncle. I wanted to ask if he was coming back, but didn't want anyone to know I was interested.

As drought had ruined our summer, now the rainy season, usually the most temperate time of year, abundant with plant and animal life, was worse than usual. Day after day clouds blew in from the ocean, catching on the cliffs above the beach, opening to rain down torrents, and the world took on a sodden and dark heaviness.

My mother and I awoke shivering many mornings, our blankets smelling musty. Mildew grew on every surface, and the driftwood was perpetually damp. I couldn't start a fire to cook or to dry out the hut. Within a few short weeks I feared that all our belongings would be ruined, including my beloved collection of foxed, warped books and passage charts.

Our roof started to leak. When the weather was the most arid, cracks opened in the clay, letting in air. In the winter rains the cracks usually closed and the clay absorbed the water, keeping us warm and dry. But our hut roofs, unlike those of terracotta tiles that graced the houses in town, only lasted a few seasons. I had helped my father mix new clay and slather it on the cracks the year before he left. Now I would have to do it on my own.

Waking into the sodden, stinking wetness of our home, my mother cleared her throat; a cough and sore throat had been plaguing her. "We could move up into the cliffs and stay in a cave until this rainy time has passed," she said.

"A cave?" I said as I dressed for work. "Like animals?"

"The caves are dry," she answered, coughing. We both knew a tea of sweet violet would help her, but without a fire I couldn't boil water. "You were born in one."

"You never told me that."

"Even though I helped the women of the beach, when it was my time all of them were frightened to come to me, frightened that they might help to birth another witch and be forever cursed. It was a night when the ocean turned into a dangerous beast, gnashing its teeth and roaring. The storm brought lightning and thunder such as I've never experienced. I had a premonition that the beast would wash over the beach and our hut would be swept away. I had to protect you, waiting so patiently to come to me. And so your father took me up the cliffs, with the wind howling and the trees bent to the ground. He knelt at my side as you came into the world."

I watched her. Her face had a faraway look.

"And with your birth the world grew calm again. The beast retreated. The next morning I carried you back to the hut, which was still standing firm and strong. My premonition had been wrong. The beast hadn't been looking for you after all. You were safe from it, Diamantina, and always will be." The dark green of her eyes glistened with either tears or the pain of speaking with her sore throat.

I smiled at her, grateful for this memory of my birth. "I'll ask Sister Amélia to let me bring home a flagon of hot water and I'll mix you up a soothing drink," I said. "But I won't live in a cave. I'll fix the roof."

I wrapped a shawl over my head and ducked out the door. Water dripped from the edge of the roof as I went behind the hut and pulled out the ladder my father had made. The middle three rungs were rotted through. I would have to borrow one to climb onto the roof.

I walked up the beach in the still, grey air, looking at the fishing boats bobbing on the water. And then there he was: Abílio, coming up from the sea.

I tried to keep my breathing even, my face calm, although I wanted to run towards him. I wanted to demand, *Where have you been, and why didn't you tell me you were leaving?* But he owed me nothing.

He was carrying a long, stout fishing pole with a dangerous hook on the end. He'd harpooned a good-sized tuna. He smiled his warm smile. "You're looking very pretty today, Diamantina," he said. I studied the rise and fall of the sea over his shoulder, remembering the last time he had called me pretty. "Your eyes are the colour of the silvery porpoise that swim alongside the ships."

My cheeks were hot, and I didn't take my gaze from the sea. "You were in Madeira?"

He nodded. "In Funchal Town, working for my uncle."

I finally looked at him. "What's it like?"

"It's Madeira's jewel, very fine, with wide streets and busy squares and tall buildings. All of Madeira is green and beautiful."

I thought of the island's misty outlines, which I could see from the point on a clear day.

"It's not like this little island, Diamantina. In Funchal one sees people of many races. And so many there are learned and worldly."

"I'll go there someday soon. On my way to Brazil to join my father."

He shifted the pole.

"Can I borrow your ladder?" I asked. "I have to fix our roof."

He glanced at the sky. "It looks like we might have a brighter day tomorrow. I'll come and help you."

I felt a surge of something, perhaps just happiness. "All right," I said, smiling, and we nodded at each other and then there was a moment of awkwardness. "I have to get to the church," I added, as if he was preventing me from going.

⁂

The next afternoon, Abílio arrived with his ladder and a big wooden bucket. As he had predicted, the day was warmer, and at times a bright sun shone through the light clouds. I took our bucket and we went together up into the hills and collected clay. We hauled our buckets back to the beach and mixed the clay with sea water to make slurry. Abílio climbed up to the roof with one of the buckets and slathered the mixture over the cracks with his hands. When he needed the next bucket, I carried it up, taking the empty one back down. The sun came out brightly as we finished, guaranteeing the new clay would dry to permanence in a few hours.

We went into the sea and washed our hands and arms. He splashed me and I laughed, splashing him back. "We don't have much, but I can offer you some fish broth and cheese," I said.

"I have a honey cake at my place. Come and have some," he said. I nodded as we waded out of the water. He carried the ladder and I grabbed his bucket.

We sat across from each other at his table and he cut thick slices of the *bolo de mel*. "I'll be going back to Madeira again," he said, handing me a slice. "I only came home to act as pallbearer for Gustavo Lopez's brother's funeral."

A sudden darkness filled me. "Back to Funchal?"

"For just a while," he said, but before I could feel relieved he added, "Like your father, I plan to go to Brazil to make my fortune."

"Any day my father will be sending money, enough for me to buy passage. How much does it cost to go all the way to Brazil?"

"The cheapest passage is one hundred and sixty réis," Abílio said, and I made a low sound, trying to imagine that amount of money. "So Arie reached Brazil?" he asked me.

"He lives in São Paulo," I said with confidence, for what else could I think?

"How long has he been gone now?"

"Over a year." Sixteen months. There had been sixteen round, fat moons hanging low over the water since he left. I had been almost fourteen, but not yet a woman when he walked away. Now I was well past fifteen. I told myself he was waiting to earn enough money to send with his first letter from Brazil. Maybe he was trying to earn enough for two passages, one for my mother and one for me, although even a single passage, at one hundred and sixty réis, sounded like an impossible amount to ever save.

"I liked Arie," Abílio said, and I smiled warmly at him, thinking of the illustrations of compasses and spyglasses, of sextants and astrolabes in the books on navigation my father had left for me. I had often traced the sea routes he had told me about sailing with the Dutch East India Company. I thought of his decision to first explore the world when he was even younger than Abílio Perez.

Looking at him now, I thought that Abílio was like my father: curious, brave, wanting more than a safe and settled life. It was why my father had to leave me. And now Abílio would leave as well. "When will you go back to Funchal?"

He smiled back at me, a smile that carried the heat of today's sun. "Tomorrow, Diamantina."

My name, coming from his lips, sounded beautiful. Even though the cake was finished, I could smell it wafting from Abílio. I had long ago stopped leaning close to people, sniffing at them as I had when a child, but at this moment I wanted to be closer to Abílio, with his tantalizing scent of warm, sticky honey.

He ran his finger along the edge of the knife he'd used to cut the cake.

"My father told me many stories of life aboard ship: the cramped quarters, the ever-present threat of shipwreck, of disease and piracy," I said. "But he also spoke of the glories of the water stretching farther than sight allowed, and the light of the stars at night. The wind that changed from the cut of a whetted knife to the breath of an angel."

"Do you actually imagine you can go, Diamantina?"

"What do you mean? Of course I can go when I get the money for the passage."

"A good Portuguese woman isn't allowed to make a sea voyage on her own." He cocked his head. "Then again, you're not exactly a good Portuguese woman, are you?" His smile no longer carried the heat of the sun, but something cool and dangerous. He put down the knife and reached across the table and lifted my necklace, heavy with shells and smooth bits of coloured glass. "I've seen you sitting at the edge of the water, reading your books. Carrying your dead birds and rabbits home." He gently pulled my necklace, and I leaned forward. "You are the oddest girl I've ever known," he said, touching each piece of glass, and I felt as if the glass were my own skin, and his fingers warmed it. "No. I can't call you a girl anymore. You're a woman."

I was unable to speak.

"And I've known many in Funchal. Both girls and women." He gave a knowing smile that changed everything. There was a heaviness in my gut, as if I'd eaten a rotten quail egg. I pulled my necklace from Abílio's fingers, with their scent of honey.

"Are you jealous, little *bruxa*?" he said, so softly I barely made out the words.

"Jealous of what?" My own voice was louder than necessary.

"That I've known many women?"

I stood and wrapped my shawl around my shoulders. "What you do with your life isn't of any importance to me," I said. "Thank you for your help with the roof. And for the cake." I turned to leave, but he stood and caught my wrist.

"I'm sorry. I was only . . ."

I stared into his face. "Only what?"

"Trying to impress you." He went from charming to infuriating and back again.

I looked at his fingers wrapped firmly around my wrist. I thought of the bruises on his knuckles after his father died.

"I'll be gone tomorrow. Stay with me tonight." Abílio's voice was almost a whisper, his eyes wide and dark.

I swallowed, shocked and excited by his words, shaken at my own thoughts. I wanted to whisper back, *Yes, yes, I will stay.*

"No," I said.

CHAPTER TEN

The inordinately rainy weather continued, although our roof no longer leaked. Abílio's hut was again closed and shuttered, and I wondered if it was sunny in Madeira.

I thought of his whispered words, asking me to stay, and the way he looked at me the night before he left Porto Santo. I had never seen that look on a man's face, but I knew it was desire. It filled me with my own.

The rain ruined the herbs and flowers in our garden, drowning their roots and putting blight on their leaves and stems, and my mother and I were unable to make any new powders. Both the birds and their eggs were fewer; perhaps the larger birds of prey were also suffering, and consuming more of the seabirds than usual. Some afternoons I would search for hours in the tall, wet grass, looking for the stone nests of the pipits and shearwaters, only to find them empty but for broken shells. Even the rabbits hid themselves deeply in their lairs, keeping dry. I sat for many long, wet hours without reward.

To my great sorrow, Benedita got loose from her tether and ate a patch of poisonous creeper. She died of bloat within a few hours. I said my thanks to her as I butchered her. Her stringy body offered little good flesh to eat, with no fat to moisten it. I boiled her bones for broth, regretting that there would be no more milk or cheese. I had tarred our fishing boat and *Dog Star*, but each time I took one of the boats a few metres from shore, it leaked alarmingly. I was reduced to wading up to my thighs in the rough, raging sea, dragging our hemp net. But the waves were too wild, and I caught nothing but a few squiggling sardines and tiny crabs.

The ruined crops affected everyone on the island. The women still came to our hut for remedies but had nothing to offer in exchange for what we could give them from our depleted supply of medicines.

Although I still had the few réis Father da Chagos gave me each week, more people in the parish needed help from the church. The food the island could no longer provide was brought in from Madeira, but prices were high. All Sister Amélia could put in my basket every few days was a very small round of bread.

⁂

I used my last réis to buy a withered, blackening potato and two eggs, and my mother and I shared them. That evening we sat at the table in the chilled hut, and when it grew dark I lit the end of our last candle. By its feeble flicker my mother slowly stitched a rent in one of her skirts, and I tried to read. But I was cold and hungry, and I could think of little but the pain in my stomach.

At a sudden tap on the door, we both jumped. Expecting it to be a woman looking for relief, I rose and opened the door. Abílio stood there, rain dripping from his hair, holding a large covered basket with one hand and under the other arm a stack of kindling and wood, kept dry by a canvas wrap. "I've brought you a few things from Madeira," he said. I stepped back and he entered, ducking his head so as not to hit it on the low lintel.

He greeted my mother respectfully as he set the basket on the table. "Please, eat." He crouched in front of the fireplace and piled the kindling. I lifted out two loaves of bread and a big wedge of cheese. There were figs and dates, onions and carrots and sweet potatoes. A dried slab of beef, and a ring of sausage. Candles, and a flagon of oil and another of wine. As I set everything in front of my mother, I kept swallowing, my mouth full of saliva at the wonderful odours.

Abílio coaxed the fire to life and there was a rush of warm air. The hut took on a cheery glow, the dark chill banished.

"Please, senhora, Diamantina, please, eat. I heard, in Funchal, of the miseries here."

With tears of gratefulness, I looked from him to my mother, but she was watching Abílio watching me.

⁕

I slept more deeply that night than I had in a long time, full with food and the thoughts of Abílio's kindness. I brought back the memory of him asking me to stay with him. How I had wanted to.

I awoke in weak sunlight. I rose and prepared a rich stew. I was not expected to work at the church, and all I could think about was Abílio's face as he handed me the basket.

When the stew was slowly simmering on the fire, I put my shawl over my head. "I'm going to return Abílio's basket," I said.

My mother only nodded. I had expected her to say something about Abílio's consideration, but she hadn't.

As I approached his hut, the door was shut. I had somehow imagined he would be waiting for me. As I stood, suddenly shy of knocking, the door opened.

"I slept late," he said.

"I've brought your basket back." I handed it to him. "And I also want to thank you, again, for all you did for us. I . . . I didn't expect it. My mother is so grateful," I said, not really lying. She had enjoyed the food as I had.

"Madeira isn't suffering like Porto Santo." He reached up and brushed his hair from his eyes. I wondered if he had actually been with a girl or woman in Funchal this time. "It's a different climate, in spite of only being a day's sail south," he said. He studied me. "You've grown so thin since I last saw you. It's the slow season for my uncle — he doesn't need me right now. I came back because I was worried about you. I'll make sure you have enough to eat from now on."

His words created a weakening somewhere inside me.

⁕

Over the next days, I saw Abílio frequently, either on the beach or when he brought supplies to our hut. Once it was a catch of long, black-skinned, razor-toothed scabbardfish, once a slab of goat meat and a dozen eggs, and another time a stack of dry wood. He would have purchased all but the fish from the Madeira packet.

On the eighth day, I invited him to come to our hut for dinner. The three of us sat before a bright fire and ate the meal I'd prepared with the food he had given us. My mother answered the few questions he asked her about her garden, but otherwise didn't speak. I was used to her silences, but in Abílio's company I realized how withdrawn she appeared.

He had brought a flask of Boal. My mother refused the wine, and I drank her share. As Abílio rose to leave, I took up my shawl. "I'll walk with you," I said. "The moon is full." My mother made a sound, and I looked at her, but she was staring at the fire.

⌒⌒⌒

"I apologize for my mother," I said as we walked under the moon's light. "That's the way she is. She's not used to a man in the hut anymore."

"My father remembered when she came to the island."

I stayed silent, not wanting him to know my mother had never spoken of her past to me.

"Did she tell you my father was one of the men who rescued her after she was tossed into the sea by the Algerian ship?"

"No."

"My father said none of the women would shelter her or even speak to her at first. They knew she was a slave but saw her strange beauty, and were afraid she would steal their men. And the men were afraid of her power." He laughed. "But only weak men are afraid of a woman with her own power. A strong man likes it." He stooped and picked up a shell. "I like a strong woman," he said.

My mother had been on a ship from North Africa. That explained her secret language, and why she looked unlike any other woman on Porto Santo. Just like my father, she had been thrown overboard. What was her crime? I stared at the cowrie he held.

"Diamantina?" Abílio said. "What's the matter?"

"Nothing," I said, and we continued up the beach.

"Did you mean it when you said you were going to sail to your father in Brazil?" he asked. "Or is it just a dream?"

I couldn't concentrate on his words. The wine had created a pleasant lightness in my head. It was sweet at the back of my throat. My mother was an Algerian slave. I carried African blood. It excited me. Abílio's hand brushed mine, and I boldly took the cowrie from it, rubbing the shell's smoothness against my cheek. It was good luck for a woman to find a cowrie, my mother told me. The shell was a symbol of womanhood and fertility.

"Is going to Brazil just a dream?" Abílio repeated.

"No. I told you I would go, and I will."

He laughed. "We should sail away together."

The lightness left my head, and I blinked. "Together?" I stopped, looking at him.

His face was open, his eyes bright in the moonlight. "Brazil is the place to make a fortune, and quickly." He picked up my hand and brought it to his lips. "Do you want to come to Brazil with me?" His lips touched the back of my hand.

I was too startled to answer. I imagined that faraway country and my father waiting for me, his arms outstretched.

Abílio shrugged. "Well, who knows?" he said. He let go of my hand and walked backwards down the sand towards his hut, his eyes on me. I was shaken by what he had told me about my mother, what he had said about going to Brazil, and by the brief touch of his lips on my hand.

"Who knows, little *bruxa*," he called, his voice floating on the still night air.

Back home, I confronted my mother. "You were an Algerian slave? Abílio just told me."

She covered the smoking bowl with a plate and went to her bed. "Soon you will know my story," she said. She turned on her side, away from me.

I felt the same irritation as always at her wariness in answering my direct questions. "Mama!" My voice was loud in the hut, but she didn't answer.

⁂

I awoke the next morning to my mother burning herbs, waving the smoke about with a cluster of quail feathers. The smell was pungent. I imagined her over a fire somewhere in the north of Africa. I knew there was no point in questioning her. She only spoke when she was ready to speak.

I thought of Abílio's face when he had said we could go to Brazil together, uncertain of his expression.

When I came out of my hut, there he was, sitting on the stone that faced the sea, waiting for me.

"Let's go for a walk, up past the dunes."

I nodded. I didn't want the others along the beach to see us walking together and start a chain of gossip.

At one particularly sharp rise, he held out his hand to help me. I had been clambering over the dunes my whole life and needed no help, but his gesture moved me.

He kept my hand in his as we walked.

"Did you mean what you said last night, Abílio?" I asked. "About us going to Brazil together?"

"I want to go to Brazil, and you want to go to Brazil. It makes sense we should go together."

"I should know where my father is before too long."

"We'll find him together," he said.

I stopped and looked at Abílio. He put his arms around me and I felt his heart, beating against my breast.

⁂

I couldn't eat any dinner. After we had come back to the beach, Abílio had asked me to come to his hut later, and I had said yes.

I knew why I was going, and what I would do. He had wanted us to be together behind the dunes. I wanted it too—I had thought of it since the night he had whispered for me to stay—but I couldn't allow it to happen until I prepared my body.

I knew the stories of the women who came to our hut. I understood the rhythms of life, and how a child started, and I would not let this happen to me. In the *latrina* I put a piece of sea sponge soaked in vinegar and wrapped in a piece of fine muslin as far up inside me as I could. I had tied it with a slender thread that would allow me to pull it out afterwards. The women of the beach couldn't use the string for fear their husbands would notice. I didn't care if Abílio noticed. I had no dreams of saving my purity for a husband. There would be no young man on Porto Santo for me other than Abílio Perez, who would take me away with him.

CHAPTER ELEVEN

I was trembling as I lay down on his pallet, the light of the fire and the candles on the table flickering over the ceiling. My breath was ragged with excitement, but there was also a drumming of panic in my throat. It was not only anxiety for the physical act, but a great fear for how my life was about to change. How I was going to be changed.

My teeth chattered as Abílio lay beside me and stroked my face. "It will be all right, Diamantina," he said softly, then slowly pulled up my skirt, running his hands over my knees, my thighs. In the flickering light I saw his pupils pulse as he pushed my skirt to my waist. I fought not to cover myself with my hands, and my legs instinctively closed. He gently pushed them apart.

He leaned down then, as if to kiss me, and I waited, but his lips did not graze mine. His breath smelled of the sweet wine we had drunk before we lay together, but there was more. His body gave off another odour, a quick, dancing smell of excitement, something musky and unfamiliar.

As he outlined my lips with his index finger, he murmured, "You smell wild, of the salty sea and the clean wind. And of . . . what is it? What is your sweetness?"

He was taking in my scent as I took in his.

I didn't answer, but when I saw his hands work at the lacing of his breeches, I turned my head away, too shy to look at him. Then he was again pushing apart my knees, which strained against his hands as if with a spirit of their own. "It's all right, Diamantina," he whispered again, and I willed my knees to fall open as he lay on top of me. I put my hands around his back. And then his flesh burned against mine and there was a sudden stabbing pain. I sucked in my breath with the shock of it, my hands tightening on his back. I kept my eyes closed the entire time, waiting for the rhythmic waves of discomfort to be over. I listened to the quiet sounds Abílio made, almost like praying, and felt his cross swing against my ear with each of his slow thrusts. Suddenly he stopped with a quiet, almost helpless cry, and then his chest dropped against mine, although he didn't allow his full weight to fall on me. I felt the scrape of his cheek, soft skin under sharp stubble.

I opened my eyes and he moved beside me, shifting so that his head lay on my breast. His eyes were closed, and I saw the length of his eyelashes against his cheeks. I put my hand into his hair and finally felt its soft thickness. I wanted him to tell me something, needed to know what he thought at this moment. What he thought of me. That he allowed me to see him so vulnerable filled me with a delicious sense of power. He breathed slowly and heavily, as if falling asleep. I waited.

He opened his eyes. "You were as sweet as you smell. I love a sweet new fruit."

It wasn't what I wanted to hear.

"What's this?" he asked, lifting the silver amulet and studying it.

"My father was born with the birth casing over his face," I told him. "His mother kept it. Inside the silver is a piece of that caul, good fortune for sailors. It saved him from drowning."

"If you believe that story," he said. As he laced his breeches, I sat up, pulling down my skirt and straightening my blouse. The candles had burned low, and the fire was only glowing embers. He urged me down beside him again. "Don't go. Stay the night."

"I can't. My mother . . ."

He sat up as I stood, trying to ignore the sudden weakness in my legs. He caught my hand and kissed the palm, and I again put my fingers through his hair. Then I left. He didn't accompany me.

As I walked down the beach, fully lit by the moon, I was glad it was too late for anyone from the other huts to see me leave Abílio's.

In front of my own hut I tucked my skirt up around my waist and waded into the sea to my knees, pulling out the slimy sponge and tossing it as far as I could into the waves. In the moonlight I saw, on my inner thighs, lines of dried blood, thin as if painted with grass strokes.

I let the cool water wash me, wanting to smell only of the sea when I went inside. But my mother lifted her head, studying me as I crossed the room to my pallet. I had to look away from her sharp gaze.

Later, as we lay in the darkness, she said, "Men do not always do what they promise, Diamantina."

I said nothing, for I had no answer. I did not feel shame, but somehow I was sorry that she knew what I'd done.

⌒◦⌒

It was raining heavily again the next morning as I ran up the beach on my way to the church. I had slept longer than usual, and Sister Amélia would be wondering where I was. But my steps slowed as I drew closer to Abílio's hut. As if pushed by the stinging rain, I stopped in front of his door. Of course, I'd known I would stop. Otherwise why had I put in the sponge?

He opened it immediately, as though he'd been waiting. I stepped inside and he put his hand on the curve of my hip, brushing my wet hair from my cheeks.

"I shouldn't have come," I said, my words unconvincing even to me, my voice breathless from running, from the pleasure of being so near him, lust filling me with a surprising strength.

"I'm glad you're here," he said, and pressed against me.

"It isn't right, what we did. We shouldn't do it again, Abílio," I said, feeling him already hard. I don't know why I felt the need to say such words. Perhaps I wanted him to convince me there was nothing forbidden in being together.

His smile was easy, apparently boyish. But there was something behind it, something not boyish at all. Not easy. Rain drummed on the roof. He poured me a cup of warm water sweetened with honey. I drank a mouthful, and then touched my mouth to his. He licked his lips, staring at me. He dipped his thumb into the cup and made the sign of the cross on my forehead with the warm, sweet water.

"*In nomine Patris, et Filii, et Spiritus Sancti.* Amen. Now you are baptized," he said, with that same, slightly strange smile.

I slapped lightly at his hand, smiling back. "I don't need to be baptized."

"But now I can marry you," he said, and I drew a sharp breath, my smile falling away. "Even without a dowry." He took the cup from my hand and we moved together to his pallet.

Later, I pulled down my skirt, still damp from the rain, and searched on the pallet for the twine he'd pulled from the end of my braid. *Now I can marry you,* he'd said. "I'm so late for the kitchen. Sister Amélia will think I'm not coming."

"Don't go."

"I have to."

"Will you come to me when you're done?"

Now I can marry you. "Of course," I said.

❧

A few mornings later, after Abílio and I had spent an hour on his pallet, I sat combing my hair with my fingers. He stretched, yawning contentedly.

"I bought you some green ribbon. There, on the shelf." He gestured to a length of shiny satin. "I thought it would be pretty with your hair," he said, stopping my busy fingers. "I'll walk into Vila Baleira with you. I'm expecting a letter from my uncle with news about a better position with him in Funchal. After a few months I'll have made enough money for the passage to Brazil," he said. As he spoke, he absently stroked my arm, running his fingers up and down my skin under my loose sleeve. "I can't wait to leave this island for good. I'm not made for island life. I need more."

I had waited, each day, for him to talk again about us marrying. I hadn't told my mother, although I wanted to. I wanted her to know that she had no reason to be suspicious of Abílio.

"Your skin is so fine, Diamantina," he said. "Portuguese women don't have such fine skin." He moved closer to the wall, making room for me, and I lay beside him again, pressing the full length of my body to his, my face against his neck.

"When will we marry, Abílio?" I whispered, needing to hear him speak to me of it as I pulled him on top of me. I wrapped my thighs around his hips, my feet over his lower back. As he unlaced his breeches, I arched to meet him and pressed my lips against his neck. His skin, under my tongue, tasted of salt.

Afterwards, we lay beside each other in silence. He hadn't answered my question. But he held my hand, winding his fingers through mine, and pulled my head onto his shoulder. He would take me to Brazil. I would find my father. I didn't know what I would do about my mother; she seemed weaker every day, and I couldn't leave her like this. But I wouldn't think about that right now. I wanted to savour my joy. I wanted to hold on to this feeling.

I hadn't felt such comfort since my father left.

⚭

I thought of Abílio as I fell asleep, and he was in my thoughts when I awoke. Slowly, fine weather returned, and I was able to coax the garden to life, and once again caught rabbits and birds and scooped living creatures from the sea.

I went to work at the church, but could hardly wait to run back along the beach to Alílio's hut. Sometimes we didn't speak, and we never undressed, simply pushing our clothing out of the way. He never even took off his boots.

Each time I came to him, Abílio had some of his day's catch waiting, as well as something for me: a small bolt of cloth and embroidery floss, or two or three candles, a painted dish and once a bracelet of hammered copper. I loved thinking of him in the shops in Vila Baleira, picking out what he would give me.

My mother didn't ask about the food or gifts I brought home, although she looked pointedly at what I held each time. Her silence annoyed me, and I stared back at her.

It wasn't just my mother who was aware of Abílio's gifts. The people of the beach watched me go to Abílio's hut and watched me leave it. They saw us walking together. And the women of the island came less and less to our hut. At first I didn't care; I would rather be at Abílio's than working with them.

The busy tongues of the shopkeepers wagged of Abílio's purchases. Soon the townspeople whispered about me as I passed.

Did I care? I had always been the subject of gossip. Soon I would marry Abílio and leave this place.

CHAPTER TWELVE

As I walked towards Abílio's on my way home from work one late afternoon, my bare feet soundless on the sand, I heard his uncle's voice. When had Rodrigo come from Funchal?

I stopped. I didn't plan to listen, but Rodrigo's voice was loud as he said my name. "You have no place for her in your life."

I couldn't hear Abílio's response.

"Make your decision, Abílio. Choose a woman, or choose your own success. We're speaking of your life, and your life here is done, with both Lía and Marco gone. There are women everywhere, both ladies and whores. You don't need to bring one with you. Find one—or as many as you like—once you have the money and power. They will always be there."

I wanted to march into the hut and tell Rodrigo Perez I was not that kind of woman. Why didn't I? I waited, hoping to hear Abílio defend me. But I heard only Rodrigo.

"Don't throw your life away for a woman. Look at me. I'm successful because I didn't let anyone hold me back. The *garum* business is thriving—fish sauce is highly sought after. Think about what I'm offering you: you have the ability to become one of my top men." His voice was loud and commanding, and reminded me of his brother. "You know I have no room for both of you in my house—and before long there'll be a child to contend with, and you'll be even more trapped. Don't do it, nephew. A chance like this doesn't come along often, but girls like the witch's daughter can be found in any alley of any town."

I backed away. I didn't want Abílio to know I had heard the deeply shaming words.

※

I waited all evening for Abílio to come to me. I was sure he cared for me as I did for him. The feelings that brought me to his bed time after time were unlike anything I'd ever imagined. He was going to marry me. We were going to Brazil together. He wouldn't let his uncle dictate his actions; he was stronger than that. I pressed the satiny surface of the cowrie shell to my lips and willed him to come.

That night I slept in small, fitful snatches, thinking I heard him tapping on the door. Twice I got up and went outside and looked up the dark beach. I blamed Rodrigo. Surely he'd taken Abílio to Rooi's to drink wine. The third time I opened the door, my mother spoke softly.

"He's not coming, Diamantina."

I slammed the door, angry with her for knowing too much.

※

The next morning, as I ran up the beach, I said hello to Rosa, who lived a few huts from Abílio's. She had often come to me for powders for her daughter's troublesome stomach. She turned her head and didn't greet me, but I was so relieved to see Abílio on the bench in front of his hut that I didn't think anything of Rosa's response.

I glanced through the open door; the hut was empty. "Where's Rodrigo?"

"How do you know he was here?"

I swallowed. "Someone in town mentioned seeing him yesterday."

"He left on the packet this morning."

My spirits soared with relief and joy. I sat beside Abílio, our arms touching. I couldn't let him know I'd overheard the conversation the day before; it was too humiliating. But now everything was all right. He took my hand and we went into the hut. He made love to me slowly, and afterwards, as we lay together, he reached up and untied the twine at the end of my braid. He ran his fingers through my hair, bringing it to his face. "You always smell so sweet and wild, Diamantina."

I sat up and put my hand on his cheek. "Abílio. I could go to Funchal with you and we could be married there, where nobody knows my . . . my circumstances. Then I'll come back here to care for my mother. By the time you've earned the money for your passage to Brazil, I'll have the money for mine from my father." He needed to work for his uncle, and yet his uncle wouldn't accept me. I wanted him to know I would wait for him. I wanted to bring him the comfort that he had brought me.

He looked at me with an odd, unreadable expression, then closed his eyes for a moment. When he opened them, his lips twisted into something between a smile and a sneer. "Do you really think I would take you with me to Brazil?"

My mouth went dry.

He got up and stood with his back to me, lacing his breeches. "I'm leaving for Funchal tomorrow. On my own. And for good this time." His voice was rough. Surely he was teasing me in the worst of ways. "You should leave now. I have a lot to do."

I couldn't move.

"Diamantina? I told you. Go." Finally he looked back at me, his face dark, perhaps ashamed, or perhaps it was just shadowed by the ugliness of this moment.

"What are you talking about? You said . . . you said we would marry and go to Brazil together. You said we would marry, Abílio."

"All women are the same. At the first hint of marriage they're willing to open their legs."

The words were so unexpected that I couldn't speak for a moment. "Stop!" I finally said. "Stop talking this way." When he didn't respond, I said, "This is your uncle, not you. You don't mean what you're saying, Abílio."

He sat heavily, staring at his hands spread in front of him on the table. "It's just part of the game," he said, his voice emotionless. "I can't help it if you're too naive to see the world as it really is."

Tears came to my eyes, tears of confusion, of horror and disbelief.

I stumbled from the pallet, my skirt still caught up at one side, my blouse slipping off one shoulder. I knelt beside him and put my arms around him. "Abílio. Why are you being so cruel? What's come over you?" I knew that Rodrigo had convinced him, but I couldn't believe Abílio would hurt me in this way, with such ruthlessness.

"Do you really think I would sail away with a whore from Porto Santo?" he asked, seemingly unable to stop the terrible words. He looked away from his hands and at me. "You'll stay here all your life, on your back, while I'll discover new worlds and make my fortune."

I looked into his eyes. They were brown and dull; why had I thought them so bright? There was nothing there. Nothing. He had called me a whore.

I rose and stepped away, wiping at my cheeks and straightening my skirt. I wouldn't let him see me like this, crying and begging. Such shock and anger filled me that my legs wobbled. "Discovering new worlds? You call me a whore, and imagine yourself sailing off as an adventurer? You say you aren't like your father, but you are. You're every bit as cruel and vicious as him. And worse. You need your uncle to hold your hand and tell you what to do. You follow his demands like a sheep." I attempted a laugh, but the look on Abílio's face frightened me.

"Don't ever laugh at me," he said, his eyes strangely focused. "But you—*you* dare to compare me to my father? You're definitely like your mother: a witch and a whore who slept with a heathen sailor. And look at you, the bastard of that union."

"I know what I am." My own smell rose from under my clothes, the rosemary fragrance I now wore, like my mother, and the remains of damp lust and of Abílio's seed. The smell filled the air, threatening to choke me. I wouldn't cry again.

"A girl like you will always find a man to give her what she needs," he went on. He wore a slightly quizzical air, as if challenging me. "Or perhaps just what she wants."

"I put a curse on you," I said when I could finally speak again, when I could trust my voice to be strong. I found enough saliva to spit on the floor in front of him, needing to get the taste of hurt and rage out of my mouth. "A curse for pox, for boils, for blindness. For a life of misery."

His face was pale. "I'm not one of your superstitious island women, Diamantina. Your hex won't work on me." He gestured towards the door. "I'm finished with you. But I'll remember you—you were made for a man's pleasure." He rose and took a small cloth bag, tied with a leather strip, from a nearby shelf. I heard the clink of coins. "Here." He held it towards me.

His words, and the offer of money, hurt more than I thought possible. "I'm glad you're going, and glad that I'll never again see you, Abílio Perez." I stepped close and slapped him, one hard blow with my open hand, my fingernails scratching his cheek. The bag of réis flew from his hand to the floor. "Burn in hell," I said.

His cheek immediately reddened, thin lines of blood oozing in the scratches, and he grabbed my throat.

"You are just like your father," I said, fighting the pressure of his fingers around my neck.

He swallowed and dropped his hand. Then he reached up to touch his cheek. He looked at his bloodied fingertips, and I saw that they trembled slightly.

I went to the door, needing to hold the frame for a moment. I was still shaking, my legs weak. I didn't look back as I made my way home. In front of my hut I waded out into the water and pounded the waves with my fists. I ducked under the water, opening my mouth in a bubbling scream. Then I rose, choking, and wrapped my arms around myself. I stayed in the ocean as long as I could, not wanting to face my mother. Finally, drenched and shivering, I went into the hut.

She stared at me, but she did not speak. Neither did I.

I lay awake that night looking up at the roof Abílio and I had repaired together, and thought of the way he ran his fingers over my eyebrow and along the side of my jaw as he looked down at me. I thought of the taste of his skin, and cried then, pressing my blanket over my mouth.

My mother sighed. "Men make promises," she said, as she had the first night I went to Abílio. I turned on my side and looked across the dark room, seeking the whites of her eyes. "At least he didn't leave you with child. This I read in the smoke today. Even with the sponge and vinegar you know there is no assurance. "

I felt something close to gratitude that she didn't force me to speak of what had happened earlier.

"A man's promise," she said. "That's how I came to the island, so long ago. I believed in the man who took me away on a tall ship. Although I had once been a slave, I had bought my way out with my powers. But those same powers made me feared, and I was condemned to be burned alive. Even those who had once sought my help joined the crowd who came for me. And yet the man convinced me he was not like others. He said we would sail far away from Algeria, far away from the danger."

I sat up.

"All went well for the first weeks at sea. But then a storm came up, and we were blown far off course, all the way to the Madeira archipelago. The wind and rains continued for a full eight days, and the crew, exhausted and fearing for their lives, looked for reasons for their bad luck. One, then another, and then more muttered that I was the cause. They said I controlled the moon with my spells, and was changing the tides. It was because of me that they would all die. They told the man I thought loved me that he must throw me overboard."

Outside, waves crashed on the beach. After a long while I said, "And he did."

"He had said he couldn't live without me. I thought he would join me, and together we would perish. But he valued his own life too much."

"Then fishermen found you," I said. Abílio's father's story.

"I don't know what happened. I only remember falling, down, down into the dark water, and then rushing through that water as if I had the body of a fish. Or maybe I was skimming the waves with the body of a bird."

I lay down, staring at the ceiling. There I saw the image of my mother floating on the air as a gull, the wind billowing her skirt and streaming through her hair.

"When I awoke, I was on this beach. I was alone. And I stayed alone for a long time. Until Arie ten Brink came."

"Do you think about him?"

"Your father?"

"No. The other man. The man you thought would save you, but who damned you."

She was silent for so long I thought she had fallen asleep, but then she said, "Yes. As you will think of Abílio Perez for some time. But then you will think of another."

I turned to face the wall and allowed myself to weep without trying to hide my sorrow. After a while I felt my mother's hand stroking my shoulder, light as the touch of a wing.

"Promises are like smoke, Diamantina—strong and visible at first, but fading into nothingness. Don't waste your tears on promises from another. Stay true to your own promises."

I fell asleep with her hand on my shoulder.

⁂

The next day, I sat on the rock on the beach in front of our hut. The sun shone weakly. I dully watched a row of busy terns running along the sand, their feet leaving tidy rows of tracks. I turned to follow them as they rushed headlong up the beach.

There was a man in the distance, walking towards Vila Baleira with something slung over one shoulder. It could have been a fisherman with his catch, taking it into town to sell. Or it could have been Abílio, on his way to the wharf.

The old memory came back, the one that still haunted me: my father walking away.

CHAPTER THIRTEEN

Something shifted after Abílio left Porto Santo. Not just within me, but in how I was treated by the people of the island. As well as a witch and a heathen, I was now seen as the whore both Rodrigo and Abílio had called me.

The women of the beach no longer came to our hut, suffering their ills rather than accept help from a woman such as I, or going to Teresa Trovão, if she would agree to their offerings.

A few weeks after Abílio was gone, a boy of only nine or ten, made bold by his friends, grabbed my skirt when I was at the back door of the church. I slapped his hand and his grin faded as I hissed at him, muttering one of my mother's incantations. He and his friends backed away. Entering the kitchen, I nodded at Sister Amélia, snatching my apron from its hook and tying it with swift, angry movements. I chopped an onion violently, the knife slamming against the board.

I stared at the squares of onion and shook my head. "This place, Sister. I mind my own business and bother nobody. And yet . . ." I put down the knife and looked at her. "I wish . . ."

She was standing in front of a mound of fragrant dough. She opened her mouth as if to speak, then closed it. She scattered flour on the table and set the dough on it, but didn't begin kneading. "What do you wish for?"

To be away from here. To find my father. To change what happened with Abílio.

It was only then that I saw she was troubled. Her skin, untouched by the sun, was as creamy as the finest linen, but, like linen, it also showed a very faint map-work of wrinkles fanning from the corners of her eyes. "Is something wrong, Sister?"

She wiped her hands down her apron and reached up to remove the heavy veil that covered her coif, then unfastened the tight wimple and pulled it off. She threw it down on the bench. She had short, dark hair, wavy and soft. "Father da Chagos is away for the afternoon, ministering last rites to one of his flock. I'm unbearably warm. Tonight I will confess this sin." She waved her fingers at the heap of her veil and wimple. "Leave the onion. I have to talk to you."

I set down the knife.

"I see who you are, Diamantina. Do you think that I didn't have a life before I was put into the convent by my father?" She lifted the edge of her apron and dabbed at the perspiration on her temples. "He condemned me, against my will, to seclusion in the convent to protect my purity. Twice he had arranged my betrothal, but both men were unsuitable to me. And then, unexpectedly, I met a man I gave my heart to and wished to marry. My father found him unacceptable. I threatened to run off and marry without my father's permission, and it was then he decided that the only way to save me from an unfortunate future was for me to live a cloistered life. I was about the same age as you, coming sixteen," she said. "I argued and pleaded with him—I tried to run from him. My mother could not stand up to him, although I entreated her as well. But she also felt they had to force a righteous path on me. In the end I had no choice." She sighed heavily. "And so I tried to be a good nun. I forgave my parents, after much contemplation and prayer, and understood their concern for me. But I did not hear the calling, either as a novice or when I took the veil."

She looked down at the mound of dough. "Every time I took Communion, I kept His body on my tongue as long as possible, certain that He was with me. I kept my heart open. I was always waiting, and listening, but not once did He come to me. I have never known a rapture or an ecstasy, as I witnessed with so many of the other Sisters. I longed to know what brought God into their bodies but not into mine."

She looked back at me. "Once a week, for one hour, we could

break our silence and converse, and I did ask the others how they had achieved this miracle. But none could give an answer that satisfied me. And those one-hour conversations once a week weren't enough for me. Over and over I broke the vow of silence. I entered into a friendship with one of the other Sisters. Friendship is frowned upon within the convent walls. We are to devote ourselves only to God. There is no room for personal feelings other than love for Him." She ran her rosary beads through her fingers.

"The nun I befriended was the one I eventually tried to help flee the convent. She was even less suited than I to a life of silence and contemplation. I don't know what happened to her, as she was taken from the convent and her name never again mentioned. And I was sent here, into exile."

I put my hand on hers.

"Another sin," she said, nodding at our hands, and then she looked into my face. "Some people are born with a pure nature, and others must try to find that pureness. For me it was a struggle, as I know it is for you. I know, Diamantina."

My face was hot. She couldn't know what I'd done with Abílio, could she? She couldn't know that even though I now hated him, hated how he'd made me feel when he left, only last night I had dreamed of his hands on me, his mouth on mine. I was full of both sorrow and anger when I awoke.

She gently pulled her hand from under mine and ran her fingertips along the flour on the table. Did she have the same lustful thoughts as I? Did she never awaken in the night, restless and desiring? How did she ignore the body's heat?

Without the heavy wimple, her head was so vulnerable. "Even when temptation arises, you do have choice," she said.

I thought of my father telling me I had to choose, and felt a surge of displaced anger. I picked up the knife and chopped again, violently. "What choice do I have here, on Porto Santo? Choice, Sister Amélia?" I shoved the onion to one side with the outside of my hand. A few pieces fell onto the floor.

"I didn't say one choice or another made for an easier life. But certain choices make it easier to live with dignity."

She was telling me to be a clean, upstanding woman. I only hoped she couldn't see the images in my head as she spoke of dignity, the images of me under Abílio, my knees gripping his hips, my hands clutching his back.

"And there is fate," she said. "Although Father da Chagos—and all those men and women of the Church I have knelt before— believe God has predetermined our lives, I sometimes wonder. I question it, especially when I see how some are born into an unfair situation. All the babies who die, the innocent children who suffer. Those people afflicted with a lifetime of pain, or those who lose their minds and are chained like animals in straw for the rest of their time on earth. I know that mistakes are made. There are accidents. There is . . ." She paused. "There is passion."

My face must have reflected my discomfort, for she said, so quietly I had to hold my breath to hear her, "I speak to you in this way because I do not judge you."

I imagined the depth of her loneliness in her narrow cell every night, with only her Heavenly Husband on the cross over her pallet, who had so far been no company.

"Sometimes others can see your fate more clearly that you can," she went on. "It's as though you're walking blind, your hands out- stretched, trying to feel your way, but you're going in the wrong direction. And at those times you need someone who is watching, who has vision, to help you. To take your hand and lead you to that path."

"You mean God," I said, my voice sharper than I'd intended.

She stared at me with an unfamiliar look that might have been impatience, or maybe it was just that she didn't look like a nun without her veil and wimple. "God sees all, yes. But He has many lambs to care for. Sometimes He asks a shepherd on earth to do His work for him."

I watched her.

"Man, every man, is tempted by his urges. If that flicker of desire didn't arise in him, he wouldn't be a man," she said. I was hot with shame. She knew that I had sinned. "A woman, while also having the desire, has to learn not to act on it. You are bigger than the island, Diamantina. Don't sink to its size."

Her words hit me so strongly that for a moment her face swam in front of me, a pale disc. "Sister Amélia," I finally said, my voice as quiet as hers, as though we might be overheard and punished, even though the priest never came into the kitchen, and today wasn't even in the church. "I do want to be bigger. I want to leave, and go to my father."

She nodded.

"And I'm waiting to hear from him, waiting to know where he is, and how to get there. He said that he would send us money to live, and then enough for me to go to him if the time was right. I'm willing to stay with my mother as long as necessary, knowing I *can* go to him. But right now I have nothing, not even the réis it would take to get as far as Madeira."

We sat without speaking for a few moments. Then she replied, carefully choosing her words. "To anyone else I would say confess all to Father da Chagos, and ask for absolution, and do your penance, and then pray for the answer. To anyone else I would say God will give you the answer. But I know that you don't have the training to look for answers from God. And so I tell you this: it's up to you to find the answers. Watch and listen for signs. Pay attention to what presents itself. You will find that there is reason in everything."

Was there no end to the ways Sister Amélia would surprise me today? "Reason in everything? Don't you mean there is God in everything?"

"Take my words as you will," she said, and then put one floury hand on her breast, leaving a dusty white print. "I was once a young woman like you. *Like you.*"

I leaned over and touched my cheek to hers. "Thank you, Sister Amélia," I said. "Thank you for being my friend. You are the only one."

At that, she stood abruptly, looking down at me. "I cannot be your friend." She put her hands on the table as if to support herself, as if she had grown suddenly weak. "Diamantina, you are no longer allowed to work here. I wanted to tell you as soon as you arrived, but you were so distraught."

I stared at her.

"It was the confession of Abílio Perez, before he left. He confessed his relationship with you to the Father, and . . . the Father sees you as a fallen woman. He can no longer have you working in the church." She gestured to a small pile of coins on a shelf near the door. "He left your last payment there."

When I didn't respond, she said, "I'm sorry, Diamantina. Father da Chagos didn't want to speak to you of this. He gave me the task of letting his wishes be known."

I tried to think of my life without Sister Amélia in it. "When will I see you again?"

"You will not see me," she said, "but some days I commit the sin of stepping outside the kitchen and watching the square, hidden behind the gate. Some days, as you cross the square, know that I'm watching you. Walk with your head high, and know that I'm smiling at you. And that you will always be in my heart."

My eyes burning, I stood and untied my apron and hung it on its hook. I took her hand, and she allowed it for a moment. Then she gently pulled away, picking up her veil and wimple. Her bare feet gliding unseen under her long robe in their usual way, she went to her room. The swirl of her robe as she softly shut the door was the last I saw of her.

CHAPTER FOURTEEN

The next day, I tried to find other work in Vila Baleira. With no healing to do, no help from Abílio, and now no more réis from the church, our situation would soon be dire. I was willing to take on the lowest job, from emptying and scrubbing the chamber pots of the few wealthier families to swabbing the blood and entrails from the wooden cutting tables of the fishmongers. But I was turned away.

And then I noticed Rooi, sitting on a bench in the sunshine outside his inn. Although I often saw him there, and waved to him, I hadn't visited him for a long while. With my father gone, it seemed we had little to say to each other.

I stopped now in front of him. "Hello, Rooi."

"How have you been, Diamantina? How's your mother?"

"She's not well, after the rains. And I need a job." I crossed my arms over my chest. "I could clean the inn."

He shook his head. "The inn isn't a place for a girl."

"I'm not a girl. I'm a woman, Rooi, and I can handle myself."

His shirt was stained and his hair long and unwashed, his pipe stuck behind one ear.

"Your customers will come more willingly if the cups are clean and the tables not so sticky." I glanced in the open door. "And the floor, Rooi. The floor." I clicked my tongue, looking at the mess.

He shrugged, taking his pipe and pressing his thumb into the tobacco still there. "My customers are sailors. They'll come no matter what. There's no other place in Vila Baleira where they're welcome to drink as much as they like."

"Please, Rooi," I said. "For only a few réis a week I'll keep it spotless."

He studied me.

"For my father," I said, refusing to move. "Help me, Rooi. He would want you to help me."

He sighed heavily, and then was silent for a long moment. "*Ja*, you're right. I give you the job for Arie ten Brink."

After I'd finished the cleaning in the afternoon, I started staying on to pour drinks behind the counter. Rooi soon realized his take was greater when I looked after things. He was often drunk along with his customers, and it was clear to me he lost a great deal of income in this way. I collected the price of each drink before handing over the tankard, and when I presented him with a full purse at the end of the evening, Rooi was happy to give me some of it. I would only leave when the last sailor had staggered back to the wharf to be rowed to his ship for the night.

The money I earned was worth being winked at or treated to a foul joke by the hard-drinking sailors. Occasionally the way one of them smiled at me reminded me of Abílio, and at those moments I would pour myself a cup of wine to wash away the memories. Because Rooi and I spoke Dutch to each other, the sailors assumed I was his daughter. When they wanted me to serve them, they snapped their fingers and called out for the Dutchman's daughter.

One afternoon as I was washing the floor, Rooi filled a jug with wine from a newly opened cask.

As the fumes wafted towards me, I called, "That one's got something wrong with it, Rooi." I leaned back on my heels, dropping the rag into the scummy grey water. "I can smell it from here. Who sold it to you? Was it Henry Duncan?"

"This one and a keg of Sercial."

English merchants came from Funchal to sell to Rooi, and Mr. Duncan was his main supplier. He was even-featured, his blue eyes bright in a youngish face, his rich brown hair streaked early with grey. He liked me to serve him, always entreating me to sit and talk to him for a few minutes. He patiently let me practise English with him, never making fun of me like some of the English sailors did.

"*Nee, mijn meisje,*" Rooi said now. "You can't tell there's something wrong with the wine from all the way across the room." Every time Rooi called me "my girl," as my father had, I felt a twinge of both pleasure and sadness.

He poured himself a cup and took a swig. As he swallowed, he made a face and shook his head. "Acch. You're right. Tangy as horse's piss." He wiped his mouth with the back of his hand. "Doesn't matter. Most of the sailors will drink anything."

"Maybe the Portuguese or the Spanish or North African sailors. But not the English—they're fussier." I got up and came to him, taking the tin cup from his hand. I stuck my nose in it and took a great whiff, then sipped it. "A Boal from the north side of Madeira. Maybe São Vicente. Get me some of our *surdo*, Rooi." Because of the intense heat of the sun on the island, Porto Santo's grapes were very sweet, and their juice produced a strong, syrupy liqueur. Rooi brought me that *surdo*, and I poured a bit into the cup of Boal, tried it, then added a bit more, swirling it to mix it and taking another sip. "There," I said, handing it to him.

He tasted it and nodded. "Much better." A sudden warm wind blew in through the open door. Rooi took another swallow and smacked his lips appreciatively. "Leave the floor and come make your magic on this keg," he said.

⁂

That evening, Henry Duncan arrived, and asked me for a cup of his own Sercial. Instead, I brought him the wine I'd blended, and watched as he lifted the cup to drink. As he breathed in the wine, he looked at me quizzically. "I said Sercial, Diamantina. This is a Boal."

"Could you try it, Mr. Duncan? I won't charge you for it."

He looked at me with surprise. "For you, of course." He took a sip, rolling it around in his mouth. "Caramel, coffee, but there's something different about it." He took a second mouthful, and when he'd swallowed, he said, "I can't say I love it, but I will admit it's interesting. I can identify most of the Funchal blenders by their signature palate. Who's the merchant?"

I smiled. "You are, Mr. Duncan. It is your Boal, slightly spoiled in the keg. So I added some *surdo* to sweeten it and bring out its fullness."

"Rooi," he called with a laugh, "your girl could teach you a lesson or two." He pressed a few réis into my hand. "Now bring me the Sercial."

⁕

The money Rooi paid me was enough so that my mother and I didn't want for food, but still there was no extra. Without money, my dream of leaving Porto Santo could never be anything more than a dream. After I was let go from the church, I had still regularly gone to the priest asking if there was a letter from my father. Each time, Father da Chagos just shook his head, closing the front doors where I had stood waiting for him. He appeared angry with me for asking, and this in turn angered me. I wished my father had arranged to send the letters to Rooi, but Rooi was drunk most of the time, and there was no sense of order anywhere in his life. My father wouldn't have trusted him.

As I passed sixteen, I stopped asking Father da Chagos about a letter. It had been three years since my father left. Why hadn't he written? Certainly some letters could have gone astray between Brazil and Portugal, floating to the bottom of the ocean in a ship that had sunk, or lost when the ship was pirated. But this couldn't have happened to every letter, could it? Perhaps my father had been unable to save the money as he had promised, and was too embarrassed to write to tell me this fact.

I thought of Abílio's brothers, who surely still did not know of their parents' deaths. I didn't allow myself to think that my father was dead, and I didn't stop dreaming about sailing to Brazil and looking for him in São Paulo.

I knew I had to earn more réis. I watched how the sailors gambled over cards as they drank, tossing their coins recklessly. I reasoned I could take advantage of their willingness to part with their money for sport.

The set of domino tiles my father had left behind had been made from the bones of a dead monk seal he found on the beach after a two-day storm. He had laid the bones in the sun to bleach them, then cut them into small rectangles and smoothed their edges with a piece of coral. To make the pips, he drilled into the bone with the tip of his knife. He stained each tiny indentation with the red blood of the dragon tree, and made a box from the hard wood of the same tree to house them.

He showed me how to play dominoes when I was very young. When I was older, he pointed out the tiny clues he had created on the backs of the bone tiles. The clues, imperceptible to anyone not looking for them, ensured that I knew the number of pips each half of the tile possessed. He also made three extra bones, hidden under a fake lid in the box, to be concealed in a sleeve or pocket while playing. He said he had made a similar set while on the ships, and in this way won extra tobacco on the long voyages.

I told Rooi I wanted to play dominoes with the sailors. If we worked together, I said, we would both profit.

He looked skeptical, and only said, "We'll see, Diamantina."

I spent the next few days studying the tiles, memorizing each secret mark. And then I carried my box into Rooi's and surveyed the room carefully, picking a sailor who looked free with his money.

I bet him a cup of rum and let him win. Then I suggested we play for money, showing him a few coins in my pocket, proof that I would pay up if I lost. But I didn't. Each time I won, the sailor had to pay me the bet, as well as buy me a cup of wine. Rooi brought me water with a drop of wine to colour it, although the sailor paid the full price.

By the end of the evening, I had played with three sailors, and Rooi and I were both surprised at the profit.

I gambled most nights after that. I learned the ways of men, and how easy it was, after they'd had a few drinks, to make them laugh and feel taller and more handsome. I remembered Abílio's words to me the last time I saw him: *It's just part of the game. I can't help it if you're too naive to see the world as it really is.* I assumed that this was what he meant. I was seeing the world as it was now.

Each night was a new crowd of sailors. I joked with them in their own languages: Dutch and Spanish and French and English. I opened every game with, "Have you ever met a Dutch sailor named Arie ten Brink?" Some kept me guessing, toying with me as I toyed with them, acting as though they might remember him if I bestowed a kiss upon their cheek.

All assumed Arie ten Brink was a lost lover, not a missing father.

Although I never allowed a sailor to touch me, avoiding their drunken, clumsy attempts to kiss me or grab my breasts, my work at the inn, along with the knowledge of my behaviour with Abílio, marked me as the lowest woman on Porto Santo.

As I walked through the square, the men who spent hours under the shade of the palms and dragon trees felt they had the right to stare at me openly, making rude comments and ugly suggestions. Depending on my mood, I would act as though I hadn't heard, or stop and look straight into the man's face and tell him to go home to his wife and ask her if she'd enjoy what he'd suggested to me.

Although a few of the women still smiled at me, most of them viewed me as a temptress, either turning their faces away from me or muttering loudly enough so I could hear them—*a disgrace, she'll get what she deserves, a sinner in the eyes of God*—as I shopped in the market or crossed the square.

I told myself I didn't care. Those who damned me—as they'd damned my mother when she arrived on the island—did not live in my situation. My way was the only option open to a woman without father or husband or any family to provide for her. At least one who wished to eat, and keep herself and her strange, silent mother alive. And maybe, one day, leave.

CHAPTER FIFTEEN

I sought out news of the wider world, reading the *Gazeta de Lisboa* brought by packet ship, and regretted that I had no one to speak to of the events I discovered: the births, baptisms, marriages and deaths of the noble dignitaries of Portugal, the representation of the royal family at court ceremonies, the sinking of a brigantine off the coast of the Algarve, or a play on the lives of saints written by Baltazar Dias and enacted in the Salitre theatre. My head filled with images of grand buildings and life in the huge city of Lisboa.

I did tell my mother about what I'd read. She listened, smiling slightly and nodding encouragement for me to continue. But she had nothing to add, and never asked a question. I wished I could speak to Sister Amélia. I missed her, and hoped she did not fall too often into her bouts of melancholy

I could have spoken to Rooi as I cleaned the inn before the first customers arrived, but he was usually suffering too much from his drinking the night before to concentrate on serious conversation. I sometimes brought him a mixture of raw eel and bitter almonds to help dispel the shaking and headache; he said it didn't help but ate it anyway. The sailors didn't want to talk of the world when they played dominoes with me. They wanted to have a good time, for me to laugh at their jokes and pretend I had purposefully touched their hands as I reached for a tile.

The only person who would speak to me of life outside the island was Henry Duncan. He too played dominoes with me, good-naturedly handing over the réis I won without making me pretend

I was drinking the watered wine he had paid full price for. Occasionally he brought along a bottle of one of his own special vintages, and Rooi pretended he didn't notice Mr. Duncan sharing it with me as we played.

When I came home late every night, my clothes smelled of alcohol and tobacco. I finally admitted to myself how much I liked these evenings, the noise and camaraderie, feeling attractive and important in a way I had never been made to feel by the righteous of Vila Baleira. I liked the taste of the watered wine on my lips and the weight of the coins on my palm. I liked the thud of the tiles on the wooden tables, and the way a sailor looked at me with surprise or grudging admiration as I triumphantly threw down my final bone.

My mother always waited up for me in the flickering candlelight, her ever-present smoking bowl of wormwood before her on the table. She would study me, her features fierce in that half-light, and I felt she saw right through me. And yet she never asked me anything.

⌐≈⌐

Of course, I intended to save as much of the money as I could. I was playing dominoes so I could leave Porto Santo. But after buying the food we needed, other temptations proved great. I bought books and sweet pastries and pretty decorated plates. I bought soft cloth that I made into skirts and blouses, and bright embroidery floss to decorate them. I bought more ribbons to weave into my hair. The first time I brought home a book for myself and a bracelet for my mother, she fingered the double circle of shiny metal etched with a leafy design, then handed it back to me. "Buy yourself what you like. But don't buy me anything."

"You don't want the bracelet?"

She shook her head. "I have all I need."

But when I brought home a pair of green-feathered, red-headed lovebirds in a finely worked wooden cage, my mother, lying on her pallet, sat up and looked at them. I hung the cage near the window so the noisy little lovers could enjoy the fresh air.

She slowly got to her feet and put her hands on the intricate carvings, leaning her face against the cage and breathing deeply, as if pulling its smell into her lungs.

"I've named them Zarco and Blanca," I said.

The birds fluttered off their perch, hopping in distress on the bottom of the cage at my mother's face so close to them.

"Mama?"

She turned to me, her eyes bright in a way I hadn't witnessed for so long, and I smiled, pleased that I had made her happy.

"The shopkeeper said they can live ten or even fifteen years."

"They're African birds," she said. "And this"—she gently traced one of the carvings of the cage—"is from Algeria. From home." Then she sat back down, still smiling as she stared at the cage.

I waited a moment. "Do you ever dream of going back? Going home?"

She was still smiling. "I will go, Diamantina. Soon." Her soft words sent a tremor through me, and I questioned her no more.

My mother grew ever more silent, ever more slender, her nose sharper, her lips thinning, her skin the texture of a parched fruit, although her hair remained black.

One warm day she had me hollow out a shallow bed in the sand for her. The sand of Porto Santo was known for its healing qualities, and many island people would lie covered in it for hours, hoping to ease the discomfort of rheumatism or skin disorders or general malaise. After I scooped sand over her, I sat beside her as she dozed. We did this every few days, and sometimes she fell deeply asleep in the warm peacefulness of the sand, with the foamy waves gently washing up at a slight distance. When she awoke, she often spoke in her secret language, as if in conversation with an unseen friend.

Otherwise she spent most of her time on her pallet, often staring at the carved cage and the twittering birds. When I asked her if she felt ill, she shook her head, but no longer showed an interest in burning herbs and watching the smoke.

It felt as though we were suspended in time, each of us waiting. I waited for the letter from my father. I didn't like to think of what my mother waited for.

❧

And then, shortly after I turned seventeen, Abílio Perez returned. I never expected to see him again, and a young married couple now lived in the Perez hut. And yet there he was, staring at me in the inn as I laughed with a sailor and tucked the coins I'd won into the pocket of my skirt.

I struggled to control my breathing as Abílio came towards me. When he was in front of me, I lifted my chin and stared at him. On his face was the same strained expression I felt on mine. We looked at each other for mere seconds, and then, as if his uncertainty had been a trick of the light, his face took on a knowing, superior look, his teeth white as he smiled at me. He leaned so close his thigh touched mine, and he put his hand on my waist to pull me towards him as he whispered into my ear. "I'm only here for a few days, for the wedding of Estevo Da Luz. I know you've missed me. Meet me on the beach when you're finished here."

Prickly heat rose up my neck into my cheeks.

"I'm sure no one else has satisfied you as I did," he added, no longer smiling.

His words thudded inside me, and I was glad for my anger. I wanted to shout at him that there had been no one else. I wanted to slap him as I had the day we'd parted. I wanted to lean forward and kiss him. "So you haven't set off for Brazil, then," I said. "Still in Funchal. And there you'll stay, as I predicted."

He took a step back, his eyes narrowing. "I already have my passage booked. I'm leaving next month. But you, Diamantina, you are still on Porto Santo, and my estimation of you has turned out to be correct."

I fought to maintain my composure as I walked into the back room of the inn, ripe with the odour of its kegs and pipes of wine and barrels of rum. I closed my eyes and tried to calm my ragged breathing.

I couldn't face going back into the hot, noisy room. I hurried out the back door, sickness rising into my throat. I smelled the cheap rum and bitter pipe smoke on my clothing and in my hair, and shuddered at the thought of the tarry roughness of one sailor or another's fingers on me. I ran down to the beach and waded out into the sea, floating under the moon as though the cool salty water and thin white light could cleanse me.

I floated for a long time, looking to the starry night sky as if it might give me the answer as to how my life had come to this.

CHAPTER SIXTEEN

That night, I was pulled from sleep by Abílio, shouting my name down the beach; surely he was drunk. I didn't know if he'd come to my door, or what I would do if he did.

I sat in the darkness until he stopped calling. Then I pulled my blanket tightly around me and lay awake, and troubled, for the rest of the night.

My mother did not speak of it.

The next day, I gave a child of the beach a coin to run to Rooi's and tell him I was ill. I'd decided not to go to work for the next few days. I stayed away from Vila Baleira too, until I knew the Da Luz wedding was over and Abílio would be gone.

When I returned on the fourth day, Rooi asked, "You feel better, Diamantina?"

I nodded.

The inn was more crowded than usual; I had noticed two big caravels sitting out in the deep water beyond the wharf. I looked around me with new eyes, imagining the inn as Abílio had seen it—and me: the coarse laughter and shouted curses, the splintered tables and benches, the sloping dirt floor, the dull flicker of candles melting in their own tallow, and Rooi, red-faced and drunk, spilling more wine than he poured.

The smells of the sailors who came to collect their tankards from me were particularly strong that day: salt and tar, unwashed flesh and hair and greasy clothes and rotting teeth. I stayed behind the counter, uninterested in bringing out my dominoes.

Then, in a far corner, I noticed a man who wasn't a sailor. I assumed he was a wine merchant, as there was little reason for anyone else to come to Porto Santo. He was well dressed in brown breeches and a long jacket with a striped waistcoat of lambswool over a white linen shirt. His black hair, gleaming in the candlelight, was smoothly combed back and tied at the nape with a strip of fabric. His skin was clear above his neatly trimmed beard. As he raised his tin cup to his lips, he looked in my direction, letting his eyes linger for a moment, and then away.

I took out a bottle I'd blended the week before, poured a cup and went to him. "Good evening, senhor," I said, my box of dominoes under one arm, holding the wine towards him with the other hand. I expected he would react as the sailors did, with a wink or gap-toothed smile. But this man stood, bowing slightly from the waist.

"*Boa noite*, senhorita," he said, and remained standing.

There was a shouted curse and a burst of laughter from the French sailors at the next table.

"May I help you in some way?" he asked.

"I play dominoes with the customers. Would you care for a game?"

"No. No, thank you."

I put the cup in front of him. "I've made a special blend of wine for you. I know you'll find this more palatable than Rooi's usual offering. A drink for those who play is on the house."

He eyed the cup suspiciously.

"Please. As my guest. As a welcome to Porto Santo."

His polite expression didn't change. "I'm perfectly fine with the Verdelho the innkeeper served me," he said. "I'm quite familiar with it."

"You're from Madeira?" I asked, wanting him to invite me to sit down.

"Yes."

"May I sit down?" I said finally, and did so without waiting for his consent. My only excuse for my boldness was my strange mood, and my renewed sense of loneliness after seeing Abílio.

As he sat, I opened the domino box. "Just a quick game, senhor," I said. "You'll enjoy it." I leaned forward as I spoke, and breathed deeply. He smelled sweet, not of some artificial scent or pomade . . . What was it? I leaned closer, closing my eyes, and breathed in again.

"Senhorita?" he said, and I realized I must appear a fool. It was grapes. I smelled grapes. Yes. He was a wine merchant.

I straightened and spread the tiles on the table. "Do you live in Funchal, senhor? I'm sure you do—such a fine-looking gentleman. I hope to go there someday. I'd love to see the—"

"Perhaps you didn't hear me," he said, his voice louder. He pushed the cup I had brought towards me. His fingers were long and slender, his nails clean. "I'm not interested in your special drink, nor in your game, or in any game you imagine I would be a willing partner in. I'm not here for that."

My hand froze over the bones. It was as if he'd punched me in the stomach. I stood, trying to breathe, setting the tiles back into their box. As I turned to go, he said, "Don't forget your wine."

I ignored him and hurried to the counter. I told Rooi I had to leave.

"You're still sick?" he asked.

Without answering, I hurried out, keeping my head turned away from the well-dressed man.

I realized how I had appeared to him. If I was honest with myself, what would I have done if this clean, attractive man had made me feel important for one night? Made me feel I was worthy of his touch?

If I had been a praying woman, I would have gone to confession.

⧫

Later, reading at the table by the light of my last candle, my humiliation faded and anger took its place—anger at myself over losing my evening's wages. What did it matter what the man thought of me? I knew who I was, and he didn't.

I slept restlessly, not quite able to rid myself of the expression in the man's eyes as he had looked at me. I thought of my mother, eating less and less, fading before my eyes. I felt the overwhelming need to be away from this place.

The next morning, as I walked up the beach, I decided to ask
Father da Chagos if he had a letter for me. It had been over a year
since I'd last stood at the church doors and waited for him. And I
doubted that he would seek me out should something actually
arrive. As to the handsome man from the inn—I hoped he had left
on the morning packet, and would never return to Porto Santo.

⁂

I stood at the open church doors, waiting for a parishioner I could
ask to please bring Father da Chagos to me. I leaned against the
door frame. The sun was hot, and I took a step inside, seeking
the cooler dimness.

The church appeared empty, but I heard the murmur of prayer.
After a moment the prayer stopped, and low weeping echoed faintly
against the high walls. I edged along the back of the church. And
then I saw him: a man, dressed in dark breeches and a white linen
shirt, prostrate on the floor, arms outstretched, his forehead pressed
against the hard stone as he prayed and wept. It wasn't an islander;
none of the men dressed like this. I first thought it must be the man
from the inn, but realized that this man's hair was shorn closely to
his head.

He got to his knees then, and I stepped back into the shadows.
Facing the altar, the man struck his own forehead with his fists. I
was shocked at the violence of his blows and the involuntary grunts
he made as he beat himself.

I left, no longer wanting to wait for Father da Chagos.

I bought a skinned rabbit and some carrots at the market, planning
to make one of my mother's favourite meals to tempt her to eat. As
I started home, the air was damp and soft on my skin. It had rained
the night before, a steady, warm downpour, and the streets were
sticky with red mud.

As I turned a corner, the wheels of a cart pulled by a shaggy-
haired donkey slid in the mud and came towards me. I tried to
jump out of the way as the driver pulled hard on the reins, but the
wheels churned and kept sliding, and I fell, my basket flying. The

cart stopped just short of hitting me. Stunned, I pushed myself to my knees.

The driver leapt out of the cart. He took me by the elbow and helped me up, brushing a clot of damp dung from my sleeve. By his shorn head and the angry welts on his forehead, I knew it was the man from the church. He had an asymmetrical face, his right eye just slightly larger than his left, and a long nose. The skin under his eyes was dark, as though he hadn't slept well for a long time.

"Senhora," he said. "Please. Forgive me. I'm sorry to have upset you."

I was rarely treated with such respect. Unexpectedly, my throat grew tight.

"And here . . . your basket." He retrieved it from the mud. As he handed me the woven basket, the feathery tops of the carrots and the rabbit's head hanging from it, he said, "I trust you haven't injured yourself." He glanced at my skirt, wet and muddy at the knees. "I'm sorry," he said again. "I was unable to keep the donkey from sliding in the mud."

"I'm fine," I told him. "Thank you, senhor." I cleared my throat, wanting to swallow the sudden hot lump, fearing I might weep from his unexpected courtesy. I took a step, and grimaced at the throbbing pain in my ankle.

"You *are* hurt."

"It's nothing." I shook my head, trying not to show my discomfort.

"Is your home close?" He glanced around.

"I live at Ponta da Calheta, the far end of the beach."

"Then allow me to drive you."

"It's a long way on the rough cart track above the beach," I said.

"You would do me an honour by allowing me to see you safely home to your husband, senhora." We were the same height, but there was a slightness to him that made him seem smaller. "I am Bonifacio Rivaldo of Madeira."

I thought of his odd behaviour in the church. When I breathed in, I detected perspiration and incense and something darker coming off his skin. "I don't need your help," I said, and started to hobble away.

"Please. I ask nothing in return. I feel responsible."

I turned back and studied him for another moment. None of the island men would ever treat me with such consideration. I imagined painfully making my way home.

"All right," I said. "I will put my trust in your generosity, senhor."

CHAPTER SEVENTEEN

He drove in silence, urging the plodding donkey along the winding, sandy path humped with patches of rough seagrass. When we arrived at the end, where a slope led down to our isolated hut on the edge of the sea, Senhor Rivaldo stepped from the cart and held up his hand to help me down.

"Thank you," I said, taking his hand. His knuckles were like a row of pebbles.

My mother came to the doorway, shading her eyes.

"Mama, this is Senhor Rivaldo. I hurt my ankle, and he brought me home," I said, as my mother stood before us in her layers of rags, circles of charms tied on seaweed about her neck.

Senhor Rivaldo appeared undaunted by her appearance. "Good day, senhora," he said, removing his hat and bowing to my mother. Then he turned and looked at the sea. "You have a wonderful view of the ocean. And you're so close to Ilhéu de Baixo," he said, pointing across the channel to the islet. "I've heard the old mines are still there." He looked at me. "Does your husband go over to collect lime for your fire?"

"No," I said, not correcting his assumption.

"I'm sure there is a profound peace in this lonely spot. Communication with God in a place such as this would come so much more easily than amidst the chaos of town."

At the mention of God, I turned from him and went to my mother, handing her the basket. She had been staring intently at Senhor Rivaldo, but now went into the hut with the food. "Thank you again for bringing me home." I stood in the doorway, waiting for him to leave.

"You're welcome. I hope your ankle heals, senhora . . ." He waited.

"I am Diamantina," I said. "Senhorita."

He nodded. "I'm staying with Father da Chagos for the festival of Our Lady of Grace. He's an old friend. I brought him a supply of wine for the festival."

"You're a wine merchant." Perhaps he had come with the other man.

He didn't answer, climbing into the cart. "I'm sure I'll see you at the festival tomorrow, Senhorita Diamantina."

"I won't be there," I said.

"You won't be attending the Mass, or the procession?"

"No."

"Not even the festivities afterwards?"

I was tired of his questions, and now wanted him to leave. "Excuse me, but I must get back to my mother." I went inside, glad to hear the creak of the wooden wheels as Senhor Rivaldo pulled away.

⁂

Two days later, I limped up from the sea with a small catch of sardines to see the cart with the same shaggy donkey in the traces on the dune track. Senhor Rivaldo stood outside our hut. He was again studying Ilhéu de Baixo.

"Senhor Rivaldo," I said, and he turned, removing his hat. There was new bruising on his forehead.

"I trust your ankle is healing, Senhorita Diamantina," he said, looking at my bare feet covered in wet sand. I had wrapped my sore ankle in seaweed smeared with a paste of honey and figs.

"It's better," I told him, although it still ached.

We stood in silence.

"Father da Chagos spoke about you," he finally said.

So now he knew I was not one of the priest's flock but a bastard of an unholy union, a fallen woman despised by the town. I crossed my arms over my chest. "And, senhor? What do you think of what he told you?"

He didn't answer, but went back to the cart and returned with an intricately carved basket of willow branches. "I noticed that your basket was close to wearing through."

I looked from the basket to his face.

"Please." He held it closer. "Since you weren't able to enjoy the festival's specialties, I brought you a few samples."

A cloth covered the top, but I smelled pork sausage and sweet potato bread. I thought of Abílio, bringing us that first basket of food when we were so hungry. But I was not that hungry girl any longer.

"How is your mother?" he asked.

"She is as before." I didn't take the basket, and gave him no invitation to speak further.

"I understand from Father da Chagos your father is no longer on the island."

I didn't answer.

"Will you not accept the basket?" he asked. "I only brought it as a further gesture of apology, for your turned ankle." He leaned forward just the tiniest bit as he spoke, inclining his head as if encouraging me to speak towards his ear. Perhaps he was slightly deaf. Today the smell of incense was stronger, the skin under his eyes darker. He set the basket on the ground between us, then went back to the cart.

"I will return to Madeira on the afternoon boat tomorrow," he said, climbing in. "May I pay you another visit before I leave?"

"Why?" I asked, frowning.

His throat flexed as he swallowed.

There was no wind, and the sky was blue and clear. Gulls hung low, gliding soundlessly as they watched the water for movement.

"I don't know what you think of me, Senhor Rivaldo, but I want you to know I am a respectable woman. I thank you for the gift, but to suggest you would wish to come back again is . . . There is nothing for you here. Nothing. Do you understand?"

His narrow face darkened, and his hands went to his waist in a practised gesture, as if searching for something that wasn't there. "I'm sorry, senhorita. I meant no offence." But his expression didn't indicate that he was sorry, and his tone verged on anger.

Before he had climbed into the cart, I was inside my hut, the door firmly shut. I set the basket on the table and unpacked it. As well as the food, there was a paper with a verse written in a tight, careful hand: *The name of the Lord is a strong tower; the righteous run to it and are safe. Proverbs 18:10*. Underneath it, Senhor Rivaldo had drawn a small circle with rays being emitted from it. Inside the circle was a cross, and the letters *IHS*. *In the name of the Jesuit Brotherhood,* he had written underneath. I took out a candle; it too was marked with the Jesuit symbol.

My mother got up from her pallet to stare at the symbol. "You see?" she said.

"What?"

"The flaming sun."

I frowned and turned from her. "Just misplaced religious fervour. It appears he thinks we need saving."

⟷

Late the next day, after the packet had left the wharf, I was washing the stoop of the inn.

I looked up to see Father da Chagos walking purposefully towards me. He held out a square of paper. I dropped my dripping rag and scrambled to my feet, running to him.

"At last," I said, my eyes filling with tears. I took the paper from him, my hands trembling, and stood in the hot afternoon sunshine as he walked away.

I went into the inn and sat on a bench, pressing the letter from my father to my chest, savouring this moment. My hands shook so badly I tore the thin paper as I broke the wax seal.

My dear Senhorita Diamantina,
Father da Chagos informed me you were literate, and so I took it upon myself to leave this letter for you.

You were correct in that I did have a reason to seek out your company. I had hoped to make this reason clear by speaking further with you, but it proved difficult for me to convey such a complicated situation in our brief conversation.

I am in need of a woman to care for a child recently come into my custody. Father da Chagos suggested you might be amenable.

Should you wish, you may send correspondence to me through Kipling's Wine Merchants in Funchal.

Bonifacio Rivaldo

Under his signature he had drawn the same Jesuit symbol, and written, *What if some did not have faith? Will their lack of faith nullify God's faithfulness? Not at all! Romans 3:3–4.*

I dropped the paper. It lay open at my feet, the crabbed copperplate mocking me.

I stepped on it, pushing it back and forth with my foot until it was torn through. Then I picked it up and crumpled it. I took it back outside to the stoop and threw it towards the wharf, as hard and as far as I could, too disappointed and angry to cry.

CHAPTER EIGHTEEN

It had been three days since my mother had eaten. I made a rich *fragateria*, filled with pieces of fish, tomato, onion and potato. I sat down at the table across from her and picked up my spoon.

"Mama, why won't you eat? You keep saying you aren't ill, and yet you look ill."

"I am changing into my old form, readying myself. That's what you're seeing."

I put down my spoon. "Readying yourself for what?" I asked, although I knew.

"It's almost time for me to leave you. It will be a time of great peace for us both."

"Mama," I said, swallowing. "Don't talk like that. And don't say I will be peaceful when—"

"There's no reason for fear," she interrupted. "It's as the fates determine. It's as it should be." She rose then and lay on her bed, smiling at me as though I were a small girl and had done something to please her. "It's a time for celebration, and for truths," she said, and then turned on her side. In a few moments she was asleep.

"Mama," I whispered, and then I put my face into my hands and wept.

⁂

The next morning, my mother was awake when I arose and uncovered Zarco and Blanca, and as usual they immediately called joyously of their love, preening each other's feathers with enthusiasm. I filled their little bowls with seeds and bits of fruit and fresh water. My mother watched me, sitting on the edge of her pallet. "Is there any honey? I would like a hot drink," she said.

"Yes, we have honey," I said, pleased she wanted something.

When I brought her the cup, she said, "Sit beside me." After she had taken a few sips, she said, "You know how your father came to me from the sea."

I nodded.

"His hair was dulled by the salt water, but I knew that when it dried it would be as golden as the sand. Like yours." Her voice was stronger than it had been in some while, and a tiny flush had come to her cheeks and lips. "I touched him with my pole, and he opened his eyes. Do you know what he thought of me, Diamantina?" She smiled.

I shook my head.

"He asked me if he was in Heaven. He thought I was an angel, with a halo of coloured jewels. He thought I was a glorious angel, Diamantina."

Tears came to my eyes, thinking of that moment, of my father seeing my mother and thinking she was an angel. I remembered what she looked like when she was her old self, her hair thick and so black it shone blue as it swung freely about her. I could see her as clearly as my father must have seen her that morning, with her glittering corona of sea glass. For one moment, she was seen as a beautiful, unearthly angel.

Now she fell silent, staring at the wall behind me.

"Mama?" I said.

She looked back at me, and again smiled. "When Arie knew he was alive, he told me he thanked his God for allowing him to survive his ordeal. But I knew why he had lived, and why he came to me from the sea. I had seen the vision in the candle flame."

"You saw him in the flame before you found him?"

"No. I saw you, Diamantina. He was brought to me so I could bring you to the world."

The gulls were screaming over the water and a cool breeze blew through the open doorway. My mother lay down, and was soon asleep again.

I lay beside her, listening to her soft breathing.

～

That evening, I was shocked to see that my mother's feet were badly swollen, her toenails purple.

"Are your feet sore, Mama?" I asked. "Surely they pain you. Let me rub them, or make a cooling poultice."

"Don't put me in the earth when I'm dead," she said. "Put me in the water."

"Mama," I said, fighting the ache in my throat. "Please. I don't want you to talk about—"

"I am a woman of the earth only while my spirit lives. When it leaves my body, I don't want my shell trapped under the soil. And I don't want to be burnt, my ashes scattering into the wind."

I was swallowing and swallowing, trying not to cry. My mother thought tears were of no use. To hide my wet eyes I knelt beside her bed, my hands clasped and my forehead resting on them. And I realized I was praying, which I had never done. I prayed to the Unknown for my mother not to die, not to leave me alone.

She put her fingers on my wrist, and I lifted my head and looked at her. "You will not be alone," she said, and it didn't surprise me that she heard my thoughts. "I will always be with you. You and those who come later—your own daughter and her daughter and so on—are tied to me forever. I told you, the night you became a woman, that it is your duty to pass on the power. My job was to protect you until you no longer needed me. You don't need me any longer, Diamantina. It's your time now."

My face was wet. "Time for what?"

"Your life will truly begin when you follow the flaming sun," she whispered. "As I followed the moon to my destiny, you must follow that sun to yours." She stared into my eyes with a look that was frightening in its intensity. "I have held you here long enough, Diamantina. When I am gone, you must leave Porto Santo."

I wiped my cheeks with my palms. "I'll go to Brazil, and find *Vader*."

"Maybe Arie could have given you a better life than what you had here. I know what you have sacrificed in order to care for me. I know what you've given of yourself."

"I chose to stay with you, Mama. *Vader* gave me the choice, and I stayed."

"It wasn't right of him, or of me, to make you choose. I have suffered guilt over this ever since he left. As I know he suffered for leaving you." She was so fragile now, and so agitated. "But I saw that he needed to go. We'd grown bitter with each other. It wasn't his fault. He knew that I was so firmly rooted that to tear me away would cause me to wither and die. In the same way, I knew that Arie trying to root himself here was causing his own slow death."

She lifted her hand from my wrist, and her fingers trembled in the air. I put my own around them.

"I loved you too much," she said then, and I held my breath. "My love kept you from a better life. I shouldn't have loved you so much." The only time I'd seen her cry was the day my father left us, but she was crying now.

Why could she not have shared these thoughts and feelings with me earlier? For these last years, I had seen a sadness, or perhaps longing, on my mother's face. I thought she longed for my father, or for her past. I thought I couldn't make her happy.

"I couldn't show my love for you because too much love makes a person soft," she said, again answering my unspoken question. "I knew you would need strength for what lay ahead. I had to keep you strong."

I carefully rested my head on her chest. I heard the steady beat of her heart, but also a murmuring as though something else lived under her rib cage. She rested one hand on my hair.

"There is one more thing you must know," she said. "It is important you speak my true name when you put me in the sea, so that those who wait for me will know it is I, coming back to them."

I lifted my head and looked at her. I thought of my father's long-ago disclosure that my mother's name was not truly Estra.

"I am Shada," she said. "It means 'fragrant smell' in my language."

I put my head on her chest again, feeling the almost unbearable lightness of her hand on my head. "You have been a good daughter," she said, and I wept anew.

Through my tears I matched my breathing to hers. It joined us, bringing a strange comfort. Although I had thought my mother as hard as one of the diamonds my father had spoken of, I knew now that beneath my cheek beat a soft, secret heart.

Eventually I lay beside her. I put my arms around her, and her thin warmth was comforting. For the first time in many years, I felt like a child again, and fell into a deep, dreamless sleep.

⁂

When I awoke the next morning, my mother stared at the ceiling as though it carried a deep, important message, and I was alone in the world.

⁂

As the lovebirds twittered, I undressed my mother, layer by layer. She had only ever rolled her sleeves to her elbows as she scrubbed her hands before working with the women. I had seen her bare feet, and occasionally her ankles, but her long skirts usually dragged on the ground.

Now her limbs, so thin, were heavy in death. As I manoeuvred her arm out of the last sleeve and pulled off the ragged blouse, I cried out, my hands flying backwards as if her cool body burned me.

And then I breathed deeply, studying her torso in the morning light. She was covered in images from her collarbone to her pubic bone, down her arms and legs to the elbows and knees. Many sailors' arms carried pictures of their past voyages and of women they'd left behind, mothers and sweethearts. My mother's marks were unlike any of those crude depictions. The black of some was dark and deep; others were faded to pale grey. There were stars and crosses, palm trees and snakes, diamonds and feathers and the sun and rows of links and many, many intricate designs in wondrous detail of beings I couldn't name. And the moon in all its ages, from thin crescent to full.

"Who were you, Shada?" I whispered, laying her back down and stroking her cheek. "Who were you?"

I washed my mother, and then dressed her in a clean skirt and blouse. I put some of her favourite necklaces around her neck, and strung her wrists with bracelets. I brushed her long black hair and wove bright red poppies through it. I twisted small rocks into a piece of old fishing net and then tied it around my mother's waist.

After I had dressed her, I folded her hands on her waist before they became too frozen in death. I wanted one more night with her. When darkness came, I lay down on my side on my own pallet, watching her. I drifted in and out of a strange sleep filled with visions. Each time I opened my eyes, I thought my mother might suddenly smile at me, and tell me more, perhaps about the images on her body, or perhaps, again, that she was glad she had been my mother. That she loved me.

I felt a strange calm, watching her still form. It wasn't grief; I had already grieved too long, wanting what she couldn't give me, watching her leaving while still with me.

As the sun rose, I waded into the sea, holding her against me as though I were the mother and she my child. In spite of her belt of stones, the water carried her weight, making her light in my arms. When the water was up to my chest, I kissed her cheek, and then straightened my arms. "Here is Shada," I said into the still air, although I didn't know to whom I spoke. "Please, take Shada," I repeated, and then I pushed her as far as I could, watching her float out, out, out on the wave I had chosen for her. As she floated away, sinking gradually, it appeared she raised her head and looked at me, a ruse of the new sun on the undulating, glinting water.

Nevertheless, I slowly waved to her. When the water closed over her, I turned and made my way back to the empty hut.

CHAPTER NINETEEN

The warning signs for calamity can be so small and insignificant. Clouds approach, the wind changes, there is a sudden shift in the flight of birds. Does one say these are simply the usual portents of an approaching storm, or of a drop in the air temperature? Are any of these occurrences so strange on an island's hot night?

It was a few months after my mother's death that I felt this difference in the air as I went to Rooi's. Living alone had changed me, and more and more I spoke to the lovebirds and to myself. I was often in an oddly unmindful state, not watching and listening closely. This night I chose unwisely, sitting with a filthy, pock-faced sailor and pulling out my box of dominoes. I smelled absinthe as we played, and knew he had brought his own flask with him, drinking the nearly lethal swill instead of rum or wine. I knew full well that absinthe could create viciousness along with drunkenness. Many of the brawls in the inn were caused by that evil brew. But I ignored what I knew.

We played three games. By the third he no longer smiled at me but caught my forearm and turned over my clenched hand, looking for a tile. I opened my hand innocently; it was empty. I had played the game long enough to never be caught using the extra tiles. He rose with a lurch, knocking over his bench and draining his cup, tossing it to the ground, pulling me to my feet. "You're cheating me. Come on," he said. "Out behind the inn. You can work for the money you stole from me."

I shouted for Rooi. He came with two other sailors, grabbed the man and shoved him to the door. I played another few games, and when the last sailor had left Rooi's, I picked up a candle as I went to the door. "That sailor will have gone back to his ship, won't he?"

"*Ja, ja,* girl," Rooi said, banging open the door and looking up and down the street. "He was just drunk. He's long gone."

My candle held high in the now still night, I counted the skiffs as I passed the wharf; all twelve were there. That meant there were no sailors still loitering, waiting for a ride back. Still, I had a sense of unease, remembering the man's pupils sharp and tiny as pinpoints, the grip of his huge hand on my arm.

A short distance from the wharf, a steely grip caught my shoulder. I cried out, the box of dominoes falling. I whirled round. In the candlelight, the scarred skin and unfocused eyes were even more frightful.

"Think you can cheat me and get away with it?" he asked, his breath foul.

I swiped at his face with the candle, but he knocked it from my hand as though it were a feather. It rolled in the sand, snuffed out, and the darkness closed in on us.

"Here," I said, my mouth dry, scrabbling in my pocket and pulling out the coins I'd earned. "Take your money." I looked over his shoulder, calculating how to duck around him and run back to Rooi's.

That second of hesitation was my undoing. Before I had a chance to act, he grabbed my arm as he had in the inn, the coins flying into the sand. His anger and the absinthe had made him doubly strong. "You think you can act like a whore and then pretend you're too good for me?"

When I opened my mouth to protest, he hit me across the face with such force I fell to my knees. He grabbed my shoulders and forced me onto my back, then straddled me and slapped me across the face again with the back of his calloused, meaty hand. I was stunned, blinking up at him. I felt something hard under my palm, and lifted it, smashing the stone into his cheekbone. He yelled a curse, and punched me in my left eye.

There was a scalding explosion and I heard a popping sound and then saw only red in the dark night, and this shock—surely he had blinded me—turned me into an animal.

I screamed as I fought him, scratching and kicking. But such was his strength that he flipped me over with ease in spite of my thrashing arms and legs. He put one hand on the back of my head and held my face into the sand. With his other hand, he forced me to my knees, and then he shoved up my skirt and violated me with shocking brutality. My face deep in the sand, I struggled to turn my head, to take a breath.

I was being ripped apart. Time faded in and out. And then I was on my back again and his hands were around my neck. As I felt myself losing consciousness, I heard someone screaming—surely it couldn't be me—and then saw, through a haze of red, a number of shadowy forms around me. I believed they were angels, greeting me upon my death. I went to them willingly.

⌘

I was carried. Every bump was a knife through my torso. I was moaning, deep in my throat, unable to stop. Eventually I was lowered, and something cold and wet was gently placed on my injured eye. I heard my name, over and over, and finally opened the other eye. Rooi came into view, holding a candle. "All right, then, Diamantina?" he asked, but I felt nothing. "Can you see me?"

I struggled to sit up. But at the movement there was a tremendous pressure in my throat, and a raw ache came over me in such a wave that my stomach churned, and I retched.

"Don't try to move," Rooi said, now holding the wet cloth to my mouth. "Lie back down."

I groaned as I did, and tried to speak, but nothing would come out. The candle came closer, and I had to close my seeing eye against its glare.

"Your neck is all purple—you probably won't be able to talk or eat for a while. And your eye . . ."

I slowly reached towards my face, but Rooi stopped my hand.

"Don't touch it. It's swollen shut, and there's a deep cut above it. I think you need to sew it up, because the goddamn bleeding won't stop. And your face. *Meijn Gott*, Diamantina. Hopefully you haven't lost too many teeth."

I couldn't move my lips.

He put the wet cloth back over my eye, and said something else in a whisper of comforting Dutch. And then there was only blackness.

⁂

That night, the pain was too great to allow me to sleep and too great to let me stay alert. I heard my mother speaking softly to me. When I slowly turned my head towards her bed, I saw a dark form sitting on the pallet that had been empty for the last three months. Was she waiting to take me into the next world?

I tried to call to her but could only whimper, and then I felt tin against my battered lips. I took in sips of cool water, and wondered how a spirit could satisfy my thirst.

I put out my hand, urging my mother to take it, take me with her, for I no longer wanted this life. But nothing touched my outstretched, trembling fingers, and again I let myself go towards the darkness.

⁂

I could see a band of dim morning light at the bottom of the shutter, and I knew I was still alive.

Rooi was asleep on my mother's bed, snoring, his mouth open. I carefully touched my puffy lips, slowly moving my index finger to the inside of my mouth. I was relieved to feel the hardness of my front teeth. It took a long time before I could find the courage to pull myself into a sitting position. Involuntarily, I groaned, and Rooi closed his mouth and opened his eyes. As he came towards me, his white hair fanned out around his head in a frothy white cloud, he looked old and exhausted.

I cried without a sound, tears running from my good eye. I hated Rooi seeing my weakness.

He frowned, but I knew he was only worried and uncomfortable with my raw emotion. He poured more water into the cup and held it to my lips. "I have to go back to the inn," he said. "I left it unlocked last night, when I heard you screaming. I'll come back later. You best see to your face when you're able. I'm no use with a needle."

I caught his hand. *Don't go,* I wanted to say. *What if he's still out there, and comes for me again? Don't leave me alone. I'm afraid.* But nothing would come out.

Rooi left.

A long while later, I gathered my resolve and then hoisted myself off the pallet, swaying. It was difficult to walk, and I knew I was badly torn. I couldn't walk as far as the *latrina* outside and so lowered myself onto a pot, which filled with blood. Making my way to the shelf over the fireplace, I picked up my mirror. The deep gash in my eyebrow was crusty, and as I touched it, it reopened, releasing a stream of hot red blood. I could see the white of bone.

Faint, I lowered myself to the bench at the table. Sitting was almost unbearable. I held the edge of my skirt against my eyebrow to staunch the flow. When I had breathed deeply for long enough to regain some strength, I again rose to find my sewing pouch. Propping the mirror against the cup on the table, I cut away what I could of my eyebrow so no hairs would be sewn into the wound. Then I stitched the gash. My hand shook, and I had to stop each time my stomach heaved from the pain. The stitches were uneven and heavy. I still didn't know whether I would have sight in the damaged eye.

I slowly fed the silent lovebirds; uncovered all night, their tiny world was thrown into confusion.

Rooi came later, as promised. He brought a bit of fish and a slab of bread and a flagon of wine, but I couldn't open my split lips to eat. "That stinking bastard, he would have left you for dead," he said, soaking a small piece of bread in the wine and gently working it into my mouth.

"Where," I whispered, flinching as I tried to chew, "is he?"

"When I heard you screaming, I ran to you. Three of the men from the beach came to help as well. The four of us made sure he won't be fucking anyone else for a while, cunt or ass, whore or cabin boy."

I put my hand over my good eye in shame. Although I was used to the coarse language of the sailors, I had never heard Rooi speak like this. I thought of him and the fishermen—my neighbours—seeing me with my skirt up, spread-eagled in the sand. The soaked bread felt like a stone in my mouth. I thought of my father as a young boy, suffering the demands of a brutish pig as I had on the beach, and how he'd tried to save the cabin boy from the same fate. Suddenly I couldn't remember what my father looked like, just the height, the bleached hair and pale blue eyes. In a panic, I looked back at Rooi, hoping his features would return my father's to me.

"We beat him senseless and threw him into one of the skiffs. This morning he was taken back to his ship. You won't see him again. Don't you worry about him."

I still couldn't remember my father's features. Again, tears rolled down one cheek.

"Is the pain terrible?" he asked, misinterpreting my reaction.

I lowered my hand and pushed the wet bread out into it with my tongue. "I'll heal. Thank you, Rooi." I could manage only the faintest of a hoarse whisper. "Thank you for saving me. For staying with me last night." What was left of my voice faltered, and we sat in silence.

"You rest for a while," he said finally. "Give yourself time to heal before you show your face again."

I wanted my mother to fix me with her potions and her spells. I wanted the comfort of Sister Amélia's words. And yet I was glad neither of them could see me now.

CHAPTER TWENTY

Rooi came every day for the next three, bringing me food and wine.

"It's not good for you here, Diamantina," he said on the third day. "This . . ." He waved his hand in a vague direction. "This mess. What happened to you—it could happen again. Or worse."

For me, worse could only mean death. Is that what Rooi meant?

"Word gets around in such a small place, my girl. Everyone knows about you and the sailor. I let you convince me you could handle the job. I enjoyed the extra profit you brought me. But I shouldn't have allowed it. If your father knew what I'd let happen . . ." He poured himself a cup of wine and drained it. "And now, you don't want . . ." Again he hesitated. It was odd for Rooi not to speak directly, not to say what was on his mind.

"I don't want what?"

"A life with the sailors. If you're at the inn every night, they'll keep after you, break you down. What happened is your warning." He poured himself another cup. "One night you'll find it easier to take the money for something other than the dominoes, or to stop this from happening to you again." For the second time he drained the cup in one long swallow.

I thought of what Abílio had said to me as he left, calling me a whore, and closed my good eye. So now even Rooi thought this might become my fate. And after my face had been so rearranged, it was possible the sailors wouldn't even want me to sit with them and play dominoes. They played with me only to enjoy some time with a woman who gave them the tiniest bit of what they'd been missing while at sea.

Was this my future, then—to become a scarred, half-blind whore?

"It's not good for you here anymore," Rooi repeated. "You shouldn't come back to the inn. I can't let you."

"My father . . ." I started. "He said . . . He said he would send money, Rooi. So that I could go to him."

Rooi shook his head. "What can I say, Diamantina? Your father was a good man, but maybe . . . Who knows what has happened to him? But you can't spend your life waiting." He made a sound in his throat. "I've got nothing but that cursed inn, Diamantina. It's falling down around my ears, and I'm in debt to all my suppliers. If I could give you money to help you get away, I would."

⌇

A few days later, when I opened my damaged eye, I saw a flash of light. By the next day I was able to make out the objects in the room, and soon my vision became clearer.

I picked up the mirror and studied myself. My nose hadn't been broken, but there was a scabby cut across the bridge. My lips were still swollen and discoloured, my neck deeply bruised. And my eye . . . The lid was grotesquely puffy and crimson, and the clumsy black stitches in my brow were caked with dried blood. In spite of my frightening appearance, I knew I would heal, but alone in the silence, thinking of Rooi's words, I was filled with a deep sense of dread.

Forcing myself to go outside, I made my way up the beach to see if I could find my box of dominoes. Each step was an effort, and I leaned on my old wracking pole for support. It was as if I had to teach myself how to walk, lifting each foot high, telling myself to set it down again. The people of the beach watched me pass; none spoke or waved to me.

And then I saw the box, caught in a patch of wet kelp. The lid was broken off, one side in splinters. This was where it had happened, then. I looked around, suddenly full of terror, as if the sailor might still be nearby, waiting for me. I was on the stretch of beach between the huts and the wharf, alone as I had been that night. I was shocked at the fear that took hold of me.

My heart pounding, I turned. I saw a tile, and another, and then a third, stuck in the wet sand. I grabbed them up and walked back to my hut as quickly as I could. If I could have, I would have run. Once in my hut, I shut the door firmly. I pulled the table in front of it and sat on my pallet, looking at the tiles in my hand. These few tiles, cast into the sand, felt like what was left of my life, thrown into the air and then falling in a random pattern, scattered on the ground.

The immensity of my aloneness hit me with force in my darkening hut. As Rooi had said, I could no longer wait in hope for some word from my father. I felt small and brittle, easily broken.

Did I really think a flimsy wooden table would stop anyone from coming in? I didn't sleep that night, but sat at the table and burned one candle after another, afraid of the dark as I had never been before.

⁂

The next morning, I pulled the table away from the door. As the sun rose over the calm water, I went to its edge and tossed the three tiles as far as I could. They were of no use to me.

Back in the hut, I tucked my fish-gutting knife into my waistband. I had stopped wearing it when I no longer needed to catch and kill my own food. If I had had it the night the sailor attacked me, I might have been able to fight him. I forced myself to think about him and what he'd done to me, and felt an anger that was new, and clean. Yes, if I'd had my knife, I would have killed him. I visualized slicing open his grizzled neck, warm blood spilling over my hands.

I will kill anyone who tries to hurt me, I thought, resting my palm on the handle of my knife, and then I said it aloud. "I will kill anyone who tries to hurt me." I vowed to do whatever I had to do to get away from Porto Santo.

I realized I was hungry. I went into the hills and found that my old skill hadn't deserted me. I caught a rabbit and skinned it and made a fire. I sat before the flames, cooking the flesh on a stick, the dried blood still on my hands. I imagined it was the sailor's.

After I'd eaten, I buried the pelt and bones of the rabbit. I lay beside the dying fire and watched the stars pulse over me, and then I slept, unafraid as I hadn't been since the attack.

Was it an hour later, or three? Something woke me, and I sat up straight. I felt as though I had been stroked, ever so slightly, by the cool milkiness of the moon. I knew then with certainty what I would do.

I carefully tore a blank page from the back of one of my books. I sharpened a quill and mixed some charcoal with water, and I wrote.

My dear Senhor Rivaldo,

I write to tell you of the passing of my mother. She died peacefully and I am relieved that she is released from a difficult life.

I am wondering if you will be visiting Father da Chagos in the near future. It would be a pleasure to see you again. I would like to discuss your offer.

I remain your servant,

Senhorita Diamantina

I folded the page. I closed my eyes and tried to remember the name of the Funchal wine merchant Senhor Rivaldo had written in the letter I threw away, but couldn't.

I went to Nossa Senhora da Piedade and waited impatiently for Father da Chagos to come to the door. He drew back at my appearance, but I ignored his expression and held out the tightly folded paper. "It's for Senhor Rivaldo in Funchal," I told him.

He stared at my badly stitched eyebrow, then at the paper. He took it and started to unfold it.

"Don't," I said, but he had already scanned the few lines.

And then he nodded, and looked . . . what did he look? Was it pleased?

I stared at him. "Do you know what Senhor Rivaldo wrote in the letter you delivered to me?" I asked.

"I do."

"Why did he speak to me about caring for a child? There must be any number of women—women who live close by, and not on another island, like me—he could hire."

He didn't answer for a moment, as if debating with himself. "I suggested to him he should consider you."

I stared at him. "You suggested it?"

"I want you gone from Porto Santo, Diamantina, although I didn't tell him why." He didn't have the courtesy to look even slightly apologetic. "I suggested it would be good for him and you."

Heat and anger pulsed in my temples. "I'm that much of an embarrassment to your parish that you would ask a stranger to offer me a position?"

He tilted his head. "He's not a stranger to me."

"Give me the letter." I reached for it. "I refuse to be pushed away from my home on *your* whim, Father."

He held the paper out of my reach. "How do you imagine you will feed and clothe yourself? I've heard Rooi will not take you back. No one will give you any work, nor will you receive any charity. It seems you've already had your first taste of what lies in store for you." He lifted his chin at my face, looking at my eyebrow again. "Yes, you can live off the island's wildlife when it is abundant. And when it's not . . ."

I swallowed. "My mother survived when she first came here."

"And a life of survival is what you want? Is that what she wanted for you?"

I remembered my mother telling me it was time to leave. To follow the flaming sun. I dropped my outstretched hand.

As I did, Father da Chagos said, "I can attest to Bonifacio's character. I taught him at the seminary in Funchal."

"The seminary?"

"He recently left the priesthood, after ten years of serving God."

I leaned against the door frame, my hands at my sides. "Why did he leave the priesthood?" My voice was low. Was I shocked that Senhor Rivaldo had been a priest? Not entirely.

"That is for him to explain."

"And the child he spoke of—is it his?"

"It is not. The child is his penance."

"Penance for what?"

He refolded the letter. "I will send this to Bonifacio at Kipling's on tomorrow's packet," he said, and closed the door.

I had to step back so the heavy wood didn't graze my toes.

CHAPTER TWENTY-ONE

I was grinding seeds in my mortar when I heard the creak of wooden wheels. I put down the pestle and went out into the late afternoon sunshine.

"Good day, Senhorita Diamantina," Senhor Rivaldo said, coming down the sandy rise. He studied me, frowning, as he drew closer.

The deep bruises on my face had faded, but there was still a faint ring of muddy saffron around my neck, and a slight mauve swelling in my left eyelid. My eyebrow was growing back, short and spiky around the heavy black stitches. It was past time that I snip out the thread.

"I'm very sorry to hear of the passing of your mother." He stopped in front of me. "What happened to you?"

I wasn't pleased to see him, and yet I had reached out to him. I had no one else. I ignored his question. "May I offer you a drink of water? Would you care for something to eat?"

"Only the water, please."

I went inside and stood in the dim coolness for a moment, then returned with a flagon and two cups.

Senhor Rivaldo was standing where I'd left him.

"Please. Sit down," I said.

He sat on the rock facing the sea, and I sat beside him. I poured water into his cup. He emptied it in one long draft, then brushed his hands down over his thighs in a quick, practised, almost womanly motion. Suddenly I could see him arranging his cassock in the same fashion. I envisioned him as Father da Chagos, in a black robe and cincture, the cross and rosary.

"Would you like more?" I asked, holding up the flagon.

"No, thank you. It appears you've been hurt in some way." He touched his own eye, looking at mine.

"Yes," I said, setting the flagon and my cup in the sand at my feet. "A clumsy accident, trying to help a neighbour push out his boat. It was deeply moored in the sand. My feet slipped out from under me and I fell forward, hitting my face." I cleared my throat.

Now he glanced at the marks on my neck. "Why did you contact me, senhorita?" He set his own cup down. It was clear he had no further interest in small talk.

I looked at the sea. Ragged clouds scudded over the waves. "My mother died, and I thought to inform you."

I could see him watching me out of the corner of his eye.

"You indicated you would like to see me. You mentioned my . . . offer."

As he reached into his jacket pocket, I looked back at him. He pulled out my letter. It was very creased and slightly darkened, as if he had handled it many times. His face offered nothing. "Your penmanship is flawless. A very careful hand."

I took a deep breath. "You're a wine merchant now? Since you left the priesthood? Father da Chagos informed me of your past."

"Yes, I was a priest. I am not a wine merchant."

"But the letter was sent to Kipling's."

"That is where I receive mail," he said.

After an uncomfortable silence, I said, "The child. He's not yours?"

His mouth was a firm line. "You know I was a priest. Why would you ask me this?"

"How old is he?"

"I'm not certain. Perhaps five. And I have an ailing father as well."

"You don't know the boy's exact age?"

"No."

"Is he a relation? A nephew?" I asked, not really caring but feeling I needed to show interest.

He rubbed his hands together as if they were cold, glancing at me, and as I returned his look, his eyes flitted away with an uncertainty I hadn't seen before. "No. The boy is . . ." He stopped. "He was alone. I am committed to seeing to his welfare. His mother died, and his father . . . There is no father worth mentioning. I wished to save him—Cristiano—and so I took him from an uncertain future."

A thin film of perspiration beaded under his eyes and on his upper lip in spite of the cooling breeze from the sea. The way he was watching me suddenly made me uneasy. I thought, at that moment, that he was regretting his offer.

"No child should be uncared for," I said, too quickly. I thought of this man and Father da Chagos discussing me, and straightened my shoulders. "Senhor Rivaldo," I said carefully, "it is difficult for me to find work on Porto Santo. It's such a small island." I took a deep breath. "And since my mother died, I am quite alone. I have decided that I'm willing to cook and clean and care for the child. And your father."

Still he was looking at me in a studied way. He cleared his throat. "Knowing your mother was no longer here, I asked Father da Chagos if he knew of someone who might chaperone my visit. But he assured me it wouldn't be necessary. That you are an honourable young woman."

I ground my back teeth. Was he mocking me? He was so difficult to read. Father da Chagos had asked him to take me away from Porto Santo, but hadn't he told him the truth about me—that I was a fallen woman, and viewed by most of the island with trepidation and disgust?

"You trust Father da Chagos to speak the truth to you?" I asked.

"Of course." He frowned. "Why wouldn't he?" Suddenly he stood, and I realized I might have said the wrong thing. Making him doubt Father da Chagos would not benefit me. Now that I had made my own decision about leaving Porto Santo with Bonifacio Rivaldo, I didn't want him to change his mind. Before I could say something to amend the situation, he paced down to the sea, and then back.

Standing in front of me, he said, "And you, senhorita? Do you speak the truth as well?"

I waited, perhaps a second too long, before answering. "What are you asking me?"

"You commit to come to Madeira with me?"

I took a deep breath and stood to face him. My eyes were level with his, in spite of the fact that he wore boots and I was barefoot. I tried to read something in his eyes, but couldn't. As well as incense and his faint smell of perspiration, I knew he'd recently eaten a dish with both garlic and parsley. I could discern no more. "I will come with you. As I said, I would work for you as your housekeeper, and look after—"

He held up one hand. "Work? You said you would work for me?"

"Yes. Isn't that what you're offering?"

He shook his head. "No. I thought . . . I assumed you knew I meant . . . as my wife."

I sat down, my mind racing. "Well then. Well then," I repeated in shock, unable to think of anything more to say.

He sat beside me. His knees, under his wool breeches, were bony and pointed. He turned his head at a sudden rustling in the grassy dunes behind us as if relieved to have an interruption.

When the small creature in the long seagrass quieted, I said, "I'm sorry I brought you all the way back to Porto Santo for nothing. To offer marriage is very kind." As I uttered the words, it crossed my mind that I did not view him as particularly kind. I looked down at my hands. My nails were ragged and broken; a fine line of dirt rimmed each one. "You know of my unholy state. My parents were not Catholic, and unmarried. I have not been baptized. So I will not be able to marry." And even if I could, I could never imagine marrying this man, this former priest with his dark look and smell of incense and anxiety.

He attempted a smile, the first I had seen. It lightened his face, and made him look younger. "I believe God does not punish one for ignorance of His ways. I'm sure that in spite of your limited knowledge, you could learn to embrace God. The sins of the parents pass to their offspring, and although you are seen as a sinner in the eyes of the Church, this type of sin is not of your doing, nor your wish."

His voice changed as he spoke, growing softer. I understood this was the voice he had used with parishioners. It was his forgiving, understanding voice. It was an improvement.

"You are no worse than the heathens of many countries. You simply need to be shown the path to righteousness. The mission of the Jesuits is to bring every heathen to God. I would baptize you myself if I still had that authority. Instead, I will have Father da Chagos baptize you, and then we can marry."

I didn't wish to marry him. I wanted to work for him, and receive payment. I studied the wool of his jacket, the linen of his shirt.

"For you to be my wife is the only way I can take you with me," he said. "As a former priest, I cannot bring a woman into my home . . . for my father's sake, and . . . and how my parish views me. I left a priest, and returned a fallen man," he said, taking a deep breath, looking away. "I will not fall further in their eyes." He looked back at me and attempted another smile. "We don't always know what God plans for us. And I am willing to accept this as His wish. I don't understand it, but I do believe it is His wish. And perhaps, once you understand the ways of God, you will see it was His plan for you as well."

No. It is my mother's plan I am following.

"I have already spoken to Father da Chagos about this," he said. "He is willing to baptize you, and marry us."

I blinked. "He would marry us?" I repeated. How desperate the Father was to have me gone. But I did not want to be baptized, nor did I want to marry Bonifacio Rivaldo.

Your life will truly begin when you follow the flaming sun, my mother had told me.

"I know you will need time to think about this," he said, interrupting my thoughts. "But there is one more thing I must make clear before you make your decision."

I waited.

"We will be married, but will not live as man and wife." Before I could react, he continued, "Although I have left the priesthood, I still hold the major tenets of my former life: poverty, chastity, and obedience to Christ. Chastity," he repeated, the slightest flush rising in his cheeks.

"I see," I said, although I didn't. But I felt a rush of relief. If I did agree to marry him, at least I would not have to share a bed with him before I could procure enough réis to buy a passage to Brazil.

"This means there will be no children, other than the boy. Do you understand the seriousness of this?" Before I could respond, he stood. "I know it's something you must have time to consider. I'll wait for you in the square at noon tomorrow. You can tell me your decision then." His voice left no room for discussion. He climbed back up the dune and into the cart, slapping the reins against the donkey's back.

I watched him drive away. He had been a priest—a Jesuit. He had been trained in a seminary, and lived a holy life; he could not be too unsavoury a character. I tried to push away the image of him weeping on the stone floor of the church, and the viciousness of the blows to his own face.

Could I do this? Could I accept this humourless man as my husband in name only for a short while? The fact that I would not have to abide his touch made my decision a little easier, and, I told myself, he offered what I needed. He would take me away from Porto Santo.

I went back into the hut and looked around at the few belongings that were the sum of my life. The lovebirds twittered, their heads to one side as they watched me with their tiny bright eyes. I sat on my pallet and stared at my mother's bed.

There are moments when one thing ends and another begins. My life here was finished.

That night, I burned wormwood and looked deeply into the smoke. I wanted to see my future, as my mother had.

Nothing appeared.

CHAPTER TWENTY-TWO

The next day, when the sun was overhead, I went to the square. Senhor Rivaldo, as promised, sat on a bench in the shade of a dragon tree. When he saw me, he stood, his hat in his hands.

"*Bom dia*, Senhor Rivaldo," I said.

He nodded. "I trust you slept well, Senhorita Diamantina."

"No. I didn't sleep. I had too much to think about."

"Of course."

"I'm sure you also had a great deal on your mind."

He looked at me for a long moment.

I tried to look agreeable, even a little pleased, but couldn't. "My answer is yes, Senhor Rivaldo. I agree to your terms."

"Fine," he said, with no more expression than me. "Shall we say I will return for you in a month's time?"

I shook my head. "No. I would like to go with you now."

His eyes widened. "But you will need to prepare for your baptism with Father da Chagos. And surely you wish to have time to say goodbye to friends. Or . . . or plan the wedding? I know ours is not a traditional situation, and yet . . . don't you want a wedding celebration?" His uncertainty was somehow comforting.

At that moment a local fisherman walked past. He looked pointedly at us, and behind Senhor Rivaldo's back gave me a knowing wink. I was suddenly overwhelmed with panic. It was my one chance to escape this life, and I couldn't lose it.

"I don't care about wedding festivities," I said. Did he not realize the actual situation: that there would be no guests, no well-wishers, no celebrations? How exactly did this man see me? "I want to leave as soon as possible, Senhor Rivaldo."

He sat down again. I remained standing.

"This seems unconventional," he said after a few moments. "But I understand that you are not a conventional woman. Had you been, I doubt you would have agreed to my proposition."

I nodded.

"And so I will do as you ask this time." I noticed the stress on the words *this time*. He appeared to be calculating something, and I waited.

"I suppose we can sail back tomorrow," he finally said. "This means that Father da Chagos will have to baptize you today—in spite of you having no preparation—and perform the marriage rites first thing tomorrow."

"Fine."

"I'll go and tell Father da Chagos you will come to see him for the baptism soon. I'll fetch you and your belongings in a cart at sunrise tomorrow."

"I don't have much. I'll meet you at the church tomorrow morning."

"As you wish," he said, and we parted awkwardly.

❧

As it was early afternoon, the inn was closed, but I went around the back. Rooi was sitting on a crate, smoking his pipe, a large tankard of wine in his hand.

"Rooi," I said, "I've come to say goodbye."

"Goodbye?"

"You said it wasn't good for me here, and you're right. I'm leaving Porto Santo."

He stood in surprise, squinting at me in the sunlight. His jowls were stubbled in bristly white. "Where are you going?"

"To Madeira. I'm marrying a Senhor Rivaldo from Funchal."

Rooi's unruly white eyebrows rose, and he took his pipe from between his teeth. "Will this man treat you right?"

I shrugged. "I'm getting away from here. Father da Chagos is baptizing me later today so we can be legally married." I smiled. "Can you believe that?"

Rooi gave a hoarse laugh. "Well, I shouldn't be surprised at anything the Dutchman's daughter does."

"We're marrying tomorrow morning, and leaving on the packet immediately after."

"This calls for a drink," he said, and drained his tankard. "Come inside and sit with me."

I followed him into the darkened inn. His white hair was flattened and matted at the back. His breeches were stained. He needed a woman to care for him. "Are you hungry?" he asked, and I shook my head.

He walked across the room and pulled open the front door. Sunlight spilled in, throwing a long rectangle of light over the floor. Benches were overturned and empty tin cups lay on the counter and the sticky tables.

"What a mess, Rooi." I thought of all the nights I'd spent here. All the sailors I'd laughed with. All the games of dominoes.

"I know," he said, chewing on a cold, greasy slab of fried pork fat. "But as I once told you, the sailors take no notice."

I sat down at one of the tables, and he brought over a big flagon and a cup for me. He wiped the rim on his sleeve, and when we had touched our full cups, I said, "I'm going to get to Brazil and find my father."

He looked at me, then probed his cheek with his tongue, chewing and swallowing whatever he'd dislodged.

"I won't believe he's dead, Rooi. I won't."

He swirled his cup, staring into the deep burgundy liquid. "I used to see Arie standing on the end of the wharf, studying the caravels and brigantines anchored out in the deeper water. I know he wanted to leave, but he stayed, at first because of Estra, and the sweet breezes and the warm water that gave up its food with so little effort. And then because of you." He shook his head. "It's hard for a father to leave a child," he said, his voice faltering, his bleary eyes suddenly wet. I wondered how many children he had abandoned, and where. I realized he hadn't been back to the Canary Islands since my father had gone.

"Arie and I were alike: the call of the sea is in our blood," he said. "Even when on land, we dream of the snap and tug of the sail, the smell of the tar, the creak of timbers, and the wind burning our faces. Sometimes, Diamantina, we miss the sea as one misses a woman we know was a true love but will never see again."

I finished my wine and we sat in silence. Outside, a canary sang to its mate, and there were the sudden shrills of the cicadas as the sun warmed them.

Rooi stood unsteadily. "*Ja*, that's the way it is, my girl." He lifted the flagon, tipping it to his mouth, but only one brilliant ruby drop ran from its lip. He banged it onto the table. "So you get married. I wish you a long and happy life, Diamantina. I will come to your wedding?"

I made a face. "No. It will be a sham. Father da Chagos is only doing it to get me out of his parish."

"The old hypocrite," Rooi said, and that was our goodbye.

⚘

After I left Rooi's, I went to find the priest, walking through the front doors and standing in the warm, dim church. From the confessional came the murmur of a higher voice, followed by Father da Chagos's response. A few women lifted their heads from their hands as I walked to the confessional and waited.

When Father da Chagos came out and saw me, he nodded once. As the final woman finished her prayers and left, he put a heavy bar across the door. "It's time for the midday meal. Few will come at this hour," he said, an annoyed expression on his face. "It's my mealtime as well. Come."

I followed him to the font.

"Diamantina," he said, looking over my head, "do you, with a contrite heart, express a true desire for baptism?"

I did not have desire of any kind for baptism. Was my heart sorry? Remorseful for what? For the deception that both the Father and I were committing?

He looked at me. His stomach rumbled, and I knew he was

thinking of his meal. "Say yes. Just say yes to everything I ask you."

I nodded.

"You have to say the word," he demanded.

"Yes," I lied.

"Do you wish to be given the seven gifts of the Holy Spirit: wisdom, understanding, counsel, fortitude, knowledge, piety, and fear of the Lord?" He spoke quickly, by rote, and his words flew over my head and up, high into the dusty rafters. They were only words, meaning nothing.

"Yes," I lied again.

He held back his sleeve and dipped his hand into the font, cupping water in his palm.

"*Ego te baptizo in nomine Patri*"—he dripped water on my forehead—"*et Filii*"—more drops—"*et Spiritus Sancti,*" he finished, trickling the last of the water onto my forehead.

I thought of Abílio and his mock baptism.

Father da Chagos stepped away, wiping his hands on a small cloth.

I blotted my wet face with my sleeve.

"You can go now."

"That's all?" Even though I cared nothing about the baptism, somehow I had expected more.

"That's enough," he said, and walked to the door and took away the bar.

I went into the afternoon sunshine, and as I walked home along the beach I thought that as the wedding tomorrow would not be a true joining of man and woman, so the baptism had been a deception. I was doing what I had to do to leave Porto Santo, taking charge of my own fate, the one my mother had told me was mine.

"Be proud of me, Mama," I said, looking at the wide, bright sky. "Nothing can diminish the power you gave me." The whole sea shone silver. "And certainly not words."

CHAPTER TWENTY-THREE

I opened my eyes into the darkness with a startled sense of dread. Today, Senhor Rivaldo was taking me to Madeira, that green island rising out of the ocean only a day's journey across the water. Into the wonders of Funchal Town. I should be feeling relieved, but maybe in this respect I was like every bride who felt anxiety on the night before her wedding day.

When the sky was grey with approaching dawn, I dressed in my best skirt and covered my snowy white blouse with a finely embroidered bodice. As always, I wore my father's talisman beneath my blouse, and I layered the last of my mother's necklaces around my neck. My wedding would not be like the weddings I had watched from the edges of the square, the brides in their traditional Portuguese family gowns and white lace mantillas. But I was not a traditional Portuguese bride. I was the daughter of the Dutch sailor and the slave witch from Algeria. I smeared my eyelids with purple dye I made from the lichens that grew in the crevices of the rocks along the north coast, and perfumed my neck and arms with rosemary. I combed my hair until it shone, falling to my waist in a flowing, bright cascade, and then settled a small circlet of delicate shells on my head.

Taking the lovebirds from their spot near the window, I set their cage and my packed shawl of belongings a short distance from the hut. I went back inside and piled driftwood around the base of the four walls. I struck my flint and went to stand beside the love-birds. Within a few moments there was the bitter reek of smoke, sparks swirling in the air, and the murmur of the eagerly lapping flames.

I walked down the grey, misted beach with my knife in my waistband, my shawl slung over my shoulder, the shoes my father had left stuck into the opening at the top. I had lived my life without shoes, but I would not be a barefoot bride. I carried the cage my mother had loved, and the birds flapped and screeched, excited to be out in the sea air. I glanced back once to make sure the hut, dry as tinder, was ablaze, sending up pale swirls of smoke. Satisfied, I turned my face to Vila Baleira, and the packet boat beyond the wharf.

Senhor Rivaldo's eyes widened as I walked across the empty square to meet him in the dim morning light. Was it the cage of birds, or my purple eyelids, or the ill-fitting shoes? Was it the protruding handle of my gutting knife or my tangle of necklaces and crown of shells?

"There's smoke down the beach," he said by way of greeting, perhaps as uncomfortable as I on our wedding day. "Is someone burning something this early in the morning?"

"Yes."

"Father da Chagos is ready for us."

I nodded and turned towards the back door of the church.

"This way," Senhor Rivaldo called, waving at the front door.

"I'd like to speak to Sister Amélia first."

"Father da Chagos has told me the Sister is to be the witness. You'll see her inside. Come here."

"I need to speak to her for a minute," I repeated, ignoring him. I found Sister Amélia on her knees in her tiny cell, and waited in her doorway until she lifted her head.

"Oh," she said as she saw me, pressing one hand to her chest as she got to her feet. "I was just coming to the church for your wedding, Diamantina." She smiled at me. "I was so very, very pleased to hear this news." She studied me and her smile grew. "My heart is full for you: you are baptized, and now you will be married and start a new life. Everything has worked out for you, as I have prayed for daily. And you look so beautiful, like a siren from the sea." Her voice was sincere. I loved her so much at that moment my eyes stung.

I blinked away my tears, holding out the cage. "I'd like you to have them," I said. "The male is Zarco—he has the darker beak. And the female—her head is a little less vibrant—is Blanca. They eat seeds of any sort, and bits of vegetable and fruit. Fig is their favourite. If they remain healthy, they will live for many years. Will Father da Chagos allow you to keep them?"

She smiled at the birds, putting her index finger between the bars. "He won't know, he doesn't come beyond the kitchen doorway," she said, wiggling her finger. "I'll hang them near the window—there's often a cooling breeze."

Blanca tipped her head and stepped sideways down the perch on her small grey feet to take a curious peck at Sister Amélia's finger. The nun laughed with a surprisingly girlish sound, and her joy pleased me so that I no longer felt like weeping. She took the cage and set it on the floor.

I wanted to tell her that I loved her, but my throat was still thick. "Could I write to you?"

"You know I wouldn't be allowed to receive a letter." And then she put her arms out, and I went to her, and we held each other tightly for a long moment. Without looking at me, she moved away, and I followed her down the hall towards the chapel.

⟶⟶⟶

I had never attended a wedding, and didn't know if ours followed the usual ritual. Before Father da Chagos started the ceremony, he put the bar across the church door as he had when he baptized me, so an over-eager parishioner arriving for Mass early wouldn't come across this strange spectacle.

I heard a whisper of cloth from the side door, and knew Sister Amélia had hidden herself behind a pillar. Senhor Rivaldo and I stood side by side facing Father da Chagos. In the warmth of the apse I was aware of the odour of woodsmoke rising from my clothes. Father da Chagos lit the censer and swung it in front of us, and its familiar sweet odour comforted me. He began with a great deal of droning in Latin, with Senhor Rivaldo answering in a practised manner. The first time Senhor Rivaldo knelt, I hesitantly knelt beside him. Nobody corrected me, and I assumed it was the right thing to do, and so I knelt and rose along with Senhor Rivaldo. He performed these functions—kneeling and rising—in supple movements, as if lowered and pulled up by invisible strings.

I felt ungainly. Perhaps it was the unfamiliar shoes, which hurt the ends of my toes when I went down on my knees, and made me lose my balance as I pushed myself up again. Once I stumbled as I tried to stand, and Senhor Rivaldo caught my elbow.

Finally, Father da Chagos murmured a final sentence, lifted his cross and kissed it. He held it out to Senhor Rivaldo, who also kissed it. He didn't extend it to me. He nodded at Senhor Rivaldo, who took a thin gold band from his jacket pocket and put it on my finger. I don't know where he got it. It felt a little tight, but perhaps it was because I had never worn a ring. Watching him push the circle of gold over my knuckle, I saw that my fingertips were smeared with ash from lighting the driftwood, and newly noticed the criss-cross of scabbed scratches from brambles on the backs of my hands. I saw the deep white scar, like a miniature crescent moon, on the fleshy pad on the back of my thumb, a slip with the gutting knife years ago. I thought of my mother.

Senhor Rivaldo took my hands. His were damp, the palms square, only slightly bigger than mine. Father da Chagos intoned another sentence, and Senhor Rivaldo let go of my hands.

"Will you perform a Mass for us, Father?" my husband asked, and Father da Chagos shook his head.

"You expect too much, my son."

Senhor Rivaldo glanced at me. "I understand."

"Please give my regards to Father Monteiro when you reach Curral das Freiras," Father da Chagos said then, and my husband said, "I will."

Curral das Freiras. I hadn't heard of it, but it must be an area of Funchal. I had one last request of the priest. "If a letter comes from my father, will you have it sent on to Kipling's?"

Father da Chagos nodded.

Even though the sun had risen as we left the church, no one was in the square. There was no ringing of the church bells or cheers of congratulations or thrown flower petals. There was just the empty street leading down to the wharf, and the anchored fishing boats bobbing on the water, the gulls shrieking and spiralling over them, the shearwaters and storm petrels silently gliding above. As Senhor Rivaldo, carrying a leather case in one hand, took my bulky shawl from me, I looked back at the gate to the church kitchen. There was a shift and flutter in the shadow, and then a rhythmic movement of paler shadow. Sister Amélia had broken the rules again, leaving the kitchen to wave a cloth at me through the gate. I waved back, tightening my lips so they wouldn't tremble.

And there was Rooi, standing in the doorway of his inn. He had risen so early to watch me leave, and now I couldn't stop the tears as he took his pipe from his mouth and lifted it in a salute.

I held up my hand, the gold band catching the first rays of the sun, and waved goodbye.

We were rowed out to the packet. I climbed up a rope ladder, and a sailor gripped my hand to help me over the side.

I was relieved that there were no other passengers to Madeira this morning, no one from Vila Baleira to stare at me with this well-dressed gentleman and start the flow of gossip. None of the townspeople would question Father da Chagos about my disappearance; to mention my name might bring ill luck. If anyone ventured as far down the beach as Ponta da Calheta, there would be nothing left to signify I had ever been there. The next few rains would work the burned remains of my home back into the earth from where it had come.

I sat on the wooden bench beside Senhor Rivaldo, my bulky shawl with all my worldly belongings between us. At one end of the deck was a pile of dusty sacks of limestone, a huge open basket of the ugly black scabbardfish, their dead, fishy eyes bulging, and three goats tethered together, bleating and restless.

I was weary from lack of sleep and all that had happened in the last few days. My throat was dry and my head pounded.

"I will address you as Diamantina now. And you will call me Bonifacio," my husband said, rubbing a small silver icon between his thumb and index finger. "Saint Christopher," he explained, lifting the icon. "Let's hope he will protect us as we journey across the water. The *travessia* can be rough and dangerous, although it appears we will be blessed today. The sea is calm."

I watched as four sailors gathered in a circle. "O Holy Lady of Navigators, Mother of God," they prayed. "Creator of Heaven, earth, rivers, lakes and the seas, with thy protection and the blessing of thy Son, the ship of my life will anchor securely and tranquilly in the port of eternity. Our Lady of Navigators, Pray for me. Amen."

Bonifacio murmured amen as well.

The sailors broke apart, and in the next moment there was a shout, and the sails were unfurled with a great whooshing and snapping, and it was as if the sound awakened me from my stupor. I sat straighter, my physical discomforts gone. As the wind took the sails, I kicked off the uncomfortable shoes and knelt on the bench, leaning out as far as I could. I closed my eyes and turned my face into the wind, feeling the spray as I held my crown of shells in place with one hand.

I was a seabird wheeling over the water, the wind caught under my wings. I remembered Rooi's story, and understood my father's longing.

Jumping from the bench, I ran to the side of the ship facing the island. As we sailed past Ponta da Calheta, with the towering shape of Ilhéu de Baixo across the channel, all I could see was a tiny grey spot on the sand, and some faint tendrils of smoke.

It hit me then: I was leaving my home. I thought of the light on the water when I first woke. Of the smell of rain approaching over the waves. The whole world of stars above me at night, birdsong at dawn. The sand: wet, dry, shifting beneath my bare feet. The seagrass that held tenuously to the earth with its tough roots. The fragrant harshness of the damp basalt cliffs. Would I ever know these things again?

"There's a decent following wind today. It shouldn't take us more than five or six hours to arrive in Funchal if all goes well," Bonifacio said, his voice in my ear. I turned to him, annoyed that he had come to stand beside me. I wanted to be alone to experience this leaving. This loss.

I knew now what had given me the unnamed dread in the night. It wasn't Bonifacio Rivaldo himself but what I was losing. Why could I see the beauty in my life only as I was sailing away from it?

"Come and sit down. You're getting wet," he said, taking my arm firmly, leading me away. He took bananas and figs and a round of bread from his bag. I recognized the loaf as one of Sister Amélia's, with its cross cut into the top. "And put on your shoes."

I sat beside him and ate a few figs and a banana, but did not put on my shoes. And after a while I went back to the side of the boat. Just beneath the cool water was a school of silver porpoise, swimming alongside us. High above in the blue sky was a long, ragged line of birds, thin as a scratch from a quill, and far in the distance sat the golden mound of Porto Santo, with its smaller islets on either side.

My husband and I said nothing more on the journey. I was lost in my thoughts of what was to come. I didn't care or wonder what his thoughts might be.

PART II

CURRAL DAS FREIRAS, MADEIRA

The sun went behind clouds and then burst forth, and eventually hid itself again as we made our way towards Madeira. Distant misty mountains peeped through the cloud caps, and as we sailed through the vapour, the phantom greyness became living colour. As my island had been barren and golden, this one was lush and green. I could make out the tiny dots of villages nestling in the valleys scoring the mountainsides.

Flying fish leapt alongside us, and shearwaters skimmed the surface of the water as the ship slowed and came into Funchal Bay. I hung on to the side as our packet tossed in the choppy water of the wide bay with its many anchored ships. I wasn't prepared for the size of Funchal Town, the glimmering whiteness of it as it lay at the bottom of verdant hills.

"It's like a giant amphitheatre," Bonifacio said, speaking loudly to be heard over the rough waves beating against our boat. I looked over my shoulder at him. "You see how the slopes rise up all around the town, framing it? There's no flat land on Madeira, and so all the planting is done on the *poios*," he said, pointing to the cultivated terraces I could see to the west. "The slopes are reminiscent of viewing galleries, and the town below a stage."

I had never heard of an amphitheatre, or seen a stage. I was determined, in that moment, never to indicate all that I didn't know. I would remain silent, and watch and listen.

"And there is Fortaleza do Pico, the fort, high, up there." He pointed over my head at a huge grey building that looked like the image of a castle I had read about in one of my books.

There was a maze of streets with white-walled houses leading straight uphill. "Where's the wharf?" I asked, seeing only a beach covered with large stones, the hard surf crashing upon it. I could make out women bending to beat bright splashes of cloth against the stones, but we were too far from shore to hear anything other than the waves.

"There isn't one. Too many rocks lie under the surface close to shore. We'll anchor here in the bay, and be transported to land by a smaller boat." Two skiffs bobbed a safe distance from us, and almost as soon as he had spoken, there was a great grinding as the anchor was lowered.

The cargo and the protesting, struggling goats were lowered over the side into one of the skiffs. After Bonifacio threw his bag and my belongings to the waiting hands of a sailor, we climbed down the rope ladder into the other skiff. As we were rowed closer to shore, the sailor carefully avoiding the stone breakers, the sounds of the town grew overwhelming. Dogs barked and cocks crowed amidst the cries of children and the slapping of the women's washing, all against the backdrop of the waves hitting the rocky shore.

When it was impossible for the sailor to row any farther, a snaking line of half-dressed, black-skinned men waded into the water and hauled our flat-bottomed skiff to shore with a rope as thick as my arm.

As we started up a rough set of stones leading from the beach to the town, I stumbled more than once in my loose shoes.

Ahead were buildings of white stone taller than I had ever known, their roofs red slate. We passed shouting vendors selling vegetables and fruit, fish and grains. As well as Portuguese, a number of English, both soldiers and well-dressed men and women, strolled the esplanade that ran along the seafront.

An older woman came towards us, her head wrapped in a twisted strip of sweat-stained cloth. On a second coiled strip of cloth sat a basket heaped with jagged pieces of red stone. She walked tall and straight, one hand steadying the basket on her head. Her face had markings—feathered lines interspersed with what looked like tiny spear-heads on her forehead and running down between her eyebrows, and small crosses on her cheekbones.

"That woman, Bonifacio," I said, pulling on his arm. "Just there, with the basket on her head. What is she?"

"She's a slave," he said. "There are many like her on Madeira."

"Why is her face marked like that?"

"She's from North Africa. The marks are a pagan practice."

I wondered what he would think if he knew about the marks on my back.

"Diamantina," Bonifacio said, his gaze fixed on my head. He took off my coronet and handed it to me. "You must attempt to fit in on Madeira. It's too late to start the journey home, so we'll stay the night here. There's an inn just ahead." He adjusted my bulging shawl over his shoulder.

"Home? But . . . don't you live here, in Funchal Town?"

He looked at me. "I didn't tell you I lived in Funchal. My home is in Curral das Freiras."

"I heard Father da Chagos speak that name. But where is it?"

"In the mountains."

I drew in a quick breath and caught his arm. "How far is it from Funchal?"

"About three leagues."

"That's not so far." I was relieved. Surely we would still be in sight of the ocean and the tall ships in the harbour, some on their way to Brazil.

"No—not so far—but it's difficult to reach. If we set out tomorrow morning, it will take us until late afternoon—a full day of walking. The valley is isolated, and the trails along the cliffs are narrow and dangerous."

The fleeting relief fled. A full day of hard walking from Funchal. A valley, surrounded by the mountains. I would not be able to see the water. "I thought you lived in Funchal," I said, my tone accusatory.

He simply looked at me, turned and walked on.

I followed, blisters growing on my heels as I struggled on the streets of slippery cobbles. Clutching my crown to my chest, I tried to push down the overwhelming dismay at learning that I would not be living here, close to the ocean.

The inn was small and clean. Bonifacio led me to a tiny room under the eaves, the window looking down into the street three levels below. Although I had climbed the hills and cliffs of Porto Santo all my life, I had never climbed steps before. I took off the shoes I had grown to hate as I followed him up the tight stairway, adjusting each of my steps to the even height of the stairs. In the room was a single narrow bed, a candle and flint on the windowsill, a small table with a jug of water and a basin, and a ceramic pot behind a low screen.

"I trust you will be comfortable here," he said. "I'll be in the next room, through there." He pointed to a door that connected the two rooms. "I have business to attend to. I'll come back to the inn later," he said, standing in the doorway. "Stay here, please. You're not ready to go out on the streets." I didn't know whether he was referring to my newness to Funchal or my appearance.

Once he left, I went to the window and leaned out, gripping the sill, delighting in the dizziness I felt as I watched the busy street below. In the window across from me was an old woman with a dark moustache and heavy brows that met over the bridge of her nose. She stared at me with open suspicion. I stared back until she closed her shutters with a slam.

I stayed there a bit longer, looking down at the tops of the heads of the people and the backs of the animals on the street below. The loudness of the city was astounding.

I didn't want to stay in my room, even though Bonifacio had told me I must. I would just walk up and down the street right outside the inn. I went to the door and turned the handle. It was locked. I rattled it. Then I went to the connecting door and tried that. It was locked as well.

I had never been locked inside a room before, and it filled me with some unknown dread. I ran to the window and leaned out, breathing deeply. My head hurt, and the room rocked as if I were still at sea. I needed to get outside. I fruitlessly tried the doors again, then sat on the bed and covered my ears with my hands, closing my eyes and humming, trying to find calm within myself.

I didn't hear Bonifacio unlocking the door, and jumped when he said my name.

I stood, relieved that the floor was now steady under my feet. "Why did you lock me in?"

"I've brought you some dinner," he said, setting a covered plate on the table. "And then you should sleep. We start early tomorrow."

"Why did you lock me in?" I repeated. "There was no need for that."

"You will have new boots tomorrow."

I looked at the old shoes, on their sides near the bed. "Will we come regularly to Funchal?"

"I've seen the difficulty you have walking. I'll buy you the boots women of the mountains need. I'll knock on the door in the morning, and when you're ready, we'll leave Funchal. Good night." It seemed he wouldn't answer any of my questions.

As he started to shut the door, I said, my voice too loud across the small room, "Don't lock it."

He looked back at me. "It's for your own safety." He shut the door firmly, and I heard the click of the key in the lock.

⁂

I ate the food. The bread was far from as light and flavourful as Sister Amélia's, and the tepid, overcooked slab of white fish full of bones. There was a pile of green, bitter vegetables I didn't recognize and didn't particularly like, but ate anyway. When I had finished, the light in the room was fading, and the sounds on the street below lessening. Men were lighting torches attached to the walls of buildings. I walked around the room four times, stopping each time I passed the window.

I looked at the connecting door, and then put my ear to it. I could make out a stealthy, rhythmic slapping, accompanied by whispers.

I pressed my ear closer, remembering Bonifacio pounding his own forehead in church. But this sound was different. It was a strap against bare skin.

"Please, Heavenly Father, let vice and concupiscence die out within my flesh," he now murmured, just loud enough for me to hear. "I strive to be holy and chaste. Please, Heavenly Father, wash away my sinful thoughts."

The slapping came faster, and I stood as if frozen, listening until it finally stopped. Then came the more mundane noises of pouring water and the closing of shutters. I went to the window once more, looking at the street lit by flaming torches.

After a time, I sat on the bed, longing for the familiar comfort of my own pallet in the hut that no longer existed.

CHAPTER TWENTY-FIVE

I was standing at the window when Bonifacio knocked the next morning.

"I'm ready," I called, and he unlocked the connecting door.

He wore a set of wide linen breeches, a rough baize shirt and boots of cowhide. He looked more a simple man of the land than the dignified gentleman I had married in Vila Baleira.

All traces of yesterday's colour were washed from my eyelids, and my scent was no longer rosemary, but that of the lye soap sitting beside the wash bowl. My crown of shells and my mother's necklaces were packed away.

"Cover your hair," he said, and I waited, for perhaps an instant too long, before I pulled my shawl up from my shoulders to drape over my head. I was barefoot. I had left the dreadful shoes under the bed.

He nodded, and I knew that apart from the colour of my eyes and my gutting knife hidden in my waistband, I would pass as an obedient and pious Portuguese country wife.

*

We walked through winding streets. There were bakers with all manner of breads and pastries, and weavers with their dyes, and tanners in narrow stalls. We went into a shop where, as promised, Bonifacio bought me a pair of *bota*—soft and supple suede boots that rose to my ankle, with a red stripe around the top.

"We mainly barter between farms to obtain the food we need," he said as we stood in a busy lane lined with shops.

"You're a farmer?" My voice rose on the last word.

"I grow grapes."

But he didn't smell of grapes. I had a sudden thought of the good-looking man with his strong, sweet smell of grapes in the inn the evening before I first met Bonifacio.

"There is one small *venda* in the parish," Bonifacio went on, "but its supplies are meagre, since everything must be carried in. Is there something else you will need?"

I thought for a moment. "Some cotton and thread. Embroidery floss. And I would like a set of dominoes." I stared at him as I spoke, daring him to deny me these things.

Bonifacio's brow wrinkled. "Dominoes?"

"I like to play dominoes. Do you? Or do you prefer cards?"

He was silent for a moment. "I am not a man for games."

"I would like a set of dominoes," I repeated.

He hesitated. "It will be a wedding gift."

For the first time, I thought that perhaps he would soon not be as stiff and awkward with me. For whatever time I was forced to be with him, it would make it easier if he appeared more . . . human. I put my hand on his arm and squeezed it to show my gratitude, but he pulled away.

At another shop he bought me a small and simple wooden set of dominoes. It paled in comparison with the bone tiles my father had made, but I put my mind from that set, and what had happened to it.

We then stopped in an open market, where Bonifacio bought food for the journey: bread and a slab of pork, a gourd of wine. He saw me looking at a pile of sweet buns and bought me one. Something lifted in me as I walked beside him on the bustling streets. My feet were comfortable in the soft boots, I carried my set of dominoes under my arm, and the sweet pastry melted in my mouth. I had done it. I had left Porto Santo. I was in Funchal Town. The harbour was filled with boats, and one day soon I would be on one of them.

And then I saw Abílio Perez walking ahead of us. I knew that set of shoulders, the way he swung his arms, the hair curling over his collar. I stopped abruptly on the crowded street, the bun halfway to my mouth.

A woman holding a child's hand bumped into me, apologized and walked around me.

"What is it?" Bonifacio asked.

I watched the man disappear into the crowd. I was wrong: of course it wasn't him. He would have sailed to Brazil by now. But for that instant I thought of Abílio turning and rushing to me, his face alight. He would tell me that he'd always known he'd made a mistake in leaving me, and that he would take me away with him after all. He would be a different Abílio, less cruel, less full of thoughts of himself only, and he would care about me.

"It's nothing," I said, and we continued walking.

⁂

I followed Bonifacio northwest into the hills.

"A horse or donkey can handle this part of the journey with ease," he said, "but once we're higher, human feet can navigate the narrow paths easier than pack animals."

As we climbed upwards, away from the harbour, we passed high gates. Behind them I could see beautiful gardens and pine forests, and occasionally a house of a size and grandness I had never imagined. I stopped at one, to stare through the gates.

"Those are quintas, country houses owned by the wealthy merchants of Madeira," Bonifacio said. "Mainly the wine merchants, and mainly English."

A number of bullock carts loaded with wood passed us, heading down towards Funchal. As we walked farther, we passed the terraces hewn from the hillsides, where the island's food was grown. Women and children were hauling baskets of soil to build up these *poios*. Water for the crops rushed down the hillside in trenches that Bonifacio called *levadas*, built by slaves a century earlier.

Sugar cane and bananas and grapes grew closer to Funchal, but as we climbed higher, the only crop was grapes, the trellised vines clinging dizzily to the *poios* on the sides of the mountains. It was clear the harvest was over, but I breathed in the scent of rotting fruit lying on the ground beneath the gnarled vines. I thought of merchants such as Henry Duncan; the wines he brought to Rooi came from these very hills. A group of wiry, black-bearded, barefoot men came towards us on the narrow path. Their rough clothing was stained with sweat, their skin burnished deep brown by the sun, and they carried sloshing, bulging goatskins slung around their necks. I stood aside so they could make their way around us, and the smell of grape was overpowering.

"*Borracheiros,*" Bonifacio said, "carrying the last of the *mosto* to be sold to the wine merchants. The grapes are pressed in the vineyards, and the juice carried down to Funchal to be made into the wine. The men are coming from higher in the mountains, where it's cooler and the harvest a little later."

The path twisted dizzily in and out of huge ravines. Each time I looked over my shoulder, the sea had grown more distant, and at a sharp curve it finally disappeared completely. I stopped a few more times as we wound along the path, looking behind me and hoping it would reappear, but it didn't.

When we came to a small wooden cross beside the trail that ran along the cliffs, Bonifacio knelt. "We will pray for the soul of the person who lost his life here."

"Who was it?"

"I don't know. But it's an act of respect. Come," he said, looking up at me. I was weary, and it would feel good to rest for a moment, and so I knelt beside him. But I didn't put my hands together or bow my head; I simply waited while he recited the Our Father. We passed seven more crosses on this most treacherous part of the journey to my new home. Seven more times Bonifacio stopped to pray.

Sometimes the path rose almost vertically through heavy woodlands of scented laurel trees. I had never seen such a thick forest, with soft bracken and ferns growing underfoot. Lichen and moss dangled eerily from the high branches. As I reached up to touch the hanging wisps, Bonifacio said, "Witches' hair," and I stopped, looking at him sharply. But he only wanted to explain. "That's what it's called. The air is so pure and the branches so high that vegetation grows from them."

When we stopped by a mountain stream, I took off my shawl, too warm from the constant climbing, and splashed icy water on my hands and face. We sat by the tumbling water and ate the bread and pork and shared the flask of wine, and then Bonifacio refilled the flask from the stream.

"You can see the difficulty of this journey," he said as I took off my boots and put my feet into the cold water. My ankle, sprained months ago when I'd first met Bonifacio, throbbed in the old way, and I rubbed it firmly, trying to ease away the slight swelling.

We finally emerged from the forest, with the mountains high and craggy all around us. My head ached and my legs were strangely wobbly. It was hard to catch my breath. Bonifacio handed me the water flask. "We're on the *miradouro*, the highest peak. Being so high above the level of the sea can cause you to feel light-headed. As soon as we start the descent, you'll feel better." He pointed downwards. "Curral das Freiras."

The flask halfway to my mouth, I stared at the incredible sight below. We were on the edge of a deep, yawning valley where, at the very bottom, a church steeple stood like a tiny needle. Wisps of smoke were the only indication that houses rose up into the terraced mountainsides. A precipitous, snaking path, hardly more than a goat track, wound down. Staring at what was to be my home, with the dramatic cliffs rising all around us, I was struck by the fact that tomorrow would be the first day of my life that I hadn't gazed upon the water. "Why do people choose to live here?"

"This is the richest growing area on the whole island. The volcanic soil creates harvests like no other. It's said that originally this valley was a place of refuge for nuns from Funchal, hiding from corsair attacks. Other stories say the land was granted to the first Sisters who arrived on Madeira. That's how it came to be named Valley of the Nuns."

A pair of unseen birds called back and forth above us, their voices ragged in the thin air, an echoing, lonely sound.

I followed Bonifacio slowly, thinking about waking each morning without looking out at the ocean that was as familiar as my own skin, without hearing the water's gentle kiss or wild crash. I wouldn't be able to stay here long. I couldn't live like this. A soft wind wrapped the smells of the trees and vegetation around me. Plants nodded in the breeze.

"Chestnuts," Bonifacio said as we walked through a thick glade of trees filled with brown clusters.

Past the forest, another odour, pungent and spicy, surrounded me. "What's that smell?"

"Eucalyptus," Bonifacio said without turning.

"Did you grow up here?"

"Yes."

"Your father owns the vineyard then," I stated.

He looked over his shoulder at me. "He doesn't own it. None of the small farmers on Madeira own their land. My father is a *caseiro*. He leases the land from a landlord in Funchal. The landlords are descended from the first settlers to whom the Portuguese crown gave large tracts of land. Every year the *caseiro* must pay his landlord part of the proceeds of the grape harvest."

At the sound of distant bleating, I gazed up at the cottages and byres scattered on the mountainsides.

"Do you have a goat?" I asked.

He faced forward again. "No."

"I had a goat once."

He didn't respond. The mountains felt like high walls, imprisoning me, hiding everything but a piece of the sky.

⸎

We stopped at last outside a small house made of whitewashed stone. Olive trees grew along one side of it. It had a thatched roof, and green shutters on the windows on either side of the door. Beside it was a smaller, similar building without shutters on its one window: the kitchen. Chickens high-stepped about the yard, pecking at the ground; a low enclosure for them backed into a thick tangle of ferns. There was an open wash house with two big covered cisterns. A large and smaller tub hung from the outside wall, as well as a collection of woven baskets and axes and shovels. Nearby, a tiny *latrina* was half hidden in the trees. There was a woodpile and a garden surrounded by a fence of gnarled sticks. Inside the garden a man swung a long-handled tool.

A child sat on the low step to the front door. Cristiano. I glanced at Bonifacio, expecting him to wave, or the child to run to us.

The man in the garden straightened and looked in our direction, then opened the gate and came out. He carried a toothed sickle caught with weedy growth. Age and work had bent him like one of the grapevines, making him shorter than both my husband and me. He wore simple baize breeches and a stained shirt and tasselled woollen hat with earflaps. Like Bonifacio and me, loose cowhide boots were on his feet. He walked as if each step pained him.

"This is my father, Senhor Vitorino Rivaldo," Bonifacio said to me when the old man stood in front of us. "And this is . . ." He stopped. The silence stretched. "This is my wife, Diamantina," he said, his voice louder than usual, leaning close to his father.

Senhor Rivaldo frowned. He lifted one of the earflaps of his hat and cupped his ear. "Did you say wife?" he repeated, in a loud, uneven timbre. He looked at my hair, my face and down my body to my feet. "A wife?" he said, staring at Bonifacio.

When he looked back at me, I dipped my head. "I am pleased to meet you, Senhor Rivaldo."

"He's a bit deaf," Bonifacio said, so I repeated myself, speaking loudly as Bonifacio had, directing my words at the old man's uncovered ear.

Seconds passed. "Welcome, daughter," Senhor Rivaldo finally said, and I took a quick, sharp breath. Nobody had called me daughter since my father had left. "You will call me Papa." He again studied my eyes, my hair. My shawl was around my shoulders. "Which parish do you come from?" Under his smell of sweat and dung I detected a fermented odour that told me he had an internal problem, something in the stomach and bowels.

"I'm not from Madeira, Senhor Rivaldo. Papa. I'm from Porto Santo." It was tiring to speak at such a pitch.

"Ah," he said, looking at Bonifacio again, but I couldn't read anything in either of their faces. "And you married there?"

Bonifacio nodded.

There was another moment's silence.

"Do you wish to drink cherry liqueur to celebrate your wedding?" Papa asked.

I opened my mouth to say yes, pleased that my father-in-law wanted to mark our marriage, even with this simplest of rituals.

"Not right now," Bonifacio said, and beckoned to the boy on the step.

The child slowly rose, clutching a piece of cloth, staring at his bare feet as he came towards us. Under his rough striped wool shirt, his small shoulders turned inwards as if to protect himself. His skin was dark—too dark even for an olive-skinned Portuguese child. He stopped a short distance from us.

"Come here," Bonifacio said sternly. The child obeyed, still staring at the ground. "This is Cristiano. Cristiano, look at Diamantina."

When his eyes met mine, I smiled. He was a beautiful child. His large green-brown eyes framed with curling lashes stood out in his dark face. His hair was the colour of ironwood bark with curling streaks of gold. But it was matted and filthy, as was the rest of him, and he smelled strongly of urine. Although he was small and slight, his face was too knowing. He was older than five.

He scratched his scalp as he stared at me blankly.

"Hello, Cristiano," I said, perhaps a little too loudly, as if he, like Papa, couldn't hear. But he had obeyed when Bonifacio told him to come closer. Was he simple?

"Cristiano," Bonifacio said. "Remember what I've taught you."

Cristiano limply put out his hand. I took it. His fingers felt boneless, lifeless and strangely cool, as if I held a small, dead bird. He immediately pulled away and ducked his head with what I suspected was a greeting. He glanced at Bonifacio in an uneasy, almost fearful way.

Bonifacio nodded at him, and the boy took a step back. "He doesn't speak, and he prefers not to be touched. I've tried to instill some manners, but . . ."

I smiled at Cristiano again and, studying his eyes, realized he wasn't at all simple.

"I'll get on with my work, then," Papa said. "I hope you will be happy in Curral das Freiras, daughter." Still holding his sickle, he limped back to the garden.

CHAPTER TWENTY-SIX

"The kitchen is there," Bonifacio said, pointing, "and the wash house and the toilet. We get our water from a stream a short distance from the garden."

I followed him inside the house.

Cristiano, the dirty cloth pressed against his mouth and nose, had returned to his place on the step.

Dominating the sitting room was a long wooden table with benches on either side. There were two plates covered in chicken bones and eggshells. Two wooden chairs faced the fireplace, which had a thick layer of soot running up its stone front. An open-shelved cupboard holding dishes, glasses and cutlery sat against one wall. On the other wall was a large crucifix made of rough, bleached wood. The thatched ceiling was higher than I was used to, giving the room brightness, and the floor, littered with crumbs and ground dirt, was made of smooth wooden planks. The stone walls were peeling; they needed whitewashing. Tattered curtains hung over the two windows.

"That room is my father's," Bonifacio said, nodding at an open door. "And you can put your belongings in here." He opened the second door and went in. I stood in the doorway.

This bedroom was divided from Papa's by a wall that didn't meet the ceiling. One narrow bed was against the partition wall and the other on the opposite wall under the window. Both were neatly made with thick wool blankets. Against the wall beside the door was a chair, a low pallet and a cupboard. Wooden pegs ran along the upper portion of the wall, and a few were hung with Bonifacio's breeches and shirts.

"You can hang your clothes on the pegs, and use the cupboard for anything else. The child sleeps there," he said, pointing at the pallet. "You can have the bed under the window, to get the breeze."

We both looked at the beds, and then Bonifacio turned away, as if they were something shameful.

I unpacked my books and took them and my domino set and my mother's mortar and pestle out to the sitting room and placed them along the top of the dish cupboard. Back in the bedroom, I hung my skirts and blouses on the pegs. I opened the cupboard; on one shelf were extra sheets and blankets, on another a long blue striped cotton shirt and a similar red one, as well as a small pair of breeches—Cristiano's clothes. I put my medicine sack, with its twists of ground powders and seeds and leaves and small pots of salves, onto the empty bottom of the cupboard. Then I sat on the bed, unsure what was expected next.

Bonifacio returned. He carried a length of rope, a hammer and nails. I watched as he hammered the big nails into two opposite walls. Then he tied the rope firmly to the nails and opened the cupboard and took out three heavy sheets. He hung them from the rope, dividing the room in half so that I couldn't see his bed. He moved the chair beside my bed. "I'm going to help my father in the garden. You'll find what you need to make dinner in the kitchen," he said.

I looked at my cubicle, and thought of Sister Amélia and her cell.

※

The kitchen was in an even worse state than the sitting room. The simple fireplace, similar to the one in my old home, was fashioned from three large stones set in a rectangle with one side open to lay the wood. There was a chimney, so although the smell of grease hung over everything, at least the low ceiling and walls weren't blackened by years of smoke, as my hut had been.

There was an oven like the one in the church kitchen, but when I looked inside, it was evident no baking had been done for some time. A big cast iron pan sitting on the fireplace stones was filled with hardening fat, and a blackened kettle and smaller pots were piled on a table along with wooden spoons, earthen jars of oil and a large cistern of water. A big basket was filled with chestnuts. On a set of shelves draped with thin muslin to keep out flies were a slab of dried beef and more baskets of cabbages and sweet potatoes and various beans. There was a bowl of eggs and a salt tub and the remains of a loaf of bread.

Another shelf held a row of jugs—I counted fourteen of them. I took the stopper out of one and smelled it: the aroma of cherry and brandy and a touch of cinnamon wafted out.

I cleaned the ashes from the fireplace and went out to the woodpile. As I stacked kindling and wood in my arms, Cristiano came from the step and followed me into the kitchen. I started a fire, then filled the big kettle with water from the cistern.

Cristiano watched me, sitting on a stool at the table. I smiled at him a few times, but his expression never changed as he followed my movements. He scratched his head vigorously, clearly tormented by lice. Eventually he put his elbow on the table and wearily rested his cheek on his hand, as though he carried burdens too heavy for such a young boy.

"How old are you, Cristiano?" I asked.

He shrugged.

When the kettle boiled, I took it off the hook and hung the pot filled with vegetables and the dried beef and water and salt and spices in its place.

I went back to the house and took my scissors from my sewing pouch. I could smell the pallet: like Cristiano, it stank of urine, and I knew there would be lice in it. I dragged the little stuffed mattress and blankets through the sitting room and threw them off the step, then went back to the bedroom and fashioned a temporary bed for him out of clean blankets on the floor at the foot of my bed.

I took the long blue shirt from the cupboard and went back to the kitchen. Cristiano still sat where I had left him. "Come to the wash house with me," I told him firmly, taking the kettle, and he did as I asked.

As he stood beside a rough bench holding different-sized pieces of flannel and a small dish with a soap mixture, I filled one of the tubs with water from the cistern and warmed it with the boiled water. Cristiano held his cloth to his nose and mouth, unmoving, as I cut off his beautiful curls. The lice had bitten him severely, and I had to cut the hair right to the skull to get rid of all the nits. His tender scalp was criss-crossed with scratches from his own fingernails. I wrapped the curls in a piece of flannel to be burned.

When I motioned for him to come to the tub, he laid the cloth on the bench, stroking it tenderly for a moment, then pulled off his shirt. As he started to undo his breeches, he stopped, staring at me, and I turned away.

As Cristiano sat down in the tub, I looked over my shoulder at him. "Do you want me to help you?" I asked, rubbing soap onto a flannel. As he looked up at me, I was startled to see the letter *T* burned into the front of his right shoulder. Under it was a second mark, a cross, this one newer. I had seen similar marks on the shoulders and arms of blackamoors on the wharf in Vila Baleira as they unloaded cargo. Shirtless, their dark skin glistening in the heat, I had studied the variety of letters that identified their owners. I assumed the cross signified they had been baptized.

I handed the soapy, wet cloth to Cristiano, watching as he rubbed it over his face and chest and arms. He was a slave child, then, but by the colour of his eyes and the lighter shade and looser texture of his hair, he was a mulatto or perhaps a quadroon. His little body was perfect, his neck long and graceful, but he was too thin, his ribs and collarbones sharp.

He rubbed the cloth over his head. "Close your eyes," I said, and poured warm water over him. He wiped his eyes with his fists, and I held out a large flannel and wrapped it around him as he stepped out of the tub.

I gave him the clean shirt and he turned his back and let the flannel drop, pulling the shirt over his head as he pushed his arms into the sleeves. The shirt fell below his knees. He turned and walked towards the house. After I had thrown out the dirty water and wiped the tub clean, I left the filthy clothes to be washed and went back to the house. Cristiano was lying on the blankets at the foot of my bed, his eyes open. I took a few powders from my medicine bag and mixed them with one of my salves. I sat on the floor beside him. "I'm going to rub some of this on your head. It will soothe the scratches," I told him.

He didn't move as I gently massaged the mixture onto his scalp, but he closed his eyes.

Poor, strange little thing, I thought, looking at his shorn head. "You don't have to go to sleep yet, Cristiano," I said. "You haven't had your dinner."

He kept his eyes shut.

"Are you hungry?" I asked.

He didn't move.

I went out and quietly closed the door.

⌘

While I waited for Bonifacio and Papa to come in for dinner, I peeked into Papa's room. It was empty but for a bed and a low stool and a few chests along one wall. The room smelled of unwashed bedding and clothing soiled by grease and sweat. I would need a full day to wash Papa's and Cristiano's bedding and clothes, and work through the sitting room as well, cleaning all the cobwebs from the walls and the dirt and dust from the floors and furniture. I didn't want to live any length of time in such filth.

When I heard the men at the wash house, I set the table with plates and spoons, the steaming pot of stew and the half loaf of bread. They came inside and Bonifacio knelt at the bench, his hands folded in prayer. Papa set down one of his earthenware jugs of the cherry alcohol and grunted slightly as he knelt. Bonifacio looked up at me.

"Kneel to pray," he said, and although I was angered at his command, I didn't want to create a fuss in front of Papa on my first evening in his home.

"Thank you, Lord, for our food and all your other blessings," Bonifacio said, and as I was about to rise, he continued in Latin. I stayed where I was. He spoke for so long that when he finally stopped I was further annoyed that the stew had grown tepid, oil swimming on the top.

We ate in silence in the flickering candlelight. I was exhausted from the day's walk, and the smell of the cooking stew had been tempting as I stirred it earlier. Now it was hard to swallow, and sat like a leaden lump in my stomach. I wasn't comfortable being in the small house with Bonifacio Rivaldo.

"Cristiano will need a new pallet," I finally said, but neither man replied.

When we were done eating, Papa poured himself a hornful of cherry liqueur and carried it out to the front step, where he sat drinking it. I took the dishes to the wash house and washed them, and when I came back, the bedroom doors were shut. I took a deep breath and entered the room I would share with Bonifacio and Cristiano. A candle burned behind the hanging sheets, throwing a wavering, muted glow. Cristiano was in a deep sleep, his little eyebrows twitching slightly, his cheeks flushed.

I set my candle on the chair and cleared my throat. Eventually, I carefully, almost cautiously, lay on the bed. Then I turned on my side to face the sheets. Papa's soft snores came over the partition. "Cristiano's head was crawling with lice," I finally said.

When there was no answer, I said, "Bonifacio? Why is the child so uncared for?"

"He's difficult to handle," Bonifacio said, his voice low. "He won't let me touch him."

I turned onto my back again and looked at the lighter square of my window. The stiff branches of an olive tree were outlined by moonlight. "I saw the slave mark on his shoulder." I waited. "Who is he?"

"I brought the child from Brazil with me," he said quietly.

"You were in Brazil?" I sat up, surprised at the secrets that were being pulled from my husband, one by one.

"I was a priest at a mission in Tejuco."

I knew nothing of Tejuco. "When did you return?"

"Not long ago," he answered, and then there was the sound of a book closing, and the candle behind the curtain went out.

"You've only just left the priesthood?" I sat waiting in the darkness, then asked, "Who was Cristiano's mother?"

After a long silence, Bonifacio said, "She was among the slaves brought from Luanda, in West Africa, to sieve for diamonds in the rivers and streams around Tejuco."

"And his father?"

Again no answer. Eventually I understood that Bonifacio would say nothing more tonight. I leaned forward to look at the sleeping child, one hand curled sweetly under his cheek. Could Cristiano truly be Bonifacio's son, even though he denied it? Was a relationship with the slave woman the reason he had left the priesthood?

After some time, I blew out my candle and lay down again. Small puffing sounds came from behind the sheets, and I knew Bonifacio slept. I stayed awake for a long time. I missed the sound of the waves on the shore. Staring at the branches of the olive tree, moving slightly in the night breeze, I remembered my father's stories of diamonds. The wind grew stronger, and the olive tree rustled.

I wondered how long I would have to stay here.

CHAPTER TWENTY-SEVEN

I was in a deep sleep when the screams awoke me. I sat straight up in the darkness, my heart pounding, not knowing where I was. Then I saw Cristiano standing at the foot of my bed, screaming in a language I didn't recognize. A candle flared; Bonifacio pushed aside the hanging sheets as I scrambled out of bed and tried to put my arms around the child. He wouldn't be comforted, writhing and slapping at me without seeing me. His eyes were open, and yet there was no comprehension in them; I knew he was caught in the dream world. His face, in the wavering light, was a show of pure terror, and he kept screaming the same sentence over and over.

"Cristiano, stop. Wake up," I said, struggling to dodge his fists and hold him. "Wake up," I kept saying, not understanding his words, not knowing what else to do. His body was rigid and hot as though he burned with fever. Finally I pinned his arms between us, and his cries softened and then faded to nothing. He began to tremble violently. I held the back of his head with one hand, pressing his face against my shoulder. I felt a growing damp patch on my blouse from his tears and running nose, and smelled an acrid odour.

I gently moved him away from me, my hands on his shoulders. He was no longer trembling, but looked confused, staring at me, and then suddenly he looked down and drew in his breath.

"It's all right, Cristiano. It's all right. Come, let me help you," I said, glancing over my shoulder at Bonifacio.

He shrugged. "It's like this every night," he said. "Every night," he repeated, then retreated behind the sheets.

The little boy, swaying with exhaustion, let me pull off his wet shirt. I took the red one from the cupboard and put it on him. The blankets were wet as well. I directed him to my bed. He got in, but squirmed as far from me as possible, his face against the wall. In a few moments he was asleep.

❧

When I awoke, there was dim light in the room. Daybreak had come later than I was used to, the sun having to rise above the mountains.

Cristiano wasn't in my bed, and I didn't know whether Bonifacio was still sleeping. I went through the empty sitting room. Once outside, I knew that it was too early for the men to have risen, as only a few birds peeped sleepily. Besides, surely I would have heard Bonifacio moving about, or he would have woken me to make breakfast. I looked for Cristiano in the *latrina* and the kitchen. As I stared around the hillside above me, I saw a spot of red, moving high on a cliff, far beyond the last house on the mountainside.

I lifted my skirt to my knees and climbed. It was so steep that small trees grew sideways out of the mountainside. By the time I reached the boy, I was panting, my bare feet scratched and cut.

Cristiano sat in his red shirt and clean breeches, staring across the highest mountain, hugging his knees. Last night, as he screamed, I saw he was missing his two bottom milk teeth. He had to be at least six, maybe closer to seven years old.

I sat beside him. He moved slightly so I had more room, but he didn't glance at me. I could see the tiny roofs of houses on other terraces, and the steeple of the parish church below. After a few moments the sun rose above the mountain we faced. I put my hand out, palm up, and it appeared the sun rested there, a glowing disc.

"It looks like I'm holding the sun in my hand. I used to do this when I was a little girl and watched the sun rise."

He didn't respond.

"What are you looking at?"

He shook his head, clearly impatient with me.

"*Ma casa*, Cristiano," I said, finally guessing what he might be thinking. I stretched my hand in the direction Bonifacio and I had come from: Funchal, and beyond, the ocean and Porto Santo.

He looked at me and nodded slowly. He had climbed up to see over the mountains. Maybe to see the ocean, which would take him back to his home.

I reached out to put my hand on his knee, but he drew away. After a time I rose. "It's time to go back."

I started down the mountain slowly, holding on to branches and rocks, constantly looking behind me. Once, Cristiano slid on his heels and grabbed my skirt, making no sound.

As we approached the house, I saw Bonifacio on the road leading to the foot of the valley, and the church.

I gathered the soiled clothing and blankets from the bedroom floor, picking up Cristiano's scrap of cloth. "You can help me scrub the clothes at the—"

Cristiano grabbed the cloth and clutched it, backing away as if I'd threatened him.

I watched him. "I won't wash it if you don't want me to. Was it a blanket?"

He didn't answer, but turned and ran. I finished the washing and hung the clean bedding and clothes over bushes to dry in the sun and breeze. Shading my eyes, I looked up the mountain, hoping Cristiano hadn't climbed so high this time.

I found him asleep on a bed of soft ferns behind the chicken house, the cloth against his face.

Dinner that evening was the same: the endless prayer while the food cooled, and then silence as we ate. Tonight Cristiano sat beside me on the bench, eating a piece of meat with his fingers. I put a fork into his hand. He set it on the table, but after a few moments he picked it up and used it awkwardly.

"Espirito came to see me while you were away," Papa said, looking at Bonifacio. Then he grimaced, pressing his abdomen with his fist.

Bonifacio didn't look up from his plate.

"I can bake bread if I have flour and some leaven," I said. Papa didn't appear to hear, his head bent over his bowl.

"My father trades eggs for bread from a neighbour," Bonifacio said.

"There's no reason to do that anymore. I can make the bread," I said. "And we could use some milk, and cheese. Could Papa trade the eggs for that?"

Bonifacio nodded, and we finished the meal in silence. I stood, reaching for the empty bowls, but Papa raised his hand and I sat down again.

"Bonifacio," he said. "The *senhorio* will take back the land when I die. He and I agreed on this—I haven't had to compensate him for a number of years. Because I believed you would never return to Curral das Freiras, I told him there would be no one to carry on after I was gone. He has already arranged for someone from his own family to take over here."

"I know, Papa. You already told me this."

"That was before you had a wife." He glanced at me. "Even with the child, you had more freedom. But now, with a wife . . . When I'm gone, you will have to leave Curral das Freiras and go elsewhere."

"There's nothing for me anywhere else."

"There will be nothing here for you either. You will make a new life somewhere. And you must do the right thing for your family. You have a family now." Again he looked at me.

When Bonifacio didn't speak, Papa said, "Bonifacio. Tell me you will do the right thing for your wife and the boy."

Bonifacio cleared his throat and met his father's eyes. "I will do the right thing."

"Good," Papa said. "We will not talk of this again."

As on the previous night, he sat on the step to drink his cherry liqueur. I mixed a tonic of ground milk thistle and wormwood into warm water. I touched his shoulder so he would look into my face.

I knew that if he watched our lips, he understood more easily. "For your stomach," I said, handing him the cup.

He studied me for a moment, then drank the liquid in one swallow. "Thank you, daughter," he said.

When I went to the wash house with the dirty dishes, Cristiano came with me. Again he just sat on the stool and watched me. As I worked, I thought of Papa's words. I would not be here long enough to see all of this: Papa dying and Bonifacio making a new life away from Curral das Freiras.

When we returned to the house, Bonifacio was already in his bed behind the sheets. I made Cristiano a bed on the floor again.

The nightmare came, and again I fought to calm the boy. This time Bonifacio stayed on his side of the room. Eventually Cristiano slept, as did I.

❧

The next morning when Bonifacio returned from Mass, he carried a small, rolled-up pallet under one arm, and in the other hand a basket with a sack of flour and lidded containers of both leaven and milk. I put down the pallet for Cristiano, then went to the kitchen and mixed up dough in the wooden oblong bowl, and while it rose I cleaned out the bread oven. Then I plucked and cleaned a chicken Papa brought me, its headless neck still dripping blood. It was the same as preparing a partridge or quail, although bigger.

"Do you want to help me pick beans in the garden?" I asked, and Cristiano nodded. I knew he had a voice, evidenced by his nightmare-induced babble, but during the daylight hours it disappeared. I watched him, trying to imagine what had happened to him in Brazil.

❧

That evening he knelt, but refused to lower his head or clasp his hands in prayer, at the bench before dinner. I saw him fighting sleep during that endless, exhausting prayer, and eventually he laid his head on his arms on the bench.

I decided to give him some bread and cheese before dinner from then on, to hold him through the long prayer. I also woke him before I went to sleep, directing him to the pot in the corner in the hope that it might help stop the bedwetting during the nightmare.

And on that third night, when Cristiano was sleeping once more, I again questioned Bonifacio through the sheets about the child's silence and if there was an explanation for his nightmares.

"He has experienced a difficult life," he said, but would not be further drawn.

CHAPTER TWENTY-EIGHT

On the fourth morning, there was a great ringing of bells as Cristiano and I collected eggs.

When we came back to the house, Bonifacio was already on the step, holding his Bible and dressed in his wool suit and white shirt and black shoes and hat. "Change your clothes for church," he said.

I shook my head. "I'm not coming."

"I will go to daily Mass alone, but on Sundays you will accompany me. Leave the boy here. I tried to take him once, but he created a terrible scene."

"I don't want to go to church," I said, walking past him.

He grabbed my shoulder, and the unexpectedness of it made me drop the basket, the eggs smashing. Cristiano sucked in his breath, looking from the broken eggs to Bonifacio's hand on my shoulder.

"You *will* come," Bonifacio said.

Cristiano's eyes were wide, his chest rising and falling.

"All right," I said, pulling away from Bonifacio. "All right." I agreed more because of the look on Cristiano's face than anything else. "But the boy is coming as well."

Bonifacio turned his back and crossed his arms, staring at the church in the valley below. Papa slowly came from his room, also dressed for church. He looked down at the mess on the stoop, stepped over it and started down the road without waiting for us.

I wondered that none of the neighbours had stopped by. Each day, when I was in the yard, people had passed on the road and stared at me openly. I always waved, and most waved back, although their expressions were more curious than friendly. The evening before, as I sat on the step fixing a torn hem on my skirt, Papa had walked by. "I'm going to visit a friend," he said.

I stood. "Why haven't I met anyone?"

He held out his hands, palms up. "Bonifacio returned to Curral das Freiras in disgrace, and is ashamed. He turned everyone away, even the woman who cooked and cleaned for me for many years. He isn't interested in his old friends, and made it apparent. So nobody cares to visit. I go to my friends when I want to talk and drink."

Now, I cleaned up the broken eggs and changed into my best skirt and blouse. I secured my braids around my head. When I came into the sitting room, Bonifacio sat at the table, and Cristiano was on the step.

"You can't enter the church without a head covering," Bonifacio said.

"I *know* that," I said. "Cristiano, come inside and put on your better shirt."

He shook his head violently, wearing the same expression of fear as when he saw Bonifacio grab my shoulder.

I smiled at him, but his expression didn't change. "Cristiano," I said softly. "Please. You don't need to be afraid."

He shook his head again.

"You will come with me," I said firmly, not wanting to leave him here alone. "Nothing bad will happen. I promise."

⌒

We walked down the road behind Bonifacio. Cristiano lagged further behind as we approached the church doors, but I stopped and waited for him.

There were tables and benches set up in the yard in front of the church. On them were big pots and baskets, bowls and dishes and cutlery.

Inside, the congregation was already gathered, and the three of us stood at the very back. In a niche to one side was a beautiful female saint. On the other side was the Holy Mother, wearing a crown. The ceiling was painted with depictions of Jesus, surrounded by saints and cherubs. There was the familiar scent of incense and the glow of flickering candles. Light filtered in warmly through the high open windows, casting rays onto the walls and glinting on the gold of the tabernacle and the Holy Mother's crown.

Cristiano was trembling. I looked down at his poor scabbed, bare head and put my hand on his shoulder to comfort him. I felt a quiet relief that he didn't pull away from me. A very elderly priest came from the sacristy and raised his arms, palms up, gazing at his congregation. As his eyes went over the crowd, they stopped on me.

He smiled. Clothing rustled and heads turned as a small sea of faces looked at me.

I kept my chin high, my face still.

"Welcome," the Father said, and I nodded, glancing at Bonifacio. He was pale.

"*In nomine Patris, et Filii, et Spiritus Sancti*. Amen," the priest began, and then turned to the tabernacle.

I knew every Latin prayer and every response from watching while hidden in Nossa Senhora da Piedade. I knelt and stood as the others did, although I didn't bless myself. When it was time for Communion, and the priest lifted the consecrated hosts from the tabernacle, I left the church, Cristiano following. I did not want to take the Body of Christ. I would attend church as Bonifacio dictated, but that was all.

We stood on the far side of the churchyard. Eventually the priest opened the door and stood while his parishioners trickled out, talking and laughing with each other. Papa walked slowly with a few older men. Bonifacio did not appear.

All of the parishioners studied me with the same open curiosity as those who had passed our house. Nobody smiled. Cristiano and I stood silently. Finally, a heavy-set older woman came to me and took my hand.

"Welcome to our parish," she said. "There is rarely a new face among us." She glanced at Cristiano. "I'm glad the child has someone to care for him. Many of the children are suffering from ringworm right now. If you need something, please come to me. I'm Senhora

Cardozo. Rafaela. I'm the *curandeira* for the valley," she said, still holding my hand, and at that I squeezed her fingers.

"I'm a *curandeira* as well," I said. "From Porto Santo."

"You're far too young to be a healer."

"My mother taught me what she knew."

"Ah. Well, you still have many years ahead, and much to learn," Senhora Cardozo said. "How is Vitorino? He's come to me for help with his stomach for the last few years, but he hasn't been by lately."

"I've been giving him a tonic of milk thistle and wormwood twice daily."

"Yes, this is effective," she said, nodding. "You can also use the oil extracted from the fruit of the laurel."

"He seems able to digest the powdered thistle and wormwood easily."

"Very good. Yes, very good," she repeated. "I'm glad he has you to care for him as well, senhora. We have worried about him since Bonifacio came home and did not wish my sister to cook and clean the house and do the laundry as she had for many years, since Telma died."

I thought of what would happen to Papa when I left, then pushed that thought aside. "I am Diamantina."

She smiled again, then said, "*Bom dia,* Father Monteiro."

I turned to see the priest coming towards us. Cristiano made a sound, and I felt his sudden grip on my skirt.

"Good morning, Rafaela," he said. "And greetings, Senhora Rivaldo. Of course, we all heard that Bonifacio brought home a wife." He looked at Cristiano and smiled. "I've met the child once before." The old priest had a gentle face, his dark eyes almost hidden in wrinkles. The clean scent of soap wafted from his robes. "Hello, Cristiano," he said.

Rafaela moved away to join a small group of women.

"I'm Diamantina," I told him, as I had Rafaela. "Your church is beautiful. Who is the saint at the front of the apse?"

"She's our patron saint, Our Lady of Deliverance, a symbol of great devotion for our parish. I'm always here for confession, Diamantina," Father Monteiro said, and then looked at Cristiano again. The boy's eyes were huge, and he was biting his bottom lip.

"For everything there is a season," Father Monteiro said. "The child will eventually come around." I saw the kindness in his eyes. "I hope you will enjoy meeting more of the good people of our parish. We always gather after the Sunday Mass, and enjoy food and wine together."

Bonifacio came up behind the priest, stepping around him to stand beside me.

I nodded. "Oh, yes, I'd like—"

"Not today, Father Monteiro," Bonifacio said firmly.

"Yes," I repeated. "Cristiano and I will stay. Bonifacio, we'll come home with Papa."

He looked at me, a muscle in his cheek jumping.

Father Monteiro left us.

"Come home," Bonifacio said.

"No. You told me to come to church, and I came. Now I want to stay."

As I defied him, the colour first drained from his face then rose from his neck. He turned and strode up the road, away from the church.

CHAPTER TWENTY-NINE

Bonifacio wasn't in the house or garden when Cristiano and I got home, and I didn't see him until dinner. His prayer was shorter, and he jabbed his fork into his food. He left the table abruptly, half his dinner uneaten.

When Papa and Cristiano had gone to bed, Bonifacio came to the wash house where I scrubbed a pot.

"You flagrantly disobeyed me," he said. "We have been married less than a week, and you dare to act this way?"

I looked from the dirty pot to him. I had been waiting for this confrontation ever since I got back. Rafaela had introduced many of the women to me, and although they appeared shy or perhaps uncomfortable speaking with me, they were not unfriendly. Cristiano wouldn't play with any of the other children, but he'd lost his usual wary expression and watched with interest as a small group of boys chased each other and kicked a ball.

"Is it a sin to eat and talk with others, Bonifacio? Even if it's impossible for you to find pleasure in these ways, you have no right to take that pleasure from me." I dropped the pot into the water, and droplets flew onto my blouse. "I know you want to maintain your former vows, and perhaps in some ways continue the life of contemplation and prayer you knew so recently, but you can't expect the same of me." I put my wet hand on his sleeve for emphasis.

He flinched as if my hand burned him, and his face flushed.

I took my hand away. "I like Father Monteiro," I said. "It's clear he's a kind-hearted priest. Unlike Father da Chagos."

"What do you mean?"

"I knew him all my life, and yet he treated me with only a begrudging generosity of spirit, as if it pained him to help me."

"Are you forgetting that were it not for Father da Chagos, you would have been left in that mouldering hut for the rest of your life, living like a . . ." He stopped.

"Like a what, Bonifacio? Say it. Say what you really think of me." I was facing him now, my voice as loud as his.

"I know you had no choice in the way you were forced to live." His tone dropped. "And Father da Chagos told me that he admired you for your purity, in spite of the temptation that came your way."

I wanted to open my mouth and laugh, a long, hard laugh. That fat old flatulent priest knew from Abílio's confessions what we'd done. And he knew, along with everyone on the island, how I'd been debased by the sailor on the beach. I wondered now if the good Father thought that beating and humiliation deserved. He had no trouble lying to Bonifacio in order to have me taken from his parish, the town and the whole island.

"Your purity was important for me, Diamantina. That you were not yet dirtied. I could not have married you if this were the case."

"Dirtied? Is this why you keep your vow of chastity, even though you're no longer a priest? Does this mean you are so clean, Bonifacio?" I was breathing heavily.

A dog barked in the distance.

He turned his face from me but didn't leave.

His silence allowed me to grow calm. Finally I asked, softly, "Why do you really think Father da Chagos agreed to marry us?"

He looked at me again. "Because he is an old friend. I told you, we knew each other in the past. I spoke to him of the difficulty I was having with the child. I wasn't comfortable with any of the women here coming into our house, then going back to whisper and gossip to the whole village about the fallen priest and the slave child. Father da Chagos encouraged me to marry, insisting that to take a wife would help me to become part of the world I was out of step with."

I waited a long moment, because I wanted to form my next words to have the most effect. "He didn't do it for you, Bonifacio,"

I said slowly. "He did it for himself. When you first told me Father da Chagos would marry us, I knew why. It was to cleanse his parish of me. Baptizing me and marrying us wasn't an act of friendship, wasn't a favour to you or charity for me. You just came along at the right time, and were the perfect solution to his problem: me."

He swallowed.

"How can he call himself a messenger of God?" I went on, growing more agitated. "How can he say that God speaks through him, if he could treat my mother and me so uncharitably? Does every priest have to be only good, or can they not be both good and bad, like the sailors and the fishermen, like the weavers and the farmers? Are priests not just men, Bonifacio?"

His face was suddenly chalky.

"What did *you* do? What, Bonifacio, did you do that was so terrible that you were turned away from the priesthood?"

He shook his head, but I persisted, newly angered by his white face and troubled look. "Why did you have to take Cristiano so far from his home? Why won't he speak, apart from his babble at night?" I stepped so close to him that my breasts touched his chest. "Tell me!"

He just stared at me. Finally I backed away, and turned to go to the house, tensing for the sound of him following me, wondering if I had pushed him to a point that he might strike me. A thud made me look over my shoulder.

Bonifacio had dropped to his knees and covered his face with his hands. He rocked, his shoulders bent as though he were as old as his father.

"Bonifacio?" I said, and he raised his face. He was weeping silently, his expression so stricken that I thought he was at the beginning of an apoplexy. I took a step forward, but he put up a palm to stop me. And then he prostrated himself on the dirt floor of the wash house, his arms stretched out at his sides, and began the Our Father.

As he said it the second time, I left him.

He didn't come to the bedroom that night.

After Cristiano was asleep, I pulled off my clothing, slipping on the white sleeping gown I'd made. It was in the fashion of the one I'd once seen Sister Amélia wear, but had a lower neckline and looser sleeves. I stroked it down my body, pleased at the feel of the soft cloth against my bare skin. The silver talisman was cool between my breasts. I thought of Abílio, and his touch. Was that him I'd seen as we walked through Funchal?

Then I thought of the sailor on the beach. I had felt safe enough, my first night here, to take my gutting knife from my waistband and put it under my mattress. Now, as I lay on my bed, I put my hand under the mattress, reassuring myself it was there. I looked out at the olive tree, the moon caught in its top branches, and then back at the hanging sheets that separated my bed from my husband's.

I closed my eyes, knowing that Cristiano's nightmare would come too soon.

⁂

Bonifacio didn't return the next day either. Papa didn't ask about him.

I went about my chores while Papa, as usual, went to his garden. His endless hours in the big patch were not work for him, but pleasure. He loved keeping the weeds cleared away, picking off insects and staking the long trailing vines of his beans. In the cool of autumn in the mountains there were only the root vegetables left to be dug up, and sometimes Papa just stood, leaning on his hoe and looking at the neat rows with a calm expression. I knew he was in constant pain by the way he kept one hand pressed to his side, the difficulty he had in straightening after sitting or bending, and the soft, involuntary exhalations he made as he reached across the table. I gave him all the powders and tinctures I could to soothe the pain, but knew, at his age, that the difficulty in his bowel would not resolve itself.

By his colour and the odour of his breath, I doubted that Papa would live beyond the next planting season.

⁂

Late that afternoon, he came into the kitchen while I was preparing dinner, with Cristiano, cross-legged under the table, watching me.

Papa lifted the lid off the steaming kettle of water and dropped four handfuls of chestnuts into it. "I'll show you how to make *licor de castanha*," he said. "It's ready much faster than the cherry. That takes twelve Sundays." He sat on the stool by the table, looking under at Cristiano for a moment. "Espirito loves *licor de castanha*."

This was the second time he'd mentioned Espirito.

I touched his arm so he would watch me speak. "Who is Espirito?"

He looked surprised. "He's my other son, younger than Bonifacio by two years. You don't know of him?"

"Bonifacio hasn't mentioned him."

Papa shook his head, clicking his tongue.

"Why haven't I met him?"

"He lives in Funchal with his wife. Whenever he comes to visit, he asks for my *licors*. My Telma made the best *licors* in the parish. Everybody wanted Telma's *licors*."

"When did she pass on?" I asked.

"Thirteen years ago. Bonifacio was seventeen and Espirito fifteen years old. She wanted her sons to live in Funchal. She was from Câmara de Lobos, on the ocean not far from there, and never liked the mountains as I did. 'Promise me, Vitorino,' she said before she died, 'promise me our boys will not spend their lives here working themselves to death.'"

He got up and scooped the chestnuts out of the boiling water with a handled sieve, dumped them into a flat wooden bowl and shook them back and forth. Steam rose from them. "Cristiano, come and watch," he said.

Cristiano came out from under the table and stood beside Papa.

Using a small knife, Papa made a cut two-thirds of the way around the flat face of the shell and peeled it away, then eased the rest of the nut out of the skin. "The chestnuts are nice and fresh, so both outer and inner skins come away. This is a good job for a boy when he's old enough to use the knife. My boys always did this." He handed the knife to Cristiano. "You are old enough."

Cristiano looked at the knife, then picked up one of the chestnuts and slowly, carefully cut it the way Papa had.

"Good. That's the way," Papa said, and Cristiano's mouth moved in the beginning of a smile. Then Papa added sugar to the hot water the nuts had been in. While we waited for it to come to a boil, Cristiano finished the peeling.

Papa skimmed froth off the surface of the boiling syrup, then dumped the chestnuts in and let them cook for a few moments. Then he fished them out again, putting them into an empty earthenware jar. "Now you can do the rest," he said to me, and pulled another jar from a shelf. "Brandy. This much," he said, holding his thumb and index finger apart. "Let the syrup boil again, and when it cools, pour the brandy over the chestnuts, but don't stir—the chestnuts fall apart easily. Then put in the stopper. In only two Sundays it will be ready." He turned to leave. "The chestnuts are delicious to eat, once they've sat in the liqueur. They were always Espirito's favourites. You will like Espirito. He's a good boy."

"We'll save them," I said, "for the next time he comes."

He nodded. "Tonight we will play dominoes, you and I," he said, and I smiled at him.

CHAPTER THIRTY

That evening, I hung Bonifacio's clean shirts, smelling of the mountain air, on his pegs. I straightened a blanket thrown over the chest at the end of his bed, and then, on a whim, knelt in front of the chest and opened it.

Under a folded pair of old breeches was a worn leather bag with a torn strap. I took it out and looked inside. There was a long black buttoned robe of coarse cotton, as well as a black cincture. I sat back on my heels. Bonifacio's Jesuit vestments. I imagined him wearing these in Brazil. At the bottom of the bag something glinted. I pulled it out. On a long strip of leather was a heavy pendant with a cross, and on the cross the sign of the Jesuit. As I put it back into the chest, I saw a small cloth sack almost hidden in one corner. I lifted it, then opened the drawstring and gazed in. I dumped the coins onto my skirt and counted them. One hundred and seventy-six réis.

I sat back on my heels. If Abílio had been correct about the cost of a passage to Brazil, this was enough. I counted the coins again, then put them back into the cloth bag and bounced it on my palm with a sudden lifting joy. I could take them and walk back to Funchal. I knew Abílio had also told me an unaccompanied woman would not be allowed on the long journey across the ocean, but that would be a simple matter to remedy: I would find a family and ask to join them.

To take Bonifacio's coins would be stealing. I had only a moment of remorse at the thought, but it was not about taking the money. It was at the idea of leaving Papa and Cristiano.

Cristiano put his head around the sheet, and I jumped up. He looked at the bag I held, and at the open chest.

I hurriedly put the money back where I'd found it, arranging the leather bag and clothing as it had been, and slammed the lid of the chest as Cristiano watched me. "Go out and wash your hands and face before bed," I said, a little more sternly than I'd intended.

He ducked behind the sheet and was gone.

⁂

I was almost asleep when Bonifacio got back. I sat up as he opened the bedroom door and went to his side of the room.

"Where have you been?" I asked.

"In the hills. It's peaceful there, with no voices, no stares. No temptations. I feel closer to God," he said, his voice muffled behind the curtain.

I lay back down, but in the next instant he pulled the sheets open and I sat up again, staring at him in the darkness. "What do you want?" I asked, not exactly fearful, but unnerved by the way he stood, so still, his face shadowed.

"Come to the sitting room," he said, glancing at Cristiano's sleeping form. "Please," he added, and at that I pushed back the blanket.

He looked a moment too long at me in my nightgown. I grabbed my shawl from the end of my bed and wrapped it around myself as I followed him. He sat at the table, and I sat across from him.

"Don't," he said, as I reached for the flint beside the candle in the middle of the table. "It's easier for me in the dark." He stared towards the window, and I watched his profile.

"I thought that with time . . ." Bonifacio glanced back at me. "I thought that perhaps time would heal. It's been almost ten months since . . . since we left Brazil. But the wound has only festered in both of us, left untreated. Left unspoken. I do want the boy to find relief from his misery. I did not bring him here to live in fear and hatred."

I waited. I heard him lick his lips.

"Father Monteiro knows. I daily make my confession and do my penance. He assures me God forgives me. But I don't feel His forgiveness. Father Monteiro suggested I tell you what happened, so that you might help the child. I know that no one will ever be able to help me. And I don't deserve help." He cleared his throat. "I have to tell you now, before I lose my courage." He gave a sudden mirthless laugh, the first laugh I had heard from him.

"Courage," he said, with another, painful, laugh. He stopped abruptly. "I told you Cristiano's mother was a slave, brought from West Africa to sieve for diamonds around Tejuco." He sat for a moment in silence, as if unsure how to continue.

"Yes," I finally said, thinking he might be waiting for a reaction from me.

"I was alone in the church at the mission. It was growing late, and I was extinguishing the last of the candles before going home. The Fathers lived in a separate dwelling a little distance away.

"A young mulatto woman, Vovo, ran into the church, dragging her boy by the hand. I had baptized Vovo and her son the year before. The boy had been sired by Vovo's owner, Nuno Travino, in a union not unusual for the owners and their female slaves.

"She was wild-eyed, panting. She spat a diamond into her hand. 'Help me, Father Bonifacio, help me,' she said. She looked fearfully over her shoulder. 'They're coming for me,' she told me, and shoved the rough diamond into my hand. It was larger than any I'd seen. 'Take it, and protect me,' she begged.

"Slaves were allowed to wear only the flimsiest of clothes, and had their heads shaved so they couldn't hide any diamonds they found. As they left the streams each evening, they were forced to lift their loincloths and open their mouths to an overseer. I don't know why Vovo took this chance. I don't know how she spirited such a large diamond from the stream, or how it became known that she had it. But three men burst into the church. I recognized them: Travino's overseers. Vovo crouched behind the altar, but they'd seen her. It was all happening so quickly, Vovo screaming as they pulled her up.

"I told them that this was a place of God, and that the woman was protected within the sanctified walls. But they cared nothing for God's house. Two of them dragged her outside, all the way to the edge of a deep ravine behind the church. The other forced me to follow, one arm twisted behind me, a knife held to my throat. The diamond was hidden in my clenched hand. There was a gibbous moon. I remember the moon," he said, his voice faltering. His shoulders had been high, as if he were protecting himself, but now they fell.

I sat very still.

"My robe and cross meant nothing to those men. I had always thought . . . I thought that my robe would protect me—that I was untouchable because of my faith."

"Why didn't you give them the diamond?"

I heard him swallow. "As I entreated them to leave, the pig cut me. He slashed through my robe, across my chest, and I fell, overcome with pain and shock, and . . ." Again he stopped.

"But why didn't you give them the diamond?" I asked again.

"You don't know?" His voice rose. "You don't realize what kind of man I am? I didn't give it to them because I was afraid. Just one slash of the knife and I turned into a quivering rabbit. I was afraid that they'd think I was helping her, that I was part of it," he said, "and that they'd kill us both."

He said nothing more for so long that I finally asked, in a quiet voice, "What happened to her? To Vovo?"

"While two of the men held her on the ground, the third pried open her mouth and stuck his fingers down her throat until she gagged. He jammed his fingers up her nostrils and into her ears. Then he ripped her shift down the front and threw it from her, and searched inside her body." He put his hand over his eyes, as if he couldn't bear to look at me, or couldn't bear to remember what he'd seen. "Vovo stared at me through all of this in her nakedness and humiliation, as that animal dug inside her. She pleaded with me. 'Father Bonifacio,' she kept calling, 'please help me. You can help me, Father Bonifacio. Stop them, stop them,' until one struck her in the mouth with his fist to silence her."

"But Bonifacio, why—"

"I lay on the ground not far from Vovo, but I watched the horror unfolding as if from a great distance," Bonifacio continued. "I lay bleeding, in a strange dream world." Finally he took his hand from his eyes. "But then the man with the knife said, 'She swallowed it. You swallowed it, didn't you?' In that instant I knew what they would do, and yet I lay there protecting myself like a frightened animal. Protecting myself. Myself. And then the man with the knife went to work on her."

I put my hand over my mouth.

Bonifacio wept quietly at first, and then with great shuddering sobs.

I didn't know what I felt at that moment. Horror at the story of brutality? Revulsion for his weakness? I watched him weep, and thought of the little boy in the next room.

Eventually he wiped his eyes and nose with his sleeve. "She didn't make a sound as they butchered her, looking for the diamond. She never once said I had it. She accepted her fate. In spite of the most unbearable agony as the men dug through her entrails, she quietly waited for her death, and she knew me for the coward I was.

"She was able to speak once more before she died. 'My boy,' she said, a whisper, but I heard her. 'Save my boy, Father.' It was only then I thought of the child. I followed her gaze, and saw him, pressing the dress they had torn from her body to his face. He saw what they did to her. And then he looked at me, and ran."

I heard Cristiano's breathing, ragged, loud, from the bedroom. His nightmare was beginning. I felt as though I'd been hammered in the throat.

"The diamond cut into my hand as I lay there. I watched, in this strange dream, as the men lifted Vovo's body and threw it into the ravine." He tried to draw in a breath, but it was shaky and uncontrolled. "I don't know how long I lay there. When I realized I was able to rise, I opened my hand. The diamond burned my flesh as though it was the devil's fork. I threw that evil gem into the dark ravine. Eventually I found myself in my room. When I took off my robe, the cut still bled, but it was not deep. It was not deep." His voice was so low I had to lean forward.

"I stayed on my knees for the rest of the night, praying for Vovo's soul, and for my own salvation. She was with God, but I was lost to Him by my own doing. My prayers felt false. By morning I was fevered, so filled with contempt for myself that I fell ill. I started to the church to confess, but instead went to the village. I told myself I would see Vovo filing with the others to the river with her sieve. That it hadn't really happened. I tried to convince myself it had been a terrible nightmare."

He laid his hands on the table in a helpless gesture and stared at them.

Finally I said, "What happened, Bonifacio?"

He raised his head. "The news in the village was that the mulatto slave Vovo had been found dead on the rocks at the bottom of the ravine. Her body, it was said, had been ravaged by wild boars after she died. The story was that she had been drinking a homemade *licor* with some of the young male slaves, and in her drunkenness fell to her death. This, all the Portuguese in the village said, was what happened when you drank and ran with men. I knew that what was spoken in the slave quarter would not be the same story, that they knew she had been killed, but who among them could stand up and be a voice for their fallen sister? Because she was lighter-skinned, the Portuguese village gossip went on, she felt herself above the other slaves. Pride, they muttered, and the wages of sin. There, in the public square, I leaned over and was sick."

Cristiano whimpered, hoarsely whispering.

"I also heard that her child was found nearby, hiding. He had witnessed his mother's immoral behaviour, the gossip continued, and her fall to the rocks below. As I stood in the warm dust of the village square, my own vomit splattered down my robe and on my feet, I knew I must go to Nuno Travino immediately. I would identify the three men who had killed his slave. I would have been believed—I was a priest and they ignorant, low-minded overseers without respect for a missionary Father. Even if they weren't punished—for slaves died brutally and often—I thought that at least the name of Vovo wouldn't have been so dirtied. At that moment, one of those overseers passed me in the square. He gave me a knowing, threatening smile, putting his finger to his lips. I saw my own body at the bottom of the ravine. Later I reasoned that surely they wouldn't murder a priest, but . . ."

Bonifacio stopped, and I smelled his fear. A spasm, as if he'd experienced a sudden sharp pain, passed over his face. "My bowels churned, and I had to fight not to soil myself. I realized that for all I had seen of the world, both here on Madeira and in Brazil, I had never really been tested. Even though I had sailed across the ocean and started a new life, I did not know what I was made of. I had felt protected by the Church, by my robe and cross, by living what I believed to be a pious, righteous existence. I didn't know who I was, or what I was capable of outside of prayers and meditations.

"And when I truly saw myself for the first time that day, I was revolted. I knew that I would not report the men because of my cowardice, just as I had not saved Vovo the night before. I knew with complete certainty that I was as low as the serpent that came to Eve and whispered, *Do as you please,* and as low as Judas in the Garden of Gethsemane. God had put a test in front of me, and I had failed. I failed God, and knew I no longer deserved to walk and live with Him."

Cristiano screamed then, and I ran to him. I did what I could to wake him and bring him back to this life, away from the one I now knew he lived at night. I soothed him, holding him until his eyes closed and he again slept.

The bedroom shutter banged in the wind, and I gently put Cristiano down and closed it. The room was dark save for a long sliver of moonlight shining in through one broken slat. It fell over Cristiano. I now understood why he was afraid of the church and the priest's robes—and why he hated Bonifacio.

CHAPTER THIRTY-ONE

When I went back to the sitting room, Bonifacio had lit a candle, and there was a jug of water on the table, and he held a cup. Before I sat down, he started talking, but now he spoke rapidly, as though he needed to finish the story as quickly as possible.

"Father Nóbrega, my superior, heard my full confession. I begged him to tell me what I could do to find understanding for the girl's suffering and death. How would I ever be granted absolution? Father Nóbrega knew how I loved Tejuco, so he suggested that as penance I leave it. Leave Brazil, and spend a full year in solitude and prayer at a monastery far in the north of Portugal. Segregated from others, with only God for company. 'This is your crucial moment, Father Bonifacio, your time of testing,' he said, 'and you must learn from it.'

"For the next three days and nights, I did not sleep or eat. I stayed on my knees, praying, like Christ in the Garden of Olives, to find the strength to cope with my penance.

"On that third dark night, He finally spoke to me. What Father Nóbrega offered as penance was not enough: the sacrifice of leaving Tejuco and spending time in isolation would not absolve me. I knew what my sacrifice must be. Like Adam and Eve, I had to be cast out. I went to Father Nóbrega and told him I was leaving the priesthood." He lifted his cup and drained it. The candle flame flickered with his movement.

"He argued that I had shown absolute willingness to do God's bidding over the years we had worked together. 'How can you abandon God?' he asked me. I wasn't abandoning God, I told him, but no longer deserved to be His messenger. He asked me where I would go. I told him I didn't know but would be shown the way. I would continue to put my trust in God, even though He could no longer trust me.

"I was twenty-nine years old, and had spent my adult life walking and living with Christ and doing His work. I knew that leaving the priesthood wouldn't change my oath to live a life of poverty, obedience and chastity. Those oaths I would keep, but I had to make further amends."

From outside came the first sleepy twittering of the awakening birds.

"And Cristiano?" I said quietly.

He lifted the cup to his lips; he'd forgotten he'd emptied it. He reached out and took the jug. His hand shook, and droplets spilled as he poured. "I vowed to take on Vovo's child. I would look after him and protect him, as she had begged me as she died." He took another deep breath. "I promised God that I would raise that innocent child to be an honourable and upright man, not like his cruel father, Travino, and not like me. It was all I could do in memory of Vovo: take on her child and raise him into a man she would have been proud of. I would bring him to Lisboa, and find some kind of life there. I couldn't come home, could I? Not as a disgraced priest, fallen from grace.

"It was dawn when I arrived at the slave quarters. Some were already moving about, drawing water and preparing for their long day of labour. I asked where I might find the child of the dead woman. I was shown a hut, one among many around a square of beaten earth. An old woman sat against the wall. I told her I was there to take away the son of Vovo. I still wore my robe. She motioned for me to follow her inside, and in the dim light I made out children of various ages sleeping on piles of long dried grass.

"She pulled one of the children up. He swayed, rubbing his eyes, clutching a colourful piece of fabric. I drew in a breath when I realized it was Vovo's dress. 'Here is Cirilio,' the old woman said.

"The child rubbed his eyes again, and then, when he saw me, his face contorted and he clung to the old woman. 'He sees something happen to his mama, and his words go dead with her,' the old woman said to me. My insides turned to liquid as she brought back the horror.

"'I won't hurt you, Cirilio,' I told him, trying to get him to look at me, but he was terrified. 'You don't have to be afraid.' Why should he believe me? Hadn't he seen that I did nothing to help or protect his mother?'"

Bonifacio held out his hand, his fingers spread, as if what he was about to say next was written on the back of them. "I told him, 'You are no longer Cirilio. Now you are Cristiano.' I wanted him to have a Portuguese name for his new life. At that, something came into the child's eyes, some skepticism that made me realize the boy considered me either a fool or mad. And that made me think that he possessed intelligence beyond his years, which I presumed to be four or five, I couldn't tell. But when I tried to take him, he screamed in a terrible way. All the other children were on their feet, watching us, the smaller ones clinging to the older ones. The old woman tried to comfort him, rubbing the dress on his face. I picked him up and put my hand over his mouth to silence him. And then . . . I carried him away."

He stopped. A grey light was washing over the room now, and the birds were louder.

"I overpowered him, and took him away. I took him all the way to Rio de Janeiro. He never spoke again, except in the nightmare, which came his first night with me, and has never stopped.

"Because I still wore my robe, we were given free passage on a ship sailing to Lisboa. Cristiano sat or lay motionless, his mother's dress over his face, throughout that long journey. He was very ill when the sea was rough. Although I talked to him in his patois at first, eventually I spoke only Portuguese, to prepare him for his new life." He stopped, shaking his head. "When finally the ship stopped in Funchal to take on supplies for the rest of the journey to Lisboa, I left Cristiano below and went on the deck. I didn't know what I'd feel when I looked out upon Madeira after so many years away. I had thought to never see it again. But as I stood in the warm and familiar air, a beam of sunlight shone upon the mountains. I believed this to be a sign: I was lost, and had prayed every day to be shown a path. The sun on the mountains was like the finger of God, pointing out my rightful place—my home, Curral das Freiras. I was being shown another part of my penance, one I hadn't imagined until that moment: to face my father and my brother, and confess that I was not worthy of being a priest. Facing the parish and all those who had seen me go off to the seminary and then to Brazil, full of a pride I couldn't hide. I knew that I had to look into all their faces, and accept that I was contemptible and undeserving, and that they knew me to be so."

Bonifacio's voice was hoarse after talking for so long, and he roughly cleared his throat. "On shore, Cristiano was unable to walk, so weak that he immediately fell into a deep, exhausted sleep in my arms. Looking down at him, seeing the darkness around his eyes, the drawn cheeks, I felt even stronger guilt. And . . . I thought the guilt would fade. But I have come to realize Cristiano's purpose is never to let me forget what I did. He is my daily reminder. To him, I am as much a monster as the men who slit open his mother's belly."

"You wanted to use him to help relieve yourself of your guilt?" I pulled my shawl up around my shoulders in a quick, angry gesture.

We sat in silence.

"You have heard it all," he said. "I can see how you look at me now. But we will have to find a way to live together. Nobody but Father Nóbrega and Father Monteiro know what took me from the priesthood, not even my father or brother. I ask you never to repeat my story. I'm only telling you so that you can understand Cristiano's behaviour." He stood. "As there was nothing for me in Brazil anymore, there is nothing for you on Porto Santo. So you may as well make the best you can of this life with me in Curral das Freiras."

He left the house. I knew he was headed for the church, where he would stay on his knees, praying, waiting for early Mass.

I blew out the sputtering candle, then went out and climbed the mountain path. I watched the rising sun, imagining the ocean far beyond.

CHAPTER THIRTY-TWO

A week later, a voice called from the yard.

"*Bom dia*, Bonifacio!"

I wiped the sweat from my forehead with my arm and came out of the kitchen. I saw him before he noticed me: the man with the long hair who had taken me for a whore in Rooi's inn. The man, smelling of the grape, who had been in Rooi's inn the night before I met Bonifacio. The man who had humiliated me.

His hair was still long, tied at the back, but now he was clean-shaven. Without the beard, he looked younger.

"You," he said, his voice incredulous as I walked towards him. "What are you doing here?"

I swallowed and fixed my eyes on him, refusing to blink. "This is my home."

"Here?"

I put my hands on my hips. "I am married to Bonifacio Rivaldo. How may I help you?"

"Married?" he repeated. "Bonifacio *married* you?"

My face burned, and my voice grew loud. "My husband is at the stream with his father. Cristiano," I called over my shoulder, and he came from the house. "Take this man to Bonifacio, and . . ." I stopped, startled, as Cristiano ran down the step and across the yard to the man, who picked the boy up.

I opened my mouth to tell him no, that Cristiano didn't like to be touched, but Cristiano didn't struggle at all. "I like this," the man said, touching the circle of shelled chestnuts I had strung together and hung around Cristiano's neck. "But where are your curls?"

Cristiano stroked the man's cheek with his fingertips. The man nodded at him. "We both lost some hair. You remember I had a beard the last time you saw me, don't you? I had to shave it off. Do you know why? I found a family of mice living in it. A father and a mother and five babies. They nibbled at the food stuck in my beard from my dinner, and they tickled so much they kept me awake all night."

Cristiano's eyes were wide.

"So I finally took them out of my beard and said, Listen, Senhor and Senhora Mouse, I'm sorry, but you tickle too much. You're going to have to find another home. I'm shaving off my beard."

Now Cristiano made a wry face.

"You don't believe me? Well, Papa Mouse wasn't happy about that, and we had a bit of an argument, but finally he took his wife and children and moved out, and I shaved. We've remained friends, however, and I saw him only last week. He told me he and his family are now living in a pastry shop, and feasting on all the sweets there. He says it's far superior to the crumbs of bread and bits of cheese they found in my beard. And now I can sleep at night." With that, he tickled Cristiano under the chin, and Cristiano made a sound that actually verged on laughter. A dimple I'd never seen appeared in his left cheek.

Without warning, tears came to my eyes.

The man, smiling at Cristiano, glanced at me. His smile faded. "How long could he have known you? He really married you?" He set the boy down.

"Yes," I said, looking aside and blinking the tears away. "Cristiano will take you to Bonifacio."

"I know where the stream is," he said in a sarcastic tone. "Come along, Cristiano." He took the little boy's hand and Cristiano's small fingers closed around his.

"Who are you?" I asked.

"I am Espirito, Bonifacio's brother," the man said, stopping. "And your brother now as well." He shook his head. "He married without telling me. And a woman like you. Full of surprises, my brother."

I was setting out dinner when I heard the rumble of voices and went to the step. Bonifacio and Papa, followed by Espirito and Cristiano, were coming towards the house. Bonifacio and Espirito each carried a bucket of water for the cistern.

Espirito was taller than Bonifacio, and looked much younger than his brother, even though I knew they were only two years apart.

Bonifacio's expression was unreadable. Had Espirito told him about me? I had thought of nothing else as I waited for the men to return.

Would Bonifacio banish me from Curral das Freiras, now that he had learned I was not as clean as he thought? "My brother will be staying for dinner," he told me, then took Espirito's bucket and went to the wash house.

"Cristiano, go with Bonifacio and Papa and wash your hands," I said.

Espirito stood in front of me. He still smelled of the grape, tinged now with tobacco.

I crossed my arms over my chest. "Well? Did it please you to inform your brother about me?"

"What do you refer to?"

I glanced at the wash house. "Don't play me for a fool. You know what I'm talking about. Did you tell Bonifacio about our meeting on Porto Santo?"

"So he doesn't know your past. You didn't divulge who you really are?"

I took a deep breath. "Your brother and I accept each other."

He made a sound in his throat. "I don't know what happened to him in Brazil, or his reasons for returning with Cristiano, but him marrying you, well . . ." His voice trailed off as the men came from the wash house.

"Diamantina," Papa said. "Get out the *licor de castanha*."

Bonifacio went into the bedroom, and Papa and Cristiano sat at the table. I poured four cups of liqueur; Papa took his. I picked up two of the cups while Espirito looked around the room, his gaze stopping on the jug of autumn wildflowers on the table, the crisp white curtains I'd made for the windows. He went to the dish cupboard and took down a book.

"Those are mine," I said, more brusquely than was necessary.

"Yours?" he asked, looking at me.

"Yes. I read," I said, stressing the word. I took a sip from my cup.

He studied me closely, and I didn't understand his expression. He returned the book to its place. "You left your family and your life on Porto Santo to come here with my brother?"

I stepped close and gave him his liqueur. "You're surprised that a woman who reads worked in a dirty inn," I said very quietly. "I'll tell you something else that may surprise you." I glanced at Papa, engrossed in cleaning under his fingernails with the tip of a knife, and at the open bedroom door. "When I enticed a drunken sailor to play dominoes with me, and when I won—as I always did—I made sure he gave me a réal and then left me alone." I spoke even more quickly and quietly. "I insisted all of them leave me alone. Do you understand? I only played dominoes to make a few coins."

He showed no reaction.

"I have no family," I went on. "I was alone in the world. Your brother offered me a new life, and I took it. He had his own reasons for what he did." I hated that my hands were shaking. When Espirito at last accepted the cup, I moved away from him.

He drank, and then said, "I'm surprised. Surely you can understand that."

My neck felt stiff. "Because you see me as—" I stopped as Bonifacio came in from the bedroom with his Bible. I drank from my cup to hide my discomfort.

Espirito turned from me and went to the table. His own liqueur untouched, Bonifacio knelt at the bench. Espirito and I set our cups on the table and, along with Papa and Cristiano, knelt as well.

At the final amen, we all sat, and Papa poured himself another cup of the liqueur. "Diamantina made this," he said to Espirito, lifting his cup. "Good for her first try. Remember how Mama made it?"

"I do," Espirito said.

After that, only the sounds of our spoons clinking against the bowls broke the silence. The tension between Bonifacio and Espirito cast a heavy pall over the table, and made it difficult to swallow. What caused the unease? Only Cristiano ate with gusto, constantly glancing at Espirito, his little face bright.

"So now you enjoy a game of dominoes, brother?" Espirito asked, gesturing at the box on the dish cupboard.

My spoon hovered over my bowl.

"You know I've never been interested in games," Bonifacio said. "Unlike you."

I set down my spoon. "It's mine. My father taught me to play." Then I added, "Would you care for a game after dinner, Espirito?" I stared into his eyes, daring him to speak.

"No. But my brother is right, I've always enjoyed games."

I looked away, wiping a thin smear of olive oil from Cristiano's chin with my apron.

"Bonifacio," Espirito said then, "why didn't you stop by when you brought Diamantina from Porto Santo, and introduce us?" His voice had a mocking quality.

Bonifacio ignored him.

"Perhaps you can bring your wife here the next time you come," I said evenly.

"She's not strong enough to travel far."

Silence.

"You work with wine?" I asked.

"My brother told you?"

"No. I can smell the grape on you."

"You have a finely developed sense of smell." His voice was unreadable now.

I watched him. "Yes. I do."

"Espirito works for Kipling's Wine Merchants," Papa said, looking at our faces as he worked at following the conversation.

That explained why Bonifacio received his post there. I cleared my throat. "What do you do?"

Espirito put down his spoon. "I'm the overseer. As well as negotiating the price of the *mosto* that comes down to Kipling's, I do some of the blending as well."

"I used to—" I stopped, about to blurt out my own small attempts at blending wine at Rooi's. Instead, I said, "I'm interested in the blending of wines." From the corner of my eye, I saw Bonifacio's head turn towards me.

"My son has a fine position," Papa said, pouring himself and Espirito and me another cup from the jug. Bonifacio still hadn't touched his. "Kipling's isn't large, but it has one of the best reputations in Funchal."

I looked at Bonifacio. "I would like to see the wine lodge sometime. When can we go to Funchal?" I took another drink of the strong liqueur.

"I don't know." His tone was curt.

Papa shook his head, then stood and patted my shoulder. "Thank you, daughter," he said. "I'll go to bed now."

Espirito rose, and the two men embraced briefly. "Goodbye, Papa. You have a full house now, so I'll stay the night with Felipe Pestana. I have to get back to Funchal tomorrow, but I'll see you in a few weeks."

Papa murmured, "Yes, yes, son. Say hello to Olívia." He went into his room and shut the door.

"He looks poorly. And this early to bed?" Espirito sat down again.

"If you cared so much about him, you would come more often," Bonifacio said.

"I come as often as I can. You left Madeira, saying you'd never return, and didn't even write to him. And you criticize me?"

Both men's expressions were tight.

"I've been trying to help Papa's stomach pain," I said, "and I know he finds some relief with my medicines."

"What medicines?" Espirito asked.

"I'm a *curandeira*."

"Really? You're a *curandeira* as well?" Espirito said, emphasizing *as well*. The warmth from the liqueur fled. "And how did you learn this skill?"

"From my mother," I said, and turned to Cristiano. "You can go and play with the baby chicks before bedtime."

He got up and went outside.

"So many surprises," Espirito said, looking from me to Bonifacio. "You are both full of surprises."

"I might say the same of you," Bonifacio said.

I perched on the edge of my seat, expecting something to erupt any moment.

But then Espirito shook his head and said, "There's nothing to be gained by this. The past cannot be undone. Look, if nothing else, Bonifacio, I'm glad you're here for Papa. It's clear he can't manage on his own anymore." He again took in the tidy room, his eyes resting on the fluttering curtains. He glanced at me and opened his mouth as if to say something more, but then closed it.

Bonifacio stared into his full cup.

"And so how has it been for you since I last saw you?" Espirito said into the silence, leaning forward and studying Bonifacio.

"Difficult, as you'd expect."

"What does everyone think of you bringing a wife here?"

Bonifacio finally looked at Espirito. "What do you want to hear?" His hands were clenched on the table, and his cheeks a dull red.

But Espirito didn't stop. "Papa is a tolerant man. One imagines that when a son enters the priesthood, he will always remain a priest, and not come home expecting things to be as they were before he left." He stood. "Thank you for dinner, Diamantina. Good night, Bonifacio."

Bonifacio didn't reply.

Cristiano was sitting on the step, cradling a yellow chick. Through the open doorway I watched Espirito bend to put his hand on the boy's head. "Goodbye, little man," he said. "Remember what I told you about talking to the mice in the wash house." Then he walked into the deepening evening, whistling, his arms swinging by his sides.

Bonifacio immediately rose and went into the bedroom with his Bible, closing the door. I waited until Espirito disappeared down the road before taking the dirty dishes to the wash house. When I was done, I told Cristiano to put the chick back with its mother and come inside.

I lit a candle as Cristiano got into bed, and when I pulled the coverlet over him, he turned on his side, clutching the cloth that had been his mother's dress. Today with Espirito was the first time I had seen him behave as any small boy might, smiling at Espirito's story of the mice and eating his dinner with noisy enthusiasm.

Ever since Bonifacio had told me the terrible story of what had happened in Brazil, I had looked at the little boy differently. Where earlier I had felt only confusion about him and his behaviour, now I felt an ache when I watched him.

I didn't want to feel this way, for when the time came for me to go, it would be hard to leave Cristiano.

CHAPTER THIRTY-THREE

On All Souls' Day, the four of us walked down the slope to Nossa Senhora do Livramento. I carried a basket of flowers Cristiano and I had collected, at Papa's request, for Telma's grave.

After the Mass, we joined others in the cemetery as they celebrated their departed loved ones. We decorated Telma's grave with the flowers, and Bonifacio closed his eyes. *"Réquiem ætérnam dona ei Dómine,"* he prayed for the soul of his mother. His face was so calm, his expression so pious, that I knew he was again in his old life. Every time he attended Mass, he must long to be the one performing the sacred rites. He longed for the holy life as I longed for the ocean.

But he was no longer a priest, and I was no longer part of the rhythms of the sea. I thought of my own mother, sinking under the waves, and sent a message of love to her.

⁂

After we ate dinner that night, Papa held out a delicate gold chain adorned with a small medallion of the Holy Mother. "It was my Telma's," he said, putting it into my hand. "I wish you to wear it always, and as you wear it, you will be reminded to honour my son. Our son, Telma's and mine."

I looked down at the medallion.

"Put it on," Papa urged, and I slipped it over my head. It rested on the front of my blouse, its slight weight touching the silver talisman underneath. I glanced at Bonifacio. His jaw was tight and his face dark.

"Should it not have been Olívia's? She was your first daughter-in-law," he said to Papa.

"Don't spoil it for your wife," Papa said. "It's not her fault."

I wanted to ask Papa what he meant, but the air was thick with Bonifacio's anger.

Apart from the daily early Mass, Bonifacio rarely left the yard. There was no work to be done on the vines during the cool months, and so apart from the daily chores of chopping wood or hauling water to the wash house or making minor repairs to the house and outbuildings, he sat on the step and read his Bible. Sometimes I felt him watching me as I crossed the yard or hung clothes on the bushes, but each time I glanced at him, his head was lowered over the page.

I heard him in the sitting room some nights, whispering the same prayer as he had in Funchal on the night we married, begging for help to be holy and chaste. I found the cat-o'-nine-tails in a sack under his bed the first time I washed the bedroom floor. Also in the sack was a shirt with strips of stiff goat hair sewn into it, and a belt with sharp metal studs on the inside of the leather.

During the fourth week I was in Curral das Freiras, I found Bonifacio's shirt soaking, the water pink, in a tub behind the wash house. I knew then that he'd been wearing the belt with the studs, cinching it so tightly around his waist under his shirt that the sharp metal bit into his flesh and made it bleed, wanting to concentrate on the pain instead of the needs of his body.

I didn't mention the bloodstained shirt, disturbed by the idea of Bonifacio's fight against his vow of chastity. And yet again, I was glad for this vow. I couldn't bear to think of him touching me.

To pass the time until I could leave, I learned to use the abundant chestnuts to make soup and pudding and cake, delighting Papa. I helped him in the garden, touching his arm when I heard birdsong.

Although he could no longer hear their voices, as I pointed to each bird, Papa told me its name. I realized I waited for him to smile at me and pat my arm or shoulder after each meal, saying, "Thank you, daughter."

There was abundant plant life in the cool dampness of the valley. I visited Rafaela one morning, and she showed me her herb garden and described the use of the root and flower and seed of each plant I hadn't known on Porto Santo. She was bringing up her grand-daughter, close in age to Cristiano. I watched the little girl stand in front of Cristiano and hop on one leg. After a while he solemnly mimicked her, his tongue caught between his front teeth in concentration. Then they caught grasshoppers in their cupped hands, the little girl squealing, Cristiano silent.

He was usually at my side, helping me as best he could. I spoke to him as we worked, telling him whatever I was thinking about. I talked to him as I had once talked to my missing father. I worried about his desire to climb the steep cliffs, but there seemed no way to stop him; he refused to listen to my admonishments. I often climbed up to fetch him from a dangerous perch. And yet I understood his need to get closer to the sky. I also felt closed in, especially when the mountains caught the clouds and mist covered the valley.

One day, I found a safer path to climb, where the incline was firmer and there were roots and small trees to hold, and showed it to him. As we went upwards together, we came upon a wide, flat shelf of rock and sat there. I tried to whistle and call back the birds' tunes: the rich, melodious song of the blackbird, the high-pitched call of the shy little firecrest, and the pleasant chattering of the blackcap. The first time Cristiano tried to mimic the firecrest, I laughed and clapped my hands, and he laughed with me.

I knew how clever he was. He learned anything I showed him almost immediately. Some evenings after dinner, I read aloud from one of my books. He sat closer and closer to me on the bench, and then let me put his finger under the words as I read them. Eventually I suspected he was beginning to understand the letters on the page.

His soft curls were growing back. At times, as I read to him, I ran my fingers over his hair, and he let me.

Every night, at the first tiny whimpers that signalled his nightmare, I went to him before he was on his feet. I whispered or sang in Dutch or Portuguese as I held him tightly, anything to wake him enough to release him from the terror before it took a firm hold on him.

His hot little body, pressed against mine each night as I soothed him, was the only human contact I had. I hadn't known I'd feel so much for him. Each time I imagined leaving here, leaving him— and Papa—I was overcome with queasiness.

⸙

Espirito came back to Curral das Freiras a few weeks after his first visit. Anxiety arose in me when I saw him come into the yard.

Again Cristiano was delighted. He sat beside Espirito on the step as Espirito and Papa talked and drank *licor de castanha* while Bonifacio stayed in the bedroom with his Bible.

While preparing dinner, I heard Espirito's laughter a number of times. He was drying his hands in the wash house as I carried a pot of soup across the yard.

"Diamantina," he said, coming towards me, and I stopped, steam rising from the pot. He looked at his mother's chain around my neck.

"Your father gave it to me," I said, my chin lifted.

He nodded. "It's good to see my mother's Blessed Virgin. How is my father doing? He says he's well, but he doesn't look any better than the last time I was here."

I waited a moment. "He's not. Every day I give him what I can to take away the pain, but . . . but it's not going to go away." I shook my head. "He's growing weaker all the time."

"Thank you," he said, and took the pot from me. "For caring for him."

I followed him into the house. I wondered about his wife, Olívia, and tried to imagine her.

During dinner, Espirito spoke of his work at Kipling's, and how he and Olívia had attended the wedding of Martyn Kipling's younger daughter. He talked about wine sales and of a problem in the blending room. He said a shipment going to Brazil had been delayed because of storms at sea, and at that I made an involuntary sound of dismay.

He looked at me, and I asked, "How often do ships leave Funchal for Brazil?"

"Once a week for much of the year. But within the next month, December, the storms are at their worst, so fewer ships depart until at least the end of February. Why?"

I shook my head as if it wasn't of great importance. But it was. I would have to get to Funchal soon, if I was to leave. Not only did I fear Bonifacio coming after me and preventing me from leaving, but I wouldn't have enough money to stay anywhere for longer than a few nights if the passage cost as much as Abílio had once told me.

After dinner, Espirito again drank *licor de castanha* with Papa for a few hours, then went to stay the night with his friend Felipe. "I'll see you in a few weeks, Papa," he said. "I'll come two days before Christmas to celebrate with you, so I can be back in Funchal for Christmas Eve."

As I lay in bed that night, I thought of him. It was almost unbelievable he and Bonifacio were brothers. Espirito was full of life, laughing easily, telling endless stories. Bonifacio was silent and distant, as if not really present much of the time.

⌒

I knew I couldn't wait any longer to leave. On Saturday, I made a large jug of Papa's special tonic of powdered thistle and wormwood, covering it with a cloth and setting it in the middle of the table. It would last him a few days at least.

Sunday morning, I remained in bed, telling Bonifacio I was ill and wouldn't go to church with him and Papa and Cristiano.

He nodded and left the bedroom. I looked at Cristiano, sitting on his pallet.

"Cristiano," I said, and he raised his eyebrows at me. "Come here." He came to me, and I took his hand. "You're a good boy," I said. "And a big boy. You are a big boy."

He was staring at me, his fingers tightening on mine.

"Go to church with Bonifacio and Papa," I said, and then put my arms around him and held him for a moment. "Go now," I said, looking away, tears filling my eyes.

He stood there.

"I'm just ill," I said, putting my arm over my eyes.

I didn't hear him leave the room. Once the house was quiet, I sprang from bed and tied everything I owned into my shawl, along with a piece of bread and cheese wrapped in a cloth. I slung my medicine bag across my chest and filled a skin with water and looped it over my shoulder. I took the bag of money from Bonifacio's chest and hid it inside my bodice. I put my gutting knife into my waistband.

Cautiously going outside, I saw a number of small figures far down the hill, heading towards the church. I ran onto the road.

I was panting long before I expected to, and the ankle I'd sprained in Porto Santo twinged as I climbed with my heavy load. I went behind a tree and took a long drink from the water skin. As I started again, I heard a faint voice, and froze.

It was Cristiano, running up the path. I closed my eyes.

"Irmã," he called, over and over, and I opened my eyes. Sister. He was calling me sister. It was the first time he had spoken aloud in daylight hours. I hesitated, but then kept climbing. His voice grew louder and closer. Finally I stopped again. I looked back at him and shook my head.

"No! Go back, Cristiano," I called, but he wouldn't stop, and in moments he had caught me. His face was contorted, wet with tears.

"No, Sister," he cried, his face against my waist, gripping my skirt. "No."

I put my arms around him. "I have to go, Cristiano. And I can't take you. I can't," I said, crying as well. "It's so far, and I don't have enough money for us both, and . . ."

He lifted his face to me, and his look was so stricken I dropped to my knees and held him.

"Don't go away, sister," he said, and his new little voice, high and sweet, was a knife in my heart. He buried his face against my neck.

We stayed like that for a long time. Then I stood and wiped his face with the hem of my skirt. I took his hand, and we walked back down the hill.

By the time Bonifacio and Papa returned, I was in the kitchen making bread, and Cristiano sat on the stool watching me. My belongings were back in place, as was Bonifacio's bag of coins.

"You are better, daughter?" Papa asked, and I nodded.

I continued kneading, my movements slow and strong as I thought about Rafaela and her granddaughter. Cristiano would surely be happier with them than here, in this house with a dying old man and a bitter former priest disappointed in himself and with the world.

But I knew that Bonifacio would never agree to Rafaela taking Cristiano once I was gone. I would have to try to work something else out for the boy. I had to.

CHAPTER THIRTY-FOUR

The next morning, I was at the stream, washing clothes, when I heard Cristiano scream. I dropped the sodden shirt I was beating and ran to the house, limping after yesterday's climb.

Papa was standing in the garden, staring at the house. Cristiano's panicked screams were unlike those in his nightmare. I rushed through the sitting room and into the bedroom. Bonifacio gripped Cristiano's wrist.

"What happened? What's wrong?" I shouted above Cristiano's shrieks. "Let him go."

Bonifacio dropped the boy's wrist, and Cristiano immediately ran to me, crying.

"He's been in my things," he said, and it was then that I saw the open lid of the chest. "I don't know if he's stolen anything, but it's clear he's been touching everything. My coins are not where I left them."

I swallowed.

"I was only trying to reprimand him," Bonifacio said. "He has to learn to be honest and truthful. He's old enough to understand that—"

"Be quiet," I said, and Bonifacio's mouth closed, and then opened. He stepped closer to me, fury on his face, and Cristiano gasped. "It's not Cristiano," I said. "He hasn't touched your belongings. It was me. I was looking in your chest." In my hurry to replace the coins yesterday before Bonifacio returned from church, had I placed them in the wrong corner?

Bonifacio was staring into my face, his own darkening. "You're saying that to protect the child."

"I'm not. I've looked in your leather satchel, and found your priest's robe and cincture. I saw your Jesuit cross. I know you have a bag containing one hundred and seventy-six réis. So." I put my arm around Cristiano's shoulders and stayed where I was, although Bonifacio's expression made me feel a thump of anxiety. "Will you reprimand *me* now?" I saw Papa's face, pale and perplexed, in the doorway behind Bonifacio.

Bonifacio turned and saw his father, and took a step back. "The chest contains my belongings. You have no right to look in it." He spoke angrily, but kept his voice too low for Papa to hear.

"I was curious."

He studied my face a moment longer, then went to the chest and took out the bag of coins. He slammed the lid and left the bedroom, his footsteps thudding on the wooden floor as he left the house.

I knew I would never again see the réis. I sat on my bed and put my head into my hands. Cristiano sat beside me, leaning against me.

"He has so much anger. He wasn't always this way. I apologize for my son," Papa said, and I raised my head and looked up at him.

"Having a good woman will help him," he said. He glanced at the sheets dividing the room. "He was a priest for too long, and has forgotten how to be a man. But he will remember. And then he will be a better husband."

⁂

Two days before Christmas, as he had promised, Espirito appeared. He immediately handed a little box to Cristiano. *"Feliz Natal,"* he said.

Cristiano took the box and opened it, his eyes shining as he took out small carved wooden animals, lining them up on the table.

"Cristiano?" I said.

"Thank you," he said, smiling, and Espirito nodded, looking both surprised and pleased.

"You're welcome. Well, look at that," he said, pointing at Cristiano's mouth. "Where did your tooth go?" Cristiano had lost his top right milk tooth a few days earlier.

Now he laughed, sticking his tongue through the little space.

Espirito glanced at me and I tentatively smiled at him. He presented four bottles of Kipling's wine to Papa, and held a package out to me. "Olívia's mother suggested you might make use of it for the *Bolo Rei* for Epiphany," he said, and I opened the container to find glazed fruit and a variety of nuts. "She said the King's Cake wouldn't taste right without them. Is that a new shirt, Papa?"

"Diamantina made it for me to wear to Mass on Christmas Eve," Papa said, and Espirito again glanced at me.

As we ate the special dinner of roasted kid and potatoes and cabbage I'd prepared, Espirito opened the second bottle of wine and spoke about festivities in Funchal.

"I can't imagine a living Nativity in the big square," I said. "And all those singers out on the streets. It must be wonderful," I said, smiling, resting my cheek on my hand as I leaned my elbow on the table.

Espirito refilled my empty cup. "The New Year has many celebrations too."

"Bonifacio," I said, dropping my arm and sitting straight. "Let's go to Funchal for the New Year. Please? Surely Cristiano would be excited by it as well. Papa would be all right for a few days. Rafaela's sister could look in on him."

Bonifacio studied me. "Why do you need to go to Funchal?"

"I don't *need* to," I said, although this was a lie. I did need to go, to see the water again, and rest my eyes on the ships in the harbour. "I just want to see the festivities."

"Is Curral das Freiras not to your liking, Diamantina?" Bonifacio lowered his head over his plate as he ate, and I studied his thinning dark hair, his pale scalp visible. "Are you so unhappy here?" he asked, still not looking up. "Do you want for anything?"

"I'd like more cloth. Both Cristiano and I need some new clothing. And a book or two," I said, perhaps too loudly, my lips slightly numb from the wine. "I should be able to get a new book."

Espirito cleared his throat. "Bonifacio, you could stay with us for a few nights. Olívia could take Diamantina to the shops."

Bonifacio lifted his head and glared at him. "I'll make my own decisions," he said. "There's no reason for us to go to Funchal. And your offer for us to stay with you and Olívia"—he stressed her name, and then paused—"is not necessary."

There was a strained silence. "If you're finished dinner, you can play with your wooden animals, Cristiano," I said, cutting him a generous slice of the sweet bread I'd made for dessert. He took it and set up his animals on the floor in front of the fireplace.

"When did he start speaking?" Espirito asked, watching him.

"A few weeks ago. He opens up a little more every day," I told him.

More silence.

"You should play dominoes with Diamantina, Espirito," Papa said. "We play often. She's good."

I ran my finger around the rim of my plate.

"Do you want to play?" Espirito asked, his voice noncommittal.

I stacked the dirty dishes out of the way and took the box from the shelf and emptied it onto the table. Papa watched, drinking his wine, but Bonifacio left his cup and went into the bedroom with his Bible.

We played in silence for a few moments. Every time it was Espirito's turn to lay a tile, I took a sip of my wine. It was a deep burgundy, sweet and rich, unlike anything I'd ever tasted in Rooi's. "I saw so many wine merchant signs as we came into the bay at Funchal," I told him. I thought of Henry Duncan and our conversations on Porto Santo as I struggled to learn English.

"They're all owned by the English. We Portuguese only work for them." He gave a small hard laugh, then looked up from the pattern we'd created on the table between us. "From the middle of the last century our wines attracted them, and they profited from trade agreements. They forbade the export of European wines to English colonies unless through English ports and on ships flying the English flag. The one exception to this rule was Madeira, so naturally it became a regular supplier to all ships heading to the outposts of the British Empire, especially to the Antilles and the

American colonies." He took a drink. "And then the Methuen Treaty at the beginning of this century allowed excellent trade relations between Portugal and England. It gave us a much lower duty on wine exported to England, in return for which we removed restrictions on the importation of English-made goods. Look at this, Diamantina," he said, smacking down his last tile and grinning at me. "I've beat you."

"You have," I said, pleased at his open, boyish smile, the smile I'd seen him give only to Cristiano. I went to the bedroom and took my medicine bag from the cupboard. I selected a twist of the ground petals of sweet violets I had brought with me from Porto Santo, as well as a small container of soothing lotion of aloe and eucalyptus. A candle glowed from Bonifacio's side of the room, and I heard the sound of a page turning.

I went back to the sitting room. "Could you please give the aloe lotion to your mother-in-law, as a thank you for the nuts and fruit?" I asked, handing him the container. "And this is for Olívia. It's to be diluted in tea to diminish coughs." I gave him the paper twist.

He frowned slightly. "Do you know about Olívia?"

"Know about her?"

He waited.

"I'm not sure what you mean," I finally said. "But many people suffer from cough in the cooler months."

"Thank you," he said then, standing and putting on his coat. "*Boas festas*. I'll see you all in the New Year." As usual, he hugged Papa and Cristiano. He did not go to the bedroom door to call goodbye to Bonifacio.

When Papa and Cristiano went to bed, I stayed at the table among the dirty dishes and the dominoes, touching each tile, and thinking about Espirito and his smile. In that moment I thought that maybe, just maybe, Espirito could help me. Perhaps I could appeal to him and Olívia. Maybe they would help me get to my father. But I would have to go very slowly, and very carefully.

After the Mass for Epiphany in the first week of January, Father Monteiro came to me as I pulled Cristiano's cap over his ears before the walk home in the damp wind.

"Diamantina," he said, and something about the way he said my name made me frown.

"Yes, Father?"

"I have something for you. I'd like you to come into my office."

I followed him, holding Cristiano's hand. In the small room, the fireplace throwing a pleasant warmth, he pointed to a folded square of vellum, addressed to him, on his desk.

"It came to me from Porto Santo," he said, "a letter from Father da Chagos, although written by Sister Amélia. She reports that Father da Chagos is very ill. He contracted a fever a month ago and hasn't been able to fight it. He grows weaker daily. He's no longer able to conduct Mass, and the Sister informed the Mother Church in Funchal. They have sent another priest to Nossa Senhora da Piedade. Father da Chagos wanted . . ." He stopped. "What's in the package belongs to you," he said, looking uncomfortable. "Father da Chagos has suffered a crisis of conscience, the Sister has written. He is certain he will not live much longer, and daily makes his confession and does his penance. He would like forgiveness from you so that he can meet death with a clear conscience."

My trembling had begun as Father Monteiro spoke, and now it was as if all the air in the room had been sucked into the fireplace, and I couldn't breathe. I took deep gulps, pressing my palms against my chest, feeling the frenzied ticking of my heart.

"Would you like to sit down, Diamantina? You're very pale."

"Thank you, Father Monteiro," I said. "I would just like to go home now."

"Yes, of course," he said. He picked up the package and held it out to me. "The religious community of the Madeira archipelago is small. We all know each other. I would like to apologize on behalf of Father da Chagos."

I took the package, then ran from the office and through the now-empty church, Cristiano at my heels. I ran all the way home. I don't know why.

CHAPTER THIRTY-FIVE

The hours until everyone slept felt like the longest I had known. I couldn't bear to open the package until I knew I would not be interrupted, and could be completely alone.

I went into the sitting room, lighting a candle on the table. I sat with the package on my lap, feeling its sharp corners. And then I unfolded the vellum.

There were two pages. The first was addressed to me in an unknown hand. I looked at the second, and saw my name, and under it the name of Father da Chagos at Nossa Senhora da Piedade, in my father's copperplate. The wax that had once sealed the letter was broken. Looking at my father's script, so familiar and yet with an unusual shakiness, I was suddenly able to remember his face as clearly as if he stood before me. Holding the thin parchment, I imagined that once I unfolded it, his words would rise into the air like a sudden rush of startled butterflies, trembling with my father's voice. Tears filled my eyes, and I put the letter to my nose, breathing deeply, hoping to be given a tiny memory of my father's smell of tobacco. The paper only carried a faint odour of mildew and, almost imperceptibly, a trace of incense.

I set it on the table and first opened the letter in the unknown hand. In a fine, spidery script, Sister Amélia wrote:

My dear Diamantina,
    As well as the letter Father da Chagos dictated for me to write to
Father Monteiro, he also asked that I write to you, in my own words.

I am filled with sadness at discovering Father da Chagos's actions. He explained to me that the reason for keeping what your father sent was that he believed you would not be able to make proper use of the réis until you had more maturity. He also worried that should you suddenly come into possession of a goodly sum— more than many on the island regularly earned—you might be exploited.

He felt it appropriate that he give the letters and money to your husband. He was of the belief that a decent, God-fearing man such as your husband could set you on the right path.

I blinked, rereading the last paragraph. Sister Amélia's writing was blotched with fallen ink, some spots round and some smeared. I saw her sitting at the table in the church kitchen in the flickering light of the candle, writing a letter for the first time in many, many years. I smelled the strong lampblack and pine of the ink, and her floury, comforting scent. I imagined her head, bare of her veil and wimple, and remembered the shape of her small ears.

I read on.

I know by now you will have read the letters from your father, and that you and your husband will benefit from your father's generosity. Enclosed is the most recent letter that came from him, only a few weeks ago.

I know that Father da Chagos wishes to redeem himself, and I hope that with your new happiness you will find it in your heart to forgive him for his sins against you and God.

I pray for you daily, remembering our happy hours together.

With my warmest thoughts,

Sister Amélia Rodrigues de Bragança

I put down her letter and sat for a long time before picking up my father's. At last I opened it. It was dated eight months earlier.

My darling Diamantina,

As always, I send you my love. I apologize again for my worsening script. The shaking sickness, as I have told you, is a cruel disease, slow and steady. I am fortunate to have others who are able to ensure the continued security of my business and to care for me as is needed now.

Of course, I could dictate future letters to you, but I have come to a conclusion. For the first few years I told myself that the ship carrying my letters to you went down at sea, or that the same had happened to those you sent to me.

But I also knew that the law of mathematical possibilities would not allow that to happen every time. I now believe what I did not let myself think at first: that my correspondence may have brought you pain instead of pleasure. I know that if something had happened to you, Father da Chagos would have informed me—my address in São Paulo is clearly marked on each letter.

And so I will no longer burden you.

Although the illness is robbing me of my physical abilities, it will never close my heart. If you ever change your mind, and wish to join me in São Paulo, I will welcome you with that open heart.

Your loving father

I sat without moving until the candle hissed and went out, and then went to the bedroom, pulling open the sheets hiding Bonifacio's bed. I looked down at him. He slept on his back, his mouth open. I looked at the crucifix over his bed, and wanted to take it down and strike him with it. I wanted to strike him until he lay bleeding.

It was my money in the cloth bag, whatever was left of the money my father had sent to me. I hadn't wondered how a fallen priest had come into possession of such an amount, or perhaps I assumed Papa had given it to him. And what had he done with my father's letters?

I would wait until morning, and then, in the bright light of day, demand answers.

I was sitting at the table holding the two letters when Bonifacio came out to go to early Mass. I hadn't gone to bed.

He frowned at me. "Why are you up?"

I stood. "Come outside."

"Don't speak to me as if I'm a child."

I walked towards the door. "I said to come outside," I repeated, my voice low. I didn't want to wake Cristiano. "Father Monteiro gave me something yesterday."

Bonifacio looked at the letters in my hand.

"From my father," I said, and at that he had the decency to look uncomfortable.

I went to the wash house, and he followed me. There I held the letters in front of his face. "One of these is from Sister Amélia in Vila Baleira, and the other is the last letter my father sent to me. I know that Father da Chagos gave you my other letters and my money."

He crossed his arms over his chest.

"Well?" I said.

"Well what?"

"I'm waiting for you to explain why you haven't given me my father's letters. Or my money. The money Father da Chagos gave you when we married. The money my father sent to me over the last few years."

My rage built as I waited for him to speak.

"It became my money once we were married," he said. "When Father da Chagos told me he held money for you—"

I held up my hand. "Stop! He told you before you married me? Father da Chagos told you there was money that was mine?"

"Every bride has a dowry," he said.

My mouth opened, but no sound emerged.

"It's mine now," he said. "As in any marriage, the dowry is paid to the husband. I used it for your passage from Porto Santo to Funchal, and for the supplies I had to buy for you: boots and cloth, the dominoes you wanted. And my father had debts. I paid them off for him. It was the least I could do. He took me back, with the boy, without question."

I was too stunned to speak. After a moment I said, "I want what is left of that money—the one hundred and seventy-six réis. Give it to me now."

He shook his head. "As I said, the money is mine."

I heard the slam of a door, and saw Cristiano on the step.

"The letters. Where are the letters?"

"I didn't see the purpose of them."

"And . . ."

"I burned them."

"NO!" I screamed then, and lifted my hands to strike him, but he caught my wrists. His strength surprised me. "I hate you," I shouted. "I hate you and I hate Father da Chagos, and I will never forgive either of you. Never!"

"Control yourself," he said firmly. "You're no longer a wild island girl. You're a wife. It was your choice to marry me, and now you will obey me, as a wife must. Wipe your face and prepare breakfast."

I hadn't realized I was crying. "How dare you and Father da Chagos decide what's best for me!"

"Never bring up this matter again. Everything will go on as before," he said. He let go of my wrists and left.

I watched him walk towards the house, hating the slope of his shoulders, the back of his head, his measured gait. Cristiano jumped off the step and disappeared behind the house as Bonifacio approached.

Everything would *not* go on as before. In spite of my fury with both Father da Chagos and Bonifacio, and the deep sorrow at what I had missed in over four years since my father left, everything was now changed. I would write to my father, explaining what had happened. I would tell him about Mama's death, and that I now lived on Madeira. I would ask him to please send more money—enough for two passages—to me, care of Kipling's. I would tell him I would bring a little boy named Cristiano with me to Brazil.

I would ask Espirito to send the letter, and when my father wrote back, Espirito would bring his letter to me.

I would have to wait for a year or more for my letter to get to São Paulo and for my father to reply. And then, finally, I would go to him, and I would once again know his love.

CHAPTER THIRTY-SIX

I wrote my letter using the back of a chart torn from one of my books.

"Give me a few réis," I said to Bonifacio at dinner. "Please," I emphasized, although with heavy sarcasm.

He looked up from his plate. "I said for you not to bring this up again." His voice was too low for Papa to hear, but the old man watched us.

"I've written a letter to my father," I said loudly, "and I need money to send it."

"Is your father on Porto Santo?" Papa asked.

"No," I said, facing him and speaking slowly. "He lives in São Paulo. In Brazil. I'm asking Bonifacio for money to send him a letter. Bonifacio? Please give me the few réis."

"The money is not here," he said.

Papa looked at him, then slowly rose and went into his bedroom. He came back with a small tin container, and dumped its contents on the table. "It's all I have," he said. "But you are welcome to take what you need." Again he glanced at Bonifacio, who ate as though we weren't in the room.

I picked up three coins. "Thank you, Papa. I don't know how much it will be, but surely this is enough."

"Take the rest," he said, "to buy yourself something when you go to Funchal. I have no need for money."

I looked at the pitiful smattering of coins still on the table, then put my arm around him and kissed his grizzled cheek. I was alarmed at the bony stoop of his back. He was even gaunter than when I'd arrived less than four months earlier. I put the rest of the coins back into the container. "If I ever need any more, I'll ask, Papa."

He nodded, and I had to swallow the sudden lump in my throat.

⌘

The next morning, I went to Father Monteiro and asked how I could have a letter taken into Funchal to be posted. "I have money for it," I said, opening my palm to show him the coins.

"If I know of anyone leaving the valley, I'll ask that they take it for you," he said. "But during the winter months, there are few who make the journey. The trails are particularly difficult because of all the rain."

"Maybe Espirito will come soon. I can give him the letter," I told the priest. I took the letter back home and waited.

Each day of January passed. Nobody left the valley. Espirito didn't come.

"Is it the weather keeping Espirito away?" I asked Papa.

"The weather doesn't bother Espirito. It's probably Olívia. He doesn't like to leave her when she's at her worst."

"What's wrong with her?"

He shrugged, patting his chest. "She has trouble breathing sometimes. She's very weak."

"Is it the bloody cough?"

"No. Not that. I don't know what it is."

"Do you think he'll come soon?"

Again he shrugged.

As February approached, my patience stretched thin. I wanted so badly to have the letter sent. And I worried daily over Papa's worsening condition.

I could barely stand to look at Bonifacio. He grew increasingly sullen, but watched me more and more closely, even when I sat reading or sewing. At times his cheeks flushed, and he got up and went outdoors. I chose not to think about his battle; I suspected he either walked among the higher rocks, shouting his anger into the wind, or gave in to his human needs in a frustrated, solitary way. I knew which it was by his behaviour when he returned. When he deprived himself, he came home more anxious, sometimes short-tempered with Cristiano if the child got underfoot. When he had given in to temptation, he returned chastened and visibly distraught. These times he would punish himself even more severely with his whip in the sitting room at night, and the whispered praying would go on far longer than usual.

One evening, as I reached for the bread across the table, my arm hit his full soup bowl. As the hot liquid sloshed onto his breeches, he jumped up. "Watch what you're doing!" he said angrily. "How can you be so clumsy?"

I stared at him. "It was an accident. I'm sorry," I said loudly, and threw a dishcloth at him. "Here."

He caught it, but instead of wiping his trousers, he flung it back at me. "If you are so unhappy here, then I release you from the marriage, and will send you back to Porto Santo. You obviously have no interest in learning to control yourself through prayer and confession and penance. I cannot allow you to stay if you're going to show me so little respect, and think you can speak to me in this manner."

His words about me returning to Porto Santo chilled me. I wrapped my arms around myself. Even once I managed to send the letter to my father, I had to wait to hear back from him. I would have to be a little more careful.

⌒⌒

When Espirito walked through the yard, I was so happy to see him I beamed. "It's been so long, Espirito. Over six weeks, since Christmas."

"How is Papa?" He put his hand on Cristiano's head. The boy had, as usual, run to him.

My smile faded. "I'm sorry," I said, glancing behind me, through the open door into the house. "He can barely eat now, and spends most of his time in bed. He has a few hours of relief when I give him the poppy."

"I've thought of hiring men to carry him out on a litter and bring him to our home, although I doubt he'll agree. But perhaps one of the English physicians in Funchal could help him."

I knew Papa was dying, and I doubted there was anything anyone could do. "I think it's just his time, Espirito." Instinctively I put my hand on his arm, and he looked down and covered my hand with his. His fingers were long and slender, so warm on mine in spite of the chill in the air.

"Thank you, Diamantina. I know Papa is grateful for your help. As am I."

After dinner, I put my letter and the coins on the table, asking Espirito to send it on the next ship to Brazil.

He looked at the name on it. "Arie ten Brink," he said.

"My father."

"I thought you were the daughter of the Dutch innkeeper at—" He stopped, glancing at me and then at Bonifacio. But I didn't care now what he said about my past, or what Bonifacio thought of me. "Your father lives in São Paulo," he stated.

"Yes. He left Porto Santo five years ago. I just . . . I only recently found out how to reach him."

"Of course I'll send it for you," he said. He took the letter, but left the réis.

"Diamantina." Bonifacio spoke through the sheets that divided us, waking me before dawn a week after Espirito's visit. "Lent is almost here, and I want you to start preparing for Easter. I know you've never had to deny yourself anything, but you're a Catholic now, and as a believer you must prepare for this, the holiest of times, through prayer, penance, repentance and self-denial."

I threw back my blanket and made a sound in my throat, annoyed by his condescending tone. "What would you suggest I repent,

Bonifacio?" I cleared my throat, scratchy from sleep. "And what, besides some of our food, do I have to give up? Exactly what will I deny myself?" My voice was mocking.

I heard a rustle, and unexpectedly Bonifacio pulled the sheets apart. He was fully dressed. When he stared at me, I looked down at his mother's medallion, its chain tangled with the thin thong of my father's talisman, which lay between my exposed breasts.

I clutched the front of my nightdress, covering my nakedness.

"Is that a heathen icon you wear with the Blessed Virgin? You desecrate my sainted mother's memory," he said in a loud voice.

From the corner of my eye, I saw Cristiano sit up on his pallet. And then Bonifacio came towards me, breathing heavily, and I scrambled off my bed. Although at first I thought it was lust I saw on his face, I almost immediately realized it was rage. Rage at me, and surely at himself, for I had seen that he was tempted.

"Get away from me," I said, and at that he lifted his hand and hit me with his open palm, hard enough to make me lose my balance. I fell back onto the bed.

And then Cristiano was between us, striking Bonifacio with his fists, kicking him, screaming with a high, desperate sound. "No! No no no no!" he shrieked, trying to protect me.

Bonifacio stepped back.

"Stop, Cristiano," I said, standing again, pulling him away from Bonifacio. "I'm all right."

Cristiano was rigid, staring into Bonifacio's face.

"Do you see yourself as Delilah, scheming to bring me down?" Bonifacio asked then, his voice low.

"I've done nothing wrong," I said, but quietly, not wanting to incite his wrath again.

"I've seen how you look at my brother," he said. "You are a temptress as evil as Jezebel."

"Your brother? What are you talking about?"

"I'll teach you to repent," he said with that same flushed, angry look, and then left, slamming the door behind him.

My cheek smarting, I looked at Cristiano. His face was so bleak my heart lurched.

"We're not staying here with him anymore," I told him, caught in my fury at Bonifacio's treatment. I couldn't think clearly.

I put on my skirt and blouse and boots and looped my medicine bag across my chest. I wrapped my shawl around my shoulders, then spread my extra shawl on the bed and laid everything I'd brought with me on it as Cristiano watched.

"Bring me your things," I said, and he handed me his few pieces of clothing and the torn cloth that had been his mother's dress and the little box of wooden animals. I added them to my shawl and tied it firmly.

"Come on." He followed me into the sitting room, and I stopped only long enough for him to put on his jacket and hat. I looked at Papa's closed door. He would be all right for a few days.

I was going to Espirito. He would do as he had said, and have Papa brought out of the valley and into Funchal. Olívia and I would care for him.

I didn't know what had caused the rift between the brothers, but I had to believe that Espirito and Olívia would understand how impossible it was for me to live with Bonifacio when I told them about my father and the letters and money. Surely they would allow Cristiano and me to stay until more money came from my father. Maybe they would even buy us our passage, and Cristiano and I could leave right away. I would repay them once I was with my father.

It was raining as we left. I didn't see Bonifacio, and didn't care if he saw me leaving. He couldn't stop me. My brain was racing, and I felt strong and full of energy in spite of my heavy shawl slung over one shoulder. Cristiano and I started up the steep incline. The rain had made the mud trail slick, and more than once we both slid, or fell to one knee. I looked behind me at Cristiano, and his face was now resolute. "Good boy," I said, encouraging him, and he nodded.

And then, when we were perhaps halfway up the steepest trail, I half jumped over a root in the path. My boot slipped and I went over on the side of my right foot, and I heard a crack, and the pain was so sharp and unexpected that I cried out as I fell. I lay stunned for a moment, then sat up. I held my leg just above the ankle, grimacing.

"Sister!" Cristiano said. "Sister, what happened?"

"I hurt my ankle," I said, furious with myself. Driven by my anger, I had rushed ahead carelessly, forgetting the weakness in my once-injured ankle. "Find me a stick," I said. "Something I can lean on."

Cristiano looked around, then reached into the brambles at the side of the path. He pulled out a short, sturdy stick.

"No, it's too short. Something longer," I said, and he went into the bushes. After a few minutes he emerged with a gnarled, longer stick. "Help me up."

I leaned on his shoulder as I stood on my uninjured foot, holding the other a few inches above the ground. Cristiano picked up my bundled shawl and hugged it; he could barely see over. I propped the stick into the mud and held it with both hands and tried to hop, but after a few steps I slid to the ground again. I looked up at Cristiano. We were both soaked and covered in mud.

"What will we do?" he asked, shivering. I looked away, not wanting him to see my tears of pain and exasperation.

"Let me think," I said, realizing how foolish I'd been. I'd started on the long, arduous journey in the cold rain with no food or water. Had I really thought Cristiano could walk all the way to Funchal?

Once more I tried to rise, but sucked in my breath at the pain of just lifting my foot. I cautiously pulled off my boot, wincing. My ankle and the top of my foot were swollen, the skin darkening. It hurt too much to get the boot on again.

And then Bonifacio stood below us on the path.

Cristiano faced him, his hands clenched. "Go away! Go away from us."

"Go home, Cristiano," Bonifacio said evenly, and Cristiano looked back at me.

I took a deep breath, and looked from him to Bonifacio, and then back at Cristiano. We had no choice. "Do as he says," I told him.

Still carrying my shawl, he edged cautiously past Bonifacio. I saw the back of his long, slender neck, the set of his small, straight spine.

Bonifacio held out his hand, and I took it. He pulled me up and, with me leaning on his arm and my stick, slowly we descended into the valley.

"Where did you think you were going?" he asked me later. I had managed to change into dry clothes, and now lay on my bed with my foot propped on a stack of blankets. Cristiano, also in dry clothes, sat cross-legged on his pallet.

"To Funchal. To Espirito and Olívia."

"What are you talking about? Do you really think Espirito would allow you to leave me, and stay with him?"

"Him and Olívia," I said.

He stared at me, then clicked his tongue. "He's my brother. He would support me, not you." He paced beside my bed, looking down at me. "Don't you ever, *ever* do something like this again. Do you understand?"

As I pushed myself up on the bed, trying to ease my discomfort, my skirt fell back over my knees. He stared at my bare legs.

"Cover yourself." He shoved the draped sheets aside and knelt beside his bed, reaching under it to pull out the sack with his cat-o'-nine tails. I was instantly alert, fearful he might beat me.

But he put the sack under his arm. "You're not leaving. I am," he said. "I don't want to be around you during Lent. I'm going into the mountains. Like Christ, I'll retreat from temptation for forty days. I'll fast and put you out of my mind." He stomped out. The front door slammed behind him.

I closed my eyes. After a while I grew aware of Cristiano pressed against me, quivering. I covered us with the blanket and put my arms around him. After some time his trembling slowed, and then stopped, and he slept.

CHAPTER THIRTY-SEVEN

I must have slept too, for when I opened my eyes, Papa was standing in the doorway. He had been sitting at the table when I hobbled in with Bonifacio, muddy and soaked. I didn't know what he thought of all that had happened.

"Are you hungry?" he asked.

"No," I said, struggling to sit up, and Cristiano stirred and sat up as well. "Go to the kitchen and bring bread and cheese for you and Papa," I told the boy, and he left.

"What happened?" Papa asked, looking at my bulging shawl beside the bed.

"I . . . I fell. It was muddy," I said, not wanting to tell him I had been running away, in spite of the obviousness of the shawl. "I hurt my ankle."

"Where did Bonifacio go?"

"Into the mountains. He said he'll stay there, fasting for Lent."

Papa frowned. "He did this his first year in the seminary. None of the others acted in such a drastic way, Father Monteiro told me. But Bonifacio was always like this. When he gets an idea in his head, he cannot let it go." He shook his own head. "I will make you a crutch."

∞

Cristiano got into my bed every night after that, and allowed me to put my arms around him as he fell asleep. With Bonifacio gone, the nightmares were fewer, and lesser in intensity. The bedwetting had stopped long ago. His small, warm body was a comfort, but in spite of it, sleep was difficult. I was always listening, conscious that Bonifacio might return in the dark even though he had said he would stay away until the end of Lent.

Using the sturdy crutch Papa had made for me, my armpit first bruising and then toughening, I slowly made my way around the house and yard. Cristiano helped me in every way he could, running and fetching. Twice a day I wrapped my ankle in a poultice. Within a week the worst of the swelling was down, but I still couldn't put my weight on my foot without discomfort.

We didn't go to church. Papa stayed in his bed most days. After the second week, Father Monteiro came to call.

"I haven't seen Bonifacio at morning Mass for a while," he said, "and when none of you attended Mass last Sunday or this, I grew concerned."

"Bonifacio went to the mountains to fast for Lent. I hurt my ankle," I said, "and Papa isn't well at all."

"Bonifacio is going to fast the whole forty days again?"

"That's what he said."

"Are you all right here?" He looked at Papa's closed door. "Shall I ask Rafaela to come and look at Vitorino?"

I shook my head. "She knows I'm doing what I can for him," I told him. "But thank you."

"I can hear your confessions here," he said. "You don't have to come to me."

"I'll ask Papa," I said, and went into his bedroom. He nodded when I told him about Father Monteiro's offer.

When Father Monteiro finished with Papa, he sat at the table with Cristiano and me and ate the food I had set out for him. "Will you make confession, Diamantina?"

I shook my head.

Before he left, he made the sign of the cross and patted Cristiano's head.

❧

With the passing of each day, I dreaded Bonifacio's return.

As Papa grew more ill, Cristiano was growing taller and stronger. He sometimes hummed as he helped me plant in the garden. The full warm weather of March was upon us, and new shoots rose in the neat rows. One sunny day Cristiano and I helped Papa walk to the garden, and he sat on the chair Cristiano brought for him, looking at the new greenery and nodding his approval.

A few days later, Cristiano asked if he could go and play with Rafaela's granddaughter, and I took him. Rafaela and I ground seeds as the children laughed and scampered about.

Papa's door was shut when we got back. I opened it, calling, "Papa? How are—"

He was curled on his side on the floor near the door, his knees drawn to his chest. The chamber pot was overturned, its contents spilled on the floor.

"Papa," I said, kneeling beside him. I called Cristiano, and between us we were able to get him back to his bed. His body was now like that of a strange, twisted boy, his head too large for his frame.

He attempted to smile, patting my hand. "I'm sorry for the mess," he whispered.

"Papa," I said. "Oh, Papa."

He opened his mouth, and I leaned closer.

"Bury me next to my Telma. I will lie beside my Telma in death, as I did in life."

"Shhh. Don't think about that."

"Promise me."

"I promise," I told him, and he closed his eyes.

⸙

I brought him warm broth and helped him drink. I ground the seeds of the poppy and put some of the tiny balls I formed into bits of soft bread, which he was able to swallow with a mouthful of warm broth. I sat beside him all night, bathing his face and hands with cool water made sweet with mint leaves.

The next morning, I gave him more of the poppy, and when he was asleep, I left Cristiano to watch over him. I went to Father Monteiro and asked if he could send someone to Kipling's Wine Merchants in Funchal to tell Espirito that his father was gravely ill.

Father Monteiro clasped his hands, his face sorrowful. "I'll send one of the village boys. You'll tell me when last rites are needed," he said, and I nodded.

I hoped Espirito would arrive before Papa died, so one of his sons could be with him for his last days. I stayed beside him, continually giving him the poppy and gently rubbing his hands and feet. "I'm sure Espirito and Bonifacio will be here soon," I said loudly, a few times each day. I didn't believe my own words about Bonifacio.

Papa did not speak, but when he was awake, he always looked at me with a tender expression.

Early on the morning of the third day, before the sun had fully risen, I held his hand and knew, by the thin, dry texture of his skin, that he would die that day. I went to the church to tell Father Monteiro it was time.

"I don't know why Espirito hasn't come," I said, as we walked back to the house together. "You sent the boy?"

"Yes. He's returned. He left word at Kipling's as you requested."

After he had completed last rites, Father Monteiro sat with me as Papa's breaths grew so far apart that occasionally I touched his wrist or neck to make sure his heart still beat.

And then he was gone.

Father Monteiro anointed Papa's body and covered him, and we went into the sitting room. "Shall I prepare for the viewing and funeral Mass even though neither of Vitorino's sons is here? If Bonifacio is staying away until the end of Lent, we can't wait for him."

"I don't understand why Espirito hasn't come yet. Can we wait just a while longer?"

"The weather is warming, and . . ." He stopped, then continued. "You see the importance of not waiting too long, Diamantina."

Suddenly I—Vitorino's daughter-in-law of half a year—was in charge of his funeral. I wondered how Bonifacio would punish himself when he came home and learned that his father had died. "Yes. Of course. We need to go forward with the funeral."

Father Monteiro held my hands for a moment, and then left.

After I had washed and shaved Papa, I dressed him in his good clothing and combed his hair. Cristiano and I picked flowers and placed them around Papa's body; we both cried. And then I took the chain from around my neck, his Telma's medallion of the Holy Mother, and placed it in his pocket. It would go with him in death. He had asked me to wear it to be reminded to honour their son, but I did not honour Bonifacio. I had only worn it to please Papa.

A cart came and took him to the church to be laid out for the viewing. I dragged his mattress outside and beat it thoroughly and rubbed it with sweet grasses and lavender. I washed all the bedding. As I scrubbed and beat, panting with the exertion, I remembered what Papa had said about the landowner reclaiming his land.

I left the bedding to flap and dry in the wind as my mother had always instructed the women of the beach to do after a death.

⁂

The next day, I sent Cristiano out to collect eggs. I knew he would play with the baby chicks for a while. I had bathed and sat at the table brushing my damp hair, hanging to my waist.

And then Espirito stood in the open doorway. I hadn't heard him arrive. I jumped up and went to him. "I'm so sorry about your father," I said. I was suddenly short of breath. What was wrong with me? Espirito was in mourning. And yet I was thinking of his hands in my hair. Of leaning into him, feeling the length of his body against mine.

I was just lonely, I told myself. I had been thinking of my mother's death, and how alone I'd felt. I only wanted someone to comfort me.

"Thank you," Espirito said. "I've been to the church and spoken with Father Monteiro. He told me how kind you were with my father, easing him in his last days," Espirito said, meeting my eyes. His own were bright with tears. "He said you were able to bring him comfort and peace, and for that I thank you, Diamantina." He came closer and took my hand. It seemed that the warmth of it transferred into mine. "For the last week I was travelling west on the island, checking on the vineyards I buy grapes from. I only arrived home yesterday and received the message that my father was so ill. We left in the middle of the night to be here. All the way I hoped I would see him one more time. But . . ."

He let go of my hand, and I felt as though I'd lost something.

"Father Monteiro also told me that Bonifacio is in the mountains for Lent. He didn't see Papa before he died either." His eyes had lost their softness, and a muscle in his jaw tightened. "Who cut the wood and hauled the water since he left?"

"I did."

"You shouldn't have had to look after everything on your own, as well as care for my father. That Bonifacio would leave when Papa was so ill . . . Why didn't you ask someone from the parish for help?"

"I managed, with Cristiano."

"Is the boy all right?"

"Yes. Although very sad over Papa. As I am. I . . . I only knew him for six months, but I cared deeply for him, Espirito."

He touched my shoulder, and then turned. "Olívia has made the journey with me," he said, and went back down the steps.

CHAPTER THIRTY-EIGHT

Two young men, soaked with sweat, stood at the entrance to the yard. They carried a large canvas sling on a long pole over their shoulders. Inside the sling I could just make out the figure of a small woman.

I was immediately anxious at the thought of meeting Olívia. My hair was loose and I was barefoot and wearing an old patched skirt and blouse. I hadn't prepared anything for dinner. I had never been able to envision Espirito with his wife. Maybe I didn't want to.

I watched as he helped her from the sling and they started for the house, Espirito's arm around Olívia's back. She was dainty and elegant. Her hair was thick and glossy, black as pitch and, in spite of her long journey, intricately twisted in a fashion I'd never seen. Her face was too sharp, and her pallor troubling, but even her obvious illness couldn't hide her beauty.

"So this is Diamantina," she said as she and Espirito came up the step.

I smiled hesitantly. "I'm pleased to finally meet you, Olívia, although sorry it's under such sad circumstances."

She studied me, something fierce in her clear, intelligent gaze. "Not as I would have imagined."

I stopped smiling. Did she mean the circumstances, or me? "The viewing is after dinner."

"Olívia," Espirito said, "you need to rest."

"With the difficulty of the journey," she said, "I saw my father-in-law very infrequently. In spite of your very recent entry into the family, I dare say you knew him better than I." She glanced through the door. "I'm sure our presence will make things awkward for you. At least Bonifacio isn't here."

What did she mean? I felt a flush of annoyance. By her dress and manner, she was of a fine heritage, and it was clear that Espirito provided a gracious life for her.

"You must rest after the journey, as your husband says," I murmured.

⌘

Olívia picked up a forkful of goat meat and studied it, then set it down.

"Is the goat not to your liking?" I asked. "Can I offer you something else? I have some soup in the kitchen."

She glanced at Cristiano, sitting beside me. "I have a delicate palate, and can't digest country food easily." She looked at Espirito. "I told you we should have brought some of Ana's dishes."

Espirito didn't speak for a moment. "There was no time for that kind of preparation."

Olívia turned from him and looked at me. "Is that what you're wearing tonight?"

I had changed into my green and black striped Sunday skirt and finely embroidered white traditional blouse, long-sleeved, with a fitted waist that flowed over the skirt. "Yes."

"Come into the bedroom with me," she said, rising, and I left my unfinished meal and followed her into Papa's room, where Espirito had set their bags. I tried not to think of Papa dying on the bed only days earlier, and Espirito and Olívia lying on it together tonight. I was glad I had so thoroughly cleaned everything, and that the room was fragrant with the scent of lavender and mountain wind.

She pulled a simple dark grey gown from one of her travelling bags. "Wear this. You're much taller than me, but you're slender enough to fit into it. If you're quick about it, you can let down the hem before we leave."

I was insulted that she had criticized my food and now my clothing, but I would not make the situation worse. I had to think of

Espirito and his grief. "Thank you, Olívia, but I prefer to wear my own clothes."

"You represent Espirito's family, and all eyes will be on us at church. Just try it on."

I looked at her for another moment, again thinking of Espirito in the next room. It would be easier to comply than have her create an unpleasant scene. I pulled off my clothes, standing in my simple cotton shift as Olívia settled the dress over my head.

"Turn around and I'll lace it up," she told me, once my arms were in the sleeves. As I did, she cried out sharply.

I looked at her over my shoulder. I didn't think her face could become paler, but it was as white as paper. As I turned towards her, she backed away.

"Why are you marked like that?" Her eyes were huge. "What are you?" She kept backing away, reaching for the door behind her.

"Olívia. They're just . . . my mother did them."

She braced herself against the door as if I might lunge at her like a cornered animal.

"Why did she do it?" She pushed open the door. "Espirito. Come here."

Nobody had ever seen my body but my mother. I had been distracted and annoyed when I turned for Olívia to lace the dress; I certainly hadn't been thinking of the markings on my back.

Espirito came to the door. "What's wrong?" he asked, looking first at Olívia and then at me, standing with the dress unlaced and loose on my shoulders. I held it against my chest with one hand.

"She's got marks on her back."

Espirito frowned. "Marks?" I saw his throat move. "Did Bonifacio beat you?"

"Not that kind," Olívia said. "Marks like a slave. Show him."

"No," I said, and Espirito said, "No, Olívia," at the same time.

"Well," Olívia said. "I don't like this one bit. Her mother did it to her," she said to Espirito, then stared at me again. "Was your mother a slave? But she couldn't be," she answered her own question. "You're so . . . you don't look like a slave, with your hair and eyes . . ."

Neither Espirito nor I spoke. Cristiano had come to stand behind Espirito, and now craned his neck to peer around him.

"*Was* she a slave? Your mother?" Olívia asked again.

"She was a healing woman."

"That doesn't explain the way you're marked."

Espirito touched her arm. "Olívia."

She pulled away. "First he brings home a dark-skinned child, and now her. What does Bonifacio think he's doing? We have a right to know what has come into our family."

I took my clothes from where I'd set them on the bed and pushed past her and Espirito. "I'm not a *what*," I said, and went to my bedroom and pulled off the grey dress and put on my own clothes. I went back to Olívia, still standing with Espirito in the doorway of Papa's bedroom. I dropped the dress at her feet and then took Cristiano's hand.

"Come, Cristiano," I said, "it's time to go to the church."

⁓

We all went in a wagon Espirito had borrowed, pulled by an ox. Papa had been well loved; the whole of Curral das Freiras came for the viewing. On the way home, Cristiano fell asleep, his head in my lap. Espirito helped Olívia down and then took Cristiano into his arms. Cristiano stirred against him.

I hurried into the house to light candles. I carried one to my bedroom so that Espirito could see to follow me.

"Put him on my bed, there," I whispered.

Espirito did as I asked and straightened, looking, with no expression, at the sheets hung between the two single beds. Even though they were pulled back, the situation was clear.

I was oddly embarrassed at him realizing that Bonifacio and I didn't share a bed. "Thank you," I said, and he said good night and joined Olívia in Papa's room. I heard the murmur of their voices over the partition for a while. Surely she was whispering about me. Eventually there was silence. I imagined Olívia in Espirito's arms as they fell asleep.

I thought of the way she had studied me, openly critical, and didn't like the image of Espirito's long, slender fingers, smelling of the grapes, touching her.

✧

The whole parish noticed that Bonifacio was not at his father's Mass and burial the next morning. And yet, as people came to us to offer their condolences, nobody mentioned him.

As soon as we were back at the house, Olívia turned to Espirito. "Please go and summon the men to bring my sling."

"It's too late to start back now. And I want to stay for a few days, until Bonifacio returns. There are issues to settle now that Papa is gone." He glanced at me. "If you're agreeable with us staying."

"Of course," I told him, although I couldn't imagine coping with Olívia.

"But Espirito, I have my appointment with Dr. McManus tomorrow. I can't miss it. You know how important the appointments are."

"I'm sure he'll see you another day," he said.

"What is your condition, Olívia?" I asked. It wasn't the bloody cough, as there was no telltale flush of the cheeks, no salty tang of blood on her breath. But she was so thin, her chest almost concave as she took shallow, rattling breaths, her complexion now verging on bluish-grey.

She looked away for a moment, then back at me. "It's a bronchial obstruction."

"What are the symptoms?"

Olívia looked either annoyed or upset by my questions.

"I'm a *curandeira*, Olívia. I've seen many illnesses."

At that, she gave a twisted smile. "A country healer can't help with this. I've had attention from the best English physician in Funchal."

"She has very laboured breathing and wheezing. She sometimes gasps for air," Espirito said, and Olívia's lips tightened. "The breathing difficulties ease during dry periods. When the rains come, they grow worse."

I remembered a little girl on the beach who had died when only eight years old. She had wheezed and gasped for many months, her lips blue at the end.

"Do you inhale eucalyptus oil? And drink a tea made of sage and camomile? I'm sure sleeping propped up helps, and burning certain herbs—I can give you some—on bricks in the bedroom can be beneficial."

Olívia blinked. "Well, yes. That's what Dr. McManus has recommended."

"Also that she avoid physical strain of any kind. That's why it's so difficult for her to travel all the way here," Espirito added.

Was this the reason they had no children, then? She was so frail; I couldn't imagine her sustaining a pregnancy and birth. Perhaps Espirito and Olívia lived in the same way as Bonifacio and I, except Espirito stayed away from his wife's bed to protect her while Bonifacio stayed away from mine to protect himself.

"I don't want to talk about this anymore," Olívia said. "We'll leave first thing tomorrow, then," she said, as if Espirito hadn't just said he wanted to stay a few days. "I'm going to rest. Can you make flan, Diamantina?"

"Yes."

"I'd like flan for dessert," she said, and went into Papa's bedroom.

CHAPTER THIRTY-NINE

After dinner, Espirito went to the church to say more prayers for Papa. I sent Cristiano to bed. Olívia was sitting in front of the fire reading while I went to the wash house to do the dishes. When I came back, her bedroom door was closed.

I sat at the table, mending a rent in the knee of Cristiano's breeches. When Espirito returned, I put down my sewing and stood. "I know that the *senhorio* will soon take back the house and land, and that we can't live here any longer. What will happen? Will we come to Funchal with you and Olívia?"

He looked at the fire. "I have to speak to Bonifacio."

"It's difficult to be around him, as you've seen," I said. "And he's growing worse. He's so unpredictable. Cristiano is afraid of him." I was too, but wouldn't admit this to Espirito. "He's deeply angry, and frustrated."

"Frustrated?"

"I just mean that he . . . I know he wishes he were still a priest. He doesn't really want to fit back into the ordinary world. He isn't interested in friendships, or . . . or anything. Cristiano is a burden to him. He had hoped . . ." I stopped, knowing I couldn't divulge Bonifacio's story. "He married me for the wrong reasons. And I him."

As my mother had predicted, I had been able to leave Porto Santo because of the flaming sun—because of Bonifacio—but she hadn't known what would happen once I left. "I only wanted to get away from Porto Santo. I want to go to Brazil, to my father."

Espirito sat at the table. "As I said, I'll have to speak to Bonifacio."

I sat down across from him. "But when my father replies to the letter I gave you to send to him, there will be enough réis for passage for Cristiano and me. And we'll leave. Bonifacio cares nothing for us—he'll probably be glad to see the last of us. It will be less than a year, Espirito." In my need for him to understand how desperate I was for his help, I reached across the table and took his hands. "We just need a place to live until I hear from my father. Is it possible we could stay with you? I know Olívia doesn't like me, and I know that will make things even more difficult, but . . ."

"You will not come with us," Olívia said from the bedroom door, and I jumped, lifting my hands from Espirito's. She came towards the table. "I heard what you said. But you're married to Bonifacio. You can't run off to the New World without him. A marriage is a lifetime commitment, as any woman knows. No matter what transpires between you, you are tied to your husband until you die." She looked at Espirito. "Isn't that so?"

She wore a beautiful green silk sleeping cloak, incongruous with the walls, the floor. The whole house.

When Espirito didn't answer, she said, "Come to bed now, Espirito. We will have an early start back to Funchal tomorrow. And you will stay here and wait for your husband to return, Diamantina. It's him you should be discussing your future with. Not *my* husband."

Espirito rose and followed Olívia into the bedroom, closing the door quietly.

&

I slept poorly, Olívia's words resonating in my head. Before anyone else was up, I rose and made breakfast, and packed a bag of bread and boiled eggs and cooked chicken for their journey. Every movement was an effort.

We didn't speak during breakfast. The young men were summoned and waited at the end of the yard with the sling to carry Olívia back to Funchal. But as we all stood on the step, Espirito told his wife, "I'm waiting here for Bonifacio, as I said yesterday."

She stared at him in disbelief. "What? You can't."

"He should be back at the end of Lent—four or five days from now. You'll go to see Dr. McManus, and have your mother come and stay with you until I get back."

"Why do you have to wait for him?"

"I want to talk about something that might help him look after his family."

Olívia's face grew tight. "You refuse to come with me?"

Espirito didn't answer, and Olívia threw up her hands. "I'll expect you home for Easter Sunday."

"I'll try."

The men hoisted the pole over their shoulders, and Espirito walked her to the sling and helped her in. I followed with the bag of food, but when I held it out to her, she waved it away, and lay back so that I couldn't see her face. The men looked at Espirito, and at his nod they started up the path.

We watched them wind upwards for a few moments. I turned to Espirito. "Thank you for staying."

He was still watching the trail. "You shouldn't have to suffer because my brother can't act like a proper husband." He looked at me then.

I knew he referred to Bonifacio going off for Lent, leaving us— me, alone, to care for Papa—but I also remembered Espirito's face when he saw our separate sleeping arrangements.

There seemed nothing more to say, and yet he didn't look away from me. I knew he felt it as well, whatever it was that hung, unspoken, between us.

❧

Espirito chopped enough wood to last a month, and brought too much water from the stream every day. He fixed a broken rail in the fence and replaced the weakened front step.

"I've forgotten how good it feels to work outside," he said, coming in from the wash house on the second day, his hair wet, not yet caught back in its usual way. He combed through it with his fingers as he sat at the table. "I hate to think of telling Bonifacio about our father when he returns." He shook his head. "Will he forgive himself for leaving at such a time?"

"He's already tortured." I set the food on the table.

"Do you know what happened in Brazil to make him like this? He's always had problems with his temper, but——" He stopped as Cristiano ran in from outside.

"Did you wash your hands?" I asked him, and he held them out proudly. "All right, sit down," I said.

Espirito prayed in gratitude for the food, and added a special prayer for Papa. As he reached for his bowl, I saw blisters on his fingers from the axe. "I have a salve that will help those," I said, nodding at his hands.

"Sister knows how to make things better," Cristiano said, his mouth full of bread.

"Sister?" Espirito said, and Cristiano nodded, smiling.

As we ate, Cristiano told a tale of a mother hen chasing him across the yard, and we all laughed. I could not help thinking of the silent, tense meals with Bonifacio.

⁂

Holy Thursday was sunny and bright. All day I waited for Bonifacio to appear, jumping at every noise and frequently looking up and down the road. But as we prepared to go to church for the evening Mass of the Lord's Supper, I told myself that Bonifacio would not return until the next day, Good Friday. Cristiano lingered over his dinner, and so we were among the last to arrive at the church. The only place left was at the back of the nave.

After the Mass and the singing of the Gloria accompanied by the bells, the twelve men from the parish representing the Apostles stepped forward, one by one, to have Father Monteiro wash their feet. The twelfth of them was Bonifacio.

I drew in a deep breath. Even from the back of the church I could see that he was emaciated and haggard, his clothing hanging from his frame and his cheekbones sharp under tautly stretched skin. I looked at Espirito and saw him staring at Bonifacio as well.

But later, as we stood outside, Bonifacio wasn't among the crowd. We went to Father Monteiro. "Did you speak to my brother?" Espirito asked.

"I was surprised to see him when he came before Mass and asked that he be allowed to be an Apostle. I had hoped he had been home first, and that you had told him about his father. But it was quite clear that he didn't know, and I was forced to inform him. I'm sorry. And yet he still wanted to be part of the Mass."

"How did he take the news?" Espirito asked.

Father Monteiro shook his head. "He's ill from his penance in the mountains. I don't know that he actually absorbed everything I said. Please, take care of him when he comes home."

"Where is he?" I asked.

"He's at Vitorino's grave. But . . ." He stopped. "I think you should leave him alone. He'll come home when he's ready."

⟶⟵

It seemed I had barely fallen asleep when I woke with a start. Bonifacio stood at the foot of my bed. Had he said my name?

I moved Cristiano closer to the wall and sat up. I couldn't make out his face in the darkness, and reached for the flint and candle. As the light flared, the candle cast shadows into the deep hollows under his eyes. He went to his own bed and sat down slowly, cautiously, as if unsure of the distance between his body and the bed.

"Are you all right?" I whispered, not wanting to wake Cristiano.

When he didn't answer, I wrapped my shawl around myself and sat on the edge of my bed.

He looked at me, his hands hanging between his legs as though defeated.

"You know about your father," I said.

"Father Monteiro told me."

"I'm so sorry, Bonifacio."

He sat for the next few moments with that same odd lack of expression. Then he nodded. "It's my final punishment."

"Still? It's about you and your punishment?" I said, trying harder than ever to hold back my anger. Would he show no grief for the loss of his father or remorse that he hadn't been here when he died?

"How long has my brother been living with you?"

"He and Olívia came for the funeral. He's been waiting for you."

He said nothing more, lying down in that same slow, careful manner, turning on his side to face the wall. I looked at his back for a moment, then blew out the candle.

CHAPTER FORTY

I was awake before Cristiano.

Bonifacio had left the sheets open, and when Cristiano awoke, he stared at Bonifacio asleep across from us, then got up and went outside. I thought he had gone to use the *latrina*, but when he didn't return, I went looking for him. I found him hidden in the long sweet bracken behind the kitchen. He held one of the new chicks in both hands, touching his cheek to the downy little body.

"It will be all right, Cristiano. Espirito's here," I said, but he turned his face from me in the old, sadly familiar way, and then put his head in my lap, still gently cradling the little chick. It peeped quietly, and I stroked Cristiano's soft curls. Eventually he sat up and I rose, intending to get some eggs for breakfast, but noticed the garden gate open. It was always shut. I went towards it, and stopped in shock.

Every plant had been ripped out. Root vegetables were pulled up and tossed aside. I was sickened at the image of Bonifacio, with only the moon for light, destroying what had been Papa's pride. Was it his anger at his father's death, or at himself for not being present? I shut the gate and went back to the house.

Espirito's door was still closed, but Bonifacio sat at the table. In the daylight his hair, long and unwashed, showed streaks of grey, and that, along with his disturbing thinness, made me realize how much he looked like his father. He held a piece of bread, studying it.

"Why did you destroy your father's garden?"

"Isn't it strange how one loses the desire to eat after a certain length of time?" he said, ignoring my question. "God always shows what is needed. He provides the answers."

I took a deep breath and held it, but couldn't remain quiet. "God doesn't always provide, Bonifacio," I said, snatching the bread from him, throwing it onto the floor, my voice louder than I had intended. "Did He provide for Vovo and Cristiano? Did He provide for me, on Porto Santo?"

Bonifacio slowly leaned over and picked up the bread and set it on the table. All of this seemed to take an endless time. I heard my pulse beating in my ears, and I wanted to sweep the bread onto the floor again. Instead, I stood in front of him, my hands clenched at my sides.

"He sent you salvation," Bonifacio said. "I was directed to you, through Him." He rose slowly, as if in pain. "I'm going to the Good Friday Mass."

Espirito came out of the bedroom after Bonifacio had gone. "I just heard my brother."

"He came home in the night, and now he's gone to Mass. But . . . he tore up the garden."

"He tore up the garden? Why?"

I shrugged.

"His temper . . ." Espirito shook his head. "Did he eat anything?"

I looked at the bread on the table. "No."

"The fasting has made him unpredictable. He'll be better once he starts to eat again. Are you and Cristiano coming to Mass?"

"No."

❧

Cristiano was off picking eucalyptus leaves for me when I saw Espirito and Bonifacio return from Church. Bonifacio sat on a stump near the woodpile. It was as though he was broken, all life gone from him. Surely, as Espirito had said, it was the result of the fasting. And yet there seemed something more. Both last night and this morning he had looked at me with the same haunted expression Cristiano wore in the aftermath of his nightmare.

I watched the brothers from the doorway, too far away to hear their words. Bonifacio frequently shook his head. Finally I went out to them.

"I'm offering Bonifacio a plan," Espirito said as I approached. "A possibility for a future."

Bonifacio shrugged, clearly uninterested.

"If it doesn't work out, the three of you will live with us," Espirito said, glancing at me. "You know you have no option but to leave here," he added, looking back at his brother.

"How could you ever expect me to agree to live with you and Olívia?" Bonifacio said. "Are you mad?"

"What is the plan?" I asked.

"Martyn Kipling recently lost his manager of the Counting House," Espirito said, looking from me to Bonifacio, "and must fill the position. It's generously paid, and others have already applied, but I'll put your name forward, Bonifacio. Should you win the post, it could offer a life for you and Diamantina and Cristiano in Funchal."

"You think life here is not good enough for me? For them?"

"Bonifacio, you're talking nonsense. Soon the *senhorio* will reclaim his property as Papa agreed. Besides, are you so happy here that you refuse to look elsewhere?"

Bonifacio stared at him. "Happy? What does that have to do with anything? I'm carrying out my duties to feed my wife and the child. I am doing God's will."

"How do you intend to support them?"

"God will show me the way," Bonifacio said, and I clenched my hands so tightly that my nails bit into my palms.

"Maybe He is using me as His instrument. Maybe it's through me that the way will be shown," Espirito said, a dangerous quality creeping into his voice.

Bonifacio looked at him. "You consider yourself a messenger of God?" His tone was harsher than Espirito's.

"I'm simply trying to make you see sense!" Espirito stared at Bonifacio with an anger I hadn't seen before. "This appears to be your only opportunity. Is it really such a difficult decision?"

When Bonifacio still didn't respond, I asked Espirito, "Is Bonifacio suited for the position?"

"It requires someone who has a fine script and a quick mathematical ability, both of which Bonifacio is blessed with."

I stared at my husband. He sat as if awaiting a beating. I imagined his small leather whip in my hand, and me striking his back as I had so often heard him strike himself. At this moment I wanted to do something—anything—to shake him from his lethargy. "Have there been many come to ask about the position?"

"Yes, but Senhor Kipling is quite particular and is taking his time."

We both looked at Bonifacio. His eyes were on his hands, upturned in his lap. He said, "I don't want to go to Funchal. This is my home. Maybe someone would hire me on here. I could work on another's vines. Diamantina could help the wife with the house and children."

Espirito made a sound of disgust. "You would be content to be a slave to some other man, and let your wife be a servant?"

Bonifacio stared at his hands.

"Bonifacio, be a man," Espirito said, and at that Bonifacio rose, colour in his cheeks—the first colour in his face since he returned.

"You have no right to tell me what it takes to be a man," he said. "No right!"

The brothers faced each other.

"So it's to be like this, Bonifacio? You would allow your wife and the child you have taken into your care to suffer, because you want to suffer? Is that God's will, or yours?"

Bonifacio picked up a piece of split wood and held it aloft. "I should have done this sooner."

"Put that down," Espirito said.

Bonifacio swung, and I cried out, but Espirito easily avoided the blow. He stepped forward and wrenched the stick from his brother and threw it to the ground. "You shame yourself, Bonifacio."

Bonifacio looked into Espirito's face and then turned and went into the house.

"I'll go and speak to him," I said.

"No, not when he's like this."

"Now or later—what difference does it make?" I hurried into the house.

Bonifacio again sat slumped over the table.

"If you can just think about it," I said. "We could rent a room to start, and maybe later we could—"

"Who do you imagine yourself to be?" he interrupted. "After only a few months away from your mud hut on Porto Santo, you're dreaming of a life you were never meant for, and can never have."

"With what you might earn, should you be hired at Kipling's," I said, fighting to keep my voice even, "more, surely, than we need for our daily lives, you could do so much good. You could donate more to the Church and to the needy. By your own hard work you could improve the lives of so many more than by staying here."

There was a subtle change in his expression, and this encouraged me. "You took Cristiano from Brazil in order to provide him with a better life. Wouldn't it be a better life for him in Funchal?"

After a moment, he said, slowly, "I thought, when I brought him from Brazil, that when he was of age he could enter the seminary."

"Cristiano a priest?"

"Why not?" He frowned. "Why shouldn't he devote his life to God? Doesn't he have a great deal to be thankful for?"

"Does he?"

"He was the child of a slave, and would have lived the life of a slave," he said. "I took him from that. I took him with the hope of making him into a man who would live a holy life in the service of Our Father. Perhaps he could be a missionary, as I was."

"Perhaps. Yes, perhaps Cristiano could enter the seminary in Funchal." I would agree with anything Bonifacio suggested, if it would persuade him to come to Funchal.

Suddenly he put his head to one side, his eyes narrowing at me. "But isn't this all about what *you* want, Diamantina? Don't try and act as though it's Cristiano who needs and wants more. You have the devil on your tongue," he said. "*People can tame animals, birds, reptiles and fish, but no one can tame the tongue. It is restless and evil, full of deadly poison.* So say the Scriptures."

I stood very still.

"You want too much. You take too much," he said. "Haven't you taken enough from me?"

"What have I taken from you?"

He got up and came to me, grimacing as he leaned close. His breath was sour, not just the odour of an empty stomach but something more. He grabbed my wrist, wrenching it painfully, and I cried out. As suddenly as he'd taken my wrist, he let it go, and went outside.

I took a deep breath and went into the yard. Cristiano was sitting in the doorway of the kitchen. I stood beside Espirito, watching Bonifacio walk down the hill towards the church.

⁓

It was dinnertime when Bonifacio returned. I went to him in the wash house.

"I spent this holy day in prayer and confession and penance, and God supplied me with an answer," Bonifacio said, rubbing his hair with a flannel. "I'll do as my brother has suggested, and see about the position at Kipling's."

"I'm glad to hear of this, Bonifacio," I said.

He lowered the wet flannel. "If it is God's will, so be it. If not, we'll live as I said, working for others." He stepped close and took my wrist, the one he had bruised earlier, and I winced. "One thing we will not do is take my younger brother's charity." He dropped my wrist and shoved me aside as he reached for another flannel. "Ever."

PART III

FUNCHAL, MADEIRA

Early the next morning, we stood in the yard, Cristiano holding his small cloth bag of clothes. My medicine bag was slung across my chest, my packed shawl sat at my feet, and I carried a skin of water and a sack of food for the day.

As Espirito lifted my bulging shawl and tied it around one shoulder, Bonifacio watched from the step.

"I'm not ready to leave," he said.

"What do you still have to do?" Espirito asked. "Just bring your good clothing for the meeting."

Bonifacio made a sound of annoyance. "It's Holy Saturday. I'm not going to miss Mass. And I have to ask someone to feed the chickens. Go on ahead. I'll follow."

"Bonifacio, I rode Adão as far as I could, and left him at the last stable," Espirito said. "Come with us now and I'll hire a horse for you to ride the last half of the way, into Funchal."

"I told you, I'll come on my own, after Mass."

"Are you strong enough to walk the whole day? After your fasting—"

"Don't pretend you care about my well-being now," he said, and then went into the house and shut the door.

As soon as we started up the tortuous trail, Espirito hoisted Cristiano onto his back, still managing to carry my shawl and his own bag. I glanced behind me just once as we left, suddenly superstitious of the valley winds whispering of my return.

When the sun was high overhead, we came through the most

dangerous paths. Stopping at a small cluster of huts I remembered passing on my way into the valley with Bonifacio, we shared the bread and cheese and olives and the skin of water. Then Espirito went into a low stable and led out a tall red-brown horse with a golden mane and tail. "This is Adão," he said, rubbing the horse's neck.

I stroked Adão's soft nose. "There are no horses on Porto Santo."

Cristiano cautiously reached up, smiling as the horse lowered its head for his touch.

Espirito tied our bags behind the saddle. "Funchal's streets are too steep and cobbled for horses. I keep Adão in the Kipling stables. Put your left foot into the stirrup," he instructed, gesturing at the iron ring hanging at the horse's side. As I did so, he put his hands around my waist, and I swung my other leg over and sat on the long leather seat, adjusting my skirt. Espirito lifted Cristiano up and positioned him in front of me. Then he mounted behind me.

I was too aware of him. I sat stiffly, the heat of his chest against my back, slightly anxious at being so high above the ground. I concentrated on Cristiano, putting my arms around him as he gripped Adão's mane. Espirito reached around me to take the reins. As Adão started with a jolting step, I involuntarily made a small cry, and then, embarrassed, laughed. "I like it," I said, and caught Espirito's smile from the corner of my eye.

He kept the horse at a steady walk along the narrow roads, and within a short time I understood the sway and gait, and settled into the creaking leather saddle more comfortably. After a time I let myself lean against Espirito. His chest was muscled and warm. If I turned my head to the side, I could feel his breath on my cheek. Cristiano also lost his fear, putting his hands on the reins and sometimes lightly kicking his bare heels against Adão's neck.

As we descended out of the mountains, we again passed the terraces of bananas and sugar cane. The lower we went, the more the crops changed. I hadn't seen so many different plantings when Bonifacio and I had walked this way over six months earlier, but now it was spring, and from my higher vantage point I kept looking to one side or another and asking Espirito what we were seeing. He pointed out fig as well as orange and lemon trees, and maize and wheat.

And then, as we came up to a slight rise, I saw it—the sea. It shone silver, like a flat plate in the high afternoon sun. I closed my eyes then opened them, closed them and opened them, over and over, experiencing the joy of seeing the ocean again, knowing it was real.

Funchal spread before us when we stopped at the top of a hill in front of a set of high gates. *Quinta Isabella* was written in scrolled letters atop them.

Espirito dismounted; I missed his body for that moment before he reached his hands towards me and lightly swung me down. Setting Cristiano down as well, he left Adão with a boy who ran out of the gates and led the horse inside. And then the three of us walked down into Funchal, down, down, and farther down into the town, through teeming, narrow streets, passing the busy plaza where oxen and carts stood in a row.

"This is the Kipling's winery, with the Counting House here, at the front," Espirito said when we stood on Rua São Batista, a street that ran all the way down towards the sea. "Behind is a courtyard with the working buildings and storage for the wines, also accessible from another lane where the *mosto* is brought in from the countryside. Olívia and I live here, above the Counting House."

I looked up at a handsome row of three balconies with finely carved ironwork.

Espirito unlocked a dark polished door with a brass handle. In the entry was a gleaming wooden staircase rising to landings on two floors. The ceiling was adorned with decorative plasterwork. "We're fortunate to have a ship-viewing tower," he said. "Many buildings in the centre of Funchal were constructed to be able to see the harbour." We climbed up the wide, spotless stairs to the second floor.

A round-faced girl in a head scarf and apron was dusting a table as we came in. I smelled cooking meat, and suddenly was hungry.

"Hello, Ana," Espirito said, but she didn't answer, staring at me, and then Cristiano, and back to me.

At our voices, Olívia appeared. Like Ana, she looked at me and Cristiano, and then at Espirito. I tensed at the anger apparent on her face, but before she spoke, another woman came to stand beside her. I knew it was Olívia's mother, for she looked like an older, softer version of Olivia.

"You've returned, finally," the older woman said. "Olívia was worried you wouldn't be back for Easter, Espirito. And this . . ." She still smiled, although I could tell she was struggling to maintain her pleasant expression. "This is Bonifacio's wife, then."

"Allow me to introduce my mother-in-law," Espirito said, "Senhora Luzia Vasques da Silva. And yes, this is Diamantina. Bonifacio will arrive later—he wanted to go to Mass."

"Good day, senhora," I said.

"Olívia spoke of you," Senhora da Silva said, "although she didn't tell me you would be coming with Espirito." She had regained her composure, and her smile was now determined. "I remember Cristiano, although he looks much different from that first time I saw him." She nodded. "Do you remember me, Cristiano?"

He nodded shyly.

"Well, it's a good thing we had Ana prepare a big dinner," Senhora da Silva said, turning to her daughter. "Isn't it, Olívia?"

"Yes, Mother," Olívia said, with an obvious lack of enthusiasm.

"And tomorrow we can all go to the Easter Mass. Take your guests upstairs and let them freshen up for dinner," Senhora da Silva said firmly to her daughter.

"Thank you, senhora," I said, not looking at Olívia.

Olívia turned. "This way," she said, and I took my bundled shawl from Espirito, and Cristiano and I followed Olívia up another set of stairs. Her breath rasped with each step. In the wide upstairs hall we passed a room with a deep copper tub sitting in front of a small fireplace.

I looked at it, imagining myself sinking under warm water. The last time I'd felt water cover my body had been the night before my wedding, when I bathed in the ocean. The stream behind the house in Curral das Freiras ran shallow and cold, only reaching my calves.

"The lavatory," Olívia said, gesturing at a closed door.

I raised my eyebrows at Cristiano at the wonder of it. I'd only known wash houses and *latrinas* separate from living areas.

"You can stay here tonight," she said, leading us into a bright, airy room. There was one wide bed. The curtains and bed covering were the green of the forest. A carved wooden screen blocked one corner. "Cristiano can sleep on that small settee."

I tried to imagine what would happen when Bonifacio arrived. I didn't want to think of us being forced into the bed together, and looked at the flowers in vases on the dressing table and chest of drawers. Directly in front of us was a long mirror on a stand.

I stared at myself, Olívia beside me. I had never seen my whole body; I only had my small bone-edged mirror. My shoulders looked strong, my hips narrow. There were brambles caught in my coarse brown skirt, a smear of dirt on the cuff of my sleeve, and dark earth stains on my hide boots. My hair was windblown, long blond strands hanging loose around my face. My cheeks were darkened and slightly chaffed by the mountain wind, and my hands red from work. Apart from the colour of my hair and eyes, I looked like my mother, long ago when she had walked the beach with long, firm steps.

Olívia's dress was soft gold muslin, her feet small in their matching satin slippers. Her hair was pulled back, sleek and shining. She folded her smooth hands in front of her waist as she stared at her reflection.

I turned from the mirror and went to the window. It looked over the harbour, with its gathering of sailing vessels. Beyond was the beautiful, restless sea.

Hearing Olívia's slow, careful exhalation, I turned back to her. The bones of her face were too prominent, her dark eyes glittering. "So you talked him into bringing you, in spite of my wishes," she said, her voice hard.

"Espirito suggested Bonifacio apply for the position in Kipling's Counting House." My tone matched hers.

"The Counting House? He wants Bonifacio to work for Kipling's? But that means you'd have to live in Funchal?"

"Of course."

At her aggrieved expression, I stepped closer and said, "Do you not wish the best for your brother-in-law? Or is it me you don't wish to be near?"

She looked at me for a long moment. "You don't know, do you?"

"Know what?"

She turned and went to the door. "We will not wait on Bonifacio. Come downstairs when you've changed for dinner," she said, and then left Cristiano and me alone in the beautiful room.

I turned back to the window. The sight of the water brought me a deep sense of comfort, and I was able to breathe deeply as I hadn't been able to do while choked by the mountains.

※

Espirito said a brief prayer of thanks as we sat down at the long, gleaming table set with candles in high silver holders. Senhora da Silva and Espirito spoke, trying to bring Olívia and me into the conversation, but I only answered in the most cursory way. Even Cristiano didn't make a sound as he ate. I knew he felt as out of place as I did in this grand house.

"Bonifacio should have been here an hour ago," Espirito said as we sat in the salon after dinner. Outside the windows, the sky grew dark. Senhor da Silva had come to fetch Olívia's mother but had waited for her downstairs, so I hadn't met him. Cristiano was asleep beside me on the settee, his head on an embroidered pillow.

Espirito kept glancing at the wood and glass clock ticking on the mantel in the salon. Now its hands pointed at the seven and the eight. Of course, I knew about clocks, but I had never lived with one. I had lived by the movement of the sun across the sky, by the ringing of church bells, and by the needs of the body for food and sleep.

"I'm afraid something has happened to him on the road. I'll go and look for him," he said at last. "Ana, please fetch me a lantern." He leaned down and kissed Olívia's cheek. "I'll be back as soon as I can. Don't wait up."

Espirito left, and I turned to Olívia. I was determined not to let her silence and accusing stares provoke me. I realized she reminded me of some of the girls in the square in Vila Baleira, the ones who had pointed at me and whispered.

"Was the doctor able to help you?" I asked.

"A bit," she said, still staring at the fire.

As the silence stretched, I stood. "I'll go to bed," I said. "Thank you for dinner."

She nodded, staring at the fire.

I roused Cristiano so that he could climb the stairs, then settled him under a blanket on the small settee at the foot of the bed. He was instantly asleep again. In the next moment I heard the rumble of men's voices from downstairs.

I went to the hall and watched as Espirito helped Bonifacio up the stairs. Bonifacio was clinging to Espirito's arm and emitting a groan as he lifted his foot to each step. His face was pasty and his hair stuck to his forehead.

"What happened?" I asked as they passed me. "Where did you find him?"

"I've sent Ana for the physician," Espirito said. "Go to bed. We'll look after him." They went into another bedroom and the door closed.

Olívia was slowly coming up the stairs.

"Do you know—" I started, but she just shook her head and went into her bedroom.

I sat on my bed, and after a while heard more footsteps on the stairs. A youngish man, led by Ana, passed my open door.

Ana went back downstairs. After a long while Espirito and the man I assumed was the physician passed my door again. I waited a few moments and then went to the salon. Espirito was alone.

"Espirito?"

As he turned from the table holding the wine decanter, his glass trembled slightly, and a few drops sloshed over the lip of it. He raised the glass to his mouth and swallowed it in one long drink, then turned and poured himself another. "I found him by the side of the road not too far outside Funchal." He drained the glass again. "He couldn't go any farther. I hired a cart to carry him back."

"Is it because of the fasting?"

He hesitated a moment too long. "He's been through an ordeal. The doctor will come back tomorrow to see that he's comfortable. I'm exhausted. You must be as well. Please. Go to bed."

"But—"

"Diamantina, please." He put his hand to his forehead, his fingers still trembling. "I'm sorry. I just . . . I need to sleep." Then he left.

I went to the table and poured myself a small glass of wine and drank it, looking at the dying fire. There had been something terribly troubling in Espirito's expression.

I extinguished the lamp on the table and went up the dark stairs. I spent a long time at the window, watching the long, wavy reflection of the moon rippling on the water, thinking about Olívia, and her expression as she said, *You don't know, do you?*

CHAPTER FORTY-TWO

Bonifacio's door was closed when Cristiano and I passed it the next morning.

Espirito and Olívia were sitting at the dining table.

"I'm sorry," I said. "Were you waiting for us?"

"As soon as we've eaten, we'll all go to Easter Mass," Olívia said. "We will meet my parents at the church. We were going to have dinner with them, but now . . ."

"We'll have them here instead," Espirito said. "I don't feel right leaving Bonifacio on his own for so long."

Olívia shook her head. "The day is spoiled now." As Cristiano and I sat down, she picked up a small bell and rang it. In a moment Ana struggled in with a heavy tray of covered dishes.

⁂

I knocked on Bonifacio's door when we returned from church, and at his low murmur went in. He was sitting on a chair near the window.

"Are you feeling better?" I asked him, and he looked away from the window, and at me.

He was still pale, but seemed a little stronger. "Yes."

"The English physician was able to help in some way?" I wondered what the physician could have done; there was no cure for the ravages of fasting but to slowly introduce food.

He stood cautiously. "Did you want something in particular?"

"Just to see that you were all right. After last night, I—"

"You insisted on coming to Funchal. And so I have."

"I'm sorry you weren't well enough to attend the Easter Mass. We went to Sé cathedral. It was beautiful." I was speaking too quickly, uncomfortable with Bonifacio in a different way than usual. He stared at me with an intensity that was unsettling.

"I've been there. A long time ago."

I nodded, and left.

⁂

When Senhor and Senhora da Silva arrived for dinner, Espirito and Olívia and Cristiano and I were in the salon.

Senhor Eduardo da Silva was a portly man with a neat moustache, his silver hair showing the tooth marks of a comb. He bowed over my hand, greeting me formally.

When Olívia and her mother went into the kitchen to confer with Ana and the da Silvas' maid, who had come to help cook and serve that evening, Bonifacio appeared. He went to Senhor da Silva; the other man stood and they shook hands. Bonifacio then went and sat on one of the elegant salon chairs.

"Dinner will be ready momentarily," Olívia said, coming back into the salon. When she saw Bonifacio, she stopped.

Bonifacio half stood, bowing his head. "Olívia," he said. "Thank you for your hospitality."

"You're quite welcome," she said, more than the usual edge in her voice. "Please. Everyone come to the dining room."

We were served the first course. Cristiano sat beside me, and I saw him studying the confusing number of utensils. I waited until I saw Senhora da Silva pick up the outside fork, and then did the same. Cristiano copied me.

"First thing tomorrow we'll go to the Counting House, Bonifacio," Espirito said. "You can meet with the men who already work there. You may have questions for them."

Bonifacio didn't respond, but Senhora da Silva kept the conversation going, chattering about the weather, the latest new shop in the square, people they knew, and how she was redecorating her salon.

Various courses were served, and I watched Senhora da Silva carefully. I followed her lead, not wanting to appear uncouth, although I quickly realized only Cristiano paid me any heed; everyone seemed ill at ease.

I took Cristiano upstairs to bed as soon as it was polite to do so. When I came downstairs again, Senhora da Silva and Olívia sat in the salon. "The men have gone outside to walk. Eduardo likes to have his pipe after dinner, and the smoke bothers Olívia." She rose and went to her daughter. "You must go to bed now," she told her. "It's been a long day."

Olívia rose silently.

"That's my good girl," her mother said. "Would you like me to send Ana up with a warm drink?"

"No, thank you, Mother. Good night, Diamantina."

I said good night.

After she was gone, Senhora da Silva settled herself by the fire again, and shook her head, gazing at the flames. "I worry so about her. She's my only child."

"Has she had the illness all her life?"

"It started when she was a little older than Cristiano, but it was mild. It steadily grows worse. The English physician says that the chronic inflammation of the airways creates the coughing spasms. She . . ." She looked away from the fire, and at me. "She wasn't always as you see her."

I waited.

"She was full of life before the grip of the illness and Bonifacio leaving her. And I must say that Bonifacio looks terrible."

I waited three heartbeats, digesting what she had just said. "He's been fasting."

"It isn't his gauntness, it's that he's changed completely from what we once knew. It must be clear to you that you came into something of a mess. I hope you're managing." She shook her head. "You couldn't have known Bonifacio long before you married him."

"Not long."

"Was it arranged by your parents?"

"The priest in Vila Baleira arranged it."

She nodded. "Espirito said you were from Porto Santo. Diamantina," she said, and I met her eyes, "I hope you can forgive Olívia's behaviour. It will alter, I'm sure, once she gets used to you, and having to face Bonifacio again. Until today she'd only seen him once since he returned from Brazil. You know he'd had no contact with anyone here while he was in Brazil, and then when he arrived in Funchal . . ."

I didn't want to move, afraid she would stop the story, not wanting her to know I didn't know what she was talking about, thinking about Olívia's cryptic statement the day before.

"It was a terrible shock for us all when he knocked on the door, having asked where Espirito lived. He was carrying that poor little boy. His face, when he saw that Espirito and Olívia had married . . . well. What a day that was. Quite awful for us all."

There was a moment of silence as the understanding that had been coming arrived. Then I murmured, "I can imagine."

"So I'm hoping you can see past my daughter's current state. It will take some time for her to accept you. But maybe someday . . ." She paused. ". . . you can be friends. Especially if Bonifacio is hired by Kipling's and you live in Funchal." I saw the neediness on her face, and what she would try to do to make her daughter happy. "She's lonely. It's hard for her to see all of her old friends so fulfilled with their children. Did you know that she's lost three babies in their five years of marriage?"

"No. But if I'm to be able to be part of Olívia's life," I said slowly, "I feel I should know more. Bonifacio has not been forthcoming about his . . . about Olívia. About how they met, or parted."

"Ah. It's natural, I suppose, that he would be reticent to disclose such an uncomfortable situation with his new wife. But I don't know if it's up to me to talk any further of it." She turned back to the fire.

After a few minutes, I said, "If I can implore you, Senhora da Silva. My own mother died not long ago, and I . . . it would help me in my marriage to have someone to speak to about Bonifacio."

Should I have felt guilty using Senhora da Silva in this way?

Her face relaxed, and she leaned forward and patted my hand. "You poor child. I do sense you are a bit lost. Alone here on Madeira, far from home. And then living in the mountains . . . it must have been difficult. Espirito said you were wonderful with his father and little Cristiano. He said you changed the house into the home he remembered as a boy, when his mother was alive. He's so grateful for you."

I imagined Olívia hearing this praise from Espirito, and understood even more fully her reaction to me.

Senhora da Silva settled back into her chair. "I would like you to feel I can be like a mother-in-law to you, although of course we have no direct connection."

"I would like that," I said, seeing the genuine warmth on her face.

"All right, then," she said with a kind of finality, as if she now had permission to continue the conversation. "I'm sure you knew that Espirito and Bonifacio both worked for my husband as apprentices. Eduardo has a fine little winery. We often hosted social events for the employees. At the time, Bonifacio had already spent a year in the seminary but was struggling as to whether to continue, and left for a year to contemplate his choices. And then he met Olívia, and it appeared he put aside his thoughts of being a priest. Their courtship continued for over a year. Eduardo and I fully expected him to ask for her hand, and we were prepared to give it. Olívia felt strongly for him. But then Bonifacio changed his mind, and returned to the seminary. Olívia told us that he gave her no real explanation, except that he felt he had a higher calling. Our poor girl was at first shocked, then humiliated and saddened, and finally grew bitter."

"I can understand," I murmured, trying to imagine Bonifacio and Olívia together.

"Much later, after Bonifacio had left for Brazil, she and Espirito grew close, although I often thought . . . well, it's just my opinion, but I wondered if she instinctively drew close to Espirito because it was a connection to Bonifacio . . ." She stopped. "Still, when Espirito spoke to us about marrying her, we gave our consent." She took a deep breath. "And Espirito has been wonderful to her, and we love him as a son. But Bonifacio's unexpected return has affected Olívia rather badly."

She was looking intently at me now. I'd thought her almost silly through dinner, as she rambled about society and decorating, but now realized she had been covering her discomfort. "When Bonifacio chose the Church over Olívia, she had to accept that it had a stronger hold on him than she did. Her marriage to Espirito is good, but Bonifacio has hurt her again by marrying so quickly after leaving the Church."

I nodded.

"And even though Bonifacio made his own choices, he is clearly angry with Espirito for marrying Olívia. I don't believe he has a right to be so. If he were a truly compassionate man, he would be glad that Olívia—and his brother—found contentment with each other.

"Espirito tried with Bonifacio. Within the first few weeks of Bonifacio coming back, he went to Porto Santo with him, when Bonifacio insisted on seeing the Father there. Oh—that would be the priest who arranged your marriage?"

She was talking about that first time in Vila Baleira, when I met Espirito in the inn, and the next day saw Bonifacio in the church, punishing himself. "Yes."

"Anyway, Espirito hoped some time together would help. But it didn't. They argued there, and he came home alone. Espirito wants to create a better relationship with his brother. This is why he's hoping he can help Bonifacio find a position with Kipling's."

"Ah," I said.

A log dropped in the fireplace, sending a small shower of embers onto the hearth. Two jumped onto the edge of the carpet. I leaned forward and pushed them back onto the hearth with the poker.

"It doesn't appear you're with child yet," Senhora da Silva said, startling me, as I was about to set the poker back in its stand. "When it does happen, it will be the next hurdle for Olívia. Each time she lost a baby, it was harder on her. The doctor says it can't happen again. The next time could cost her her life." She pulled a delicate scrap of linen from her sleeve and wiped her eyes. "It's unnatural for a woman to remain childless. Olívia daily struggles with this failure. And of course it's difficult for Espirito to have such a fragile wife. He is . . . well, I'm sure he is deeply disappointed as well not to have children." Again she touched her eyes with the handkerchief. "I talk too much. It's a fault to not know when to stop speaking. Eduardo often tells me I create trouble with this trait."

I set the poker back and reached to put my hand on hers. "I'm sure it's very difficult for everyone, Senhora da Silva. I'm so sorry."

She took a deep breath and tucked the handkerchief away. "Eduardo and I will never be grandparents—this is difficult for us as well. But I hope you don't feel I've spoken out of turn about Bonifacio. Does it help you to know these facts?"

"Yes, it does."

"I'm also hoping I've made you understand Olívia a little better. I'm sure you would like a friend as well, having left all of your own friends back in Vila Baleira."

I attempted a smile, and hoped it looked sincere.

CHAPTER FORTY-THREE

When Cristiano and I went downstairs for breakfast the next morning, there was no sign of either brother.

"Espirito has taken Bonifacio to the Counting House," Olívia said. "Eat quickly. You're going to be fitted for some new clothing."

I knew that all I would be able to think about today was the past. About how Olivia and Bonifacio had loved each other, and how Espirito had stepped in and married her once his brother was gone.

"New clothes . . . No, that won't be necessary. We don't know if Bonifacio will get the position." I had no money, and was ashamed to tell her. "Also, it would take a number of days to have anything made, and we may not be here after tomorrow."

"It's my mother's idea to take you to a dressmaker, not mine. She wants to outfit Cristiano as well."

It didn't appear I had a choice.

As we slowly walked up the hilly cobbled street to the house on Rua São Batista with our purchases that afternoon, my feet, in soft new leather shoes, ached from the hard stones. Cristiano was tired as well; he lagged, and I kept turning to check that he hadn't fallen too far behind.

Senhora da Silva was still chatting. She loved flowers, and was an expert on Madeira's natural plants and trees, as well as exotics brought from other lands that thrived in the island's glorious temperate climate. In the pretty decorated squares, we walked under the shade of banana and guava, pomegranate and fig trees, and she named the English flowers set in borders among the walkways.

"The ornamental gardens at Kipling's Quinta Isabella are magnificent," she told me. "I have gone there a number of times as a guest, because of Espirito's position. Senhor Kipling had seeds and cuttings brought from other parts of the world, and cultivated them. There are bougainvillea, hydrangea, fuchsia, belladonna and camellia, mixed with Madeira's own earthly treasures, the myrtles and lilies, lupines and violets, and so many ferns. My favourite scent is lily, but Olívia loves camellia. Don't you, Olívia?" she said, adding, "She always wears it."

"Yes," Olívia said.

My face was sore from smiling. Senhora da Silva was attempting to make me feel comfortable, but I was unused to endless talk.

"Do you care to wear scent?" Senhora da Silva asked.

"I used to wear an oil I made from rosemary."

"Rosemary? But that's not a flower. "

"I know, but I love its fragrance."

She shook her head. "You are an unusual young woman," she said, but her voice was kind. "I'm quite excited to see you in your new frocks. With your lovely colouring, both the pale green and the silver-grey will be beautiful on you."

Olívia walked a little faster, leaving us a few steps behind.

Senhora da Silva clicked her tongue. "It appears I've upset her. Don't rush, Olívia," she called. "Be cautious."

But Olívia didn't heed her. As her mother hurried after her, I stopped abruptly.

"Come, dear," Senhora da Silva called.

"Convento Catarina of the Cross," I read from the plaque on one of the pillars outside the grey stones of a convent. "I know . . . I knew a Sister from this convent. In Porto Santo."

"Do you?" Senhora da Silva said, distracted, watching Olívia. "Please hurry. I want to make certain Olívia is all right. She shouldn't rush."

Espirito was coming down the stairs as we came into the salon. "Bonifacio is resting," he said. "I brought him home, but have to return to work."

"We've had a lovely time, Espirito," Senhora da Silva said. She glanced at Olívia, sitting in a corner of the sofa, her breath sawing the air, her eyes closed.

"Thank you again for today, Senhora da Silva," I said, then turned to Espirito. "Could I come with you, to see the wine lodge?" I couldn't bear to think of sitting in the salon with Olívia and her mother for the next hours, with Senhora da Silva's non-stop chattering and Olívia's dark silence but for her rattling breath.

He glanced at Olívia.

"Olívia needs to lie down," Senhora da Silva said. "I'm going to have Ana make her a poultice, and then I must go home as well. Take Cristiano with you, Diamantina, so Olívia has complete quiet."

⌘

Espirito led Cristiano and me across a courtyard behind the Counting House. We entered a long, dim room lit only by small square windows. The floor, like the courtyard, was paved with pebbles. The room was very hot, and the smell of alcohol overpowering. I had a dizzying, pleasant sensation immediately, as though I'd drunk too many cups of wine in Rooi's inn.

"This is the *adega*, where we store the wine as we let it mature. These vats are made from enormous old timbers from ships," Espirito said, gesturing to the hundreds of massive kegs resting on low wooden braces. Each keg was chalked with the name of the grape and a year. Some had huge funnels atop them. I ran my fingers along a keg, and Cristiano did the same. The wood was silky to the touch in spite of its age. Large bottles in wicker baskets sat in front of each keg. "The bottles are tasting samples." There was a wooden ladder to climb to a second floor of wide wooden planks and supported by immense beams. More kegs sat under the roof. There was an apparatus of ropes and wooden turning wheels, used, I imagined, to raise and lower the kegs.

A young man put his head in the open doorway. "Espirito, when

will the shipment of new bottles arrive?" he asked in English, and
when Espirito answered him and he left, I asked, "Where do you get
your bottles?"

"You know English?" he asked, surprise in his voice.

"A little. I learned it on Porto Santo," I answered, hesitating, then
added, "From English sailors. And from an English wine merchant
who sold to the innkeeper. I often spoke with him."

"Ah," he said. "We have our bottles sent from the mainland."

He took us into the sunlit cooperage with its woody scent.
Cristiano looked around with interest. Under a high window, an old
man was working at a table. "Jorge is making bungs for the kegs
from the outer fibre of the banana tree. The malleable nature of the
fibre ensures that each bung fits perfectly. Jorge has been doing
this for thirty years." The old man reminded me of Papa. He smiled
at us, dipping his head.

"Although some winemakers prefer to blend in the *adega*, I like
working here," Espirito said, leading us into a smaller room where
a wooden table with stools around it sat in the middle of the floor.
Some tasting bottles sat beside it, and there were funnels and small
glass pipes. "I like riding across the island, choosing grapes from
the different terraces before each harvest, but this is my true love—
creating the blends."

I ran my hand over the bottles.

"Would you like to try one of our best?" He poured me a small
glass.

I held up the glass, admiring the rich mahogany glow of the
wine. I put it to my nose and breathed in its odour, then took a sip.
I let it wash over my tongue and touch the sides and roof of my
mouth. I opened my lips the slightest bit and sucked air in, to give
myself more of a sense of the flavour as I swallowed. "It's a wonderful *vinho da roda*," I said, handing the glass back.

He studied me. "How do you know about round-trip wine?"

"From the English merchant I mentioned. Mr. Duncan told me it
was the Dutch who discovered that warming the wine they took on
at Madeira speeded the aging when they sailed with it to India. The
intense heat of the hold and the constant motion of the sea seemed

to improve the taste, so the Madeira producers started to purposely place kegs of wine on ships for the voyage to India and back, creating this *vinho da roda*. That's why you keep your casks high under the roof, isn't it? To keep them warm?"

Espirito nodded. "It's Henry Duncan you're referring to?"

I smiled. "Yes. He was always kind."

"He's our competitor, but is a good friend of Martyn Kipling. And to me as well. Now, if you'll excuse me, I should attend to matters in the *adega*."

I nodded, and as Cristiano and I went towards the door, I took one long, last, deep breath of the warm, familiar odour of the wine.

Olívia didn't feel well enough to join us for dinner.

I took my place across the table from Bonifacio. "Did you find the Counting House interesting?" I asked, trying to imagine him with Olívia. He was thirty now; he must have been sixteen or seventeen in his first year at the seminary, and had met Olívia the year after that.

"It was all right." He looked into his steaming soup bowl.

"Martyn Kipling is returning from Lisboa in a few days," Espirito said. "He left his son-in-law in charge of meeting the prospective employees and giving his recommendations. They have an office at the quinta, so we should go there tomorrow, Bonifacio, and I will make the introduction." He sat back as Ana served his soup. "Diamantina and Cristiano can come if they wish. Unless you two have anything else you'd rather do," he said, looking from me to Cristiano and back at me, smiling.

"We'd like to come, wouldn't we, Cristiano?" I said, and the boy nodded.

Bonifacio picked up his spoon. "There's no reason for that. They should stay here."

Espirito frowned. "What is your objection to them coming? It's a beautiful place."

"Fine, they can come," Bonifacio said tersely, pushing his spoon back and forth in the soup. "My opinion counts for little anyway."

CHAPTER FORTY-FOUR

"Why do you want to go to the quinta?" Olívia asked me the next morning, when she heard that Cristiano and I were accompanying the men.

"I looked through its gates as we came to Funchal. The house looked so wonderful. I think it will be interesting to visit such a place," I said.

"You're certainly welcome to join us, Olívia," Espirito said.

"No, thank you," she replied, and then touched her napkin to her lips, although she hadn't yet begun to eat her breakfast.

We rode to Quinta Isabella in a bullock cart pulled by two oxen. The high, wide gates were opened by the same boy who had taken in Adão on our way to Funchal. The house—glowing white in the bright sun—stood high above the gardens on either side, graced by treetops moving softly in the breeze. Along one side of the drive was a vineyard, where men worked under the pergolas supporting the vines.

The house was tall and stately in what I took to be the English style, with a grand front entrance that included a fountain in a circular drive. Espirito directed the oxen along a lane that ran beside the house, and after we all climbed down, he left the cart in front of some stables.

Behind the big house were more gardens and a terrace with broad arches supporting the vine-twined trellis overhead. Portuguese as well as black-skinned men were busy in the gardens, while women worked in a big kitchen set in a yard of well-brushed earth. Visible through another set of open doors were lines strung with clothing and linens; steam billowed from the unshuttered windows. Beyond the kitchen and wash house I could see a low, open-sided building housing a huge *lagar* for treading grapes, and behind that, backing onto a forest, were a number of simple, tidy houses—homes, perhaps, for the servants.

As a black-skinned woman carrying a huge basket of sweet potatoes on her head passed us, Espirito greeted her. "Good morning, Nini." The woman smiled and continued towards the kitchen.

"Senhor Kipling and his deceased wife, like many Madeirans, don't hold with slavery. When they purchased slaves from West Africa to work on Quinta Isabella, they immediately gave them their freedom papers in exchange for five years of work. But often, after the five years, they stay on, living as free men and women, working for a wage, given a pleasant house and enjoying the charms of the quinta."

I thought of the many mulattos and quadroons I had seen on the streets of Funchal. Senhora da Silva had told me they were descendants of the slaves from North and West Africa brought to Madeira when it was still minimally populated. They had originally worked in the sugar industry, the island's specialty before the grapes. Cristiano fit in on the streets of Funchal as he hadn't in Curral das Freiras, where there were only island-born Portuguese.

"Diamantina, you and Cristiano should first go to the kitchen for something to drink while I take Bonifacio to meet Senhor Kipling's son-in-law. And then you might enjoy walking through some of the gardens as well. Binta will take care of you," Espirito said, smiling at another dark-skinned woman. Her thick, wiry hair was neatly bound in a red cloth, and her striped skirt and white embroidered blouse were clean and of a richer fabric than mine. She had a ring of keys on a belt around her waist.

Binta took us to the big kitchen, smelling of baking bread and grilling meat and boiling fruit, and offered us glasses of cool, sugared lemon water and a plate of biscuits. Cristiano and I ate and drank, and then went out into the verdant gardens that surrounded the back of the big house.

We wandered among the flowers, and I touched the nodding heads of the blossoms. The air was rich with their perfume, and cool and fresh this high above the town, with breezes from the ocean. Wasps and bees were drawn to the flowers' sweetness, and when I closed my eyes and breathed in all these scents, it was as if I had entered another life. As we wandered closer to the house, I picked a mint leaf and gave it to Cristiano to chew. A row of open floor-to-ceiling glass doors curved gracefully along the back of the house, and all the windows on the second floor were open as well. There was a wide door at the back of the house, through which servants came and went.

And then, from one of the upstairs windows, came a sound I knew well: low notes of despair rising to a crescendo, and then the wavering, quieting sound as the pain loosened its grip. I listened to the pattern of cries three more times, in quick succession. A stout middle-aged woman, her bodice soaked with sweat and her face flushed and wet, came out of the back door. She lifted her apron and fanned her face, then beckoned. "Are you a servant here?"

"No."

"I need more linens. And hot water. I don't know where the Dona's servant has got to."

"You're the midwife?"

"Gracinha," she said, nodding. As the cries began again, she shook her head.

"She sounds near," I said. "Who is it?"

"Dona Beatriz, the daughter of Senhor Kipling. Far too old to be a mother for the first time—close to thirty." She lifted her apron again and mopped her face. "She's wearing me out. This has been going on since the middle of the night, and it should have been over long ago." A young dark-skinned girl came around the side of the house. "Jacinta," Gracinha said. "There you are. Hurry and fetch more linens, and another kettle of hot water from the kitchen."

"Can I be of help? I'm a *curandeira*, and have delivered many times."

As the girl ran off for the water and linens, Gracinha wiped away the sweat that ran down the side of one plump cheek. "You may as well come take a look at her. It can't hurt."

I sent Cristiano back to the kitchen to wait for me, then followed Gracinha through the back door, along hallways and up a flight of stairs into a bright, spacious bedroom.

Dona Beatriz lay on her back, her long dark hair tangled over her shoulders. Small diamonds twinkled in her earlobes. She gripped a corded rope tied to one of the bedposts. The room had the heavy, salted smell of sweat and fear.

"Here is someone else to help us, Dona Beatriz," Gracinha said as she bustled towards the bed. "Another *parteira*."

I poured the last of the warm water in a kettle into a basin, and washed my hands as I smiled at the woman. "*Bom dia*, Dona Beatriz," I said.

"*Inglêsa?*"

"No. But I can speak it a little."

"But your hair . . ."

"I'm a Dutchman's daughter," I said, going to the foot of the bed. "May I see how close your baby is?"

She nodded, and I pulled away the sheet and knelt, feeling for the baby. "Yes. The head is there," I said, standing again.

Her panting groan began again.

Gracinha whispered, "She doesn't work hard enough. She should have been able to push the child out hours ago."

I looked at the woman's face, contorted with pain as she pulled on the rope. "Have you tried other positions?"

Gracinha shook her head and spoke quietly. "I'm afraid to suggest she squat like a peasant. The husband keeps coming by the door and he wouldn't like it." The groans grew louder. "The Dona told me that her father wished to bring up an English physician from Funchal when her time came. The baby is a few weeks early, and the father is away. All the wealthy English use one of their physicians for childbirth. But the husband is a true Portuguese: he didn't want another man to see his wife in this situation. So they called for me. It's my first time to deliver a child on an English quinta. I'm afraid if something goes wrong I'll be blamed. I'm just trying to keep her calm and praying to the Holy Mother that she delivers safely."

Jacinta came in with an armload of linens, a kettle swinging from one hand, and set everything down and stood in the doorway.

The woman's voice rose in a warbling cry, then she fell back, panting, still holding the rope, her eyes wild.

"All right, all right," Gracinha said soothingly. "Just keep pushing. It will be over soon."

It was clear that Dona Beatriz panicked each time the pain came, and that fear made her body clench and close, the pushing ineffectual. I thought of my medicine bag in my room at Olívia's; I could have made Dona Beatriz any number of calming tisanes to drink, and applied salves to allow her to open more easily.

"You're so young to be a midwife," she said as I wiped her forehead.

"I learned from my mother," I said. "Dona Beatriz, it will be over soon if you listen to me."

She nodded, gripping my hand.

I looked over my shoulder at Gracinha. "I'll stay with her now. Go and get something to eat."

She didn't argue. "Good luck with her," she said under her breath.

I helped Dona Beatriz control her wild, ragged panting with each rise of pain by breathing with her to show her a soothing rhythm, and holding up her head and shoulders so she could push with more strength as she pulled on the rope. I kneaded her lower back between the pains, which brought her some relief.

Suddenly Dona Beatriz squeezed her eyes shut, deep guttural noises coming from her throat. I knelt at the foot of the bed, and Gracinha returned just as I guided the child, choking and then squalling, into the light.

"A boy, and healthy, God be praised," Gracinha said, taking the infant from my hands after I'd cut the cord. She rubbed the baby briskly, then stopped to cross herself. I knew she was as relieved for herself as she was for the mother.

"You did well, Dona Beatriz. You were very brave," I said, smiling at her and brushing the damp hair from her forehead with a wet cloth. She lay back, exhausted.

Her large dark eyes sloped downwards at the outer corners, giving her a slightly melancholic appearance. "Let me see him," she said, and when Gracinha held the alert baby towards her, Dona Beatriz smiled. Her nose was too long and her mouth too wide for beauty, but her cheekbones were high and fine, and her smile brought a pleasing warmth to her face. Gracinha handed the baby to me and I washed it and swaddled it as Gracinha attended to the afterbirth and changing the bedding and helping Dona Beatriz into a fresh nightgown. She called over her shoulder for Jacinta to find the husband.

As Dona Beatriz lay quietly, smiling at her baby in my arms, Gracinha bustled about, restoring the bedroom to order. A shadow filled the doorway. "Your husband, Dona Beatriz," Gracinha said, "here to meet his son."

I glanced at the door, but the light falling from the bright hallway behind the man was dazzling, shadowing his face. "A son, Beatriz. You have indeed given me the son you promised."

At the familiar voice, my hands were suddenly numb, although I held the child tightly against my chest.

"Yes, your boy is here," Dona Beatriz said.

As the man walked towards me, all sound fell away. I willed myself to stand strong in the deafening silence, and look into the face of Abílio Perez.

CHAPTER FORTY-FIVE

Abílio opened his mouth as if to speak, then shut it abruptly.
"See how beautiful he is, Abílio," Dona Beatriz said.

"Yes, let me hold my son." Abílio's voice was flannelled. He had
to clear his throat: a normal reaction for a man seeing his first-born.
"Give him to me," he said in the demanding tone I remembered so
well. He looked even more handsome and confident than when I had
last seen him on Porto Santo, and now wore fine English clothing.

As I passed the swaddled newborn to him, his knuckles grazed
my breast. I drew in a breath at his touch.

"This woman is Gracinha's helper, although she came almost too
late. What is your name?" Dona Beatriz asked. She spoke with the
authority of someone used to giving commands, and of having her
demands met.

I let two heartbeats pass. When Abílio remained silent, I under-
stood how it was to be, and felt a surge of relief. "I am Senhora
Rivaldo. Diamantina Rivaldo. And . . . I don't work with Gracinha,
Dona Beatriz. I came to the quinta with my husband. He was meet-
ing with . . . your husband," I said, knowing now that Abílio was
the son-in-law Espirito had spoken of. "I heard your cries, and . . ."
I stopped. Feeling Abílio's gaze on me, my heart thumped so loudly
I thought they would hear.

He sat on the edge of the bed with the baby, and Dona Beatriz
reached out and stroked her husband's shoulder. He stared down
at the child in his arms, then unwrapped the blanket. The baby
stretched his legs and yawned.

Abílio picked up one little hand, and then the other, studying them. He did the same with the feet. Then he looked at his wife. "He is a fine child, perfect in every way. Thank you, Beatriz," he said with a soft smile, and Dona Beatriz returned it.

I stood as if stone, wanting to be away from Abílio, from Dona Beatriz and their baby and this moment of intimacy. Watching him with this woman—his wife—as he looked at her with tenderness and thanked her, in a voice of wonder, filled me with a terrible rawness.

"I will go now," I said briskly.

"I want you to stay," Dona Beatriz said. She looked at Gracinha, standing in the doorway. "Gracinha, you will be well paid, but you can leave. Summon the wet nurse as you go."

"I'll return tomorrow," Gracinha said.

"No, Diamantina will stay and look after me," Dona Beatriz said. Then, looking at me, said, "I wish you to remain here for the next few days."

"No," I said loudly, going towards the door. "I can't stay."

"Abílio," Dona Beatriz said, "reward her as she asks. But it is my request that she stay."

"I'm sorry, Dona Beatriz, but it's truly impossible," I said firmly. I needed to get away from Abílio. "My husband is waiting for me. I have to go back to Funchal."

Still holding the baby, Abílio came to me. "You must stay, Diamantina. I just met your husband. Bonifacio, isn't it? I'm certain he would wish you to do as my wife asks. After all, I will soon be choosing the man for the new position."

I understood. I swallowed, then took a step to one side so I could speak directly to Dona Beatriz. "I must talk to my husband first."

"Tell him I have demanded that you stay," she said again.

"Yes, Diamantina," Abílio echoed, with the warm, familiar smile I knew so well. "You have to stay."

⁂

Gracinha and I went down the back stairs and out of the house together. "Such ingratitude," she grumbled. "I spent so long with her, and then she tosses me aside. I was hoping to stay much of the week, and expected a more handsome payment than this." She slapped the pocket of her apron and the coins there jingled.

"I'm sorry," I said. "It wasn't my intention—" But she had turned from me, headed down the road leading to the wide gates of the quinta. I went to the kitchen, walking slowly, trying to compose myself, trying not to let my face betray my shock. I remembered my first day in Funchal, how I believed my eyes were tricking me when I thought I saw Abílio Perez.

Bonifacio and Espirito and Cristiano were eating with some of the others in the kitchen. Jacinta had given everyone the news about the birth of Senhor Kipling's grandson, and they were all talking about it. I sat beside Bonifacio, but shook my head when a woman offered me a bowl of stew.

"Where have you been?" Bonifacio said. "I was finished some time ago. Cristiano said you went into the big house. Is this true?"

"I helped Dona Beatriz."

"With the birth?" Espirito asked, and I nodded.

"She wants me to stay, Bonifacio," I said.

He frowned. "Stay? Why? And for how long?"

"She preferred that I care for her and the baby for a few days, but I don't really want to."

Espirito said, "If you don't want to do this, perhaps I can speak to Senhor Perez and—"

I interrupted. "Since Bonifacio is hoping to work for Senhor Kipling, I feel pressured to agree. I'll go back to Funchal with you to get some clothes and my medicine bag, and then return."

"Very few can deny Dona Beatriz's demands," Espirito said, smiling.

Bonifacio stood, and I looked up at him. "How did the meeting go?" I asked, trying to visualize Abílio talking to him.

"He has others to see. Now I just wait to hear his verdict."

⁂

When I came back to Quinta Isabella with my small case and my medicine bag, Binta greeted me and took me to the back door of the big house. "You're expected. Whenever you wish to eat, go to the kitchen and Nini will serve you."

I went up the narrow back stairs, glancing at the portraits and the paintings of country fields and seascapes that lined the walls. At the top of the stairs I went through a doorway onto the huge landing. When I had followed Gracinha in and then out of Dona Beatriz's room, I hadn't been able to take in all I saw, but now I walked slowly around the square landing. A wide, broad staircase descended to an even larger entry hall below.

I stopped counting the bedrooms at seven. As in Olívia and Espirito's home, there was also a lavatory and a room with a tub for bathing.

The wet nurse, a young Portuguese woman, sat in one corner of the room nursing the baby while Dona Beatriz lay on her bed. She was very still, very pale, and her eyes were closed. I looked around the room, now tidy and calm. There was a pretty dressing table with a frilly skirt. On its top were open cases of gold and silver bracelets and necklaces, gemstones glinting in rings and ear bobs. A number of glass flagons of perfume sat in an organized row.

Two huge wardrobes lined one wall. The bed of dark polished wood had four high posts, and overhead the canopy was of the finest lace. A lacy cover was spread over the bed, and the mounds of pillows were crisp and blindingly white. I tried to imagine Abílio in this room, in this bed.

"How do you feel, Dona?" I asked, setting down my bags.

She opened her eyes. "I'm glad you're back." She grimaced. "I still have pains, the same pains as before. I don't understand why."

I pulled back the coverlet and gently pressed her abdomen. "Everything feels as it should. Sometimes the womb keeps tightening. I'll make you an infusion of herbs that calm the womb after birth." As I put my medicine bag on a table and opened it, Abílio came in.

"Will it stop the pain right away?" Dona Beatriz asked.

"Very soon," I told her, and turned my back to Abílio and set out my mortar and pestle, as well as an earthenware jar and two paper folds of leaves. Abílio's presence made my hands shake, and I didn't want him to witness the effect he had on me. As I bruised tansy leaves, I breathed in the rising smell of camphor. I sent Jacinta for boiling water, and when she returned with a kettle, I mixed an infusion of the tansy with a pinch of rue. I took out an earthenware jar and removed the stopper.

"What's that soapy smell?" Dona Beatriz called.

I turned to her, holding the earthenware jar. "This is oil of flea-bane, very effective and very powerful."

"Fleabane?" she repeated.

"It's poisonous to both animals and humans unless used very carefully. The leaves are salty when crushed, so animals spit it out at the first bite."

"You're not giving me poison," she said with a slightly alarmed tone.

I smiled at her. "Just the tiniest amount won't hurt you. There are many medicines that can either help or harm. It's how they're used." I tipped the container and let a drop fall onto a spoon, and then stirred it into the tea as she watched me closely. "It's very hot," I told her, handing her the cup. "Just take small sips. In a short time the pains will lessen." I hadn't looked at Abílio, who was little more than a shadow on the other side of the bed.

"Thank you," she said to me, blowing on the tea. "Please go and enjoy your dinner in the kitchen. My husband will stay with me until you return. Jacinta will make you a bed on the settee, and you can sleep there tonight, in case I need you."

I tidied my medicines, then left for my dinner.

❧

I was relieved Abílio was gone when I came back to Dona Beatriz's room, where Jacinta was preparing her for the night. The Dona's after-birth pains had stopped, and a book lay open and face down on her bed. I glanced at it: *Os Lusíadas* by Luís Vaz de Camões.

When Jacinta left, Dona Beatriz picked up the book, but then dropped it. "I'm too tired to read, and yet don't feel like sleeping just yet," she said.

"Would you like me to read to you?" I asked.

"You read?"

"Yes."

"But this poetry is perhaps a bit dense."

I picked up the book and smiled at her. "We'll see how it goes."

⁓

Dona Beatriz slept well, only waking once to ask for a drink of water and for me to help her to the *latrina*. In the morning the wet nurse brought the clean, fed baby to her.

She took him and looked down at him, jiggling him a little. "Leandro," she crooned. "My little Leandro."

"The whites of his eyes and his skin are a bit yellow," I told her. "It's common in many newborns." A thin line of milk dribbled from the baby's bottom lip, and he fussed and squirmed. I turned to the wet nurse. "I'll make you an infusion of comfrey leaf to drink for the next few days. That will help. Also, unwrap the baby and lay him in sunlight twice a day, letting the sun shine on his bare skin for a few minutes each time. After three or four days his colour will be fine." I held him against my shoulder and patted his back firmly. In a moment the baby let out a resounding belch, and immediately quieted.

"Do you have children?" Dona Beatriz asked.

I stroked the white silk ribbon running through Leandro's layered white dress. "No. Although my husband and I are raising a boy, Cristiano." I lifted the baby closer to touch my lips to the velvety new skin of his forehead, then stopped, realizing I had no business taking such a liberty.

"I'm sure your own child will arrive soon," she said.

"We've been married less than seven months. Not a long time yet." I looked down at the baby again, admiring his long dark eyelashes.

"No," Dona Beatriz said softly. "Not a long time. We have only been married a little longer, less than a year."

I smiled at her. "You have named your son Leandro."

"Leandro Martinho Duarte Kipling Perez."

"A fine name."

"Martinho for my father, of course. And Duarte for my mother. She was Isabella Duarte. My father built this quinta for her when they married." She paused. "She died last year."

"My mother also died in the last year," I told her.

"And my younger sister too. They . . ." She stopped, blinking. "They died of the black pox." She looked back at me and held out her arms for her baby, and I set the child in them.

I crossed the yard to have my breakfast in the kitchen. Partway there, Abílio met me.

"I was waiting for you. How do you find my wife and son today?" he asked, looking at me with a slight smile.

"They're both well. But the birth was hard on your wife. You have to give her time to heal," I said, hoping he felt my accusation.

Abílio looked around the yard and, obviously satisfied that no one paid us any attention, said, "Would you like your husband to be given the position in the Counting House?"

I crossed my arms over my chest. "You implied that it would help your decision if I stayed as your wife asked."

"Now that you know I am to be his superior, are you still so interested?"

I didn't answer. Of course I had thought about this through the long night on the settee in Dona Beatriz's room.

"Surely this would be an improvement over your life in . . . your husband said Curral das Freiras?"

"Yes."

"You've given up your dream of Brazil, then, and married a poor man from the mountains?" One side of his mouth pulled up in a half smile.

"No. I haven't given up my plan. It was never just a dream, as I once told you."

He kept looking at me with an expression I didn't recognize.

"And what of you?" I said. "You married a wealthy woman, older than you, a woman who can assure you of a prosperous career and lavish life. No future with your uncle in fish sauce, then?"

He didn't answer.

"So you're thinking that you have won out over me, Abílio? Is that what you wish to hear? That you have won?"

He waited a moment before speaking. "As you were perhaps surprised to see my choice of a wife, I was surprised to see your choice of a husband. Definitely not the kind of man who would inspire passion in you, Diamantina."

"I don't care what you think of my choices."

"You got away from Porto Santo, but I think it's important to you that your husband is employed by one of the most prosperous wine merchants on Madeira. Yes, I do think you would like this. I know you. Don't forget that, Diamantina." He glanced at the calluses on my hands, and in my mind I saw the smooth perfection of his wife's highly polished fingernails. "Life in Funchal would be a great improvement for you," he said softly, as if truly caring about my happiness and well-being. "So maybe"—he tapped his bottom lip with his index finger—"maybe you and I can work something out. I'm sure we can find a way that will guarantee your husband the position."

A slow and ugly sensation, like dark, heavy air, came over me. Just as he said he knew me, I knew Abílio Perez all too well.

"At one o'clock you will tell my wife that you are taking your midday meal. And then I'd like you to visit me in my office, just there," he said, lifting his chin towards a building set to one side of the yard, "so we can discuss how I might be able to persuade my father-in-law to hire your husband."

I hadn't taken my eyes from his face.

"Your future is in your own hands, Diamantina. I'm sure your husband is no more capable than many others who have come seeking the position. With my marriage to Beatriz, I became an important part of the Kipling management. My father-in-law will ask my opinion, and he will take it seriously. Should you visit me as I ask"— he paused—"and we come to an agreement, I will tell Martyn that without a doubt the best man for the post is Bonifacio Rivaldo."

I could simply say no and turn away. I would tell Dona Beatriz I could not stay another day. Bonifacio would be informed that he had not obtained the position. And then? I knew now that Olívia would never allow Cristiano and me to stay with her and Espirito until my father's letter came. I would be forced to return to the mountains, where Bonifacio would try to find work after the *senhorio* took back the land and house. And there I would spend much of the next year scrubbing dirty clothing and cooking for another family. We might have to live in an outbuilding, or a cow byre. But it couldn't be worse than a mud hut. I could do it. I had done many things I didn't want to do.

"You certainly don't want to live out your life in Curral das Freiras, do you?" Abílio said, as if reading my thoughts.

In my mind, I saw the shaky scrawl of my father's last letter. Until today I had refused to allow myself to think that he might die before he received my letter. Or that the ship crossing with either my letter or his would go down at sea. I had to believe that my father would live a long time. That he would receive my letter, and send the money that would allow me to leave Bonifacio and come to him.

This is what I had to believe.

"This may be your only chance to better your life, Diamantina," Abílio said then, and I realized I was looking into his face without seeing him. "Your *last* chance," he said, and a chill ran over me as we stood in the warm morning sunshine.

CHAPTER FORTY-SIX

As midday approached, I excused myself from Dona Beatriz and used the lavatory to fix myself with a sponge. I crossed the yard and knocked on the frame of the open office door. Abílio looked up from the desk and smiled. "Well, Senhora Rivaldo," he said, "you have not disappointed me. Come inside and close the door behind you. And lock it."

I did as he asked and then turned to face him.

"Of course, I expected you. Once a whore, always a whore."

"What guarantee do I have that you will do as you say, Abílio?" I asked, my back against the door. "I know you won't disclose that you know me, because then you would disclose your own truths."

He watched me.

"I'm right, aren't I? I'm sure you haven't told your father-in-law or wife the truth about your past. It's clear you've passed yourself off as something more than an island boy, the son of a fisherman. What guarantee do I have," I repeated, "that my husband will be given the position? How do I know you won't betray me?" I tilted my head, and added, "Again."

He came close enough to take my chin in his hand. He ran his other palm over my cheek. I smelled his familiar odour of excitement, high and sharp, and tried to stop myself from quivering.

I remembered the old feelings so strongly, and fought them.

"Even my wife, born of noble Portuguese and fine English heritage, doesn't possess skin like yours." He continued to caress my cheek, then his index finger traced the scar in my eyebrow. "Life has played with you, hasn't it, Diamantina?" he murmured as his other hand slowly enclosed my breast.

"You haven't answered me," I said, looking into his eyes. "What assurance do I have?"

He pressed against me, hard and insistent. "You have my word." There was a whiff of fermented sweetness on his breath: Kipling's Malvasia. In that moment I shocked myself, realizing I wanted to taste his lips, to lick and suck the sweetness from them. Why? Didn't I hate this man? And yet my body wanted what it remembered. I wanted to be touched. To feel something.

"Your word?" I said, struggling to control my voice. "Do you think I believe in your word?"

"Diamantina," Abílio said, the smile emerging again as the pressure of his hand on my breast and the front of his breeches against my hip increased. "What choice do you have but to believe me?" He pulled down the front of my blouse and my shift and put his hands on my bare breasts, then kissed each nipple. I drew in my breath, repulsed, and yet at the same time the tiniest involuntary flicker of pleasure flooded through my body.

He undid his breeches and pushed up my skirt. He guided himself into me, and I was further disgusted with myself to know I was ready for him.

He shoved me up and down against the door, the back of my head softly bumping with each of his thrusts. Eventually he removed himself and pulled me with him to the settee. He lay down and positioned me atop him, again tracing my scar with his fingertips. I fought not to lose myself, not to let him know some very small part of me wanted this. That it both felt terrible and yet brought something like relief.

Was I really this simple, like an animal in heat? My marriage was not a real marriage, and I did not feel guilt as much as a sense that I was debasing myself with Abílio Perez. It made me feel ill, made me feel I hated myself. I closed my eyes and let the sensations of my body take over my thoughts.

Afterwards, as we lay together on the settee, I tried to imagine him with his wife. She was a dignified noblewoman. Surely he didn't treat her with the same abandonment he had just shown with me.

Surely, after he had made love to her, he pulled down her sleeping gown, stroked her cheek and whispered good night.

Then again, this was not making love. This was an act of lust.

He unexpectedly laughed, and I propped myself on my elbow and looked at him. "What do you find amusing?"

"I was thinking of your long-faced husband. He doesn't satisfy you when he fucks you, does he?" So he was imagining me with Bonifacio as I was thinking of him with Dona Beatriz. "Does he enjoy fucking you, or does he feel it his duty? He seems a rather dull man. Tell me, Diamantina, when your husband fucks you, do you excite yourself with memories of the other men who have satisfied you? Do you excite yourself with thoughts of me?" He picked up the hem of my skirt and wiped himself with it.

I yanked my skirt away and rose, walking to the door.

"Come back," he said, patting the side of the settee. He hadn't bothered to pull up his breeches.

"Why?"

"This is part of the bargain. I waited for you to come to me, and now you will wait until I tell you you're allowed to go."

I stayed where I was for a moment, and then slowly walked back to the settee.

"Tell me about it, Diamantina. Tell me how your husband fucks you." He was looking up at me, and took my hand. I pulled back, but he held it tightly.

"What happens between my husband and me is no concern of yours," I said, and studied a whorl in the painted wood of the wall. I felt the heat of Abílio's hand around mine. I didn't want to look back at him. "I have to go."

"No you don't. Beatriz will survive without you a while longer." His hand was caressing my fingers. "Tonight her father will arrive from Lisboa, and tomorrow morning he and I will meet. After that I'll inform the lucky man I have decided most deserves this position, with its substantial wage. It affords a definite change of life from poor provincial ways, I guarantee you."

I looked back at him, and he finally let me take my hand from his.

He stood and pulled up his breeches and tied them. "I may need

one more reason to choose a particular man. After dark tonight."
When I said nothing, he added, "Well? Do you plan to help me make
my final decision? It seems absurd to only go half the distance,
Diamantina. When Beatriz is asleep tonight, come here again." He
smoothed back his hair with his palms. "One more thing. Let us be
very clear. I'm not forcing you into anything. What you are doing,
you do out of free will. You do it because you are a whore, and will
always use what lies between your legs to get what you want. Isn't this
true? Say it, Diamantina, say, I will come to you, Abílio, because I am
a whore. I am a filthy whore, and I enjoy it. Say it." His pupils pulsed.
What pleasure he was deriving from making me humiliate myself.

Without blinking, I stared into his face. "I am a filthy whore.
And I enjoy it."

"Ah." A wide smile. "That wasn't so difficult, was it?"

I turned to go. I wanted to slam the door with all my might, but
as I stepped out into the bright sunlight and the hub of the courtyard, I closed it gently behind me. I couldn't afford to draw attention to myself.

That evening, as Jacinta took away the tray of food she'd brought
Dona Beatriz, I gathered up my herbs and jars from the table, packing them into my medicine bag. The baby was in the nursery with
his wet nurse.

"I'm glad you've recovered so quickly," I told her. "I'll be leaving
tomorrow morning. My husband is coming to take me back to Funchal
first thing."

Dona Beatriz rubbed sweet-smelling lotion onto her hands. "I
find it lonely with my father away."

"Isn't he returning tonight?"

"Yes. I'll be asleep when he arrives," she said, smiling now, "but
wait until he sees Leandro. He'll be so happy," she went on. "He
hoped for a grandson, and Leandro will be the next Kipling to run
the business." She fiddled with her hair, yanking out a silver ribbon.
"Abílio likes me to wear my hair like this, but I know it doesn't suit

me." She held out the ribbon to me. "You wear it. It will pick up the colour in your eyes."

I remembered the ribbons Abílio had bought for me on Porto Santo. I took it and set it on the table. "You should sleep now, Dona." I went to her and arranged her bedding. "I'll be on the settee should you need me."

She lay down and turned away from me, and within moments was breathing in a slow, quiet rhythm.

⁂

Once the estate was in darkness save for a white, cold moon, I crossed the deserted yard. The dogs knew me now, and although one rose, nose in the air, it immediately lay down again.

Abílio waited with his door open, a lantern dimly lit. An opened bottle of wine and two glasses were on the desk. "Sit with me, and have a drink, Diamantina," he said as he shut and locked the door. "We will toast Porto Santo," he said, pouring the rich amber liquid into the first glass. "To the past. To you, and to me, Diamantina, and to our secrets."

"No," I said, going directly to the settee and sitting on it. "This isn't a visit between friends, Abílio."

Abílio drained his glass. "Are we not friends?" He came to the settee. "I can think of nothing more friendly than you giving yourself to me so willingly." As he put his arms around me and kissed me, I willed myself not to respond. But my will wasn't strong enough.

⁂

Afterwards, as I was smoothing my hair in the mirror over the settee, Abílio stood behind me. He put his hands on my shoulders, then down around my breasts, and ran his fingers over my rib cage.

I pushed his hands away. "Bonifacio is coming to the quinta for me tomorrow morning. You will tell him he has the position then."

"As we discussed," he answered. "But for now, take off your clothes."

I stared at his reflection in the mirror.

"I have never seen all of you. I want to, now." He undid the lacings at the back of my blouse. I was watching his face in the mirror, and was pleased to see the look that came over it as he saw my shoulders and the top of my spine. He stepped away.

"What's wrong, Abílio? Don't you like what you see?" I undid my skirt and pushed it down, then pulled my arms out of my sleeves and dropped my blouse on the floor beside my skirt. I yanked my shift over my head in one swift movement and stood naked so that he could see my entire back. "You don't like it?" I repeated, watching him in the mirror.

"Who did it?"

"My mother. She wrote my future on my back." I let him stare for another moment, remembering how, long ago, I'd envisioned his fingers tracing the vines. "Do you see yourself there, Abílio?" He didn't answer, meeting my eyes in the mirror, and after a moment I put my shift back on, then pulled on my skirt and blouse. "Lace it up, please," I said, and he did as I asked. Then he moved away from me and poured himself a drink. I liked that the bottle shuddered against the wineglass with the smallest tinkle as he poured.

I turned from the mirror and arranged something like a smile on my face, opening the door. "I'll see you tomorrow, then, when you give my husband the good news."

As I closed the door behind me, clouds moved across the moon, creating brief, shifting shafts of pale light. I looked back at the office. Abílio had turned up the lantern as if to dispel the shadows in the room, and the glow through the window was bright.

And then Espirito was in front of me, his own lantern held high. We both stopped. He glanced at the office behind me. Had he seen me coming down the steps? We stood for a moment. Crickets screeched.

"What are you doing here?" I asked.

"I brought Senhor Kipling up from the bay. I'm just on my way back to Funchal." He was studying me. "And you, Diamantina?"

"What?" I pulled my shawl tighter around my shoulders, moving my face from the light of his lantern.

He lowered it. "What are you doing out so late, away from Dona Beatriz?"

I cleared my throat. "I've been with her all day and evening. She's sleeping, and I . . . felt the need of some air."

"Ah," Espirito said. He bowed slightly, and I couldn't see his face in the shadows. "May I accompany you back to the house? It's difficult walking without the benefit of a candle or lantern, and I see you've come out with neither."

"Yes," I said, annoyed at the faintness of my answer.

Espirito put his hand on my elbow to guide me, holding the lantern high to light our way. I was sure he could smell Abílio on me. We didn't speak, and I felt such an awkwardness that I knew Espirito also felt it. At the back door of the house, he removed his hand.

"Sleep well, Diamantina," he said, and such was my discomfort, my shame, threaded with the tiniest hope that he really hadn't seen me coming from Abílio's office, that I couldn't even utter the words to wish him a good night.

CHAPTER FORTY-SEVEN

"**F**ather!" Dona Beatriz cried, sitting up.

The early morning sunlight flooded Dona Beatriz's bedroom as her father came to her. I stepped away from the bed as he leaned down to kiss her on both cheeks. "I just saw my grandson in the nursery," he said in English. "What a fine boy, and the next owner of Kipling's! You have made me proud, daughter." He patted her hand. "You are well?"

She nodded, answering him in English, "I feel much better now."

Senhor Kipling turned to me. "And this is . . ." He studied my face.

"This is Diamantina, Father," Dona Beatriz said.

"Which family are you from? What is your surname, miss?" He was unthreatening, his face pleasant.

"I am new in Funchal," I said slowly. "And I am not English."

"Oh. Well, I thought . . . well," he said, glancing at his daughter.

"I am a *curandeira*," I said. "I helped Dona Beatriz with the birth, and afterwards."

Senhor Kipling looked back at his daughter. "The physician I chose to attend wasn't here?"

Dona Beatriz looked at the coverlet, picking at a loose thread. "Abílio didn't wish him to come."

Senhor Kipling shook his head, frowning, but in the next moment smiled again. "Well, it appears both you and Leandro are well, so there was no harm done."

"Yes, Father," Dona Beatriz said.

I excused myself and went to the nursery.

When I heard Senhor Kipling leave Dona Beatriz's room, I returned to gather my things, accepting the purse of coins Senhor Kipling had left for me. I said goodbye to Dona Beatriz and wished her well.

"Thank you again, Diamantina," she said.

As I walked around the broad upper landing, I heard voices from the open hallway below and looked over the railing. It was Senhor Kipling and another man. As the man congratulated the senhor on his new grandson, I realized it was Henry Duncan.

I drew back a little as Abílio came in and shook Mr. Duncan's hand and was congratulated about the baby.

"Have you found the right man for the Counting House, Abílio?" Senhor Kipling asked, continuing to speak English.

"I don't . . . what did you say?" Abílio asked in halting English.

"The Counting House. Did you find a man for the position?" Senhor Kipling's voice held an edge of impatience.

"The Counting House. Yes." Abílio said, struggling with each word.

"Good." Senhor Kipling turned to Mr. Duncan. "Let's discuss our partnership further over breakfast, Henry. Combining our resources will double our power and export each year."

"In Oporto, is . . ." Abílio started, then stopped. Both men looked at him. "In Oporto is good. We sell port to America . . . more good than wine to Brazil."

Martyn Kipling's voice rose. "Damn it, Abílio, your English has to improve. How can you be influential if you can't converse confidently? You'll be dealing with more English than Portuguese. And the nonsense about port . . . I'm sorry, Henry. And not just for his English. My son-in-law, after less than a year in the business, has his own ideas."

I saw Abílio's hands fisted at his sides, and could imagine his expression.

"We can speak Portuguese if it makes it easier," Mr. Duncan said as the men moved towards one of the open doorways.

Martyn Kipling shook his head. "I've told him it was part of his responsibility to speak English fluently if he expects to play a major role."

Mr. Duncan cleared his throat awkwardly as the three men disappeared into what I assumed was the dining room.

I went to the kitchen and sat with my bags at my feet. Eventually Bonifacio appeared.

"How is Cristiano?" I asked, but before he could answer, Abílio stood in the doorway.

"I was watching for you, Bonifacio," he said.

My empty stomach churned. Would Abílio do as he had promised, or would he smile the smile I hated and tell Bonifacio that I had come to him, twice? Would he tell him it was my old habit—that I was simply repeating my sins from Porto Santo?

But he bowed low to me, the very picture of good breeding and respect. "Good morning, Senhora Rivaldo. I'm sorry to see you're looking a little tired. Did my wife make many demands on you through the night?" He was a brilliant liar. I was not. I kept my hands clasped in my lap to hide their trembling. "I don't know if you're aware, Bonifacio, how very helpful your wife was during my wife's lying-in, and in these last few days."

"I was glad to be of comfort to Dona Beatriz," I said after a moment.

"And were you treated well during your brief stay?"

"Yes."

"What do you think of the quinta, senhora?" Abílio asked. He was enjoying this little game.

"It's beautiful."

"And you, Bonifacio? What do you think of the grounds and the glorious view from our prominent position on this hill?"

"Very peaceful, Senhor Perez. And, as my wife says, very beautiful."

"Does it compare to your home in Curral das Freiras?"

My breath was ragged in my ears. Was he making fun of us? Forcing us to compliment him on his wealth and stature?

"It's a different part of Madeira, as you know," Bonifacio said.

"So you would admit that it's a better life here, high above Funchal, with our glorious view of the sea, than in the belly of the mountains?"

Bonifacio frowned slightly.

Abílio clapped his hands together, once. "Well, I'm taking too long to get to the point. I just wanted to make sure that you were impressed by our quinta," he said, stepping closer to Bonifacio, "because I'm offering the position to you, Senhor Rivaldo. I would like you to take on the title of manager of the Counting House of Kipling's Wine Merchants."

A small sound came from my throat. Relief, but I hoped it passed as pleasure.

Bonifacio's eyes widened as if he hadn't really expected to hear this news.

"That's not all. I'm also offering your good wife the role of *curandeira* for the quinta. There are a number of servants and slaves, as you've seen, and there's always need for some medicinal assistance. Although Senhor Kipling himself likes to enlist the help of an English physician from Funchal, the islanders are more comfortable with one of their own. Especially the females." He looked at me. "Your wife is such a competent woman, from what Dona Beatriz has told me. I'm sure Senhora Rivaldo's many talents will serve her well here on Quinta Isabella." He extended his hand to Bonifacio. "I would like to offer our guest cottage to you and your family. Living here will ensure that Senhora Rivaldo is always close at hand for those who might need her."

A tick beat under my left eye. So Abílio assumed that I would continue playing his whore?

"In case I haven't made myself clear, the cottage will be yours to live in, with no payment necessary, as long as you both work for Kipling's in the capacities I have offered."

Bonifacio took Abílio's hand then and shook it. "Thank you, Senhor Perez. We are, of course, very pleased. Both of us," he said, glancing at me.

"It's done, then," Abílio said. "We wish you to begin at the Counting House at the start of next week."

"Certainly," Bonifacio said.

"If you'd like to come to my office, we can sign the necessary papers."

As he and Bonifacio went towards the door, he looked back at me. "Your wife, Bonifacio, has arrived as if an angel from above. I don't know how my Beatriz would have fared without her gentle touch." His eyelids lowered just the slightest. "Welcome to Quinta Isabella, Senhora Rivaldo."

CHAPTER FORTY-EIGHT

Bonifacio and I rode back to Funchal in a bullock cart. Both of us were silent. I didn't know whether he was pleased at all, or simply accepting, about his new life. My own thoughts circled dangerously. Abílio would be able to call on me at any time, threatening to dismiss Bonifacio if I didn't submit to his wishes.

When Espirito came to the table for dinner, he smiled at Bonifacio. "I'm happy it's worked out. And that you were offered the cottage to live in . . . Bonifacio, this is very unexpected."

"It's because Senhor Perez wants her as *curandeira* for the quinta," Bonifacio said. "It's not my doing." I fussed with my napkin, not wanting to meet Espirito's eyes. I was afraid if I looked into his face, he would guess why I had been near Abílio's office.

By the time we had finished the meal, I uncovered another truth: what disturbed me most about my sinful and adulterous behaviour was the thought of Espirito suspecting me of it. And thinking less of me.

❧

The next day, Bonifacio and Espirito were to return to Curral das Freiras to fetch all of our belongings from the house, and would be gone three to four days.

As Bonifacio went ahead down the stairs, I touched Espirito's arm.

"Thank you."

"For what?"

I cleared my throat. "For offering Bonifacio—us—this opportunity."

"Bonifacio is my brother. I have made it my duty to do what I can to help him. Protect him, if necessary."

Although his words were said in a completely natural manner, I drew in a breath as if rebuked. But he didn't say anything more, and then disappeared down the stairs.

⌒

On the afternoon of the third day after the men left, Ana was polishing furniture and Cristiano playing with his wooden animals while Olívia and I sat reading in the salon. I was wearing my new green gown, and kept smoothing it down over my thighs, unable to stop touching it. There was a sudden knocking on the front door. Olívia and I jumped.

"I'm not expecting anyone," she said, and sent Ana downstairs to see who it was.

"Could it be Bonifacio and Espirito back early?" I asked.

"Espirito would use his key."

Ana reappeared, followed by a man I didn't recognize. He turned his hat in his hand. "I must speak to you, Senhora Rivaldo," he said, and I put my hand to my chest. My first, unreasonable thought was that Abílio had sent for me.

"Yes?" I said.

"No. The other Senhora Rivaldo," he said. "Is your husband here? He's not in the *adega*."

"He had to go away for a few days, Raimundo. He should return tonight or tomorrow," Olívia said, standing. "What's happened?"

"I was sent to tell him the news." Raimundo was turning and turning his hat. "It's very bad, senhora. Very bad."

Olívia felt for the chair and sat down.

"It's Senhor Kipling, senhora. He is dead."

The clock ticked on the mantel. Outside, a child cried, its voice echoing against the tall stone buildings. I looked at Olívia. She was ashen, her chest rising and falling in trembling breaths, her mouth open. I went to her and put my hand on her shoulder.

"What happened?" I asked Raimundo.

"I don't know, senhora. He was found early this morning. The estate is in great shock. And Senhor Perez also told me to bring you back."

Here it was. I swallowed. "Me? Why?"

"I am the messenger, senhora. I am here to bring the terrible news, and to take you back to the quinta."

I looked at Olívia. "Should I go?"

She took a long, ragged breath. "You must. You work for them now."

"I don't like to leave you like this." It was clear the shock of the news had affected her deeply.

"Ana will fetch my mother. It's all right. Go." She sat in her chair, her chin up as she struggled for breath.

"You stay here, Cristiano," I said to the little boy, who had moved to Olívia's side. I ran up to my bedroom for my medicine bag and shawl, and then left with Raimundo.

⚮

There was a hushed air about the whole quinta. In the yard, the servants were gathered and talking in low voices, some of the women weeping quietly.

Jacinta came to me, telling me that Dona Beatriz had sent for me, and I closed my eyes in relief that it hadn't been Abílio. The wet nurse sat on a cane chair outside the door. Jacinta knocked and, when there was no answer, opened the door and stepped aside for me to enter.

Dona Beatriz lay in the wide bed, almost disappearing into the white bed linens, apart from her hair. It was undone, hanging over her shoulders. The baby was in her arms. She looked at me, her cheeks wet and her eyes swollen.

"Dona Beatriz. I'm so sorry about your father," I told her, coming close and putting my hand on Leandro's head. He was alert, and

I was pleased to see his colour pink and healthy now. He was a handsome child, with his mother's down-turned eyes and his father's full lips.

Dona Beatriz drew in a stuttering breath, and a sob erupted from her throat. "I need you to make me something to calm me. My grief . . . I don't feel I can bear it."

"Of course." I opened my medicine bag and took out two vials.

"I don't know what to do. I can't . . ." She was trembling as she picked up one of Leandro's tiny curled hands, gently caressing it as if for strength. "My mother and my sister. Now my father." She wept. "Stay with me. I can't be alone."

"Where is your husband?"

"He went into Funchal," she said through her sobs, "to speak to the priest about the funeral. I told him not to go until tomorrow. I wanted him here with me, but . . ."

I poured water from a jug into a glass and stirred in the powders. I brought the glass to her. "Drink this, Dona Beatriz. Was your father ill?" I asked as she took a few sips. He had seemed full of good health when I'd met him four days earlier. She handed me the glass and I put it on the table beside the bed.

"Nothing was wrong with him. He had dinner with us last night—with Abílio and me. It was the first time I'd left my bed since I had Leandro. We were all happy and laughing. My father entertained us with stories from Lisboa. He ate a full meal, and enjoyed his usual glass of Verdelho. But he did say that his hands felt numb."

"A sign of the heart failing, perhaps," I said, drawing a chair close to the bed and sitting near her.

"He decided to go to bed early. When he stood, I saw that he was dizzy. Abílio gave him another glass of Verdelho to take to his bedchamber, telling him it would help him sleep."

Something grew cold in my chest, and my arms felt prickly.

"Early this morning, when the maid went in . . ." Dona Beatriz wept harder, holding the baby against her with one hand while pressing the delicate embroidered bed linen to her face with the other, her shoulders shaking. She lowered her head, and her scalp looked pale and tender. When she again looked at me, I saw tiny broken blood vessels around her eyes from crying.

Leandro's mouth opened, searching, and he made small sounds of distress. I lifted him from Dona Beatriz's arm and took him out to the wet nurse.

When I came back, I stood at the foot of the bed, and she continued. "The maid said that when she'd gone in to ask if my father wanted anything last night, he'd spoken to her in an odd way, as if he was seeing something that wasn't there. He also seemed unable to walk. I asked her why she didn't come and tell me, but she said my father frightened her, and threatened her. She thought perhaps it was intoxication. But my father would never behave like that, ever.

"When the physician came this morning and looked at . . . at my father, he said he suspected he'd suffered a number of seizures through the night. He said we might never know what it was—perhaps he had caught some unknown disease in Lisboa, or on the ship, and . . . Diamantina? What's wrong?"

I gripped the post of the bed, a loud buzzing in my ears as the room took on the whiteness of the bed linens and pulsed with a bright light. I heard Dona Beatriz's voice as if from far away and, without permission, lowered myself onto the end of the bed.

"I apologize," I said, blinking as my vision cleared. "Perhaps it's heat . . ." She had described poisoning by the oil of fleabane: the dizziness and numbness in the extremities, the hallucinations and seizures leading to death. I remembered talking about fleabane's toxicity in front of Abílio.

Dona Beatriz lifted the glass again, drinking until it was empty. I watched her, and wanted to leave. I couldn't stay here, thinking about Abílio poisoning Martyn Kipling. Poisoning him because I'd talked about the fleabane.

"Please. Stay with me for a while," Dona Beatriz said, curling on her side. "Stay until the potion begins to work."

I rose from the end of the bed, going to the chair beside her again.

"Talk to me about something," she said. "Anything. Anything so I don't think about it all. It scares me. I'm so afraid."

I couldn't think of one comforting thing to say. Finally I said, quietly, "I'm going to live on the quinta with my family. Your husband has asked that I be the *curandeira* here."

"Yes. Yes, that's a good idea." She drew a deep, jagged breath. "I don't know what I'll do without Father." She sat up and took my hand. Her fingers were cold, and so pale in comparison with mine, sun-darkened and hardened.

"You have your son. And of course your husband," I murmured, unable to shake the terrible vision of Abílio putting fleabane into Senhor Kipling's wine. "You have Abíl— You have your husband," I repeated.

We sat in silence for a few moments, and when she next spoke, her voice was less agitated. The powders were working. "My husband," she said, and I didn't understand the strange tone. "I had given up the hope of ever marrying," she said then. "The suitable time had long passed. My sister Inêz despaired of waiting for me to marry first. Finally my father gave her permission to marry. It was wrong, the younger sister marrying before the elder, but, as I said, it appeared I had lost my chance. There had been men when I was younger, but it was clear their interest was in the Kipling name." She let go of my hand. "Please. Give me my hairbrush."

I handed it to her. She brushed her hair with long, slow strokes.

"It was through Inêz's husband that I met Abílio at a ball in Funchal. He was very attentive. I was flattered. He was younger and, as you've seen, so handsome. He courted me with great insistence. And charm. After a few months, Abílio was bold enough to ask my father for my hand. My father said no."

Her strokes were slow and even. "My father knew, and I knew. Abílio was like the others, wasn't he, interested in marrying into my family. Not interested in me." She sighed, her eyelids heavy now. "But I no longer cared. I spoke honestly to my father. I told him it was my last chance to marry and have children. I begged him to allow Abílio to marry me, and take him into the business. I wanted to be a wife, and a mother. I didn't want to grow old alone." The brush fell to her lap. "Still my father wouldn't relent. He didn't want me to be hurt.

"And then the black pox came, taking first my mother and in another week Inês. It was so fast. We were in shock, and in mourning. Inêz's husband left in sorrow. But Abílio came and helped in so many ways. My father seemed unable to think or act clearly, and it was Abílio who made many of the necessary arrangements. And then afterwards, he just . . . stayed."

I could picture it all so clearly.

"My father barely left his room for a few months. He allowed Abílio to look after everything, the business and the quinta. Abílio seemed very good at managing things." She stared at me as if not really seeing me. "I'd lost my mother and my sister, and my father had become little more than a ghost. Abílio . . ." She stopped. Her lips were dry. "Abílio looked after me. You don't know my husband, but he can be very charming. Very persuasive."

"I'm certain he can," I said after a moment.

She went back to brushing her hair.

I kept my face expressionless, watching her fingers on the handle of the brush. I imagined Abílio's hands, his mouth, on her body as they had been on mine only the week before, and felt ill.

Dona Beatriz's strokes grew ineffectual, her voice slow and heavy as she drifted into the dreaminess created by the powders. "I miss them so much. My mother and my sister. My mother was very beautiful. Leandro reminds me of her in the shape of his face, and his fine eyebrows. Her name was Isabella Sobrinho Duarte. Her family was descended from royalty . . ."

The brush fell from her hand, and now Dona Beatriz's head bobbed as she fought sleep. "My father had no interest in fighting anymore, and gave in to our marriage." She closed her eyes, and I took the brush from her lap. "And now everyone I loved is dead. It is God's punishment for . . ." She was almost asleep. "For not listening to my father."

"All of this will pass, Dona Beatriz. It will pass." I quietly repeated the platitude as I stroked her arm.

Suddenly, she drowsily opened her eyes. "But I have my baby," she whispered. "My baby is all I need." Her eyes closed again, and she slept.

CHAPTER FORTY-NINE

Martyn Kipling had been a well-known and respected figure in Funchal, and his funeral filled the huge Sé cathedral. I stood at the back with Bonifacio.

Two days after the funeral, Bonifacio and Cristiano and I moved to Quinta Isabella, my belongings—including my two new dresses—packed neatly in a fine tapestry travel bag I had bought with some of the réis Martyn Kipling had paid me for helping his daughter.

Raimundo brought our bags from the yard to the cottage on a low-wheeled cart.

We followed him up a shady footpath, past a small, elegant chapel nestled in a copse of cypress trees. Bonifacio made the sign of the cross in front of the painting beside the open door. It was of a sainted woman holding a child in one hand and grapes in the other. "Our Lady of the Grapes," Raimundo said. Beside the chapel was a small cemetery with two headstones, the marble new, unmarked by time. Martyn Kipling was buried there too, his grave still a humped mound of earth. I knew Dona Beatriz would have a matching head-stone carved for him.

As we came through a small stand of trees into the front yard of the cottage, I stopped for a moment. Cristiano stayed by my side while Bonifacio went ahead. I wanted to look at it for a moment, this beauti-ful little cottage. It welcomed me with its bowed front windows and green door and long veranda with furniture made from the island's willow. In front of the veranda were rose bushes, their branches tipping with the weight of the flowers, white edged with pale pink. Behind the house was a stand of juniper and pine. The heat of the afternoon drew out their essence; it wafted from their blue-green needles and swirled around me. There was a sunny spot to one side of the house I knew would be perfect for a herb garden. Swallows flitted about in front of us, twittering and complaining.

"Come, Cristiano," I said. "This is where we'll live."

Inside was a large sitting room with a gracious fireplace flanked by two long settees. Fine curtains hung on all the windows, and as I knew from what I'd seen of the big house, the furniture was in an English style, gleaming wood and soft stuffed upholstery. A polished table and four chairs sat in front of the bowed windows, and glass-doored cabinets held pretty painted china figures and dishes. Paintings of landscapes were on the walls. There was a separate room with a long, high tub, and another with the lavatory, as well as three bedrooms. Each bed had wooden posts and a canopy of fabric, and was wide enough for two people to sleep comfortably. There was also a small fireplace in every bedroom. We would take all our meals at the kitchen in the yard of the big house.

Raimundo carried in our belongings and set the cases of clothing in the largest, brightest bedroom. After he left, Bonifacio took his own case into one of the other bedrooms.

The only thing that spoiled the cottage was the fact that Abílio was so nearby.

⁂

I came face to face with him as I passed the chapel on my way to the kitchen with Cristiano for dinner that first evening.

"Good evening, Senhora Rivaldo," he said. "And whose child is this?" he asked, nodding his head at Cristiano.

"My husband has taken him under his care. Cristiano, this is Senhor Perez."

"*Bom dia,*" Cristiano said politely.

"Go down to the kitchen and have your dinner, Cristiano. I wish to speak to Senhora Rivaldo," Abílio said.

"My husband will be coming along any moment."

"And so? Do I not have a right to speak to my employee?"

I swallowed. "How is Dona Beatriz?"

"She's in mourning. It's a difficult time for us all," he said, sounding sincere.

I glanced behind me. "Abílio," I said, my voice low. "I know what you did."

He looked startled. "What do you mean?"

"The symptoms of Senhor Kipling's death were of fleabane poisoning."

He took my arm and pulled me into the chapel, past the depiction of the Madonna with the Christ child in one arm, grapes in the other hand. "What are you talking about?"

I looked at the few flickering candles and the crucifix, and the small white marble statue of Our Lady with her child and the grapes in its niche. "Why must we talk in here if you have nothing to hide?"

"I'll ask you again. Why do you mention fleabane?"

I looked into his face. "I think you know."

"Are you accusing me?" he asked after a moment.

"Yes."

He wiped perspiration from his upper lip. "Do you have proof?"

"I could speak to the English physician. Would he believe me? I don't know. I have nothing more than my knowledge to offer as evidence."

"If you were going to talk to him, you would have done it before the funeral."

I stared at him. "I considered it. But I wondered what good it would do. Senhor Kipling was already dead. I could say I wanted to see you brought to justice. But who would investigate, and what would they look for? What would my husband think? What would your wife think?"

His face relaxed. "Then there's no reason to speak of what goes through your head."

"But I'm right, aren't I? Of course, Martyn Kipling knew why you wanted to marry his daughter. Surely it's clear to everyone."

He crossed his arms over his chest.

"And now you are in sole charge of the illustrious Kipling's Wine Merchants."

"You've figured it all out, have you?"

"Haven't I? I know you killed him, Abílio." I looked at him a bit longer, remembering his bruised knuckles after his own father died. "As you killed your father," I said, and held my breath.

He sat down on a wooden bench along one wall, his legs stretched in front of him. He lost his cockiness sitting there, staring at his boots. "My father was an ignorant brute. He wore my mother down with his fists, and eventually she gave up. He only got what he deserved. As for Martyn, in my defence, it wasn't the plan that he die."

"The plan? You admit it then?"

"As I said, it wasn't the plan."

"What did you plan?"

"I only wanted to make him ill for a while. Just weaken him so I had control for a few weeks, a month. He was going into a partnership. It was a mistake—he was about to throw half of the business away."

I remembered the overheard conversation with Henry Duncan.

"I couldn't let that happen. Once Martyn recovered, he'd see that what I was doing for Kipling's was right. I used too much of the oil, that's all."

I studied him. "Where did you get it? It wasn't mine, was it?" I wanted him to say no. Since Senhor Kipling's death, I had tried to remember if I'd left my medicine bag unattended in Dona Beatriz's room for any length of time. It would make Senhor Kipling's death all the worse if I had provided not only the information but the poison itself.

He put his head to one side and raised his eyebrows. "There's nothing more to be said about this. Kipling is dead. I'm sorry. But now I will make all decisions. For the business, and for the quinta. It's all mine now."

A candle on the altar sizzled and then went out. "What's made you the way you are, Abílio? You are willing to do anything to get what you want. Wasn't it enough to be married to Dona Beatriz, and work with her father? Isn't this beautiful home and more money than you can spend enough?"

He stood now, straightening his shoulders. "Diamantina, I'm in charge of everything and everyone. I suggest you run along to dinner now, and never speak of this to me again. If you insist on making some kind of scene, you will only appear a fool. I can't have a fool working for me on the quinta. I would have to dismiss you, and your husband. All your work"—he smiled lazily—"to make sure your husband got the job would be for nothing."

I turned my face from him.

"Besides, I could retaliate further."

I looked back. "What do you mean?"

"You're forgetting that I have certain proof—proof that I know you intimately. The pictures on your back are certainly not something I would know about without having seen you undressed. It would be an easy matter to mention to your husband that you were responsible for him securing the position. I have no doubt that would make the rest of your life with him much less comfortable."

I walked to the front of the nave and studied the serene, gentle face of Our Lady of the Grapes. Then I went back to Abílio. "You will pay me for my silence."

He smiled, the first real smile I had seen since our conversation started. "Ah yes, the Diamantina I know so well. You are so much like me."

"I'm nothing like you." I'd known all along that I had no credibility in Funchal. If I accused Abílio, I would sound like a madwoman. "I want money so I can take Cristiano and go to my father, as I've wanted to do since he left Porto Santo. You know how important this is for me. Give me the passage money and I'll be gone from here, and with me will go your ugly secret."

He nodded slowly. "I need time to think about it," he said.

Footsteps sounded on the gravel path outside the chapel. I moved to the shadowed wall. The footsteps stopped for a moment, and I knew it was Bonifacio, crossing himself as he passed the chapel. The footsteps moved on.

"I'll let you know my decision," Abílio said then, and left.

┳

I was relieved that Abílio did not call on me for the next week, although I waited to hear his decision.

I found beneficial herbs and plants growing in the big gardens, and made more medicines. I worked with the women in the kitchen and dealt with the minor health issues some spoke to me about. Bonifacio went to his new job in Funchal every day. At night he said little to me about it. Cristiano made friends with Binta's son Tiago, and each morning ran down to the yard to play with him.

Dona Beatriz sent for me two weeks after her father's funeral, as I was eating my midday meal in the kitchen. I left my plate and went back to the cottage to fetch my medicine bag, thinking Dona Beatriz wanted a tonic. But instead of leading me to the Dona's bedroom, Jacinta took me to a room lined with shelves holding hundreds of books. I stood in the doorway for a moment, letting my eyes rest on the books.

Dona Beatriz was standing by a wide desk. She had a straight posture that commanded attention; her close-fitting gown was of rich-looking satin, her body already returning to shape after the birth. Her face was flushed, her jaw tight. "My husband hasn't made the announcement yet, but by tomorrow everyone will know."

I set my bag on the floor, trying to cover my terrible sense of foreboding. Had she found out about Abílio and me? I took a deep breath.

"I wanted to inform you that my husband has decided that we will move to the mainland, and live in a house my family owns just outside Lisboa, in Santa Maria de Belém," she said.

I let my breath out, perhaps too loudly. My first thought was of the liberation I would feel with Abílio gone. I could live without fear that he would call upon me again, continuing to coerce me so that Bonifacio would retain the job. Then I thought of the passage money, and whether or not he would give it to me before he left.

After a polite moment had passed, I asked, carefully, "Is this decision to your liking, Dona Beatriz?"

"No. My father wouldn't want me to leave Quinta Isabella." Her voice was loud. "This is my home. He wouldn't have ever given permission for me to be taken so far from home. And from him. He made that clear to Abílio before we wed."

Again I wondered why she had called me here.

Her eyes were bright with angry tears and her mouth trembled as she fought for composure. "And now, my father barely . . ." She stopped and took a shaky breath. "And now Abílio is insisting we leave. He says he wants more than island life."

I remembered Abílio saying those words on Porto Santo.

"I'm leaving Binta and Nini and Raimundo to keep the house and property in order," she said. "I've already spoken to them about their duties. The wine lodge will operate as usual, with your brother-in-law remaining as overseer. I have always been involved with my father's business, and will be kept informed of our sales through Espirito. You and your husband will remain in the guest cottage." Her mouth was firm now. "Neither Binta nor Nini nor Raimundo are literate, so I would like you to be in charge of the ordering of supplies for the estate: food and linens basic to the needs of all of you, what the horses require, and necessary repairs to any of the buildings. You will sign the receipts, and everything will be paid for through the Counting House. Those receipts will be sent to me so I can stay aware of the estate's expenses."

"Of course," I said.

"And I would also like you to write to me regularly about Quinta Isabella: the gardens and the grapes and horses and the state of the house. Send the letters to me at this address in Santa Maria de Belém. I want to be assured that everything is running smoothly here." She held out a paper, and I took it.

"That's all," she said, dismissing me. I picked up my medicine bag and left.

I didn't like to think of disappointing Dona Beatriz should Abílio give me the money to leave, but she would find someone else to do her bidding once I was gone.

I was in the cottage with Cristiano when a note was delivered to the door by Raimundo a few hours later.

I opened it.

I have what you requested. Wait until the others are at dinner and then meet me in my office.

I tried to find a way to pass the rest of the afternoon. As the dinner hour approached, I prepared my sponge. I never knew what Abílio might do, and had to be prepared.

Bonifacio came home and changed his clothing.

"Please take Cristiano with you for dinner. I'm not hungry tonight," I told him, trying to appear normal. He nodded and they left.

I hurried down the path some minutes later. As I passed the chapel, I saw Abílio waiting for me in the doorway.

"I watched your husband and the boy go by."

"Why aren't you in your office, as you told me?"

He shrugged.

"You have the money then, as you said in your note," I said.

"Come inside."

I went into the cool, shaded room. He shut the door, then stepped close to me and put his hands on the laces of my blouse. "I want to see your back one more time."

"Abílio. Not here. The chapel . . ."

"You know I'll be leaving Madeira. I couldn't go without a last farewell." He already had my blouse undone.

I glanced at the statue. The Holy Mother's eyes watched.

"No, Abílio," I said, pushing away from him. "Stop. I won't do this. I said stop!"

But he yanked me closer and forced me to the floor. I had to close my eyes tightly so as not to look into the face of Our Lady of the Grapes as Abílio took me with a brutality that made me cry out in pain as I struggled against him.

He covered my mouth with his hand and did not stop.

⟡

When I was dressed, my back to him as I wiped away my tears with shaking fingers, I said, "Where is it?"

"The money?"

I turned to face him. "Of course, the money."

"It's better if I buy the passages for you and the boy. If you try on your own, they'll turn you away. And I'll find someone for you to travel with. When do you want to leave?"

"On the next possible ship." I never wanted to see him again.

"All right." He pulled open the door, and the early evening sunshine flooded in. "I'll look after everything for you."

⟡

Three days later, as I walked down to the yard for breakfast, I saw carts full of travelling cases. Jacinta and the wet nurse, holding Leandro, sat in a carriage. Five more servants were in another cart.

"Jacinta," I said, running to her. "Are you leaving this morning?"

"Yes," she said, and looked over my head.

Abílio, holding Dona Beatriz's arm, was coming our way.

"Senhor Perez," I said, staring at him. "And Dona Beatriz. I didn't realize you were leaving so soon."

"Goodbye, Diamantina," Dona Beatriz said. "I'll wait to hear from you, as we discussed."

As Abílio helped her into the carriage, I cleared my throat. He turned from his wife and looked at me.

"I know you and the rest of our trusted servants will keep Quinta Isabella well. Thank you," he said.

"But . . ."

He climbed in and sat beside his wife. He looked over his shoulder at me as the carriage pulled away, and touched the brim of his hat.

CHAPTER FIFTY

Dear Diamantina,

I have received the first receipts for the estate's expenses. It's been five weeks, and I await a letter from you with the news of Quinta Isabella.

Respectfully,

Dona Beatriz Duarte Kipling Perez

As I read her letter, I thought, for the thousandth time, of how Abílio had once more made a fool of me. I had been tricked into trusting him because he'd given Bonifacio the position as he had promised. I had fallen prey to his story of buying me the passages to Brazil in the same way I had believed he would take me with him from Porto Santo. I was filled with self-loathing, remembering how I had submitted to him so easily in his office. The last time, in the chapel, was not submission.

Now I had nothing but hatred for him. As long as I lived at Quinta Isabella, I would not be free of him; he could arrive any time, coming back to Funchal to inspect the winery and the quinta. But, I vowed, I would ask him for nothing, and give him nothing. I would never again let him touch me.

I had sent the letter to my father in December. It was now the beginning of June. He would have received it by now, surely. I could expect his reply between November and December. I had waited this long; I could wait another six months.

With Bonifacio away at work all day, I found pleasure and companionship with Binta and Nini. I loved the gardens, and had started my own herbs growing on the sunny side of the cottage. The women from nearby villages had heard about me through Gracinha, and came to the gate asking for my help. Raimundo allowed them in, and I sat with them outside the kitchen, listening to their symptoms and giving them what cures I could. I felt useful and fulfilled in a way I hadn't since the days of helping my mother at Ponta da Calheta.

As much as I enjoyed living in the pretty cottage, I loved the summer house best. I discovered it while exploring the estate, coming upon an almost-hidden, mossy path through a small forest of lofty pines. It was an eight-sided structure open on all sides, and the surrounding foliage gave it a sense of privacy. It was built on the highest point of the property, and caught the breezes blowing from the sea. Visible from three of its sides were the harbour and the ocean beyond. The flowers growing wild around it perfumed the air. I brought cloths to dust the soft cane sofas and chairs, and beat the cushions until they were fresh and plump. It was a small, hidden jewel, an unexpected little open-air villa that I felt was my own private retreat.

At one time it had been used for entertaining guests on hot summer nights, Binta told me when I asked her about it, but it had fallen into disuse since Dona Beatriz's mother died. Every day and many evenings, sometimes with Cristiano and sometimes alone, I went to the summer house to watch the ocean and its moods. On sunny days the water turned from blue to green and back to blue; sometimes the sun glazed its surface a bright slate. When rains came and clouds scudded low, the winds stirred and ruffled the water into dark grey. In the darkness of night I admired the cast of the moon, its long, wavering shaft of light on the sea's blackness.

The day after I received her letter, I wrote to Dona Beatriz. I left Cristiano playing with Tiago and walked into Funchal to take the letter to Kipling's so it could be mailed.

As I came into the Counting House, Espirito and a merchant stood beside Bonifacio at his desk, looking over a bill of lading. "*Bom dia*, Bonifacio," I said, the respectable wife. "I've brought a letter to be sent to Dona Beatriz, at her bidding."

Bonifacio nodded, but Espirito smiled at me. I hadn't seen him since Bonifacio and Cristiano and I had moved to the cottage after Senhor Kipling's funeral. He looked slightly drawn, his skin tone unhealthy, and I wondered if Olívia's health was worse.

"You can leave the letter in that basket with the rest of the post," he said.

"How is Olívia keeping?" I asked.

"She's had good health this last while."

"I'm glad. Please say hello to her for me."

"I will." He gazed at me. "It seems life on the quinta suits you." I had worn my silvery green dress, which complemented my eyes. I had taken special pains with my hair. I told myself it was because I was going to Funchal. I told myself it was only because of that.

"The quinta does suit me. Thank you."

"And Cristiano is happy there?"

"Yes. He—"

"Espirito," Bonifacio interrupted. "We're waiting on you."

"Goodbye, then," I said, and turned to leave. But the door opened, and Henry Duncan came in.

"Carry on without me, Bonifacio," Espirito said, going to shake Mr. Duncan's hand. "Hello, Henry," he said, smiling broadly.

"Espirito," Mr. Duncan said, then smiled at me in a delighted fashion. "Well, the Dutchman's daughter," he said in English. "Diamantina, isn't it?"

"Yes, Mr. Duncan. Diamantina Rivaldo," I replied in English.

"It's been at least three years since I last saw you. You've left the inn and your dominoes behind, then?" he asked, still smiling. "As well as your father?"

"Rooi wasn't my father," I said.

"You're not the Dutchman's daughter?"

"I'm a Dutchman's daughter, yes. But not Rooi's. He was a family friend. I haven't played for a while. I can't find anyone who dares to take me on," I said with a small smile.

"Ah. I see. But you said Diamantina Rivaldo. I never knew your surname. So you're related to Espirito?"

Espirito cleared his throat, and there was a brief, odd moment when neither he nor I spoke. What caused our discomfort?

"She's my sister-in-law," he said. "Married to my brother." He gestured at Bonifacio, who still conferred with the other merchant.

"Ah. I'm sure she's a treat to have in the family."

"She is," Espirito said, and I was surprised at how his natural response to Mr. Duncan's statement filled me with warmth. "How can I help you, Henry?"

Mr. Duncan set a leather case on the table. "I have a proposition. I know I should be dealing with Abílio Perez on this, but he's not here. And frankly, I've never liked the man. Martyn Kipling and I had a good, competitive relationship, but Perez is bad for business of any sort. There's already talk from Lisbon that he's meeting with some wine sellers in Oporto. They've signed on to sell port to the American colonies. It's a quickly growing enterprise."

"Selling port? Not our wine?" Espirito asked.

"You and I both know Perez shows little genuine interest in Kipling's. He wouldn't even meet with me to discuss the partnership Martyn and I were working on." He glanced at me. "Perhaps I shouldn't be speaking so openly."

"Diamantina knows Perez," Espirito said, and I was suddenly cold. Was his glance at me suspicious in some way? Surely it was just my guilt; I had tried to forget that he had seen me coming out of Abílio's office that dark night. "She and her husband now live on Quinta Isabella."

Mr. Duncan opened his case and took out a bottle. "I have a new client in England. One of the biggest—the Church of England. They've hired me to supply much of their sacramental wine. Perhaps all, one day."

Espirito made a low sound of approval.

"Would you like me to leave?" I asked.

When Espirito didn't respond, Mr. Duncan smiled again. "Not on my account." He set the bottle on the table. "I took on the job because it's one of the most lucrative I'll ever know. It will change my business, and put Madeira's fine reputation as wine producers on an even higher level." He pushed the bottle towards Espirito.

Espirito took the cork from it and breathed deeply. "It smells fine."

"It *is* fine. That's the altar wine they've always used. Their wine merchant is in the Douro valley, but because of bad crops due to the last two wet winters in that area of the mainland, the merchant has raised his prices to a level the Church isn't willing to pay. They heard of my company's reputation, and approached me."

Espirito handed me the bottle. I felt a sudden rush of pleasure at being included, and put it to my nose.

"What's the proposition, then, Henry?" Espirito asked.

"That altar wine is blended from a crop similar to Madeira's Sercial. But many of my grape suppliers in the higher regions were down on their production this year, and I haven't got enough of the Sercial *mosto*. Kipling's always has the greatest abundance of Sercial on the island. I want to buy all of your *mosto*—I'll take whatever you have. Don't worry about the barrels—I'll supply them, of course."

"I'll have to confirm the amounts," Espirito said. "And talk to my brother about the price we would require. And of course we'll take a percentage of your profit."

"That's only fair," Mr. Duncan said, raising his chin at the other merchant, who was leaving after shaking Bonifacio's hand. "I see Rutherford is doing business with you. He likes to buy your Sercial as well, so I want to make sure this can happen quickly."

"I can let you know by tomorrow," Espirito said.

"Good. When you approve this transaction, we will need to address the blending. My winemaker has just left me—decided he wanted to live out the rest of his life at home and went back to Scotland a few months ago. I've been looking for another good man, but haven't found anyone to my liking. Who's the best blender in Funchal?" He held his hand, palm up, towards Espirito. "It's you, Rivaldo. I know you can match this wine better than anyone."

Espirito ran a hand up and down the open bottle.

"What do you say? One old friend helping another?"

"Come back tomorrow afternoon, Henry, around three, once I've thought this through."

"All right." He shook Espirito's hand. "Good day, Diamantina," Mr. Duncan said. "It was wonderful to see you. I trust I'll see you more, now that your marriage has brought you into the Kipling empire." He smiled with the same charisma I remembered as he encouraged me to speak English and agreeably accepted my every victory with the tiles.

As the door closed behind him, Espirito called across the room, "Bonifacio, I'll need you to check on our supplies of Sercial *mosto*."

Bonifacio came to us. "You're not doing business with him, are you?"

"Why not?"

"Isn't he a rival? Why should we help him?"

"It would be beneficial for Kipling's. He'll buy all our Sercial *mosto* and pay us a percentage of his profit. I've told you that Senhor Kipling wanted to partner with him before his death."

"But Senhor Perez is in charge now."

"Senhor Perez has chosen to spend his time in Lisboa, doing as he pleases. This will be highly advantageous, as I've said. Besides, Duncan is highly trustworthy, and an old friend."

"It appeared that you're all old friends," Bonifacio said now, looking at me. "It sounded as though you were talking more than business. Did you speak English on purpose, so I was unable to understand you?"

"You should try to learn English, Bonifacio," Espirito said with strained patience. "Henry Duncan wants to buy all our Sercial *mosto*," he repeated. "He'll pay well, I guarantee. So please, check on how many barrels of the *mosto* we have."

Bonifacio's lips pursed as he turned and went back to his desk.

"I'll get home, then," I said. "Goodbye, Espirito. I'll see you at dinner, Bonifacio," I called, but he didn't answer.

I had only taken a few steps up Rua São Batista when Espirito came up behind me. "Could you stay another moment?"

"Yes. Why?"

"I'd like you to come into the blending room with me."

I nodded and followed him through the lane and across the court-yard into the warm room.

"Please. Sit down," he said, taking two small glasses from a shelf.

"You've known Henry Duncan a long time?" I asked him, sitting on one of the stools at the table.

"After I was apprenticed to Eduardo and before I married Olívia, Henry Duncan offered me a job. I took it, and learned what I know about blending from his former winemaker. When that man took a job on the mainland, I became the blender for Duncan's. After a few years Martyn Kipling came along. He offered me higher pay, and the home above the Counting House. Henry couldn't match Martyn's offer, so I took it. I was sorry to leave him, but he accepted it as the gentleman he is, and we've remained friends." He held the open bot-tle to me. "What do you smell?"

I breathed it in. "It's not Madeiran Sercial, but close, as Mr. Duncan said."

He poured a mouthful into each glass. "Try it. Please."

I held up my glass. "A little cloudy," I said, looking at the warm amber with greenish highlights. I drank. "A bit acidic at the finish. Surely blended with an older *tinta*." I licked my lips. "If you decide to blend for him, we should suggest that newer barrels would be a wiser choice."

Espirito let the wine sit in his mouth. Finally he swallowed, and said, "I agree." He set the glass down. "Let me explain why I asked you to try this. I've been ill for the last few weeks."

"I thought you didn't look quite as usual."

"It's nothing serious, just a stomach disorder that Dr. McManus assures me I'll recover from soon, but right now my palate is not as it was. I thought another opinion couldn't hurt. I'll work on the blend the rest of the afternoon. Thank you."

I didn't want to leave, but I knew I must. As I rose, he said, "Could you . . . would you be willing to stop by tomorrow to try the blends I come up with? To assure me you're tasting what I am, before Henry returns?" He smiled, but it was somewhat awkward.

"Yes, of course," I said. "I'll see you tomorrow, then."

CHAPTER FIFTY-ONE

The next afternoon, as I walked down Rua São Batista again, I told myself not to appear overeager. Over dinner the previous night, I hadn't said anything to Bonifacio about helping Espirito. Everything between Bonifacio and me was as always: we never shared anything of our days, or our thoughts.

I tried the two blends Espirito had worked on, and we agreed on which one matched the Anglican blend the best. When Henry Duncan arrived, he didn't seem surprised to find me in the blending room.

"Well, Espirito?" he asked. "What news have you for me?"

"I'd like you to try this first. I think you'll be happy with it." Espirito offered Mr. Duncan samples from the original bottle and from the new blend. "Of course, it will alter upon maturing and further fermenting, but it's as close as possible for now."

Mr. Duncan swirled a mouthful of the sample bottle first, then spat it into a little pitcher. He next took Espirito's blend, gave it a brief sniff, then repeated the process. He sat for a moment. "Yes. It will be a good match in another year," he said, smiling broadly.

"Diamantina agreed on the blend. My sister-in-law has a fine palate."

"I know. Even when I met her in that dingy inn in Vila Baleira," Mr. Duncan responded, "it was obvious that her knowledge of the grapes and their varietals surpassed many already initiated in the wine business. I take it you have the *mosto* to sell me, and you will do the blending?"

"Yes. There's just the cost to decide on."

"You set the price, Espirito. I've made it clear I need you. I don't see us having to bargain over this."

Espirito extended his hand. Mr. Duncan shook it firmly. "How I wish you'd decided to make your future with me. Even though Perez has ruined the hopes of Kipling's and Duncan's merging, maybe one day I'll find a way to buy him out, and you'll be my blender again." He smiled. "For now, we have cause for celebration." He looked around at the bottles on the shelves. "What can you offer me of my competitor's wines?" he asked with a laugh.

Espirito poured us each a large glass of a rich old Malvasia. And then another. I should have left then, but maybe because I was pleased to be part of this friendly exchange, I stayed. By the time I'd emptied the third glass, I felt light and happy, smiling as I watched Espirito's lips on the rim of his own glass.

"Diamantina? Do you ever go back to Porto Santo?"

I turned from Espirito to meet Mr. Duncan's gaze. Without warning, the last mouthful of wine rose back up my throat, and I felt horribly ill.

"No. Excuse me, please," I said to them both, standing. I had to steady myself for a moment with my fingertips on the tabletop. I went out into the courtyard, concentrating on walking slowly and deliberately. I took deep breaths, then drank two cupfuls of water from the cistern. I splashed my face and drank another cup of water. I had to sit on a step and close my eyes, willing the nausea to lessen.

At the sound of voices, I patted my damp forehead with my sleeve and stood. "I'll say goodbye for now, Diamantina," Mr. Duncan said, coming towards me. "I spend more of my time in Lisbon than I do in Funchal these days, but I'm sure our paths will cross again before too long."

I tried to swallow my queasiness. "The barrels you bring us should be of newer wood," I told him, and again he smiled.

Once he'd left the courtyard, Espirito asked, "Are you all right, Diamantina?"

"I didn't eat much today, and shouldn't have accepted the third glass. My own fault," I said, and had to sit down again.

"I'll get a cart to take you home," he said. "Wait here."

I had made a fool of myself. By the time Espirito came back, I was walking in the courtyard, attempting to appear as though all was well. He helped me into the cart.

"Thank you again. I hope you feel all right. I shouldn't have—"

"Oh no. It's entirely my fault," I repeated. "I'll be fine once I get home."

He nodded, and the cart jolted forward. I concentrated on staring straight ahead, over the plodding ox, as the driver took me back up the hill to Quinta Isabella.

In the cottage, my bedroom walls were white, the curtain fluttering over the open window also white. I had never slept in a room so filled with light. The morning sun shone through the window in slashes of buttery yellow. From my bed, I could see the blue, cloudless sky, and hear the soft cry of a mourning dove. There was the scent of heliotrope and juniper. From outside my door, in the sitting room, came the muted sound of wood hitting wood. Cristiano was playing with a set of blocks Tiago had lent him.

I imagined Cristiano building up the blocks, one on top of the other, his movements cautious as he added the final pieces to his tower, and then his smile when they tumbled to the floor. I should have risen long ago and taken him to the kitchen for his breakfast. He wouldn't come and bother me for it; he had uncanny patience for a child.

Bonifacio would have left, as usual, with the rising of the sun, to be at his desk in the Counting House before the lodge opened. He liked to be there early, to set up his quills and ink and run his fingers over the smooth ledger pages. It had been two weeks since I had gone to help Espirito, two weeks since that first warning in the *adega*.

I could no longer fool myself. It was time to do what must be done. I rose and went out to Cristiano, running my hand over his soft hair. I told him to go by himself to the kitchen for breakfast, then stay and play with Tiago for the morning.

When he had gone, I concocted a tea from the bitter leaves of rue and mixed it with tansy. I carefully added only the tiniest pinch of the ground seed from the lethal yew. I would have to drink the infusion throughout this day, and the next and the next. I was careful with my measurements, knowing the danger of the combination of herbs. I thought of poor Martyn Kipling, and his rapid, painful death. It would take three to four days of nausea and cramping before the actual bleeding began. The sponge and vinegar weren't infallible. I had always known that.

⁘

For the next few days, I spent much of my time on my bed with a bucket on the floor beside me, watching the curtains lift and sway.

I told Bonifacio I had influenza, and asked that he tell Binta to let Cristiano stay with her. Binta and Nini were quiet and helpful; one of them brought me a tray a few times a day, although I was unable to eat anything.

On the fourth day, more severe cramping gripped me, and I waited hopefully for the blood and tissue to pass from my body. Nothing appeared. By the sixth day, I couldn't bear the illness without the hoped-for results, knowing it was a danger to my own life to continue to take the herbs. The child was as tenacious and stubborn as its father. It would not be shifted from its hold on me.

⁘

I'd conceived from the rape in the chapel at the beginning of May.

I walked through the small, tidy graveyard with its three headstones. I ran my fingers over the names of Beatriz's family—her father Martyn, her mother Isabella and her sister Inêz—and wished the forming child gone. Birds sang quietly, and a breeze blew up. I was faint suddenly, and put my hand onto the headstone of Beatriz's mother. The stone was cool, somehow comforting. I thought of my own mother, refusing to perform the act with the hook. She would help with herbal infusions, but not the hook. Too many women bled to death that way, she had said, or suffered agonies from the damage for years after.

And yet it was my only recourse now: the long, cruel hook, scraping out what grew inside me.

I slowly walked back to the cottage and sat on the veranda. Cristiano came home with Tiago, and I watched them play with little round stones, rolling them into small depressions they'd hollowed in the dirt.

Tomorrow. I would do it tomorrow.

I prepared the hook and took it into the *latrina* of the cottage.

I lifted my skirt and began to insert it. As I slowly pushed it higher, I felt the first nudge of pain. I pushed further. Now my legs trembled, and although I was not afraid of pain, I stopped. I thought of myself dying here, on the floor, in my own blood.

Who would find me but Cristiano, when he came in with Tiago in a few hours, chattering and laughing? Would seeing me in that state bring back his terrible visions? He only rarely had the nightmare now.

I imagined what it would do to him should I not withstand this assault. What would happen to him, left alone with Bonifacio?

Holding my breath, I carefully withdrew the hook. I sank to the floor, my face in my hands.

After a long while, I rose and washed my hands and face and put away the hook. I had no interest in this child; it was Abílio's bastard. But if I was forced to carry and give birth to it, the only way I could continue my life at the quinta while waiting to leave was by persuading Bonifacio that the child was his. It seemed an insurmountable task. And yet I had to make it work. If I couldn't, he would turn me out. I would be disgraced and destitute.

That evening, when Bonifacio returned from Funchal, I had a plate of *cabra* and a pitcher of wine, covered with a cloth to keep away the flies, sitting in the middle of the table.

"Why are we not eating in the kitchen?" Bonifacio asked, lifting the cloth and leaning forward to smell the contents of the pitcher. "It smells like Kipling's finest Boal."

"It is. I took it from the big house. Dona Beatriz gave me permission to occasionally help myself to a bottle of wine." It wasn't true, but there were dozens of bottles in a wine cupboard in the dining room. I had gone in while Binta and Nini were dusting, and felt no guilt in taking it. "And it's just this once, for a special occasion."

"What occasion is that?"

"We have never properly celebrated our new lives," I said. "So I thought we could toast to the good luck that has come to us."

"Life is not about luck. It is God's will, coupled with hard work."

"Yes," I said pleasantly. "You're right. But I had Nini make *cabra*. I know it's your favourite."

He still stood, looking unconvinced. "Where's Cristiano?"

"He asked to stay with Tiago tonight." It was I who had asked Binta to keep Cristiano. "Come, Bonifacio. Think of how God's grace has shone upon you. You no longer have to carry the burden of the fallen priest as you did every time you went to church in Curral das Freiras. You can use the quinta's chapel whenever you like, and go to any cathedral you choose in Funchal. You have a fine new position in Kipling's Counting House, and we have this beautiful home. If ever there was a time to be a little carefree, it's now, Bonifacio. It's a cause for celebration, this new life God has blessed us with."

I hated myself, but it was all of our futures at stake: Bonifacio's, mine, Cristiano's. And that of the tiny child unfolding inside me.

"I suppose so," he said at last, and sat down.

I served him the tender goat in tomatoes and herbs, pouring him a glass of the Boal. "You're not having any?" he said, looking at my empty glass.

"I will, after I've eaten a bit," I said, watching him taste the wine. "Since I was ill, my stomach isn't back to normal."

He swallowed another mouthful. "Full flavoured and sweet, but it's got an odd aftertaste."

I smiled, raising a forkful of the *cabra* to my lips.

By the time he'd finished his second glass, Bonifacio set down his fork and ran his hand over his eyes.

"Are you all right, Bonifacio?"

He didn't answer, frowning down at his plate. When he looked up, his pupils were large. I'd made an infusion of valerian oil and mixed in the ground seed of the poppy, creating a heavy sleeping potion that I'd stirred into the Boal.

"I'm suddenly so weary," he said, rising, putting one hand on the table to steady himself.

"Maybe you're sickening with what I had," I said. "You should go to bed."

He stood there a moment longer, as if slightly dazed, then went to his room.

I waited as long as I could. Dusk was turning to darkness. When I heard him snoring, I went into his bedroom and looked down at him. He was sprawled across the bed on his back, still fully dressed. "Bonifacio?" I whispered, and then said loudly, "Bonifacio!" His snores continued.

I went to my own room and put on my nightdress. I fetched the tiny container of blood I had collected after killing a chicken behind the kitchen that morning. Back in Bonifacio's room, I sat beside him on the bed and started to undress him. His snores had stopped, and he was breathing slowly and deeply. I hoped the drugs would keep him asleep through most of the night, but I couldn't be totally certain of the effects, as I'd never made this particular concoction. I could only believe that when he woke up next to me in bed, the spot of chicken blood on the sheet evidence of my lost virginity, he would accept what I eventually told him about the child.

He worked in the Counting House; he would not be fooled easily by a too-early baby. I would eat lightly, try to keep the baby small, so that it appeared premature when I gave birth.

I fully knew it was a flimsy plan, but it was the only one left to me.

I unlaced the top of his shirt and worked his arms out of it, pulling it over his head. He was in such a deep slumber that his limbs were deadened, and hard to manoeuvre. His shoulders were narrow, his chest a little concave. I took off his boots and his stockings, and then unlaced the leather thongs of his breeches and carefully, slowly, worked them down over his hips. For that first instant all appeared normal, but suddenly, when I realized what I was seeing, my own breath trembled in my ears.

He had been castrated.

I sat back, my hands over my mouth.

The jagged scar was still an angry pink, crossed with rough, clumsy stitching lines.

I remembered his return to Curral das Freiras after Lent, so ghostly and emaciated. I remembered Espirito bringing him to the house on Rua São Batista our first night in Funchal, and the English physician attending to him.

The few bites of *cabra* I had eaten came back up my throat, and I had to close my eyes and keep swallowing. The castration had been his punishment for wanting me. This was what he felt was necessary to ensure he was not lured into sin by me.

Such was my horror and pity that I dropped down beside him, my head on his shoulder, my arm across his chest. I softly wept for him then.

After a while, I sat up and slowly dressed him again. Holding the vial of chicken blood, I stood looking down at him, filled with deep sorrow for what this man thought he had to do to remain true to his God. For the first time, I felt something almost like tenderness for him. I stoked his hair, and then leaned down and kissed his forehead.

He stirred, blinking and opening his eyes. They were unfocused, and I knew he was in a strange dream. "Sleep now, Bonifacio," I whispered. "Sleep."

⚬⟨⟩⚬

When he came out of his bedroom the next morning, he rubbed his face with his hands. "I feel unwell."

I had tossed through the night, terribly disturbed by Bonifacio's self-inflicted mutilation and that it had killed my final, desperate hope. This baby would destroy my future, and leave me homeless and destitute. Bonifacio would send me away, back to Porto Santo, for where else could I go? I would never again see Cristiano. I would not receive the expected letter from my father—it would not be forwarded to me after I had been cast out in shame.

I would have to write to my father again from Porto Santo. It would be another year of waiting, with a child and no charity from anyone. Would I be forced to live in a cave, as my mother had once spoken of?

"You drank the whole pitcher of wine," I said, turning so he wouldn't see my face as I wound the clock. How quickly I had started to rely on it for the rhythm of my days. A strange thing, I often thought now, that I'd lived without need of a clock for more than eighteen years, and now glanced at it frequently throughout the day. "Usually you just enjoy a glass or two. Then again, that blend of Boal was of a particularly high quality."

"I do remember drinking one glass, but . . ." He stopped.

I turned back to him, running my hands down my skirt. "Or, as I said last night, you may be sickening with what I had last week. Are you well enough to go to work?"

He took his jacket off the peg by the door. "The walk down to Funchal should clear my head."

CHAPTER FIFTY-TWO

I tried twice again to rid myself of the child, but both times came to consciousness on the floor of the *latrina*, the wadded cotton still in my mouth, the hook still in me. But not deep enough. I could not drive that sharp end far enough to dislodge what grew there without fainting from the pain. As unflinching as I was in my decision, my body betrayed me.

I spent many afternoons in the summer house, looking at the sea, knowing my days were numbered and there was nothing I could do but wait.

By the middle of my fourth month, Binta and Nini guessed at my condition, but assumed it was a happy occasion. Why wouldn't they? Wasn't I playing the part of a respectable married woman?

I did not venture into Funchal, not wanting to see Espirito. No invitations came from the house on Rua São Batista, and I was relieved.

As I began my fifth month, and felt the quickening of the child as I ran my hands over my newly rounded belly, hidden from Bonifacio beneath loose blouses and voluminous aprons, I tried to think of how I would survive when he cast me out.

The day I knew I could hide no longer was a Friday, dark and rainy. Although it was only early September, a sudden cool rain had blown in from the sea. Leaving Cristiano in the sitting room with his playthings, I had wrapped a shawl over my head and walked into the field behind our cottage. On my way back, I stopped on a slight rise and looked down upon the quinta. Although the summer house was hidden by high trees, the rest of the buildings—the big estate house, the stables and pressing house and kitchen and wash house, the chapel, and my home—were all visible in the mist. I gazed at their outlines in the rain and knew that after today I might never see them again. I felt this world I had never imagined to be mine now slipping from my grasp.

The thought of telling Bonifacio made me so sick that I sat down in the tall, drenched grass and took deep breaths, my face wet with both rain and tears.

⁂

Once home, I changed into dry clothing. Bonifacio came in from work. We went down the path and ate dinner in the kitchen with the others. It appeared to be like every other night. Back in the cottage, I stayed with Cristiano in his room until he was asleep, fearing for him and his future as I feared for mine. I put my gutting knife into my waistband. And then I came back to the sitting room. It was still raining.

Bonifacio sat by the fire, staring into its flames.

"Bonifacio, I must speak to you."

He glanced at me. "I'm weary, Diamantina. There was a problem with one of the shipments today, and all the paperwork had to be redone. Can it wait until morning?"

"No. It's . . . it's of utmost importance." I sat across from him, my hands clasped to hide their trembling. Outside, the clouds roiled and churned, and I felt a dark cloud above us, one that would, within the next few moments, burst open and rain down all manner of despair.

Bonifacio looked from my face to my hands, then back to my face. "What's wrong?"

He asked quietly, with a certain sense of concern, and in that instant I knew I would cry, even though I'd promised myself that I wouldn't. That I would remain calm and focused, and speak in an ordinary voice, and accept Bonifacio's reaction, however terrible.

I deserved it fully. And yet somehow the tone of his voice, and the look on his face, softer in the firelight than in harsh sunlight, started a sob in my throat. I would cry because I was about to tell him that I was a low woman. I had betrayed and deceived him in the worst way, and had no excuse except that I'd done it to help myself.

I put my hands over my face and wept.

He reached out and touched my hands, and I lowered them and looked at him. "Are you ill in some way, Diamantina?"

I took a deep breath, and wiped my eyes with my arm, and looked into his face. "I am with child." I had to say it in one quick breath, one four-word sentence, or I wouldn't be able to speak at all.

It appeared, for those first few seconds, that Bonifacio hadn't heard me, or was still waiting, patiently, for me to speak. And then, slowly, his expression changed. I didn't blink or look away. I faced him, sitting in front of the dying fire. The flames cast light upon my husband's features, and as I watched him, he aged.

And then he sighed, heavily and deeply. He placed his hands together, as if about to pray, lowering his gaze, and then touched his lips to his fingertips. It wasn't the reaction I had expected, nor was what he said next. "You will leave me, then?"

"Leave you?"

"You wish to be with this man, so go to him." He was still looking downwards. "Leave Cristiano, take your things, and go. I shouldn't be surprised. Perhaps I'm not."

I stood. It sounded as though Bonifacio was giving me a choice. "Bonifacio, I don't want to leave. I . . . the man . . . it's—he's not what I want."

At this, his body grew rigid. He spread his hands on his thighs, the fingers flexing and relaxing, flexing and relaxing in an odd rhythm. "But it's clear you did want him. *For the lips of a strange woman drop as a honeycomb, and smoother than oil is her speech; but in the end she is bitter as wormwood, sharp as a two-edged sword,*" he murmured.

"What?"

He looked up at me, his fury barely concealed now, and I drew in a deep breath, moving behind the settee. I had been waiting for this. He stood. *"But every man is tempted, when he is drawn away of his own lust, and enticed. Then when lust hath conceived, it bringeth forth sin: and sin, when it is finished, bringeth forth death."*

I backed away, my hand on my knife as I glanced behind, measuring the distance to the door.

"Get out of here. Get out!" he shouted. "Sinner! Jezebel! Get out of my sight. You sicken me. Leave!" he shouted. Such was his look that I feared for my life.

I turned and fled, leaving the door swinging behind me.

⌒

I ran down the path, the wind lashing the trees. After a few minutes I had to stop, pressing a hand into the ache in my side. I looked behind me, but the wind in the trees made too much noise for me to hear whether Bonifacio was coming after me.

I envisioned running down to the yard and pounding on Binta's door, or Nini's or Raimundo's. Surely they could shelter me from Bonifacio's wrath. But as I approached the chapel, I was unable to run any more. I had not gone into it since the day Abílio had taken me on its floor. It could no longer be a place for comfort or contemplation. But now, gasping, my feet sliding on the wet gravel, I stumbled inside and shut the door, my back against it, trying to catch my breath.

After what felt like a long while, I slid down until I was sitting on the wooden floor. I was shaking violently with both cold and fear. Then I lay on my side, cradling my belly.

Bonifacio hadn't come after me. I would wait here until morning's first light, and then go down to the yard and tell Binta and Nini and Raimundo that my husband had cast me out. I would ask to stay with one of them just until I knew what to do.

I rose and went to the front and lit a candle with the flint always there. The Holy Mother's face came into view. I went to my knees and clasped my hands.

"What have I done, Mother?" I whispered, looking up at her. "What have I done? Can you help me?"

With no warning, the door was flung open with a crash, and I leapt to my feet so quickly that for a dizzying second it was as though two Bonifacios stood there, soaking wet. I blinked, seeing the branches behind him swaying and bending in the wind as though wildly dancing to an unheard melody. He had the appearance of one truly mad, his hair plastered against his forehead and his eyes wild. I took my knife from my waistband as he stepped inside. He slammed the door with such force that the small building shook, and in that instant his eyes widened as he looked behind me.

"No!" he shouted, lunging forward, and I lifted my knife above my head. But there was a thud, and he stopped, his expression stricken.

As I followed his gaze, I realized he hadn't been coming for me, but trying to catch Our Lady of the Grapes. The slamming of the door had shaken her from her niche. She lay on the floor, the hand holding the grapes broken at the wrist.

Bonifacio dropped to his knees in front of her, praying in Latin. He murmured the same sentences over and over; I didn't recognize them from the prayers during Mass.

I watched him as I stepped back towards the door.

But before I reached it, Bonifacio raised his head and got to his feet and tenderly lifted the small statue, setting it back in its niche. He picked up the hand with the grapes.

"It can be repaired," he said quietly. He kissed the hand and set it beside the statue. "I will repair it tomorrow."

He looked at me then, his face contorted with grief. "It is a sign," he said. "The Lord has not yet forgiven me. Again he has set an obstacle in my path. I thought marrying you might help me in my quest for redemption. And maybe someday I will find it. But this"—he waved in the direction of Our Lady of the Grapes—"this is evidence of the work—the repairing of my soul—that still lies ahead. I understand that the work must involve allowing you to bear this bastard child." He put his face into his hands. "And me accepting it." His voice was muffled.

I stood without moving, my back against the door.

"Go back to the house," he said, lifting his face and looking at me. "And put away your knife. You don't have to fear me."

I realized I still held the knife aloft, ready to strike. Would I have driven it into him, maimed or even killed him in order to protect myself? I remembered my promise on the cliffs of Porto Santo.

I put it back into my waistband. I went out in the dark night and slowly walked back to the cottage.

CHAPTER FIFTY-THREE

I awoke to the sun high through the bedroom window, thinking, for an instant, that I was glad the storm had passed.

And then I sat straight up, shocked that I had fallen asleep. My sodden clothes lay on the floor beside the bed, and I put my hand under the pillow, feeling for my gutting knife. What good would it have done me had Bonifacio come into my room, his fury restored? I had slept as though an innocent child. For the last month, as soon as I lay down, the infant began to move. The movements through the night sometimes woke me. But last night he or she was still, as if waiting to know our future.

I rose and dressed. When I walked into the sitting room, Bonifacio was sitting in front of the fireplace, although no fire burned. I stopped, my heart thudding.

He looked at me, his mouth twisted and his eyes shot with blood. "I've sent Cristiano down for his breakfast, and told him to stay with Tiago this morning."

I nodded.

"Sit down," he said.

I did as he said, pulling my shawl more closely about me, used to trying to cover my growing bulk. Then I realized it didn't matter, and let it fall open.

Bonifacio studied my belly. "When will it be born?"

"The end of January or beginning of February."

"It's Espirito," he said, and my mouth opened. "It's my brother, isn't it? My own brother!" he said, his voice low but his face dark, pinched with suspicion.

"No! No, Bonifacio. It's not Espirito. How can you even think that? Bonifacio, no." My words ran together. I took a breath and spoke more slowly. "Of course it's not Espirito. That's a ridiculous assumption. He's like my own brother," I said, although I did not think of him that way.

"Give me a name," Bonifacio demanded.

I couldn't name Abílio, for then Bonifacio would leave, refusing to work for him. I would be forced to go back to Curral das Freiras with him.

"I will never speak his name, Bonifacio. Never," I said, wiping my eyes.

He studied the cold fireplace.

After a long while, I asked, "Will you still allow me to stay, as you said last night?"

"Yes."

I exhaled, a long, slow breath.

"But I don't do this for you," he said. "As I said last night, it is part of God's plan, another test He has put in front of me. The child is a test."

I nodded, and we sat in silence. Finally I said, "Others will think . . . they will think it's your child."

"You imagine I care what others think?" He stared at me for a long moment, then left for work.

I stayed in front of the cold fireplace, my hands on my belly.

⌒⌒⌒

4th November, 1750

Dear Dona Beatriz,

I was pleased to receive your letter, and hear that Leandro brings you so much happiness.

All is well on Quinta Isabella. Fortunately everyone has been in good health throughout the autumn. The roan Chico had an abscess inside the hoof from a badly placed shoeing nail, but Raimundo was able to treat it quickly and effectively.

The harvest, as you would have heard from Espirito, was a
success, and with the advent of cooler weather, the grapevines are
glorious in their reds and golds.

We attended the All Saints' Day service at Sé cathedral, and,
the day following, I put fresh flowers on your family's graves for
All Souls' Day. I have taken it upon myself to maintain the chapel
and cemetery, and you may rest assured both are treated with my
utmost respect.

I await the birth of my own child; it is due by February.
I remain,
Yours faithfully,

Diamantina Rivaldo

I did not go into Kipling's to post the letter, as I did not want to run
into Espirito. For the first few days after Bonifacio learned of my
pregnancy, I had worried that he would confront Espirito. I knew
that there was already so much tension between them; now I couldn't
imagine the situation as they worked together at Kipling's.

As each day passed, I lost some of my anxiety, but I remained
very quiet around Bonifacio, cautious of saying or doing anything
that might give him reason to grow angry with me. And so I gave
the letter to Raimundo to take to Kipling's to post.

I was sitting on the veranda reading. Cristiano played in front of the
cottage with a wooden stick, brandishing it as if it were a sword,
swiping at low-hanging branches. Bonifacio was inside the house
with his Bible.

I looked up as Cristiano gave a cry, dropping his make-believe
sword. He ran down the path, where Espirito and Olívia very slowly
walked towards the cottage. Espirito supported Olívia with an arm
around her waist, and held a large basket in his other hand.

I wrapped my heavy shawl closely around myself as I went to the top step. Cristiano was walking beside Espirito with a cheery, marching step.

"Hello, Diamantina," Espirito called out, and I lifted my hand in a half wave. "We have come with cakes for Bonifacio's birthday," he said, and I swallowed. I hadn't known it was Bonifacio's birthday.

"How kind of you."

Olívia was gasping, one hand on her chest as she bent forward with each slow step.

"Since he said you weren't feeling well the last few times we've invited you all for dinner, and when he also declined our invitation to celebrate his birthday, we took it upon ourselves to come to you," he added as they stopped at the bottom of the step.

"I see," I said, holding my shawl tighter. Bonifacio had never mentioned these invitations. "Olívia, you must come in and sit down." I stepped aside, pulling open the door.

"Henry Duncan sends his regards," Espirito said. "We have begun the production of his altar wine."

I nodded. Cristiano ran into the cottage ahead of us. Bonifacio was standing, his Bible on the settee. A fire roared behind him.

"Espirito and Olívia have brought cakes for your birthday," I said, certain he'd already heard what Espirito had said. I stared at him, willing him to be polite.

"Thank you," he said to the two of them, though his eyes were on Olívia.

I took the basket from Olívia and set it on the table, then went to the cupboard and took out the fancy plates we never used. With my back to the room, I wiped them with my shawl, then turned, holding them in front of me.

Olívia had taken off her woollen cloak and was holding it out, waiting for Bonifacio to take it. He hadn't moved. The room was very warm. I set down the plates and reached for her cloak. As I did, my shawl fell open.

Olívia stared at me, then turned to Espirito. "Why didn't you tell me?"

It took Espirito too long to respond. "I wasn't aware either," he finally said. And then he looked into my face. I was trembling with the strain of trying to smile naturally, as though my condition were a blessed event. But I imagined I resembled a horrible spectre, a skull with bared teeth. Bonifacio stood straight and unmoving. We were both so rigid it was as though we would crack if we moved too quickly.

"When is it due?" Olívia asked.

"The beginning of February."

"You're that far along and haven't told us?"

I looked at her, unsure of how to respond.

"Oh. Now I understand. Surely my mother told you . . . If you were trying to spare me, I thank you. But there's no need. You have every right to the happiness of your own child. You and Bonifacio." She looked at Bonifacio then.

I remembered Espirito's face in Curral das Freiras after his father's death, when it was clear Bonifacio and I didn't share a bed. I thought of Espirito coming upon me as I left Abílio's office in the dark of night. But he didn't know of Bonifacio's mutilation. Or did he? I suddenly thought back to the night, seven months ago, when he brought Bonifacio home after finding him unable to go any farther on the road into Funchal. How he had sent for the physician. The way his hand shook as he drank when I asked him what was wrong with Bonifacio.

He knew. Surely he knew it would be impossible for Bonifacio to father a child.

All of these thoughts passed through me in less than thirty seconds. I lowered myself onto the settee, my legs weak.

By the hard look in Bonifacio's eyes, I understood that he still believed this child was his brother's. As Espirito had wed the woman he had once loved, he now believed Espirito had also had possession of his wife. Would Bonifacio confront Espirito here and now? It would be humiliating to announce that he suspected his brother of sinning with his wife, but even worse would be the disclosure that his wife was a whore.

I felt so small and ugly and filled with self-hatred that tears filled my eyes.

Olívia straightened her shoulders and opened the basket and

lifted out the small cakes, setting two on a plate. "*Feliz aniversário,* Bonifacio," she said, handing him the plate, then looked at me. "Could you direct me to the *latrina?*"

I led her to the hall and pointed at the door.

A few minutes later, when she hadn't returned, Espirito went down the hall. Bonifacio and I remained in the sitting room, the cakes untouched. Finally I gave Cristiano a cake, and he ate it quickly and looked at the basket. "Have another," I said, and he smiled with delight, unaware of the strain in the room.

I went to the hallway. Outside the *latrina*, Espirito stood with Olívia drawn against his chest, one arm around her thin back. With his other hand he slowly stroked her hair. I silently turned and went back to the sitting room, not wanting them to know I'd witnessed their shared moment of grief.

CHAPTER FIFTY-FOUR

1st December, 1750

Dear Diamantina,

I trust you are well, and that your confinement is progressing with ease.

My husband has informed me that he will be sailing to Funchal shortly, and will stay in the estate house. He intends to have repairs to the house carried out, and possibly replace some of the furniture. I have also begun a large restoration of this Belém house, and because of those responsibilities cannot leave at this time.

I write to ask a favour. Please go to my bedroom and open the second left-hand drawer of the larger wardrobe. Feel for a small latch at the very back of this drawer. Press it and the back of the drawer will fold down, revealing a small compartment. Inside is a piece of paper of great importance to me. I ask that you keep it for me and not disclose its whereabouts to anyone.

I cannot take the chance on having it sent to me by sea. It is for you to place into my hands and my hands only. Upon leaving the quinta, I felt it best that it remain there. Now I am concerned it will either be lost, should the wardrobe not remain, or fall into the wrong hands. I hope I am clear on this.

I apologize for the nature of this request. From knowing you the short time on the quinta, and our letters over these seven months— as well as the fact that you are the sister-in-law of the finest overseer

Kipling's has known—I believe you to be trustworthy, and must now put my faith in you.

I will take this opportunity to wish you Feliz Natal.

In appreciation,

Dona Beatriz Duarte Kipling Perez

Two weeks later, Bonifacio came in from work and said, "Senhor Perez arrived from Lisboa today. He's staying in the estate house for a few days."

I stood, a book in my hand.

"He asked about you, and said he hoped he would have a chance to speak to you about the quinta."

I turned, pressing the book against my chest. "I can't see anyone like this, so close to my confinement. Tell him it's impossible."

"All right," he said, and went down to the kitchen for dinner.

I went to my wardrobe and took out my travel bag. At the bottom, under my old shawl and my mother's jewellery, lay the unsealed scroll I had taken from Dona Beatriz's bedroom. I understood Dona Beatriz's concern that it be kept safe. Now I read it again. It was the deed for all of Martyn Kipling's holdings, in which he willed everything to Beatriz. It was dated ten years earlier. Inêz was named as second successor, should anything befall Beatriz. After their deaths, the dynasty would pass on to the offspring of Beatriz, or, should she not produce any, to those of Inêz. It could thus never be owned by a man marrying into the Kipling empire. Should both daughters die without progeny, the company and quinta were to be sold, and the profits donated to the Sé cathedral.

After I rolled up the scroll and put it back into the travel bag, I went to bed, thinking about Abílio. Surely he wasn't aware of this deed.

That night, I woke with a gasp, thinking I heard him calling my name, remembering how he had drunkenly shouted for me down the beach on Porto Santo.

I sat up in bed, my face and chest damp, and listened. But the night was quiet.

For the next few days, I stayed in the cottage, telling Cristiano to ask Binta to bring me my meals from the kitchen, fearful of running into Abílio.

⁂

A few days after Christmas, Raimundo knocked on the cottage door.

"This was just brought up from Funchal for you," he said, stepping inside and handing me a lumpy square of parchment, sealed with blue wax and tied with twine. "The messenger said it was sent by Espirito."

Cristiano came to stand beside me.

Senhora Diamantina Rivaldo, was written in unfamiliar copperplate. *Kipling's Wine Merchants, Funchal, Madeira.* The return address was São Paulo, Brazil. The letter was edged in black.

"Cristiano," Raimundo said, still looking at me, "do you want to come to the stable and take Chico for a slow walk around the yard? He needs some exercise."

"Can I go, Sister?"

I looked down at him without seeing him.

"Come, Cristiano," Raimundo said, and as soon as the door shut behind them, I put one hand over my mouth, feeling behind me for the settee. I lowered myself onto it and slowly untied the twine and opened the seal. A small packet fell from the folds onto my lap. I ignored it and unfolded the page.

São Paulo, Brazil

Dear Senhora Rivaldo,

My husband and I have been in your father's employ for the last two years, and have cared for him with great respect. It is my sad duty to inform you that he passed to the arms of Our Maker on July 14 in the Year of Our Lord 1750. He was buried according to his wishes, in the cemetery of the Dutch Reformed Church in

*the colony of Vitória da Conquista. But before he drew his last
breath, he received your letter, and wept with happiness.*

*I am setting down your father's words, spoken to me a week before
his passing, and I have enclosed the package as he requested.*

I am respectfully yours, and in sympathy,

Senhora Dores Horta de Melo

I cried out, and fell from the settee to my knees, the letter pressed
against my face.

My darling Diamantina,

You cannot imagine my joy at receiving your letter.

*I truly believed I would die without ever knowing if you
continued to live, hating me or, maybe worse, simply forgetting
me. So to receive your letter has given me the strength to die
in peace.*

*You were my blessing, Diamantina. The miracle of a child is
like no other. I can only hope that one day you will know this truest
gift from God. To hold your own child changes you forever. It is
then that you understand you have a purpose greater than you
ever imagined.*

*I am sending you all that is left of my legacy. I am sorry it
is not more, but I know you will use it for whatever your heart
directs. And as you look upon these gems, think of me, and of
our stargazing when you were the little girl I left behind. That's
how I still think of you, with your bright, shining hair and your
wide eyes, flashing the glowing basalt of the island or the silver
of the fish.*

*Although I know that we will never again meet on this earth,
I trust in God's power to bring us together in His own way. I bid
you farewell now, beloved daughter.*

Always, your loving father.

I keened then, wailing in the empty room. On my knees I rocked,
heavily, weeping for so long that when I finally pulled myself to my

feet, needing one hand on the settee to support myself, my head throbbed and my throat ached, my eyes swollen and tender. I reached forward to pick up the package that had fallen from my lap.

I lowered myself back onto the settee, the terrible weight of my father's death pushing on my chest as if a load of stones sat on it. It was not only the grief of losing him forever, but the death of my dream. For the last five years it was all I had gone towards—my father, and his love.

Now it was over. What did this mean? That I would stay forever trapped with Bonifacio, with a child I couldn't even envision, sired by a man I hated?

I dully tore open the paper, tightly sealed with wax all around, and looked down at the six small, sparkling diamonds on a square of dark blue velvet: the stars in the night sky. What good would they do me now?

I went to my bedroom and lay on my bed, holding the letter and the folded velvet with its spray of diamonds. In my other hand I clutched the talisman I never removed from around my neck. These things were all I had to remember my father by.

&

When the first pains came, a few weeks earlier than expected, I wasn't ready. I hadn't been able to prepare myself for the day I knew would come. Since receiving my father's letter, I hadn't left my bed, spending most of my time sleeping or staring at the sky through the window.

Cristiano had been my constant companion, running up and down from the kitchen to bring me meals, although I had little interest in food. He was taller now, his adult teeth grown in. He read fluently, and a few months earlier, when both he and I were tired of the sentences I wrote for him to read and then copy, I had gone into the library in the estate house and chosen books I knew he would be able to comprehend. As Cristiano read each, I returned it. I too was reading books from the library. Now, as I lay so still, he sometimes sprawled at the foot of my bed, reading. Once, just once, he looked up from his book and said, "I don't want you to die when the baby comes out."

I took a deep breath. "Why do you think I might die?"

He looked down again. "I just don't want you to die."

"I won't die, Cristiano." I said it with as much conviction as I could. Some days I thought that he was my only reason for waking up, my only reason for putting food I couldn't taste into my mouth and chewing and swallowing. Who else would care if I lived or died? I knew my grief had dragged me into a mire of self-pity, and yet I felt powerless to rise from it.

After lying awake since early morning as the mild pains gripped and then released, I waited until Bonifacio had gone to work and then called Cristiano into my room.

"I want you to go and ask Binta to come. The baby is going to be born today, Cristiano. You stay with Tiago and Nini and Raimundo until Binta tells you to come home."

He stood beside me, then reached out and wiped my face with his palms. "Don't cry, Sister," he whispered.

I didn't realize I was crying. It wasn't the pain; it was still the early stages. I caught his hands and held them in mine for a moment. "Get Binta," I repeated, and he left.

CHAPTER FIFTY-FIVE

After all the children I had helped into the world, I didn't expect that my lying-in would prove difficult. I rose, slowly, and made myself a herbal remedy to relax and open the mouth of my womb.

Binta was a comfort, but as the day progressed, I spent too many hours in heavy labouring, and knew the child was not coming with the ease I had envisioned. I had Binta send Raimundo for Gracinha. She was beside me within the hour.

"Something's wrong," I told her, surprised at how relieved I was to see her. "It feels as though the baby has dropped, but hasn't moved far enough to push."

Gracinha walked around and around the cottage with me. I kept drinking my potion, and to relieve the pain went to all fours and swayed as the beasts do. Every hour Gracinha felt inside me for the baby's head.

"Ahhh," she said finally, and I knew that her tone indicated some danger. "Diamantina, I feel the feet. The feet," she repeated, wiping her hands on her apron. "The child is coming out the wrong way. I wouldn't usually tell a woman this, but you know about these things. What do you want me to do? You could go on all night like this, Diamantina. It's not good for you, or the child."

Now it appeared my wish might come true. The baby might die. And I might die too, after another day of exhausting labour, if it couldn't be extracted. I kept the flat stick wrapped in cotton between my teeth at all times, not only to bite on during the rise and peak of the pain, but also so that I would not utter something Gracinha was not meant to hear. In my head, I cursed Abílio Perez. If I died, it would be because of him.

"Diamantina," Gracinha said again an hour later, "what do you want me to do?"

When the last pain subsided, I spat out the wood. "Cut me to make more room for the baby to come out."

"No. No, I've never cut."

"I don't care. Cut me open as much as you have to, and reach in. Reach in and pull down on the feet, carefully. See if you can feel the cord. Hopefully it isn't around the neck. And then when the legs are out, wrap a cloth around them and work out the rest of the body. The head should follow. Get it out, Gracinha," I cried, my voice rising as the next wave came so soon upon the heels of the last.

"I've never done it," she said again, when the rise of the pain had ended. "My other mothers do not ask me to cut them. They rely on God to make the decision as to whether they and the child will live or die."

"Do it," I panted. "I am making the decision." I lifted my head to stare at her.

Gracinha was pale as she bent over me with a knife she'd first held to a flame. The agony of the trapped child was so severe that the pain of the blade blended with it. I screamed as Gracinha worked on me, screamed until everything behind my eyes was red, and suddenly I was back on the beach on my belly, blood in my eye, the sailor forcing his way into me, and I was screaming, *No, stop, no more, no more.*

And then all was quiet save soft whimpering. I thought it was the baby, but as I opened my eyes I realized the sounds came from my own lips. I fell silent. The pain was different now, huge and almost unbearable, but not the same pain as the labour. Gracinha had turned away and set the baby on a sheet on the low cupboard. I watched her arms working rhythmically, and heard light slapping sounds.

She glanced over her shoulder at me, then left the baby and took a thick pad of cotton folded over fleece and pressed it between my legs. "We have to stop the bleeding right away, Diamantina," she said, turning back to the child.

"Is it alive?" I whispered.

"Yes. You have a daughter. But her colour isn't good, and she's having trouble breathing. God will decide whether to take her or leave her with us," she said, and at that moment there was a snuffling sound, and then a thin wail.

Gracinha crossed herself with one bloody hand. "Listen, Diamantina. God has shown us His compassion."

"A daughter," I repeated.

The child cried more lustily, and after Gracinha had put her into the padded basket, she threaded a needle and came to me. She put the wood between my teeth again. "I will do what I can to repair the damage. Courage," she said, "and pray, Diamantina. Pray to God to keep you on earth."

I went in and out of consciousness as she stitched. Finally I was aware that Gracinha was holding a cup to my lips. "Drink this, Diamantina," she urged. "You've lost so much blood, and will be weak for some time. And your body underwent great trauma. I can't say with certainty, but I suspect you won't carry another child." I stared at her in the lamplight. "It appears it is not your time to leave the earth yet, thank the Father and the Blessed Virgin." She crossed herself.

I wanted to thank her, for it was she who had saved the baby and me, but was too weak to speak.

She patted my hand. "You must treasure this child. She may be your only one."

I was so tired, so spent, that tears rolled down towards my ears.

"Now, now, I spoke too quickly. You may heal after all. One never knows God's will. He may reward you generously. You and Bonifacio may have seven or eight more. Perhaps all boys." She smiled encouragingly, but I turned my head on the pillow.

I wasn't crying over what she'd said. I was crying from sheer exhaustion, from the pain in my body, and, listening to the baby's wails, from the knowledge that for the rest of my life, every time I looked into the face of my child, she would remind me of the man who'd made me hate myself.

⁂

A weak morning sun filled the room. I was in a fresh nightdress, and the bedding was clean, smelling of the wind. Gracinha had piled pillows behind me, and helped me lean against them.

"Thank you," I said. "I would never have believed I would have had such difficulty."

"Every birth is different, and we can never predict," she said. The baby had been silent for a while, but now was making small mewling sounds. Gracinha brought her to me and set her in my arms.

I stared down at her. Her skin was pale and looked rich, like pearl. Her head was downy with dark hair. Her eyes, murky and dark, were open. She looked somehow weary, or worried. "I'm sorry," I whispered to her—sorry for her gruelling journey, and sorry for how she had come to be. Sorry that I didn't love her, and for what lay ahead for both of us.

Gracinha folded back the end of the blanket. "Look, Diamantina. A tiny imperfection. An extra toe, attached to the fifth on her right foot."

I stared down at the six tiny toes. Each had a minuscule nail, no bigger than a sliver of almond.

"Thank the Lord it is such a small defect. Nothing that will affect her life," she said, and I quietly echoed, *Yes, nothing that will affect her life.*

"A pretty baby, is she not?" Gracinha said, as if trying to make up for the extra toe. "Her colour has calmed, and she is delicate, like her mother. Nice full lips."

I thought of Leandro. Had he looked anything like this? I suddenly remembered his long eyelashes. His lips. Other than that, I couldn't tell if he and my daughter would resemble each other.

"I'll fetch the father now," she said, smiling. I looked from the baby to Gracinha, but said nothing.

⁂

She came back alone. "Your husband went to Funchal, Binta told me. To work." She frowned, shaking her head. "I have never known a new father to leave before knowing the outcome. Before even knowing if his wife . . ."

"It's all right," I said, perhaps too quickly.

Gracinha stayed with me for the day. I slept on and off, and fed the baby when she wailed. "You can't rise for at least a week," Gracinha told me as she prepared to leave that night. She lit the candle on the small table beside my bed. "I'll tell Binta and Nini to care for you, and I'll come by every day until I know you are recovering as you should."

Bonifacio's footsteps sounded in the sitting room.

"Here he is," Gracinha said. "The proud papa." She went to the bedroom door. "Come and see your beautiful daughter."

He stood in the doorway.

"Thank you, Gracinha, for everything," I said. "Please, go home to your own family. I'll see you tomorrow."

When she'd left, Bonifacio came into the room. All day I'd been trying to ready myself for whatever he would say to me.

He stood beside the bed and looked down at me. "Is she normal?"

Did he think the child would be a gargoyle, a two-headed monster, something inhuman that announced my sin to whoever looked upon her? Punishment for my immoral behaviour?

"Yes," I said. "She's normal." I couldn't be bothered to speak of the tiny extra toe. I looked up at him. "Would you like to have Telma as one of her names?" I had thought of this as I lay waiting for him. Perhaps it would soften his feelings towards the child.

He flinched. "After my mother? She was a good, God-fearing woman. Do you think I would put a curse on her memory by calling this abomination after her?"

"Abomination, Bonifacio?" I said in the same quiet voice, and pulled back the cover so he could see the child, with her tender skin and tiny curled fingers. "She's not to be blamed. Don't denigrate her because of my sin."

He sat in the chair beside my bed. "Choose any name to your liking. But not my mother's," he said, still looking at her.

"Candelária," I said after a strained silence. "Her name will be Candelária Rosemaria." Through the long hours of labour, I had focused on the flame of the candle beside the bed. As my body rose and fell with the pain's rhythms, I stared at the flame, willing it to hold still at the height of the pain, and then flicker as the grip of it weakened.

"Candelária," he repeated slowly.

"And Rosemaria for my mother."

He hadn't known my mother's name, neither Estra, as she was called on Porto Santo, nor Shada, as she had been named at birth. *Shada* means sweet fragrance, she had said. And every time I smelled rosemary, I thought of her.

Bonifacio took the baby from my arms, surprising me. In that instant I missed her comforting weight, her small, tired face. As he held her, I could see him as he must once have held infants over the baptismal font. He touched her cheek with his knuckle, as if tenderly nudging a sleeping ladybird, then made the sign of the cross on her forehead with his thumb. I saw the trembling beat on the top of her skull. When he looked up at me, his eyes were wet and filled with sorrow. In that moment I saw a shadow of what Olívia must have seen in him so long ago, when he was younger and softer, not yet so damaged.

He drew a long, shaky breath, wiping his eyes with his sleeve. "It's all a mistake," he said in a hushed voice.

"The baby?"

"Yes, her. Everything. Leaving the priesthood, taking Cristiano from his home and all he knew. Coming back and finding that my brother . . ." He stopped. "Marrying you. It's all led to bewildering chaos for me, emotionally and spiritually. I will admit that I was wrong to leave you alone with my father during Lent. I have been wrong about many things."

I looked at the sleeping baby. Her lips stretched into something that could have been a smile, or perhaps a grimace, and a spasm crossed over her face. She stretched and yawned, putting one tiny hand against her ear.

He set her back in my arms, then knelt and prayed. He prayed for the soul of the child, and for my soul, and that the evil surrounding us would be lifted. I closed my eyes and turned my face from him, not wanting to hear his pleas for mercy, not now, and not ever.

When he was finally gone, I held my little girl close. She could not be assigned guilt for her being. I would have to find a way to feel something for her beyond responsibility. She had no one in the world but me, and I would have to find a way to love her.

CHAPTER FIFTY-SIX

"Come, Cristiano," I said when the boy came with Binta for the first time to see me. He approached the bed cautiously. I put my free arm around him and hugged him, but instead of looking at the baby, he looked at me.

"I was afraid, Sister," he said.

"But it's all right. You can see that everything is all right," I said.

The baby sneezed. He jumped at the unexpected sound, then smiled at her. "But Sister?" he said, his smile disappearing. "Don't have another baby."

I remained in bed while my body healed, and Binta and Nini cared for me with gentleness and affection. Cristiano came to see me every day, although at night he stayed with Binta and Tiago.

⁂

I could not find any joy in my child, since every time I looked at her, I saw Abílio. My thoughts swirled around me like heavy, dark clouds as Madeira's winter sunshine flooded over my bed.

I was inordinately weary, even though I slept too much. I tensed each time the baby cried, and during the dark of night felt guilty for being angry when her cries awoke me every few hours.

"You should get up, Diamantina," Binta said to me after ten days. "You'll only grow weaker if you don't move."

I looked away from her kind face, towards the window.

"A number of women have come to the quinta's gates to seek your help. You are needed." She was holding Candelária as the baby fussed, hungry. "This little one needs you. I'm happy to keep Cristiano with me, but he needs you, too. This is his home. Here, with you and Bonifacio."

Bonifacio had come to my room every day to pray over us. Each morning, when I heard his door open and his footsteps in the hall, my stomach tightened, hating that he thought he had a right to pray for my innocent child's soul.

"Why do you cry?" Binta asked me now.

"I'm crying?" I asked, and reached up to touch my face. My fingers came away wet.

Candelária wailed lustily, her voice filling the room.

"You know how this sadness comes to some women after childbirth," Binta said above the baby's howls, "but you can't let it hold you. Would some of your own medicine help this after-birth sadness?"

"I have no more," I whispered. I had plundered my medicines to assuage my grief over my father for those weeks before Candelária's birth. I'd drunk my diluted powders to let myself drift above the bed with a sense of both weight and weightlessness, eventually falling into deep, dreamless sleeps. I had eaten all the opium, floating in a cloudy stream of colours and images that didn't let in thoughts of my father's death, or of the coming child. Oh, the child.

"It's time to feed your baby," Binta said, and put Candelária into my arms.

I held her loosely, watching her as she nursed, and wanted, with all my heart, to feel more than sorrow.

⁂

The next day, I heard voices outside the cottage. Candelária lay in her padded basket beside me on the bed.

I sat up at a quiet knock on the bedroom door. It opened, and Senhora da Silva looked in at me, smiling. "Diamantina? We have come to see the baby. May we come in?" She entered the bedroom without waiting for me to reply. Espirito followed, carrying Olívia, whose elegant face had withered further. He gently set her on the chair near the bed.

"Are you all right?" he asked her, and she nodded.

The bedroom, although spacious, felt too crowded. I struggled to breathe evenly.

Senhora da Silva took my hands and kissed me on either cheek. "Bonifacio only informed us of the birth yesterday, when Espirito asked about you. When we learned she was almost two weeks old . . . well, we didn't want you to think we weren't pleased for you." When she brushed back my hair, I realized what a dishevelled state I was in, but didn't care. "You're very pale," she said. "And your eyes . . . do your eyes pain you?"

I nodded; they were sore from weeping.

"The birth was difficult?" she asked, compassion in her voice.

I turned my face, not wanting to see how Espirito and Olívia looked at me.

"We're sorry, aren't we, Olívia, that we weren't told sooner," Senhora da Silva said, and I heard Olívia's quiet "Yes."

I looked at her again. She was so much weaker since I'd seen her last. Espirito stood beside her, his hand on the back of the chair.

"May I hold her?" Senhora da Silva asked and, once more without waiting for my permission, reached into the basket and picked up the baby. "What name have you and Bonifacio chosen?"

Bonifacio hadn't even told them what I'd named her. "Candelária."

"She's a beautiful child," Senhora da Silva said. "She doesn't have your colouring, but there's something of you about the mouth and chin. Come and see her, Espirito. Does she look anything like your mother?"

"It's hard to tell," he said, coming to stand beside his mother-in-law.

"I don't see anything of Bonifacio at all," Senhora da Silva continued, studying her. She pulled away the warm blanket to look at the soft little wool gown Nini had made for her. Candelária stretched her legs, waving her bare feet in the air. "Oh, *meu bebê*, such long legs," Senhora da Silva cooed, and Espirito took a step back.

"Excuse me," he said abruptly, and left the room.

I stared after him, then glanced at Olívia.

"He wanted a child as much as I did," she said. "And some days, under some circumstances, even . . . ." She touched her lips with her gloved fingers. "Even on such a happy occasion as this, his grief surfaces unexpectedly." Her face was white and damp, like plaster on a humid day.

"I'm sorry, Olívia." I wasn't sure what I was apologizing for.

She looked towards the door, then back at me. "You needn't apologize for having a child," she said, and I dully watched as she held out her arms and Senhora da Silva placed Candelária in them.

As Olívia looked down at Candelária, she said, "A child is always a blessing. I will only see this little girl as a blessing."

Senhora da Silva sat beside me and patted my hand. "It's all right to cry, Diamantina. Cry for the wonder of God's will and His mysterious ways."

To my horror, my quiet crying turned to sobs. "My father died," I said, too loudly, the words somehow shocking in the quiet room where the talk was of the baby and new life. I had no warning I would speak of my father. I covered my face with my hands.

Senhora da Silva cried out, "No!" and put her arms around me and rocked me. She made soft sounds of comfort, and I leaned against her and wept as if I had received the letter announcing my father's death that very day.

"Olívia," she said quietly, "take the baby to the sitting room."

After a long while, listening to the slow beat of her heart against my face, my breathing calmed, and I could cry no more. Senhora da Silva wiped my face with her own lacy handkerchief, smelling of lavender. "Now," she said softly, giving me the handkerchief. "We will mourn the loss of your father, but as we also celebrate the birth of your child, you must remember that he lives on through her."

I hadn't even thought of that simple, comforting notion, and nodded.

"What was your father's name?"

"Arie. Arie ten Brink," I said, his name stuttering in my throat.

"A Dutchman? Ah. Yes, of course. The hair and eyes. And yet your skin . . . it's such a rich colour—from your mother?"

I nodded.

"And you loved your father very much," she stated. "Is he buried on Porto Santo?"

"He sailed to Brazil a number of years ago. I was to go to him there, one day. But he died before . . ." I tried to take a deep breath, my chest heaving, and again Senhora da Silva held me.

"How will we mourn him, buried so far from here?" she asked. We sat in silence for a few moments. Then she said, "Perhaps you could inquire of Senhor Perez if you could put a marker in the grave-yard at the chapel of Nossa Senhora das Uvas here on the quinta. It would be a place for you to pray and remember him, and find comfort, as we do when we visit the graves of our loved ones."

I thought of the three stone markers—Dona Beatriz's family—in the shady, fenced cemetery at the side of the pretty little chapel.

"And your mother? She is buried on Porto Santo?"

I thought of my mother floating away from me.

"You could put up a marker for her as well," Senhora da Silva said.

I nodded.

"Does your little girl look like your mother? There's a lovely shape to her eyes."

I had forgotten the beautiful almond contour of my mother's eyes. "Yes. Candelária's eyes are shaped like my mother's. Her eyes were green. Dark green."

"We can't always tell with a newborn. Perhaps Candelária's eyes will be green too."

I knew Senhora da Silva was trying to keep me talking, trying to keep me from falling back into my near-hysterical weeping.

"We will plan the baptism. I assume you and Bonifacio will wish Espirito and Olívia to be the godparents?"

I took a deep breath.

"And if you will allow it, I would like to be known as Avó to the baby."

I stared at her, her damp handkerchief balled in my hand. "You wish Candelária to call you grandmother?"

"The poor child has no living grandparents. She isn't our blood, but she is our son-in-law's blood, and this is as close as we will come to being grandparents. I have already asked Olívia and Espirito their opinion, and they do not disapprove. Would you speak to Bonifacio about it, and ask his permission?"

Poor Senhora. I was deceiving her as well. "Of course you shall be Avó. Bonifacio won't care," I said truthfully.

"And I wish you to call me by my given name, Luzia. It would bring us all closer, don't you think?" she asked wistfully. "I'm not going to allow you to lie here alone, grieving. It's terrible that you've had to bear this news with only Bonifacio to comfort you, and he's . . ." She stopped, then straightened, smoothing her bodice over her ample bosom. "Well. Certainly he's been some comfort."

I hadn't told Bonifacio about my father's death.

"I'm going to visit you every day, until you are weary of me and tell me to stay away," she said, smiling. "And I am going to spoil that sweet child, and maybe, if you'll allow me, I'll spoil you a little, as I spoil my own daughter. Every young woman needs a mother at the time she becomes a mother herself. You'll see. Soon you'll feel better," she announced, with complete authority.

⁂

The next day, Luzia came, as promised, and took charge. She asked Binta to send Cristiano home, and I was surprised at how his presence helped to prod me from my darkness.

A few days later, Luzia brought Candelária a beautiful baptism gown of finest linen, gathered with bows and ribbons, and a handsome suit of clothes for Cristiano. The week following, I rose from my bed, and sat on the sofa while Luzia played cards with Cristiano as Candelária, bathed and fed, slept deeply in her basket beside me. I felt as though I were recovering from a terrible illness, one that had ravaged not just my body but also my spirit. Some days I still wept, but more and more time went by without morbid thoughts. Each day, Luzia stayed until Bonifacio returned from Funchal, and then she walked down to the yard, where Eduardo waited for her with a cart and ox to take her home.

When Candelária was five weeks old, we had a family baptism,

held in Our Lady of the Grapes with a priest from Funchal officiating. I knew that Bonifacio hadn't given up the notion that
Espirito was Candelária's father, and he watched me more closely
than ever whenever Espirito's name was mentioned, or when he
was in our presence.

Bonifacio stared at Espirito while he held Candelária, and a small
thump of danger beat in my throat, standing in the chapel near the
spot where Candelária had been conceived. Then Bonifacio studied
Candelária as the priest anointed her. I saw only her small, tidy nose,
the pursed pink lips, the smooth little eyebrows. He couldn't see
something I didn't, could he? I didn't like how he looked at her. I
was surprised at the sudden wave of fierce protectiveness I felt for
this tiny new being, something I'd never expected to feel.

Later, between Cristiano's excitement at the sweets Luzia had
brought for him, and the passing around of Candelária so everyone
could admire her gown and the tiny gold cross Espirito and Olívia
had given her as a baptism gift, I hoped that no one noticed that
Bonifacio was the only person who did not hold Candelária.

CHAPTER FIFTY-SEVEN

1st March, 1751

Dear Diamantina,

I am so sorry to hear of the passing of your father, but hope the birth of your daughter softens that terrible blow. I give you my permission to place markers for your parents in the cemetery of Nossa Senhora das Uvas.

Thank you for assuring me that you have carried out my wishes with regards to my request in my earlier letter. I hope to come to Funchal when I can leave my duties.

I am surprised to be enjoying living in Santa Maria de Belém as much as I do. It is a parish a league and a half outside the heart of Lisboa, established in the previous century by the monarchy and nobility hoping to escape the sometimes fetid confines of the city. It's an area of wealth surrounded by countryside; the Palace of Belém is nearby, on a hill overlooking the parish, where King José and his family usually reside in the summer months.

I am also enjoying the rebuilding of the house in which my mother grew up. It has fallen into some disrepair, and while contemplating its renewal, I decided to add a new wing. It is time-consuming but a pleasure to help with the design and plan the new gardens and furnishings. It will be some time before it is even near to completion.

Another very unexpected pleasure for me here lies in the company of my mother's family. Her two sisters live in the parish, while another lives in Estoril. My aunts and their families have opened

*their arms to us, and we have gathered for a number of large
and joyous family celebrations. I'm sure my mother missed her
family when she moved to Funchal to marry my father, yet she
never complained.*

*My husband spends more time in Oporto than in Belém, as
business takes him there.*

With regards,

Dona Beatriz

⌘

During the spring and summer following Candelária's birth, I
sometimes went into Funchal, to the house on São Rua
Batista, mainly at Luzia's request. While Cristiano played happily
with the growing collection of wooden toys kept in a chest in the
salon for our visits, Olívia and Luzia and I made a fuss over
Candelária. In spite of Olívia's own grief at her childlessness, she
grew slightly warmer to me through the baby.

We celebrated when Candelária first reached for a plaything,
when she rolled over, and clapped at her comical attempts to sit up
unaided. At times I left the children with Olívia and Luzia while I
ran errands.

And on my way back with my baskets, I often crossed the courtyard behind the Counting House. Sometimes I stopped in the *adega*
and looked at the huge kegs of wines made from Madeira's grapes:
the large, pale green Verdelho and sweet Terrantez, the heavy Boal
and smaller, compact Sercial, the sturdy red *tinta* used mainly for
blending. I breathed in the aromas of wines so full-bodied and sweet
they were fantasized about by the English on their own damp, cool
island, according to what Henry Duncan had once told me. I tried
to imagine the statesmen in the American colonies recently enam-
oured of our wines, and those in the West Indies who had long
known of Madeira's elixirs. I thought of the dark, broiling hold of a
caravel with its casks of Kipling's wine pitching and tossing below
deck, the heat turning the wines sweeter by the day.

I talked to old Jorge as he made the bungs for the casks, and watched the coopers at their work. During that year's September harvest I often saw the *borracheiros* arrive in the courtyard, exhausted and filthy and sometimes slightly intoxicated from drinking from the goatskins of *mosto* they carried from the terraces to Funchal. I watched as Espirito weighed the contents of their goatskins as they emptied them into vats. The aroma of the pressed grapes was so heady that I felt as though I, along with those hard-working carriers, had been quenching my thirst.

❦

After harvest that year, I found two round stones approximately the same size in the field of wildflowers on the quinta. I asked Raimundo to bring them back in a cart, and whitewashed them and wrote *Arie* on one and *Shada* on the other. I chose not to purchase headstones with one of the gems my father had sent, as I had no wish to have to explain anything to Bonifacio.

I chose a small sunny patch a distance from the graves of Beatriz's parents, and Raimundo helped me work the stones into place. I dug up wild myrtle and lupines, and took cuttings from the cultivated hydrangea and heliotrope in the big estate garden, and created a tiny but beautiful garden around the stones.

But that evening, when Bonifacio came into the cottage, his face was dark with anger. "How dare you desecrate the graveyard with the names of non-believers?"

I stood and faced him. "Dona Beatriz allowed me to put markers to honour my parents in the cemetery. Besides, my father was a believer of his own faith."

"It's blasphemy." His look made me glad that Candelária was asleep and Cristiano reading on the veranda. "You will remove them tomorrow."

I stared into his face. "I won't. I have permission, as I told you. The graveyard is not yours. You hold no authority over what is placed there."

He took a sudden step towards me, and I drew in my breath but didn't move. He was close enough for me to see his pupils contract. "I have authority as your husband to tell you what you may and may not do."

"I will not remove them," I said quietly, and at that, he closed his eyes for a moment, and then turned and walked into his bedroom.

⁂

That night, a huge storm blew up, the trees contorted black shapes thrashing as though caught in a maelstrom.

We had all slept poorly because of the thunder and lightning, and Bonifacio was later than usual rising that morning, so we left together to walk down to the kitchen for breakfast. The yard outside our cottage was littered with fallen branches, and my herb garden flooded. As we turned the curve of the path and saw the chapel, both Bonifacio and I stopped in shock. The roof had been crushed by a huge limb. Tiles lay scattered on the path, and there was an ominous feel in the heavy grey air, water dripping from the leaves through the ruined roof. I put Candelária into Cristiano's arms and followed Bonifacio inside the chapel, stepping over more roof tiles and chunks of plaster from the destroyed wall. Shattered glass candle holders were scattered over the floor. Our Lady was tilted in her niche, her hand broken off along the repaired seam.

"I'll have to arrange to have a new roof built," I said. "I'll write to Dona Beatriz about this today."

Bonifacio didn't appear to hear me. He straightened the small statue and picked up her hand, holding it as gently as though it were human. "It is a sign of God's displeasure," he said, but before I could open my mouth to argue, he looked from the statue's hand to me. "God's displeasure," he repeated. "I tried once to repair the damage, but He has shown me I haven't worked hard enough." He laid down the hand and went into Funchal without breakfast.

⁂

Dona Beatriz came for a visit in mid-November. Espirito drove her up from Funchal, and as he helped her out of the cart, I realized I had forgotten the warmth of her smile. Jacinta followed her, with Leandro struggling in her arms.

At Dona Beatriz's nod, Jacinta put Leandro down. He was a sturdy, red-cheeked boy, who gazed at us all with open curiosity. He immediately toddled towards Cristiano and Tiago. Cristiano was holding a small wooden cart Raimundo had carved, and Leandro held his hands out for it. Apart from the dark hair and eyes, I realized he bore no resemblance to Candelária. I had been holding my breath and now I let it out.

Dona Beatriz had no reason to suspect that Leandro and Candelária were brother and sister. And she never could.

At that moment, Leandro fell to his hands and knees on the soft dirt in front of Cristiano, and Jacinta sprang forward to help him up. But Cristiano put his hands under Leandro's arms and set him on his feet again. When Leandro pulled at the little cart, Cristiano graciously relinquished it. Jacinta bent down to brush the dust from the knees of Leandro's velvet breeches and polished the toes of his little boots with the edge of her apron.

Dona Beatriz greeted Binta and Nini and Raimundo, then turned to me. "This is your little one," she stated, studying Candelária.

"Not quite ten months," I said.

I could see Espirito out of the corner of my eye, standing beside the cart.

"Please come to the house in an hour," she said to me.

"Certainly, Dona Beatriz," I said, and she left, Jacinta slowly walking behind her, holding Leandro's hand.

I asked Binta to look after Candelária and went to the cottage, where I took the deed from my travel bag and waited until the hands of the clock struck the appointed hour.

⁂

Dona Beatriz opened the scroll and ran her eyes over it.

When she'd finished reading, she rolled it up and set it on the desk. "Thank you again for keeping this this for me, and for your discretion." She went to the sideboard. "Would you care for a glass of sweet lemon?"

I accepted the glass, noticing the tick at the corner of her mouth.

She saw me looking at it. "Something I've developed from living with Abílio," she said, putting her fingers to it as if to hold the frenzied ticking in place.

"I'm sorry, Dona Beatriz, I didn't mean to—"

She waved her hand in the air. "It comes and goes. When he's not around, it stills, and as soon as he's in my presence for more than a few days, my nerves put on a display. It should disappear now that I'm here." She smiled. "The quinta appears to be in excellent order. I'm pleased how you've kept an eye on everything."

"Binta and Nini and Raimundo do all the work."

"Yes, and I'm very grateful to them as well. But it's a comfort to have someone here who can read and write and converse in both Portuguese and English. I'll go down to the wine lodge tomorrow to talk to Espirito. How is his wife? Is she still suffering badly from her asthma?"

"Asthma." I repeated the strange English word. "I didn't know its name, but have seen the disease before."

"It's how the English refer to it. From the Greek word for panting."

"Olívia is never truly well, although at times a little stronger."

Dona Beatriz touched the tick again. "It makes my small condition of the nerves seem trivial."

⌒

Over the next week, Dona Beatriz invited me to visit her every day in the big house.

I lost my stiffness with her and we laughed together as we shared funny stories about our children's antics. Although noble-born, she had a very easy air, and wasn't overbearing or arrogant. On the day before she was due to sail back to Lisboa, she arrived at the cottage, leading Leandro by the hand and carrying a basket.

Surprised to see her, I glanced around the sitting room, relieved it was tidy.

"I gave Jacinta the day to visit some of her friends in Funchal, and thought Leandro and Candelária could play together while we visit here for a change."

"Yes, of course. Please come in," I said, feeling odd inviting her into the house she owned.

"I always liked this cottage," she said. "It feels even more pleasant now, a real home with the children's things. Where is Cristiano?"

"With Tiago. They're probably down in the stable with Raimundo. They love the horses."

Beatriz took a flask with a silver cap from her bag and set it on the table.

I fetched glasses from the cupboard and poured the wine. As we sipped, I made a sound of pleasure as the liquid went down my throat. "Round and soft," I said. "A wonderful Malvasia *velhissimo*."

Beatriz looked at the unmarked flask. "How do you know what it is?"

"It's the smoothness, combined with a slight bitterness of flavour underneath. It has to be at least twenty years old."

She tilted her head. "What is your connection with wines?"

"When I was growing up on Porto Santo, my father often took me to a friend's inn, where they discussed and tasted wine." There were many ways to carve the truth; my story sounded almost respectable. I suddenly thought of Bonifacio in Curral das Freiras, telling me I had the devil on my tongue.

"Not many women are interested in the making of wine. Drinking, yes," she added with a smile, "but the production and blending, no. We are alike in this, it appears. I'm so glad I have you here. You are like the overseer of my property," she added with a small laugh. The wine was loosening her; her face looked warm. "As my father did not have a son, he took me into the business with him, teaching me all aspects of it. What did your father do?"

"He was a sailor, but then worked in the diamond trade in Brazil." I took another drink. "He taught me to read and write in both Dutch and Portuguese."

"It seems our fathers influenced us greatly, and made us into the women we are today. And your mother?"

"She influenced me as well. As I have told you, she taught me the skills of *curandeira* and midwife. She . . ." I saw her floating in a pale sky, her body undulating, beautiful in its design. "She taught me about strength. About what we must do to survive."

"In contrast, my mother was very gentle, and perhaps too accommodating. My sister Inêz resembled her in both appearance and nature. But I am my father's daughter." She looked at the children on the carpet near our feet. They ignored each other but were both busy with the scattered playthings. "I hope to impart the strengths I have learned to my son. And your husband, Diamantina?" She poured us each another glass.

"What of him?"

"You don't speak of him. When I visited the Counting House this week, I had a conversation with him. He seems . . . efficient."

I nodded. "He is. Efficient and single-minded."

Dona Beatriz tilted her head. "It's not my place to say. But you seem unsuited." She smiled. "As I'm sure people say of me and Abílio."

I didn't return the smile. "We marry for different reasons, don't we, Dona Beatriz?"

Now Candelária cried out as Leandro snatched a small cloth dolly from her. She looked at me and howled in protest. I laughed and went to her, picking her up. "It's not that bad, little one," I said, pressing my nose against her sweet-smelling hair. Then I sat again, with her on my lap, caressing her little white leather boots with my fingertips.

"Do you hope for more children?" Dona Beatriz asked.

"No," Bonifacio said, standing in the doorway.

I gasped, shocked at his unseen presence. How long had he stood there? It was early; he usually didn't arrive home from work until later in the day.

"Hello, Bonifacio," Dona Beatriz said, looking from him to me and back to him.

He didn't return the greeting. "No," he repeated, coming into the sitting room. "Candelária will be Diamantina's only child." He stared at me.

I took a deep breath, feeling the need to respond. "Her birth was damaging."

"I'm sorry to hear that," Dona Beatriz said. There was a moment's silence, and then she said, "Do you care to sit with us, Bonifacio?"

"No, thank you. I will go to the chapel. There is much to pray about on this quinta." He still looked pointedly at me. Candelária slid off my lap and crawled back to the toys.

I was embarrassed by his comment, but Dona Beatriz only said, "Good day, then," as Bonifacio left without another word.

"Dona Beatriz, I apologize for my husband's behaviour. He . . . he is often distracted after work," I said, unable to come up with a better excuse for his rudeness.

"Never mind," Dona Beatriz said.

We watched the children again. After what felt like a long, uncomfortable time, Bonifacio's presence still lingering in the room, she said, "Leandro will be my only child as well."

"Why is that, Dona?"

She looked at her son. "Abílio is wandering. I knew he would, as my father warned me. He has a woman in Lisboa, and I suspect another in Oporto. There are few secrets in the world I live in." She looked back at me. "He is rarely with me, and it's clear we feel no attraction any longer. I don't mind. I like my life in Belém. When we're together, we do little but argue over the business. He's not interested in it, not the way he should be." She raised her eyebrows. "But I got what I wished. I have a child, and I have a new and unexpectedly happy life in Belém. I have nothing to complain about."

I waited a moment. "Nor do I," I said, attempting a smile, sure that in Dona Beatriz's eyes I had nothing to complain about apart from a husband with a lack of manners.

CHAPTER FIFTY-EIGHT

In late May of 1752, I sat in the salon with Olívia and Luzia, Candelária toddling about our feet. At sixteen months, she was stringing her first words together and making us laugh with some of her attempts at conversation.

Ana ushered in Bonifacio.

"What is it, Bonifacio?" Olívia asked.

"I am here to escort my wife to the *adega*."

I rose in alarm at his expression. "Why? Why am I wanted?"

"We will speak of it downstairs," he said.

"Could you watch Candelária for a few moments?" I asked Luzia and Olívia, picking up my cloak.

"Dr. McManus is coming later," Olívia said peevishly.

Luzia waved her hand at me. "Go, go, it's all right."

I followed my silent husband out into the street. "What's happened, Bonifacio?"

He stopped and looked at me. "The Englishman Duncan is meeting with Espirito. He expressed a desire for your opinion. Your opinion," he repeated, shaking his head. "Espirito told him you were visiting upstairs. Duncan sent me to fetch you, as if I were his messenger." His jaw tightened, and then he grabbed my hand and hurried me along after him, down the alley that led to the *adega*.

I tried to pull my hand free, but he held it too tightly as we went to the blending room together. I was embarrassed to stand in front of Espirito and Mr. Duncan like this, Bonifacio gripping my hand as if I were a child or a lover.

"I'm glad you were nearby, Diamantina," Mr. Duncan said, and nodded at Bonifacio.

"Hello, Mr. Duncan," I said, hiding my hand in the folds of my skirt, trying to untangle my fingers from Bonifacio's. My face was hot. I didn't look at Espirito.

"Please. Call me Henry," Mr. Duncan said. "We're sampling the altar wine from that first harvest two years ago. I'm considering sending it to England." He lifted a tasting glass. "Espirito and I are debating whether it's ready for us to ship it now, or should we wait until fall to let it ferment further." He spoke English, and I knew Bonifacio couldn't understand him.

Bonifacio finally let go of my hand and stepped forward, taking the glass. He sniffed it, looked at Henry, then handed it to Espirito.

There was an awkward silence as Espirito held the glass. Then he took a sip and let it sit in his mouth. He spat it into a small dish.

"Well, Espirito?" Henry said. "What are your—"

Bonifacio interrupted. "I have to return to my desk."

We all looked at him.

"All right, Bonifacio," Henry said, in Portuguese. "Thank you for bringing Diamantina." He looked at me as Bonifacio left. "Your husband seemed offended. It was not my intention."

I shook my head and cleared my throat, further embarrassed.

"Perhaps it was discomfort," Henry said. "It appears he's not at ease in the *adega*. Well. What are your thoughts on the wine, Espirito?"

"I think we should wait. It would benefit from another few months."

"And you, Diamantina?" Henry said. "Try it, and see if your opinion is the same as Espirito's."

I tasted it and spat it out, trying to push aside my discomfort over Bonifacio's behaviour. "It's important, isn't it, Mr. Duncan—Henry— that this first vintage is perfect? You want to show them that your altar wine stands apart, in the hopes they offer another contract. Am I correct?"

"Yes."

"Then I agree with Espirito. It's full-bodied, and perfectly acceptable as it is, but another few months in the warmth would benefit it."

"As I feel too," Henry said. "Those in my *adega* are saying we should be sending it now, though. They're anxious to get it into the pipes to be shipped because they want to start a new vintage in the barrels with the fall's harvest."

I looked at Espirito. "Surely we can have more barrels made. Our cooperage is bigger than yours, isn't it, Henry?"

Henry crossed his arms. "I can see why Dona Beatriz is so trusting of your judgment, Diamantina." I smiled, and he added, "Sit down, please. Both of you." As Espirito and I sat, he continued, "I've returned from Lisbon recently, and while there visited with Dona Beatriz and Perez. I have little regard for either the palate or business acumen of Perez, but I've known Dona Beatriz since she was younger than you, Diamantina, and I consider us friends. Dona Beatriz was very happy about this new arrangement I have with Kipling's to make the altar wine.

"As you and I originally discussed, Espirito, after the sale I was prepared to give Dona Beatriz twenty-five percent of the profits." He laughed. "But she's a good negotiator, and knows the business. At her suggestion, we will partner on the altar wine contract, with the split at sixty percent to me and forty to her. It will provide sufficient monies to keep the winery going as Martyn wished, but also give her more funds for her pursuits in Belém. Her husband isn't overly concerned about the Madeira operations, and had pulled me aside to broach the subject of selling Kipling's to me. He'd rather have a great deal of money outright than depend on a yearly income."

"You? Buy the winery? But Martyn Kipling . . ." I stopped, not wanting to disclose that I knew what was in the deed Dona Beatriz's father had left her.

"Perez is simply greedy. He proposed a ridiculous sum, one I would never even consider." Henry shook his head and pulled a sheaf of papers from his case. "Here is the copy of the contract Dona Beatriz signed." He set the papers on the table.

Espirito picked them up. "Barrels apart, your *adega* doesn't have such capacity, Henry."

"You're right. Dona Beatriz has asked me to work on her behalf to obtain the building next door and have a second Kipling *adega* built. But this partnership on the altar wine necessitates other changes here. Espirito, instead of bringing in another blender, Dona Beatriz and I decided that we'd like you to look after the production of the altar wine and its shipping. How do you feel about that?"

Espirito smiled. "So, Henry, you're finally getting me to work for you again." He grew serious. "That's a lot of responsibility. I'm not sure I can handle my duties between two *adegas* during harvest."

Henry held up a hand. "Yes. Dona Beatriz and I discussed that as well." He turned to me. "She's very taken with you, Diamantina. Her father taught her to be a good judge of character. She would like you to help Espirito oversee the operations here during the busiest periods."

She had called me the overseer of Quinta Isabella when she was last there. I looked from Henry to Espirito, and back to Henry. "I'm honoured, but I know nothing about the job. What would I do?"

"She didn't specify, except to say you had an excellent brother-in-law to give you direction. She thinks everyone benefits when business ventures are kept within a family. This means there would be three Rivaldos working for Kipling's."

"Dona Beatriz didn't want to hire another man?" Espirito asked.

"She wants someone she can trust, and she openly contested her husband's choices for a part-time overseer. Then she asked me about Diamantina's knowledge. I told her the truth—that Diamantina has a taster's tongue," he said, looking at me and smiling. "Her palate is excellent."

I sat very still, an excited beating in my temples.

"We must do whatever makes Dona Beatriz Kipling Perez happy," Henry said, nodding first at Espirito and then at me.

Espirito's expression was less certain. "I don't think the men Diamantina would have to deal with would accept her."

"They would have no choice, would they?" I said.

Henry laughed. "Come, Espirito. You won't throw her into it without help. It doesn't have to happen all at once. I'm sure she's already a familiar figure around the *adega*. It will take some time for the wine growers and shippers to get used to her, but if they want to deal with Kipling's, they'll have to deal, at times, with Senhora Diamantina Rivaldo."

"What would I be expected to do, Espirito?" I asked.

He thought for a moment. "You can work with me, to begin, checking on the *mosto* the *borracheiros* bring down from the vineyards, weighing it and making sure our payment to the vineyard owners matches what they delivered. If you find that within your grasp, you can relieve me in negotiating prices with the owners, depending on the season and quality of the grapes. You have to regularly check on the barrels, tasting the wine to make sure it's progressing properly. When it's ready, you will supervise the emptying of the barrels into the pipes before they're loaded onto the ships. That sounds like a lot, but, as Henry said, you can go slowly at first."

I looked from him to Henry. "So I would start this harvest?" When he nodded, I said bravely, "I can do that." Inside I was trembling with eagerness at this unexpected opportunity. "I can do it," I repeated.

I crossed the flagstone courtyard and stood on Rua São Batista, letting the cool breeze from the ocean take the excited heat from my face before I opened the front door and climbed the stairs. In the salon, Ana was cleaning out the fireplace. She pointed towards the bedrooms. I went up, and found Dr. McManus with Olívia. She was lying on her bed while he pressed his ear against her chest. Candelária slept soundly on the settee under the window.

Olívia's breathing was laboured. As her eyes went to me, the physician rose.

"My sister-in-law, Senhora Rivaldo," Olívia whispered.

"I shall be done my examination in a moment," he said, dismissing me.

I went back into the hallway to wait, and when he came out, I walked down the stairs with him. "Is there anything more we can do, Dr. McManus?" I asked in English.

He buttoned his jacket before speaking. "There's little to do but continue as always, making her comfortable."

I felt a chill. "Thank you," I murmured, and went back upstairs.

Olívia was coming into the hallway, smoothing her hair into place. "It's just the weather affecting me."

"Your mother left?"

"My father arrived early for her."

"I'm so sorry. I didn't know you would be left alone to cope with Diamantina."

"It's all right." She studied me. "You have much colour in your cheeks today. I'll have Ana make us some tea while we wait for Candelária to wake." She went down the stairs, gripping the banister, and I followed, thinking of the look on the physician's face as he spoke to me. "Why were you wanted in the *adega*?" she asked, sitting down and looking up at me.

"Mr. Duncan had a message for me from Dona Beatriz," I said after a tiny hesitation. I wasn't comfortable telling her I'd be working with Espirito, but wasn't sure why. I would leave it up to him to tell her, as I'd tell Bonifacio. "Has Candelária been sleeping long?" I asked, wanting to change the subject.

"She fell asleep almost as soon as you left. She rarely slows down."

"I know. She wakes up full of energy and runs about all day. Sometimes it's difficult to get her to stop long enough to feed her."

"She clearly takes after you, quick in movement and, I can already tell at her young age, in her thinking." As she picked up the bell to ring for Ana, she began coughing. I went to her and rubbed her back. By the time she was able to stop, Candelária was calling, "Mama, Mama," from upstairs.

"I'll go and get her," I said, but as I crossed the room, Olívia said, "Your daughter already appears fearless. She shows no caution."

I stopped and looked back at her.

"She gets that from you as well." Her gaze was piercing, and I felt compelled to turn away from it. "We all know *you're* not cautious at all," she called after me as I went up the stairs.

When I came back down carrying Candelária, Bonifacio was standing in the middle of the salon. "I went to see if you were still in the *adega*," he said, and I busied myself straightening Candelária's ribbons.

"Obviously I wasn't," I said.

"It's time for you to take her home," he said, nodding at Candelária. She was rubbing her eyes.

I wanted to ask him what business it was of his how I raised my daughter. He had never before shown any concern for her physical well-being. I glanced at Olívia. Was it for her benefit, this act of the doting father?

"Take her home, now," he said.

"I was on my way," I said tightly. "Thank you again, Olívia." I picked up Candelária's little cloak.

"It was no trouble," Olívia said quietly.

Bonifacio followed me down the stairs. We didn't speak as he turned into the Counting House and I went towards the square to hire a cart to drive Candelária and me home.

CHAPTER FIFTY-NINE

20th October, 1752

Dear Diamantina,

*Thank you so much for your work in the wine lodge this fall.
When I saw Henry recently, he informed me it was a year of high
yield on the island, producing the most successful harvest to date.
He stated that your assistance allowed Espirito to devote more time
to the preparation and shipping of the first vintage of altar wine to
England. I'm also happy to hear from Henry that the expansion
of the second adega progresses as hoped.*

*In spite of Abílio's losses as he attempts to move some of the
business into the port venture, I must do whatever I can to protect
Kipling's. It is Leandro's legacy, as my father wished.*

*My life continues to be full. I particularly love to visit my aunt
in Estoril, a number of leagues west of Lisboa. I stroll through her
citrus groves and take the healing baths.*

*I also visit Lisboa frequently. There, life is very different from
provincial Belém. Only slave women, maidservants and women
of the working masses are seen on the streets. Upper-class ladies
remain respectably cloistered unless in the presence of husbands
or fathers. There is the terrible fiery madness of the autos-da-fé
and the pomp and ceremony of the royals as they parade through
the streets in their opulent carriages. There is splendour in
the churches with their gold and silver altars studded with
precious stones.*

*I do enjoy these forays, but am always happy to return to the quiet
streets of Santa Maria de Belém.*

    *I hope all is well for you. Although I am grateful for the speed
of the ships passing between the mainland and Madeira, carrying
our letters back and forth, I would prefer to sit and talk face to
face as we did almost a year ago.*

    With my warm thoughts,

Dona Beatriz

I had loved my first taste of working in the *adega* that harvest. The
only unpleasantness had been Bonifacio's reaction. I told him
about the offered position that same evening after Henry had offered
it to me. Bonifacio's first reaction was disbelief, and then he shook
his head.

"You will not work in the *adega*. It's not a job for a woman. Your
role is here, on the quinta."

"I've already accepted."

"Go back and tell Duncan your husband won't allow it."

I frowned. "No. Dona Beatriz wishes it, and I work for her. As
do you," I added.

"You work on the quinta, in your various capacities, not in a
lodge with—"

I interrupted loudly. "This quinta that is your home, thanks to
me. Senhor Perez gave us this cottage so I could be of use as a *curandeira*. And then Dona—"

"All right, all right. Do you think I'm not reminded of that all too
often?"

We were both breathing heavily.

"Kipling's wine lodge is my place of work," he said. "I do not
want you there, surrounded by men. It's bad enough . . ."

"What is? What's bad enough?"

He went to the front door and opened it. "You can't stop yourself, can you, Diamantina? No matter how I pray for you, you

continue to be driven by your own evil desires."

"What's evil about agreeing to work for Dona Beatriz in the wine lodge? It's you who has the suspicious and evil thoughts, Bonifacio, not me. As you could not dictate to me about putting headstones in the chapel cemetery, neither can you dictate whether I will work for Dona Beatriz. She is my superior. Not you."

He came at me, his fists clenched, and I raised my chin. We stared into each other's faces for a moment, and then he unclenched his hands and let them hang, limp, at his sides.

"I'm going to the chapel and will stay on my knees all night, praying for you," he said, his voice quiet now. "You grow further and further from God's grace. I don't know that you will ever find redemption." He went back to the door.

"Isn't it you that looks for redemption?"

He stopped in the doorway, not looking back at me, and then went out into the night, leaving the door open.

⤙⤚

We never spoke of it again. When I received word from Espirito that I could begin helping him, I arranged for Binta and Nini to keep Candelária while I was away from the quinta.

At the end of the season, as our own crop on the quinta was harvested, I decided to have a small Festa do Vinho. I invited Espirito and Olívia and the da Silvas.

But only Espirito arrived on the evening of the festival, after the long tables had been set up in the yard and the locals who had worked on the harvest were eating and drinking and making music. "Olívia sends her regrets," he said. "She hoped to be able to come, but her breathing is more laboured than usual. I can't stay long. Her parents are with her, but I don't like to be away from her when she's in this state."

"Tell her I'm thinking of her," I said, and started as Bonifacio was suddenly beside me, his arm around my shoulder. I looked at him, pulling away slightly from his touch. "Bonifacio, please pour your brother a cup of wine. Sit, Espirito, and I'll have a plate brought to you." Bonifacio kept his possessive hold on me, and I felt a flush rising in my cheeks. "Bonifacio, please," I said, and finally he left my side and poured Espirito a glass of wine.

In the end, Espirito stayed for an hour. When he rose to leave, he handed me a small but heavy sack of coins.

"What's this?" I asked, shifting Candelária to my other arm. She was tired after running around and playing with some of the other children who had come, and now lay with her head against me.

"You didn't think that Dona Beatriz expected you to work without pay, did you?"

I glanced at Bonifacio, who was standing nearby, watching the musicians. "I never thought . . . because we're living at the cottage, and . . ."

"You are in the employ of Kipling's Wine Merchants. You will be paid for your work." Espirito stepped closer and ran a finger down Candelária's cheek. "Good night, little one," he said, and she smiled at him, and then she said, "Down, Mama."

"Bonifacio," Espirito called as I set Candelária down. "Thank you for your hospitality."

"Good night," he said, starting across the yard towards the path to the cottage.

"You're leaving?" I called, and he waved his hand in a gesture that might have meant either *Yes* or *Leave me alone*.

But Candelária ran after him and unexpectedly threw her chubby arms around his legs.

"*Adeus,* Papa," she said, and I started. I hadn't heard her call Bonifacio Papa before. It must have been Binta or Nini who spoke of Bonifacio as Papa to Candelária.

Bonifacio looked down at her, and then turned his gaze to Espirito, watching his brother until he climbed into his cart and was gone.

⁂

Olívia's breathing took on a permanent rasping wheeze that winter, after we had celebrated Candelária's second birthday.

Olívia was exhausted by struggling to draw air in, but more so to expel it, and there was no further remedy to relieve her pain. Eventually she was too weak to rise from her bed, and her mother stayed with her every day. It was hard on Luzia, and I often left Cristiano and Candelária with Binta and Nini and walked into Funchal to help her.

Olívia's back and ribs ached when she coughed; although she was uncomplaining, she involuntarily moaned after each harsh bout. I made her endless poultices of heated mustard, flour and water.

As I placed the warm, damp flannel on her flat chest, I had to look away from the parchment of her skin, her tiny shrivelled nipples, the way her narrow rib cage strained against her skin.

Dr. McManus announced she had caught an infection that was putting even more stress on her weak lungs.

For those few weeks, as I sat on a chair beside her bed, I found myself growing breathless as her breathing became more and more laboured. It sounded as though each inhalation became trapped inside her ribs and remained there, rattling, until she was finally able to expel it in a terrible gasp. Even the small amounts of poppy paste I rubbed on her gums only allowed her to drift into a half-hour of restless twilight. Eventually she could barely swallow the warmed broth I held to her lips.

She was suffering horribly, not only from the struggle to breathe but from starvation. And yet I knew, by the way she looked at me as I sat holding her limp hand, that the disease hadn't dulled her brain. She knew with terrible clarity what was happening.

CHAPTER SIXTY

One morning, when both Binta and Nini were too busy to watch Candelária, I brought her with me to the house on Rua São Batista, walking into Funchal with Bonifacio.

Luzia held a handkerchief to her eyes, and turned away when I came into the salon with Candelária.

"Luzia?" I asked, touching her shoulder. "Perhaps it wasn't a good idea to bring Candelária. Would you rather I go home with her? Is it too much to have her here?"

She turned back to us and smiled shakily at Candelária. "No. A child is good at these times. A child reminds one of life. Come and sit with Avó, Candelária. Soon we will go into the kitchen and Ana will find you a biscuit." She held out her arms, and my daughter went into them. She patted Luzia's wet cheek, her little brow furrowed. At just past two, she understood tears.

When I went into Olívia's room, Espirito was there. He had spent the last week sitting beside her through the long nights. He was unshaven, and pale with fatigue. Olívia was propped up on her pillows, and the muscles of her neck were corded in her attempt to breathe. Her eyelids and hands were puffy, and there was a bluish tinge to her skin.

Espirito and I spent the next few hours sitting with Olívia, trying to comfort her with our presence. As I read to her, she stopped me by lifting her fingers off the blanket. She opened her mouth, trying to speak.

I put my ear to her lips.

"Help me," she whispered.

I straightened, pulling her blanket higher. "I'll make you a poultice," I said, and glanced at Espirito.

He looked away.

"Help me," Olívia breathed again, and as her eyes stared into mine, I stopped breathing myself. I left the room.

Espirito followed me into the hall. He shut the door and took both my hands. "You heard her. Help her, Diamantina," he said, his chin trembling. "Please. I can't watch her like this any longer."

I swallowed and swallowed, not wanting to cry, because I knew he was fighting to stay composed. "Espirito. You know I do all I can. There's nothing more—"

"There is," he said, his hands tighter on mine.

I looked down at them, then back to him.

"There is," he repeated, so quietly I leaned closer to him. "Help her so she doesn't suffer anymore." He met my eyes, his own unblinking. "Do whatever you need to do, so she's finally at peace. It's what she wants. You know what to do. I don't. Please. Do it for her."

We stood in the hallway, listening to Olívia's desperate wheezing through the door. From downstairs came the sound of Luzia weeping.

"Do it for all of us," he begged.

"Mama," Candelária said, and I jumped.

Bonifacio stood at the top of the stairs, holding her. His eyes were on our hands, Espirito's and mine, still joined.

"I think you should take Candelária home," he said as Espirito and I dropped our hands. "It's not the atmosphere for a child. And it's hard on Luzia to be expected to care for her, don't you think?" He came closer. "How is she?" he asked Espirito.

Espirito shook his head.

I took Candelária from Bonifacio. "I'll take her home," I said, but to Espirito, not to Bonifacio.

"You'll come back," Espirito said, staring at me. "Tonight. You'll come back tonight."

"Yes," I said, and went downstairs with Candelária and my husband.

"You should stay home tonight, with your child," Bonifacio said behind me on the stairs. "You're letting others care for her while you run about as if you have no responsibility to her, first working in the *adega*, and now spending so much time with Olívia."

I didn't speak until we were on the street. I set Candelária down and tied her bonnet ribbons, then took her hand. "Olívia is dying, Bonifacio. You know that."

He stared at me.

"You once loved her. Maybe you love her still. She's dying, and yet all you speak of is my behaviour. You and I both know it's not the child"—I glanced down at Candelária, eating a biscuit Luzia had given her as we left—"you're concerned with. Are you so unfeeling? She's dying," I repeated.

It was the first time I had indicated that I knew what had happened between him and Olívia.

Candelária tugged on my hand. "Go, Mama, let's go."

"It is up to God to decide whether she lives or dies," Bonifacio finally said. "My feelings have nothing to do with it."

⌒

I awoke to the unfamiliar sound of birds twittering on the roof outside the open window. I was on a chair beside Olívia, resting my head on my folded arms on her bed. I blinked in the first rays of morning light. Realization came slow. I hadn't heard the birds these last weeks because Olívia's laboured breathing had been the only sound in the room.

The previous evening, I had tipped a fatal mixture of the crushed leaves of purple monkshood, infused in warm water, tiny drop by tiny drop, down Olívia's throat. I had long applied the leaves of the plant to the skin of those who came to me with open sores, or deeper aches of the muscles. The leaves first caused tingling and then numbed the afflicted area. But ingesting any part of the plant was poisonous, and the plant was always pulled out if found in areas used for grazing by domestic animals.

Taken internally, a tiny amount caused the pulse to slow, gradually, and I'd used it sparingly to calm a racing, painful heartbeat.

Because Olívia was already so weakened, and her body so frail, the small amount of monkshood I gave her would simply make her heart beat slower and slower, until it finally stopped.

She would not know pain.

As I mixed the tincture in Olívia's bedroom, I remembered my mother's words: *The only difference between a medicine and a poison is in the dose.*

When I went to her with the first drop on the end of a spoon, she knew what I was doing, and parted her lips, her eyes wide and searching mine. She tried to help me, tried to swallow. Sometimes I had to massage her neck and often she choked, but after the first few hours I saw that the gentle poison was making its way through her body by the contraction and then dilation of her pupils, and by the slight sheen of perspiration on her face and chest.

Through that long night, her face little more than a pale oval in the dim candlelight each time I bent over her with the spoon, Espirito watched. When the candle sputtered in the breeze from the window, he and I looked at it as if it would tell us something important. Suddenly it blew out with a tiny whoosh, and neither of us lit another. When Olívia was no longer capable of opening her lips, we sat on either side of her bed in the warm darkness and waited, each of us holding one of her hands.

I hadn't expected to fall asleep.

In death, Olívia's face was calm, the swelling and blueness gone. In spite of the tightness of her skin stretched over her bones, she looked more like she had once. Espirito still held her hand, his face ashen.

I rose and went to him and leaned down to put my arm around him and press my head against his. Then I brushed Olívia's hair and arranged it over the shoulders of her nightdress. I put salve on her lips, and touched her neck, smooth and no longer distended, with her favourite scent of camellia from the bottle on her dressing table.

Finally, Espirito stood. He put his arms around me, but he didn't weep. Perhaps he had nothing left in him. I felt the stubble of his cheek against my temple, and the length of his body against mine.

"Thank you," he whispered against my hair, and I tightened my arms around him.

CHAPTER SIXTY-ONE

The following months were long and quiet. Every week, I went to the cemetery in Funchal to place flowers from the quinta on Olívia's grave.

The da Silvas, seeming to have grown older overnight, invited Espirito to live with them. He did, saying the home over the Counting House was now too big for him. It was, I knew, also filled with memories of Olívia's life and death. Luzia still wished to see Candelária, and I took her to visit, but the air felt thick with grief.

Through the emptiness of those first few months after Olívia's death, with little to take me to the *adega* between harvests, I worked in my herb garden and still welcomed the local women, dispensing potions and salves and tisanes. I read both the Portuguese and the English books in the Kiplings' library, and enjoyed my daughter.

I tried to keep her away from Bonifacio. Too often he would take Candelária onto his lap and look into her face, as if searching for something. Was he hoping to find evidence of Espirito in her features, or was it something darker he wanted to see, some imagined malevolence?

The first few times I observed this, Candelária obviously expected him to speak, and smiled at him. But after a few episodes she came to understand it was something else, something that made her uncomfortable. She would turn her head, pulling away, sometimes saying, "Don't, Papa," and then jump from his lap and come to me.

As I watched Candelária busily play on her own, chattering to herself in both Portuguese and English, I too studied her, but I looked for anything that reminded me of Abílio. I saw nothing of him in her physical features or in her mannerisms, and for this I was thankful. She didn't resemble me outwardly either. Her hair was black and shiny as a swallow's wing, and her eyes were also black, long and slightly tilting up at the outer corners.

She reminded me more and more of my mother in the way she lowered her head and looked up at me from under her little brows. I noticed that she sometimes abruptly stopped what she was doing and fixed her gaze on something I couldn't see.

Did she have the gift of sight, as my mother had? She was mature and somehow solemn, although easily coaxed into a bubbly laugh. Even now I saw her fearlessness and spirit. I thought of her as only *my* child, through and through, as though she had grown within me without Abílio's seed. I almost let myself believe this.

And although I would never forget my old sins, they grew less troublesome as time passed. Apart from Bonifacio's strange behaviours, I could gaze at my daughter and think that the past was forever finished, and held no threat.

But the past is indelible. It isn't like the unwritten future. The past may grow shadowy, but it never leaves.

⁓

Summer arrived, and I was filled with anticipation about the coming harvest and my second season of work in the *adega*.

One hot evening, Cristiano was at the stables and I sat sewing in the light of the candle on the table. Candelária was on the floor nearby, playing with her rag dollies.

Bonifacio came from his bedroom and stood in front of me. I looked up at him, the needle poised above the cotton. Something in his expression gave me a whispering sense of approaching upheaval.

"The sham of our marriage cannot continue," he said with no preamble.

The needle was suddenly cold in my fingers, in spite of the steamy air. "What do you mean?"

"Marriage is a sacrament, a contract with God. In God's eyes we are joined forevermore. But the deception . . . You brought a bastard child into our home. Every day it's a burden difficult for me to bear."

I glanced at Candelária and tried to swallow, but I had no saliva. As if I had called her, she left her dollies and came to me. She put her hand on my knee, watching my face.

"The ordination of a priest is permanent," Bonifacio said. "It is not a sin to leave the priesthood, but it is a sin to break vows. I have struggled with keeping my vows of poverty, chastity and obedience. I am no longer living in poverty. I strive to be obedient. As for the third . . ." He stopped. "As for chastity, I fell into temptation, and this led me to take irreversible action. When alone and denying myself food, my powers of perception were sharpened. I had visions. I relied on 1 Corinthians 10:13: *No temptation has seized you except what is common to man. And God is faithful; he will not let you be tempted beyond what you can bear. But when you are tempted, he will also provide a way out so that you can stand up under it.*"

I steeled myself for his confession, thinking of the self-inflicted disfigurement he lived with now. *Not like this, Bonifacio, in front of the child.* I picked up Candelária's hand.

But he said nothing more of that horror. "When I took my vows, I received a spiritual mark that cannot be erased. I have decided that I will begin the process to be reinstated into the priesthood."

I opened my mouth then closed it, still holding Candelária's hand.

"I am going to apply for dispensation from the Superior of the Order of the Diocese of Rio de Janeiro. I will put my faith in God's understanding to allow me to return to my life's work of bringing God to the indigenous people of Brazil."

My mind was spinning. I was an employee of Kipling's now. Dona Beatriz liked me living on the quinta. Even if Bonifacio left the Counting House, surely she would allow me to stay here.

I had my diamonds.

"It will take a full year or more for all of this to be resolved. But I am confident of God's plan for me. And when I leave, I will take Cristiano back to his home." At this I stood, dropping Candelária's hand, my sewing falling to the floor. "Perhaps I'll find him a position at the mission. In this way he has a better chance at growing up to live by God's holy rules."

"No. No, you can't take Cristiano, Bonifacio," I said.

He looked at the floor. "This is another of my sorrows. I have not been able to help him as I hoped."

"This is his home now," I said firmly, waving my hand towards the walls of the cottage.

"It will never be my home." As his voice rose, Candelária moved closer against me. "It's a place of evil."

I clicked my tongue impatiently. "What do you mean, evil? It's a beautiful place."

"Evil lives here," he said, and looked at Candelária.

I drew a deep breath and put my hand on Candelária's hair. "Run into the bedroom and play with your dollies there," I told her. She looked up at me, unblinking. She understood so much. "Go, darling," I urged, attempting a smile, and she slowly left me, picking up her dolls and going into the bedroom.

Bonifacio had waited to continue. "I need to take Cristiano back to Brazil before too much more time passes. He's becoming too soft, too much a carefree Portuguese, instead of what he really is."

"A slave?" I said very quietly.

"No. As I just said, he could work in a mission, assisting his own people."

"Do you really care about his future, Bonifacio? You don't care about her, and I can accept that," I said, just above a whisper, glancing at the bedroom. "But Cristiano cannot help you find your way. This is his life now. You can't take him back there."

Bonifacio's face was worn and troubled.

"He can have a good life in Funchal," I said. "He speaks English well. With all the English here, it's beneficial to him—and to Candelária—to know the language."

"Beneficial? What is beneficial for the girl is to know my influence. She came into this world at a disadvantage, born of sin. As I just said, of evil. I have to make sure she's on the right path."

"She's two and a half years old. Stop talking about evil."

"It's never too early for one to start knowing God. I must make things right. Keeping Candelária on the path of righteousness is the start. Going back to Brazil with Cristiano will come next."

He looked at me with sudden hope on his face. I knew it was the hope of escaping the muddle of our lives to restart his own, clean and forgiven. "But things can never be as they were, Bonifacio. Time has changed them. Cristiano is not the boy he was when you took him away. And you are not the man you were."

He turned from me and went down the hall, and I heard the sound of his door closing. I didn't know how he'd interpreted my words.

At a creak in the floorboards, I looked towards the open doorway. Cristiano stood on the verandah there. I went to him. There was an odd pallor to his skin. "Cristiano," I said, putting my hand on his shoulder, but he jerked away from my touch, and ran across the sitting room and into his own room, slamming the door.

I got Candelária into her nightdress, and once she was settled in her small bed near mine, I knocked softly on Cristiano's door.

"Go away," he called, and so I left him.

⌒

In the middle of the night, I was still awake. I went to Cristiano's room and silently opened the door and crossed to his bed. He slept, but his breath came quickly, his lips pursing, uttering tiny threads of sound, a dream-whisper. Although he hadn't had even one nightmare for well over a year, I wondered if his hearing Bonifacio's words had allowed the demons to begin their haunting again.

I stayed there for the rest of the night, watching over him should the nightmare come. I thought of his bright smile and his straight white teeth, the dimple in his left cheek. Only yesterday I had seen his patience and gentleness as he sat on the floor across from Candelária and tried to teach her to catch a ball he rolled to her, and how to roll it back to him. I hated thinking of him frightened and confused by what he'd overheard.

As the first light of morning came, he stirred and sat up, blinking at me in surprise. And then his face cleared, and I knew he was remembering what had happened the evening before. "I'm not going with him," he said, his voice foggy with sleep. "I'll run away. I hate him," he said, his voice clear now. "I hate him, sister."

I sat on the edge of his bed and picked up his hand. I had never spoken to Cristiano of what Bonifacio had told me had happened in Tejuco. Now I felt I must. "I'm so, so sorry for what you have suffered. Bonifacio suffers also, because he knows he did the wrong thing, and should not have allowed that to happen to your mother. It's part of what makes him . . . how he is. But he thought it was the right thing to take you away from there."

"But why does he want to take me back?"

I took a deep breath. "I think he's confused about right and wrong. He wants to fix mistakes, but he doesn't know how."

"It won't fix anything to take me away from here. From you, and Candelária, and . . . and everyone. I'm not going," he said more loudly, his voice suddenly a shade deeper, his face so grave. At that moment I knew what he would look like when he was a man.

"I know," I said, leaning closer and speaking softly. "You're not going. I will never let him take you."

"Do you promise?"

"I promise, Cristiano. You will stay with me, no matter what."

"Will he try to take Candelária?"

I put my hand on my throat, shocked at the thought. "No! Oh no. He'll never take her. She's mine," I said, and then put my arms around him and spoke against his head. "As you are mine, my own little brother." His curls were soft, and smelled of the sun and dust and growing boy.

CHAPTER SIXTY-TWO

Over the next few months, Bonifacio spoke more and more about returning to Brazil. In July, he told me he'd written the letter and sent it to Rio de Janeiro and would wait patiently for the ship that would bring his message from God.

I was not as patient, for as soon as he had announced his plan to leave, I felt a growing anticipation. As I had promised Cristiano, Bonifacio would not take him. He could not bully Cristiano into going with him.

Thinking of my life without Bonifacio felt like a gift. I would be free of his suspicions and increasingly troubling conduct. I was often on edge, as he had acquired a habit of silently appearing where and when I didn't expect him. When we were in the presence of others, he now kept a hand on me—on my shoulder or forearm or the back of my neck, as if claiming his ownership of me.

He began praying at the foot of Candelária's bed as she fell asleep every night. I asked him to stop, but he wouldn't, and Candelária was confused by his presence and whispered prayers. I would lie beside her, holding her until she was asleep, anxious about Bonifácio's concern with what he saw as my daughter's inborn evil.

⁂

Quinta Isabella's harvest of Malvasia Babosa had been successful. The day the grapes were pressed, Candelária and I watched the pickers hired by Espirito carry huge baskets of grapes to the *lagar*.

There was room for four men to work in the rectangular wooden trough raised above the ground. In the centre was a huge hinged crossbeam balanced by a stone so heavy it must have been transported there by dozens of oxen. As the first group of four men climbed into the trough, two more strummed a slow, steady melody on small *cítaras*, and the workers, knee-deep in the grapes, lifted their legs high to step in rhythm. The *mosto* began flowing along a gutter, through a strainer and into a wide, low barrel. It was then dumped back into the *lagar* for the second treading. When the workers had extracted all they could with their feet, the stalks, skins and remaining pulp were raked into the centre of the trough and bound by thick rope. By the turning of the massive stone wheel, the crossbeam was slowly lowered onto the coiled rope of grape leavings, forcing out the liquid known as "wine of the rope." By now the workers were covered in sweat and breathing heavily.

The remaining grape skins and residue were put into clean water and strained, and the resulting refreshing drink was given to the pressers. One of them brought a hornful to Cristiano. He tasted it and licked his lips, and Candelária jumped up and down and said, "Me, me too," and was also given a sip of the sweet grape juice.

Then the pulpy debris still left in the *lagar* was cleaned out to be mixed into manure for fertilizer. Another quantity of grapes was dumped into the *lagar*, and the second group of men began the next pressing, giving the first men time to rest. The pressing went on through the day.

That night, as I lay in bed, the music and rhythm of the treading remained a steady beat in my head. When I brought my hand to my face, I still smelled the sweetness of the pressed grapes. I thought of Espirito's long, slender fingers on the baskets as he helped dump the grapes into the *lagar* in the pressing house with the ease of someone who seemed at home in every room he entered. As he worked, his face lost the stiffness that had been there since Olívia's death, and he had, for a short while, looked like the old Espirito, full of life.

The day after the last of our *mosto* had been transported to the lodge, we again held a Festa do Vinho on the quinta for the workers. Espirito, Eduardo and Luzia agreed to come to the small *festa*— one of their first social outings since Olívia's death almost eight months earlier.

There was a small replica of a *lagar* built long ago, Espirito said, for Martyn Kipling's own daughters when they were children. He had Bonifacio help him carry it into the yard for Cristiano and Tiago and Candelária to tread a basket of less superior grapes we'd kept for them. They stomped and squashed and danced upon the grapes, laughing and splattering the juice, Candelária frequently falling into the pulpy mush.

As we sat at the long table set up in the shady yard, eating and drinking wine and smiling at the children's frolicking, a lone man walked up from the gates.

It was Abílio.

I tried to swallow my mouthful of food, but it caught in my throat.

"That looks like Senhor Perez," Bonifacio said, standing. "Espirito? Did you know he was coming to Madeira?"

"No," Espirito said, rising and walking to meet Abílio. I watched the two men shake hands, and then they came to the table.

Abílio greeted us all, and then said, smiling, "It's been too long since I've been back." He wore fine leather breeches and a long frock coat. "Luckily," he said, waving his hand at Espirito and Bonifacio, "I have reliable people to ensure that the business runs smoothly. And, of course," he said, looking at me, "Senhora Rivaldo keeps my wife assured that all is well on the quinta."

"Dona Beatriz didn't come with you?" Espirito asked.

"She prefers to stay in Belém with our son, spending money on her grand new house," Abílio said, his eyes still on me. "My wife tells me you and your husband have also been blessed."

My blood thrummed in my ears, and I looked at Bonifacio. When he remained silent, I pointed at Candelária, laughing with Cristiano and Tiago in the little *lagar*. "Our daughter," I said flatly.

Abílio glanced at her but was clearly uninterested in the children, and I took a deep breath.

"May we offer you some wine?" Espirito asked.

"I hope you're not drinking too much of Kipling's profits," Abílio answered. Nobody knew what to say. In the awkward silence, he smiled again, the smile I knew so well, the one that attempted to disarm and beguile. "But no, thank you. Please. Continue to enjoy your festivities."

Espirito and Bonifacio sat down again.

"I wish to check on the state of the house," Abílio said. "When I start to bring prospective buyers to look at it sometime in the next year, I want it to fetch the highest price possible. I bid you all adieu," he added, and bowed to us with an exaggerated flourish.

As he walked towards the house, I asked, "Do you know anything about this, Espirito? Why is he talking of selling the house?"

"According to Henry," Espirito said, "Perez is still determined to sell the business—and he's including the quinta. But Henry doesn't think it will actually happen."

We sat in silence. Then Eduardo said, "It looks to me like you're all glad his visits are infrequent."

For me, the afternoon was ruined, and I could no longer concentrate on the conversation.

When Eduardo and Luzia and Espirito left, Bonifacio went to the cottage. I was still at the table, watching Candelária. The boys had gone to the stables, and Candelária was alone, content to squish about in the trough.

I jumped as Abílio put his hand on my shoulder. He had come up behind me soundlessly, as Bonifacio often did now. I glanced towards the kitchen, and pulled away from his touch.

"You're quite the fine lady now, Diamantina," he said. "Nothing left of that ragged young wife who trudged down from the mountains a few years ago."

I didn't respond.

"Do you enjoy living off my riches?"

"It was you who invited me to live here, and your wife who asked me to stay. I believe I work for what I receive."

"My wife speaks highly of you. If she only knew, Diamantina. If she only knew," he repeated, smiling as though we shared a joke. "But who am I to turn down good fortune and argue with my wife's choices? She spends money as though it will always be there. But I'm speaking to Duncan about him buying the whole operation. And I've come back to ready the house in order to get the highest profit."

Obviously, Abílio still didn't know about the deed. Candelária climbed out of the *lagar* and ran to me, her dress wet and purple with grape juice, her bare feet stuck with bits of grape skin and seeds. She stopped, looking up at Abílio.

"This is Senhor Perez, Candelária," I said briskly. "Here, let me wipe off your feet." I picked up a large napkin.

Abílio looked down at Candelária. "Ah yes, the child. Well, you're a pretty little girl. You remind me of your grandmother."

I looked at him sharply, glad no one else was around to hear such a casual remark, then lifted Candelária to my lap so I could clean her feet. "How long are you planning to be here?" I asked him. When he didn't answer, I glanced up at him. He was staring at Candelária's feet. "There," I told her. "But your dress is so wet and dirty. I'll take you home to change in a few minutes."

Candelária smiled at Abílio, and then turned and ran towards the kitchen.

"How old is she?" Abílio asked. His face had coloured slightly. I had never seen quite this look.

Before I answered his question, he said, pouring a glass of wine, "Have a glass with me."

"I have to go to the kitchen and talk to Nini about the dinner, and I need to change Candelária's clothes," I said, wanting to be away from him. I stood.

"Stay. Only for a moment," he said, gripping my wrist. I sat again, not wanting anyone to witness the intimate way he touched me. He let go of my wrist and poured wine into a second glass and pushed it towards me.

I lifted it. He touched his glass to it. "What are we drinking to?" I asked him.

"Old friends," he said. "And *vida*. Life, and its unpredictability. Look at us, you and I, Diamantina, sitting here at Quinta Isabella, sharing a glass of Kipling's wine. Do you not think that quite remarkable, given where we've come from?"

I drank, but the wine held no sweetness.

CHAPTER SIXTY-THREE

After dinner, I was in the kitchen helping Binta and Nini wash the dishes. The boys were climbing in the trees by the pressing house, and Candelária had been near my feet, playing with small cooking pots. Suddenly I heard her laugh, high and overexcited. I looked at the floor where she had been playing, but she was gone. I went to the doorway. Abílio was holding her by the hands and swinging her around.

I went out. "Stop—she'll be sick. She's just eaten."

He stopped, as I'd asked, and set Candelária on the ground. Dizzy, she listed and then fell to one side, but he caught her before she landed. He picked her up, smoothing her hair from her forehead. "Do you like playing with Tio Abílio?" he asked, and she smiled, nodding. He kissed her cheek, and I stepped forward.

"Put her down," I said, and again he did as I asked. "Candelária, go back into the kitchen with Binta and Nini, and stay there."

She held up her arms to Abílio. "Again, Tio," she said, her eyes sparkling.

"Candelária. Go to the kitchen." My voice was harsh, and she looked at me with her bottom lip extended. "Now," I said.

As she passed me, she waved at Abílio. "*Adeus*, Tio."

He waved back.

Once she was out of earshot, I said, "Leave her alone. You're not her uncle."

He stared at me in the falling dusk. "You're correct. I'm not her uncle."

I turned to leave, but again he caught my wrist. "Come here," he said, gesturing towards a bench under a lacy willow.

"What do you want?"

"To show you something."

He pulled me to the bench and I stood in front of him as he sat down and started unlacing his boots.

"What are you doing?"

He straightened. "I'm not Candelária's uncle," he said again. "I'm her father."

Hundreds of tiny black insects skittered in front of my eyes, and for a moment I was blind. I swallowed, blinking. "What are you talking about?" I said, when I could be sure of my voice. He was again bent over his boots. "She's Bonifacio's."

"Really? Are you certain?"

"There's no possibility. I only slept with you a few times—and always used my mixture to stop a child from starting. I slept with my husband every night, without the potion," I lied. "Of course she's his child."

Abílio looked at me again with a strange, sly expression. He pulled off one boot, then the other. He removed his stockings.

He had a sixth toe on each foot.

I closed my eyes.

"You didn't know about this, did you?" he asked. "It's a Perez family trait. My father had six fingers on one hand. You never noticed?"

I opened my eyes and slowly shook my head.

"Leandro doesn't carry it. But my daughter does. My daughter, little Candelária."

The earth seemed to be moving, and, like Candelária after her spinning, I took a step sideways, and then another, trying not to fall. Abílio caught me and lowered me to the bench. After what felt like a long time, watching him put his stockings and boots back on, I asked, "What will you do?"

He stood, the last of the light streaming through the leaves casting dappled shadows across his face. "Do? Why, nothing. She means nothing more to me than any of the other children I have sired, scattered about the islands and mainland."

"You won't speak of it to anyone?"

Now he put his finger under my chin. "That's up to you."

I pulled away from his touch. "What do you mean?"

"Diamantina. Don't be coy with me. It doesn't suit you. After your husband is asleep, come to me in the house," he said, as Binta came out of the kitchen with a tub of dirty water and threw it to one side. The water arced gracefully through the air before splashing onto the ground.

She stared at us.

"Have a pleasant evening, Senhora Rivaldo," Abílio said, and then walked across the yard to the house.

That night, when the quinta was in darkness, I got out of bed. I took my old gutting knife from a drawer and put it in my waistband.

Without need of a candle on the familiar path, I slipped down the hill and into the big house. My bare feet didn't make a sound on the thick rugs of the entrance hall. Light showed from under one of the closed doors. I put my ear to it and, hearing nothing, opened it.

Abílio sat in front of a fire. He rose as I came into the room. "I hoped I wouldn't have to wait too long." He shook his head, smiling. "You never disappoint me, Diamantina. Come and have a drink with me."

I crossed the room and waited beside him until he had poured two glasses from a decanter. As he handed one to me, I flung out my arm and knocked it from his hand. In his moment of surprise as the glass crashed to the floor, I stepped against him, pulling out my knife and pressing it to his throat.

He laughed, but his throat contracted as he swallowed. In the next instant he'd composed himself and wrapped one arm around me. As he reached for the knife with his other, I pressed the tip, hard, and his flesh opened like the belly of a fish and blood ran down the blade and caught in the hilt. I knew exactly where the important vein in the neck was, and I cut just to one side of it, a place that would bleed freely but not kill him.

He froze.

"Take your hands from me," I said, and he dropped his arms to his sides.

"Diamantina, there's no reason for this. Surely you—"

"I can move this knife, just the slightest, and you will bleed to death. So now be quiet and listen carefully. Never bother me, or my daughter, again. I will do my work in the *adega*, and we will live on the quinta. But you will never again demand that I come to you." I pressed harder, and the blood came over the low hilt and onto my hand, and then trickled down to my wrist.

There was a fine sheen of perspiration on Abílio's forehead and upper lip. "You can't threaten me like this, Diamantina. All I have to—"

"I am threatening you. If you don't like my terms, then tell Bonifacio about Candelária. Take off your boots and show him. He'll quit. You'll be without a head of the Counting House—an efficient and honest man, whom you know has benefited Kipling's more than most would. You will lose me, and your wife and Henry Duncan will be most unhappy. We'll move away from the quinta, and again, Dona Beatriz will wonder why, won't she? You know we correspond regularly, that she awaits my reports on the state of the house and land. Would you like to tell her why Bonifacio and I left Kipling's? Not that you would tell the truth, for you are so used to lies that they come more easily than truths, but don't worry. I'll do it. I'll tell her that while she lay in bed recovering from childbirth, or mourning the death of her father, you forced yourself upon me, and I bore your child as a result. She won't question me, Abílio, knowing the kind of man you are. Do you think she doesn't write to me of your escapades with the whores of Lisboa and Oporto? So. Do you relish living with her fury at this? Do you not fear she might take things a step further in terms of how she views your role in the business?" I pressed even harder with the tip of the knife, and this time there was a spurt, and Abílio cried out in anger and alarm. I kept pressing. "Do you not, Abílio, fear that I could bring your life down to a level you can't imagine?"

"Diamantina, you've lost your mind."

"I'm very clear right now, Abílio, and I'll say all I want to say. There was no way I could prove that you stole the oil of fleabane from my medicine bag and put it into Martyn Kipling's wine, but if I ever choose to tell Dona Beatriz that truth, she'll believe it as well. Because she knows by now that you're capable of doing anything to get what you want."

A log fell in the fireplace. Abílio's blood continued to flow.

"And you aren't capable of doing anything to get what you want as well?" he said, against the knife. "Have I not told you, more than once, that we are alike?"

At that, I grabbed his genitals and moved the knife, in one quick movement, from his throat to the front of his breeches. "I would suggest that if you want to keep bedding women, you do not bother me again." I gripped tighter, the leather smooth against my palm, and his face contorted. As I pressed the blade against him, he stared at me. "Do you understand me, Abílio?"

Of course, he could have grabbed my arm, taken a chance that he could overpower me before I had a chance to cut him. He could have grabbed the knife and slit *my* throat. And yet he didn't. I recognized his expression now. It was admiration.

I let him go and stepped back, the knife extended in front of me.

"You're still the hardened girl of the beach, still the daughter of a witch, aren't you?"

"I will always carry that girl within me. But now I'm also a woman of Funchal. I'm a mother and a healer and a blender of wine. I am many things. What I am not, Abílio, is afraid of you."

He pulled a large white handkerchief from his pocket. "If you were any other woman, your threats wouldn't have lasted longer than a moment, and I would be fucking you right now. But we share a bond, Diamantina. We know each other. As you've pointed out, it will make my life easier not to worry about the business or the quinta or to put up with more harping from Beatriz. And so I'll say and do nothing. For now."

I stared at him a moment longer, then turned and walked away, alert for any sudden movement behind me. At the door I stopped and looked back. He stood in front of the fireplace, watching me, while the handkerchief pressed against his neck bloomed crimson. "I don't expect you to speak to me again while you're here," I said.

⁂

Instead of going back to the cottage, I slipped through the woods to the summer house, feeling so shaken that I had to sit on its step. I stared at the blanket of stars over the water, clouds moving in front of the moon.

I could do nothing more about Abílio's discovery. I hoped what he had said was true: it would not benefit him in any way to disclose that he was Candelária's father. I also knew the depth of his deviousness. Should it ever be to his advantage to use this irrefutable fact, he wouldn't hesitate. And if that time came, I would have to be ready to stop him.

CHAPTER SIXTY-FOUR

I lived in a state of jumpiness until Abílio had decided what repairs and changes he would one day make to the house, and then left. I saw him occasionally over those few days, but only across the yard or disappearing down the road. When I finally heard from Binta that he had left Madeira, the heaviness that had made breathing difficult lifted.

When the next letter came from Dona Beatriz a month later, talking of her life in the usual way, and asking the normal questions, I felt further relief.

And yet I knew that from now on I could never completely let my guard down. Not where Abílio Perez was concerned.

Bonifacio grew ever more vigilant in his prayers over Candelária. He also grew thinner, and his face took on the haunted look he had when he'd returned from the mountains in Curral das Freiras after Lent. It frightened me. I suspected his anxiety and lack of appetite were caused by waiting to hear from Rio de Janeiro.

I waited anxiously as well during this time. Whenever I was enjoying myself in some small, simple activity—sitting at the table in the kitchen talking to Nini or Binta after dinner, or playing a noisy game of tag with Candelária in the sitting room, or laughing with Cristiano over a game of dominoes on a Sunday—Bonifacio stared at me as if I were engaged in some wrongdoing.

As the winter passed and spring came, Tiago was apprenticed to a tanner in Funchal. Cristiano continued to help Raimundo with the horses and with repairs around the quinta, but missed his friend.

"Tiago is a bit older than you," I told him. "But it's almost time for you to begin an apprenticeship as well."

He looked at me, very still.

"I've thought that you could learn the work of the *adega*, like Espirito and me." I planned to speak to Espirito about this: by the time of this year's upcoming harvest, Cristiano could be helpful in many small ways, running up and down the steps of the hot storage room, chalking the barrels with the year and rankings, and delivering messages as needed.

Something I didn't recognize passed over his face. "I could work in the *adega*? I'll . . . I'll always be here?"

I understood then. "Yes. You'll always be here. I told you that. You don't have to worry about what you heard Bonifacio say last summer. You're not leaving. Your home will always be with me, and with Candelária."

He smiled then. "Can I tell Tiago about my apprenticeship tonight?"

"Just wait until I make sure it's all right with Espirito. But I'm sure it will be," I said, and he smiled at me then, and I realized I hadn't seen his dimple for a while.

That evening, both children asleep, I asked Bonifacio when he expected to hear from Rio de Janeiro.

"It hasn't been a full year since I wrote, not enough time for the issue to have been resolved and the letter of my acceptance to come back."

I nodded, hoping my face was unreadable.

⁂

I looked forward, more and more, to time spent with Espirito when I took the children to visit Eduardo and Luzia. It had been a year and a half since Olívia's death, and Espirito was the man he had once been, and now often laughed at something Cristiano or Candelária said. I had missed his laugh.

Espirito had welcomed the idea of Cristiano apprenticing, and so I took him with me to the wine lodge during my third harvest. As always, I was proud of his ability to learn quickly and to carry out duties with maturity. Some of those steamy late summer and early autumn days, Espirito and Cristiano and I would leave the *adega* and walk down Rua São Batista to the square. There we ate a meal at one of the wooden tables set up under the arching trees. We always politely asked Bonifacio if he would care to join us, and each time I held my breath, not wanting him to come, and was always relieved when he said no, he was too busy to waste time.

One afternoon, Espirito dropped his fork onto the stones at our feet, and as he bent to retrieve it, I saw a small birthmark on the back of his neck, under his tied-back hair. It was a burgundy stain small as the nail of my last finger, and shaped like a leaf, tapering on one end. In one sudden, unexpected instant, I wanted to kiss that tiny imperfection.

Our hands touched as we passed each other dishes—had they always? I began to wonder whether he let his fingers linger even a moment longer than necessary. Was I creating this phantom intimacy, or had he begun to look at me in a different way?

At the end of one long, hot day in the *adega*, I sent Cristiano home; I could see he was flagging. "Tell Binta I'll be there soon to fetch Candelária," I said. "I just want to finish the last weighing of this *mosto* with Espirito."

When Espirito and I were done, I sank onto a bench in the courtyard and smiled at him. "That's it for this year, then. It feels good, having it all done. It's been another successful harvest."

"Your third."

I nodded. "The first when Candelária wasn't yet two years old. She'll be four on her next birthday."

He sat beside me, close enough for our arms to touch if I allowed mine to move just slightly. I felt alive, full of energy in spite of working in the heat all day. I turned my head and looked at him, and he looked at me, and there was a knowingness in his eyes that made something leap inside me, an ache of possibility.

But then he stood. "You should get home. You must be hungry."

I nodded.

"Cristiano shows promise," he said. "He's a hard worker."

I licked my lips. "Could we have a glass of wine to celebrate this season's last day in the *adega*?"

He looked at me a moment too long. "Luzia will have kept dinner for me. Shall I call you a cart?"

Embarrassed, I turned and started across the courtyard. "No. I'll walk home."

He called after me, "You've forgotten your pay packet." He had given it to me when I arrived that morning, but I'd left it on the table of the blending room.

"I'll come for it tomorrow," I called over my shoulder, feeling somehow humiliated.

When I went to Kipling's late the next afternoon, the door of the blending room was closed. I knocked, and at Espirito's murmur I opened it and stood in the doorway. I was uneasy, as if I'd displeased him. All night I thought of how I must have been completely mistaken about the way he looked at me, and felt a fool.

He was sitting at the table, a wooden box in front of him. He had the air of someone waiting.

"I've come for my pay packet," I said, approaching the table.

He stood. "I bought you something. I saw it in a shop, and I . . ." He gestured at the finely carved box. "Open it."

"Oh," I cried in pleasure as I lifted the lid on a beautiful set of dominoes, running my fingers over the rounded edges of the bone, the tiny indentations of the ebony pips. "So beautiful." I smiled at him, concern about my behaviour yesterday disappearing in that instant. "Why did you do this?"

He smiled back. "You've worked hard this harvest."

"I'm paid for it, like you."

"Seeing it reminded me of playing dominoes with you in Curral das Freiras. It made me remember my relief in knowing my father was cared for, and that Cristiano was not so bereft."

I sat down, my fingers still running over the tiles.

"Shall we play?" he asked, and when I nodded, he poured two glasses of wine. The clink of glass upon glass and the steady chirp of a bird in the courtyard were the only sounds. I thought of Bonifacio, still in the Counting House, and wondered what he would think should he find me here, drinking wine and playing dominoes with his brother.

But at this moment, I didn't care what Bonifacio thought. I set the tiles on the table, face down, then reached across them with my glass and touched it, with just the tiniest tinkle, to Espirito's, and took a sip. "A game of simple draw, to a score of one hundred," I said, looking at the bone yard between us. "High doubles to start." I turned over a tile: a double five, five ebony pips on either end.

He turned over the six-two.

"As it should be," he said, and we slipped the two tiles back with the others and mixed them on the smooth surface of the mahogany table. "Ladies play first."

I took another sip of my wine as we each picked our seven tiles and stood them up facing us. "The wine is full-bodied," I said. "It will perhaps soothe your loss when I win this game."

He laughed, his pupils widening just the slightest. "You're quite sure of yourself, aren't you, Diamantina?"

"About some things, Espirito. About dominoes, and about wine." The thinning afternoon light from the open door shone on the smooth surface of the tiles. "And now, shall we begin?"

I smacked down a bone. At the sound, there was the old familiar rush of pleasure through my body. How I loved laying the first tile on the table; I had forgotten how much delight it brought me.

I watched Espirito's fingers as he deliberated. My own fingers caressed the smooth, cool bone of my tiles.

He laid his four-three against mine. "Look out, Diamantina. I'm planning to win."

"I may let you," I said, and he looked up at me without smiling.

"Your turn," he said.

We played the rest of the game in silence. There was a tension between us, as if the end of the game would signal the start of something else. The room grew dimmer; I was too warm, the setting too intimate suddenly, even though I'd often spent time in the blending room with Espirito. I had to concentrate on breathing slowly, evenly. I heard his boot move on the stone floor, and wanted to extend my own and touch his. Was there a sudden fragrance in the air? Outside, the bird's rhythmic cry suddenly reached a fevered pitch, and then stopped.

I laid my last tile.

Espirito stared at me. "You've won, Diamantina."

I looked from him to the tiles, unable to keep meeting his eyes, and then lifted two tiles and set them in the box, but my hands shook. Espirito put his hands onto mine, and I was forced to look back to his face.

"Why do you tremble?" he asked quietly.

I stood, overwhelmed at his touch, and pulled my hands from his, afraid of what I might say or do should we sit like this any longer. I quickly piled the rest of the tiles into the box and closed it. "I must go," I said. "I've been gone too long."

He stood as well. "Don't forget your pay packet," he said, going to a shelf and taking the bag of coins from it. He held it towards me, and I went to him as if drawn against my will, stepping so close that the back of his hand touched my bodice. I felt an immediate visceral reaction, and drew an audible breath.

I pressed closer, and he looked down at his hand against my breast, then back into my eyes. He didn't move.

I held his gaze, and his lips parted. The heavy sweetness of the wine we'd drunk hovered in the space between our mouths. As I pressed even closer, the bag fell to the floor and opened, the réis pinging as they hit the stones. Espirito blinked as if suddenly awakened, and then there was the clatter of wheels in the courtyard, and a shout. He quickly left the blending room, left me standing with coins scattered around my feet, and full of desire.

CHAPTER SIXTY-FIVE

It was difficult to sleep, thinking of Espirito—his hands on mine, the feel of his body against mine. Wanting him, knowing he wanted me.

Not knowing what would happen next. If anything.

The next afternoon, I gathered a bouquet of violets and lilies from the quinta's garden, and took Candelária with me into Funchal Town. At the cemetery, I handed her the flowers. "Put them there, in the vase, for Tia Olívia, please," I said, pointing to the receptacle at the base of the headstone.

She did as I asked, then stood back and lifted her little nose into the air, smelling the breeze. I remembered my father calling me *klein vos*. Little fox. "I smell something nice," she said.

"It's the flowers we brought," I said.

"No. Not our flowers. The other flower smell, Tia's smell," she said, looking intently at Olívia's headstone.

I went to my knees on the grass, my legs weak. Ever since she'd started speaking, I had suspected even more strongly that Candelária had my mother's vision. She had been barely two when Olívia died, too young to remember Olívia or her scent of camellias.

She blinked then, and looked around as if awakening. "Look at that angel," she said, pointing at a small cherub on a grave. "Can I touch it?"

"Yes, you may touch it," I said, and she went to it, running her fingers over the stone features.

Olívia, I'm sorry. Sitting back on my heels, I stared at the headstone, my hands in my lap. *I'm falling in love with Espirito.*

"Does it hurt to burn?"

I looked over at Candelária, standing beside the cherub. I got to my feet and went to her. "Hurt to burn? What do you mean?"

Her cheeks were red, and I put my hand on her forehead to see if she had a fever. It was cool. "Papa said to be an angel you have to be very, very good. And if you're not good, you burn."

When had Bonifacio said this to her? When had they been alone together? I knelt and put my arms around her. "You're my angel, *querida*," I told her.

Damn you, Bonifacio, I thought, sending the curse out into the air of this resting place for the dead. *She's not even four years old. Damn you.*

⁂

A week later, Cristiano went down to the *adega*, saying Espirito had errands for him. I hadn't seen Espirito since I'd behaved so shamelessly with him. As the evening lengthened, I knew Espirito would have taken Cristiano for dinner in the square or back to the da Silvas'.

It was dusk when they came into the cottage together. I had already put Candelária to bed, and Bonifacio was stacking wood in front of the fireplace.

"I wanted to make sure he got home all right," Espirito said, although we all knew Cristiano had long been capable of walking home in the growing darkness.

"Thank you," I said.

"He ate with Eduardo and Luzia."

"It's late, Cristiano," I said. "You should go to bed."

"Thanks, Espirito," Cristiano said as he went down the hall. "I'll see you tomorrow."

"He's coming with me to Henry's *adega*. I have some work to do there," Espirito explained. The air in the room was thick with pressure, like the atmosphere before a storm. "Did you find the error in the Cramer order today, Bonifacio?"

"Yes. His men hadn't loaded two of the pipes." Bonifacio stood, brushing his hands together. "I'm going to bed," he said, turning from us.

"I'll walk down with Espirito," I told him. "I have to get Candelária's clean clothes from the wash house."

Bonifacio shut his bedroom door.

⚒

We didn't speak on the path. All my senses were heightened. Darkness was close. The air was too humid, the evening perfumes too strong, the cicadas too loud.

I stopped at the hidden entrance to the summer house, and then looked at Espirito and took his hand. "Come with me," I said, and we went together, me leading, as the overgrown, mossy path was only wide enough for one.

My heart was racing, and after I climbed the four steps of the summer house, Espirito beside me, I was breathless as if I'd run all the way up the hill from Funchal to the quinta.

I could feel the heat from his body, and smell his scent of grapes. I was aware of something else, something I could only define as desire coming from him, or from me. From us both, so different from the straightforward odour of lust I had known with Abílio.

Without speaking, Espirito encircled me in his arms, holding me tightly against him. But after only a moment, a moment when all was possible, he gently pushed me away.

"He's my brother, Diamantina," he said. "I can't do this."

"But you want to," I said, just above a whisper, my hands on his arms. "Tell me you want to. That you want me."

He stroked my neck, his touch as fine as a breath of wind across my skin. "I've wanted you since I first saw you on Porto Santo," he said, and I closed my eyes at the pleasure that ran through me at his words. And then he turned me, gently, by the shoulders. He unlaced my blouse. "I have dreamed of these," he murmured, and I pulled my blouse from my shoulders. I heard his intake of breath, and then felt the first tender touch of his lips on my shoulder blades.

I turned to face him, and loosened my hair from its ties. I put my hands on his hips as he ran his fingertips over my lips and then down my neck. His hands came to my breasts.

"I have wanted you for so long," he murmured.

"When you first thought me a wicked woman," I answered with a small smile.

"You *are* a wicked woman," he said, "and I am not a good man." He untied my skirt, slowly, as around us the cicadas shrilled.

As I walked back to the cottage after Espirito's final kiss, the dew was already starting, damp and cool on my warm feet and legs. My body was humming. I could think of nothing. In my bedroom, Candelária slept. I threw off my clothes and lay down, but could not settle. I rose again, and took my travel bag from the wardrobe and pulled out my mother's necklaces.

I stood naked, my hair loose, my face flushed, the necklaces draped around me, their shells and glass cool and smooth against my heated skin. I watched myself in the mirror over the dresser as I touched the necklaces and ran my hands down my body. I thought myself beautiful for the first time.

And then I lay on my bed again and relived each moment, remembering the sensation of Espirito's skin against mine and all that we had whispered to each other. And I felt myself coming apart, breaking into scraps of images, flashes of both urgency and timelessness.

I had felt a beauty within me as well as what I'd seen in the mirror. And suddenly, in the middle of that great swooping joy, I was filled with such a terrible loneliness that I wept, not only for the realization that this feeling was possible, but also out of the despair of knowing it would never fully be mine. As Bonifacio had said, in God's eyes we were joined forever. Even if he returned to Brazil, I would still be his wife.

When I came out of the bedroom the next morning, leaving Candelária to put on her little frock, Bonifacio was sitting at the table, sharpening a quill. An open pot of ink and a sheet of paper were in front of him.

I was surprised and disturbed that Bonifacio hadn't left for work at his usual early hour. I felt so soft and open, the intimacy still so raw, that surely my sin was written on my face. I swallowed. "Cristiano's already gone down for breakfast, I see," I said. "Are you not going to work?"

"Yes. I will, later."

"You're writing a letter? Is it another to the Diocese?" I needed to act as though all was normal. My heart raced, and I hoped he didn't see the quick rise and fall of my chest.

"Is it any concern of yours whom I write to?" he asked, and I turned and went back to the bedroom and tied the ribbon of Candelária's frock. I glanced at Bonifacio as she and I came back into the sitting room. He set down his sharpening knife but didn't dip the quill into the ink. He simply sat there, holding the quill over the pot in an odd, detached manner. "Do you not have a clean dress to wear?" he asked Candelária, and I saw the jam on her bodice, the grass stains on her skirt.

Never before had Bonifacio mentioned Candelária's appearance. She shrugged. "Will you come with us for breakfast, Papa?"

"Not today, Candelária," he said, and we left him at the table, the quill still suspended, motionless, over the ink pot.

CHAPTER SIXTY-SIX

In a mere twenty-four hours, my life had changed so dramatically that I didn't know myself. The night after I had been with Espirito, as I lay in my bed, I realized I was smiling. Smiling, alone, into the darkness.

I needed to see him, to be near him. There was no explicable reason for him to come to our cottage, and so the next afternoon I took Cristiano and Candelária and went into Funchal, telling the children we would have a treat in the square.

"Can we have a sweet cake?" Candelária asked.

"Yes, of course," I said, distracted as we walked down São Rua Batista, knowing I would stop at Kipling's, hoping to see Espirito.

"Two? Can we have two?"

"Don't be greedy," Cristiano said.

"I'm not greedy. I'm not, am I, Mama?" she said, and I looked down at her, realizing I was annoyed by her chattering.

I stopped. "You're not greedy. You shall both have what you wish in the square." I smiled. "Let's stop and ask Bonifacio and Tio if they would like to come with us."

"Espirito will probably come," Cristiano said as he pulled open the door for us, staying in the open doorway of the Counting House. "He likes cake."

"We're going for cakes," Candelária announced before we were in the room. "Cakes! Will you come, Papa? Where's Tio? We want him to come too."

Bonifacio sat at his desk in the empty room, a paper in front of him. He wasn't looking at it, but at the wall over his desk. He didn't move.

"Papa? Where's Tio?" Candelária said again.

Finally, Bonifacio pulled his gaze from the wall, staring at us as though he hadn't heard us come in. "What?"

"Where is Tio Espirito?" Candelária demanded loudly, with a three-year-old's impatience.

"I don't know," Bonifacio said.

"I'll go look for him. He's probably in the *adega*," Cristiano called from the doorway, and ran off.

Candelária held my skirt as Bonifacio stared at us. His face was so white that his eyes appeared to be sunken coals. His lips were chalky.

"Are you all right?" I asked.

"Cakes, cakes!" Candelária said loudly.

At that, Bonifacio rose and came towards us, and Candelária fell silent and edged behind me. "What is the cause for celebration?" he asked.

"Celebration? There's no celebration. I just brought the children into Funchal for a treat," I said.

"Why are they deserving of a treat? What have they done to be rewarded?" Although he questioned me, he stared at Candelária, his tone dull.

I clicked my tongue. "I'm taking them to the square. Do you want to come or not?"

The door opened and Espirito came in. "I hear cakes are in order," he said, lightly clapping his hands and smiling broadly. "Cristiano's waiting outside."

My breath caught in my throat at the sight of him. He looked at me, and I couldn't take my eyes from his.

Bonifacio turned, going back to his desk and looking down at the paper.

"Come with us, Tio," Candelária said.

"All right," Espirito answered, and put his hand on Candelária's head. I glanced at Bonifacio's back and then put my hand on top of Espirito's, and he turned his hand to clasp mine. He squeezed it, once. Desire swept through me with such force I gasped, immediately clearing my throat to disguise the sound, and Espirito let my hand go.

"Bonifacio," I said as he left his desk, "are you coming—"

But he walked right past us, and out the door.

"Where's he going?" Espirito said, then went to the open door. "Is he going home?"

I stood beside him, watching Bonifacio's slow steps up the middle of the street towards the road leading out of town. His shoulders were bent. "He's left his coat. I don't know what's wrong with him." I went to the desk, where his coat was draped over the back of his chair. As I put my hand on it to lift it, and have Cristiano take it to Bonifacio, I saw the paper he had left on the desk.

At the top was the Jesuit symbol of the flaming sun. In that instant I knew what had happened. I knew.

"Diamantina?" Espirito said as I stood at the desk, my eyes skimming the paper. "What is it?"

I looked up from the paper and across the room at him, unable to speak.

⚬⚬⚬

Espirito came with us to the square; I couldn't disappoint the children.

I brought the letter with me, and silently watched as they ate their fill of cake. Then I asked Cristiano to take Candelária and walk in the square.

"We can feed the birds," Candelária said, taking the last uneaten piece of her cake in one hand and holding Cristiano's with the other.

"Now will you tell me?" Espirito asked when they'd run off. "Is it . . . does Bonifacio suspect? Has he said something to you?"

Suspect? Bonifacio had suspected me of illicit behaviour with Espirito since before I conceived Candelária. But Espirito didn't know that.

"It's not that," I said.

I took the letter from the Superior of the Order of the Diocese of Rio de Janeiro out of my bag and set it on the table. Espirito picked it up.

"*Dear Senhor Rivaldo,*" he read. "*You write us to request to be reinstated into the Jesuit community.*" He stopped and looked up at me, then back to the letter. "*This, as you know, is a highly irregular circumstance. You left your mission and the priesthood without official review from the diocese. Because you were a devout brother, we have given your request due consideration. But doctrine does not permit your ordination vow to be reinstated, nor your marriage vow to be annulled, by simple written request.*

"*We have informed the Cathedral parish in Lisboa that our decision is final. As for your marriage annulment, the Church requires written submission provided by the officiating Father of the marriage vows that this union was unconsummated.*

"*You may serve Our Lord through prayer and penance. May God bless you and forgive you.*"

Espirito hadn't looked at me again, and was still studying the script. "Did you know that Bonifacio wanted to re-enter the priesthood?"

"Yes. I . . . I was hoping he would. He told me a year and a half ago. Some days the thought of him leaving was the only glimmer of light I could see for the rest of my life. But now . . ." I couldn't stop my tears.

"Don't cry," he said, dropping the paper and reaching for me, but as I took my handkerchief from my bag, Cristiano brought Candelária back, sobbing.

She had fallen while chasing a bird, and now held out her palms. I bent over them, hiding my own tears, brushing the grit and dust off the slight abrasions with my handkerchief and then kissing each palm.

I stood then. "Let's go home."

"Will you be all right?" Espirito said quietly, and I nodded. "Send word when you want me to come to you. To the summer house," he said, so only I could hear. And then he called a cart for us, and lifted Candelária in and helped me up.

As we rode home, Cristiano glanced at me frequently, and when Candelária started singing, he shushed her. As the cart let us out at the quinta's gates, he hoisted Candelária onto his back; she wrapped her arms around his neck. They went up the drive ahead of me and I remembered how Espirito had carried Cristiano out of Curral das Freiras on his back.

I had been full of excitement then, daring to picture a different life, an escape from the high mountains that had made me a prisoner.

Now I was once more a prisoner.

Bonifacio would never leave. I would have to guard my daughter against his influence, and spend every day of my life seeing his accusing face, his glower of disapproval, his own darkness within attempting to obliterate any light that I welcomed.

I heard him as I passed the chapel. I went in. He was prostrate, weeping and praying, as I had first seen him on the floor of the church in Vila Baleira.

"Bonifacio."

His prayers stopped, but he didn't rise.

"Here is your letter. I read it," I told him, and dropped it onto the floor and left. In the short distance from the chapel to the cottage I knew that I would make my own happiness with Espirito. Bonifacio had always suspected me of immoral behaviour with his brother.

What had I to lose?

CHAPTER SIXTY-SEVEN

The summer house was our island, cut off from duty and responsibility. No one asked Espirito to account for his time, but I could only steal an afternoon here and there.

When I was with him, I felt surrounded by an aura of unreality. It wasn't only the sharing of myself with a man who had a true and tender affection for me, and was not afraid to demonstrate it, but also because he opened something in me that allowed me to talk as I never had before. I felt as though nothing I said would shock or dismay him. He listened with a quick smile or with consternation, holding me closely, sometimes stroking my hair or my cheek as I disclosed the saddest memories. I told him about my life on Porto Santo both before and after my father's departure. I talked of my mother's teachings and her death, of Sister Amélia, of Rooi's inn, and the sailor on the beach. I never mentioned Abílio. That was the only part of my life I did not want Espirito to know.

He spoke at length of his boyhood and his fond memories of his parents, and made me laugh with descriptions of his escapades. He filled my head with images of his visits to Lisboa. He was cautious in mentioning Olívia, and I knew he took such care out of sensitivity for my feelings.

I had never before known this, the easy talk that comes with an intimate relationship, and was astounded at the closeness that continued to grow with our disclosures. I felt comfort at knowing there was someone who carried my secrets, and who was not afraid of their weight. I had never known another person as

I knew him, and I trusted him never to hurt or disappoint me.

I gathered rosemary and made its perfume as my mother had, letting the herb sit in a jar filled with oil in a sunny window. I wore the oil freely, and my skin and hair and clothes always smelled of it. The warm afternoon air on the days we met was seductive, and we lay on the soft settees and fed each other fruits from the quinta's garden, sated and drowsy after lovemaking in the heady, bee-filled air.

Bonifacio's name never came to either of our lips.

***

It was Easter of 1755, and the da Silvas invited us for dinner.

I walked to their home with Candelária and Cristiano; Bonifacio said he would rather attend the Easter evening Mass, even though we had already gone to the morning service.

As Eduardo and Luzia and Espirito greeted us at the door, I felt that Luzia, standing so close as I kissed Espirito on each cheek in what I hoped appeared a sisterly fashion, would hear the pounding of my heart. He squeezed my waist with one hand before I stepped away, and I glanced in Luzia's direction. But she was too caught up in the children, hugging them and exclaiming over their new Easter clothing.

It felt like a game—hiding our feelings for each other—that was both uncomfortable and exciting.

After we had eaten and while Espirito accompanied Eduardo on his usual walk to smoke his pipe, Luzia and I sat in the salon.

"Can I play with your jewels, Avó?" Candelária asked. It was one of her favourite pastimes when we visited. Luzia brought out the velvet box, and Candelária happily picked through the sparkling pieces, trying on rings and bracelets. She took the filmy black lace shawl Luzia had taken from her shoulders and set on the settee, and draped it over her head. "Look at me," she said, her face solemn, a string of beads wrapped around her clasped fingers. "I'm a nun."

We had watched a procession of nuns in the Easter Mass in church that morning. "You are a very pretty little nun for only four years old," Luzia said.

"Nuns can't be pretty," Candelária announced gravely, pulling off the shawl.

"Why ever not?" Luzia asked.

"They are brides of Christ. Papa says a bride of Christ is the best thing for a girl to be, but he says if she's pretty, she won't be a good bride, because she'll think more about herself than God." She slid from the settee to join Cristiano, who was arranging Eduardo's old metal soldiers in neat rows on the carpet in front of the fireplace.

I shook my head as I rearranged the jewellery in its box. "Bonifacio fills her head with strange thoughts."

Luzia fingered her shawl and looked from Candelária to me. "You still haven't had a reply from Sister Amélia?"

A few months earlier, as we walked together past Convento Catarina of the Cross, I had told Luzia about being friends with Sister Amélia on Porto Santo. "But she's a Carmelite, if she's from Catarina of the Cross," Luzia had said. "How could you see her and speak to her?"

I had bent to fuss with Candelária's hair as she sat in the small wheeled cart I was pulling. "Vila Baleira is very small. The rules are not as stringent as in Funchal Town. I write to her regularly, although I haven't heard from her."

Sister Amélia had told me, when I left, that she wouldn't be allowed to receive letters, but that had been when Father da Chagos was alive. I hoped the new priest would take pity on her and pass on my letters. I often thought of her in the kitchen and her narrow cell, and hoped she still had the lovebirds to keep her company.

Now, as we sat in the salon, I told Luzia, "No. There's been nothing. I've thought of going to Porto Santo, to see for myself if she's all right. What if she's ill, or perhaps . . . perhaps has even died, and I don't know. She's so alone, Luzia."

"I'll see what I can do," she said. "We'll go together to the Convento Catarina of the Cross, and speak to the Madre Superiora."

Espirito and Eduardo returned, and now joined Candelária and Cristiano on the carpet to stage a mock battle with the metal soldiers. Watching them, Luzia shook her head.

"It does my heart good to see such a happy family gathering," she said, and a flush of guilt ran through me. "I know Olívia watches from above and smiles her approval today."

I went to the open window and looked out, unable to face Luzia at that moment. I wanted to grow wings and fly into the scudding clouds that blew over the sea. I didn't deserve to be in the presence of this dear woman, unsuspecting of the shadowy truths in that sunlit room.

⌖

That evening, as I opened the bedroom door to see if Candelária had readied herself for bed as I'd asked, she looked up, startled, and tried to hide something under her blanket.

"Please show me what you have, Candelária."

She slowly pulled out a Mass card with a picture of Saint Francis and handed it to me.

"Where did you get this?" I asked, sitting on her bed.

She shrugged, picking at the edge of the blanket.

I took her hand. Her palm was damp. "Candelária? I asked you where you got it."

"Papa gave it to me."

"For Easter?"

"No. He always gives them to me. He tells me who the Saint is, and what we must pray to him or her for. But I can't always remember, Mama." She rubbed her eyes. "I like the way Papa's face looks when I remember, but when I can't . . . I'm afraid that God will be angry with me when I can't remember."

"Papa has given many of these to you?"

She looked down, but in the instant before she lowered her gaze I saw something verging on panic.

"Candelária? I want you to tell me."

She slid off her bed and went to the little chest holding her playthings. She took out a handful of Mass cards and solemnly gave them to me. "Papa said it was our secret. But I don't like the secret, Mama." Her mouth trembled.

I sat in silence, looking down at the stack of cards, not wanting her to see the anger on my face. But it was difficult to hide my emotions from her.

"Are you mad at me, Mama? Is it a sin because I've told you the secret?" She got back onto the bed. "Papa says I must talk to God before I do anything I think is wrong, and wait for His answer, but . . ." Now the tears spilled from her eyes.

"But what, darling?" I said, setting down the cards and wiping her face.

"He doesn't answer me. Papa always says if I'm a very good girl with only good thoughts, I'll hear God's voice, but if I'm evil, I won't. He keeps asking me what God has told me, and if God has a message for him. He said I am a messenger from God, and I must tell him whatever God tells me. But I don't hear His voice, Mama, even though I listen hard with my eyes closed so tight that sometimes they hurt." Her smooth little brow furrowed. "Does it mean I'm evil?"

My poor child. "No. You're not evil at all. Not one bit. You're a very, very good girl." And then I couldn't speak any further, my own throat too heavy with the struggle not to weep. "Lie down," I said, and covered her. "I'll ask Papa not to give you any more prayer cards, all right? You go to sleep now, and think of the nice time we had at Avó's today."

She nodded, and I stayed with her until she slept.

I went to the sitting room. Bonifacio was at the table, whittling. I had never seen him do this before. As I came nearer, I saw he was whittling a cross from a soft piece of wood, whispering a prayer along with the steady rasp of the blade.

"What are you doing to her?" I demanded, throwing the prayer cards onto the table in front of him. "You're frightening her. She's only four years old."

He slowly set the knife and the half-carved cross on the table amongst the cards. "Do you think I can look at her without seeing her as the child of an evil union?" he said. "She carries your blood, the blood of a fallen woman. She has said things to me that indicate she is possessed. And I have taken it upon myself, as a man of God, to help her remain in a state of grace, and teach her to cast out sin with prayer."

I stood in front of him, arms crossed. "She's not possessed," I whispered harshly, leaning towards him. "She's clever. She's just a clever little girl."

In spite of my confident words, I had felt a chill when he spoke, wondering what Candelária had said, what unknowing comment—part of my mother's legacy—she had made. But I would never admit that to Bonifacio.

"You should commit yourself to joining the inquisitors in Lisboa," I said. "You would surely be the first to light the flame under the feet of those accused of heresy. You find great pleasure in feeling you are so far above others in your fervour. But I know better. Never forget that, Bonifacio. I know what happened in Tejuco, and what kind of man you really are. You strive to drive out what you see as evil around you, but we both know it was—is—inside *you*."

His face flushed, and his eyes were too bright, as though he was fevered. "There *is* evil here, on the quinta, and in your daughter. And as I cannot carry out holy duties with the heathens of Brazil, I will carry them out here. I will cleanse this place of its evil."

"What evil? What are you talking about?" I knew what he didn't: that I had slept with Abílio here, that Abílio had killed Martyn Kipling, and had raped me. Those were evil doings, yes. But in spite of that, I felt the quinta to be a place of love. In spite of the pain Abílio Perez had caused here, I felt so much love: love for my daughter and for Cristiano, love for Espirito, love for the kind Binta and Nini and Raimundo, love for the beauty of the fields and forests and flowers.

"I will work with her as long as I can," Bonifacio told me, "but there is a convent—Convento Teresa de Jesus—in Lisboa. It has a high reputation. They take very young girls, in order to start their religious training before they have seen and heard too much immorality."

I blinked, staring at him. "My daughter? She's not going to a convent, not at any age. So stop filling her head with any more thoughts that upset and confuse her. I won't let you."

In a sudden, unexpected move, he rose. As his chair tipped over, I backed away.

"Be very careful, Diamantina, about telling me what to do," he said, picking up the half-formed cross. There was spittle on his lips. He made the sign of the cross in front of me with that rough piece of wood. "You tread a narrow path."

"I don't know what you're talking about."

"I think you do." He sat down and picked up the knife. "I think you do," he repeated, and then bent his head over the wood and slowly, carefully, worked on it.

CHAPTER SIXTY-EIGHT

A few days later, I left Candelária with Binta and met Luzia in Funchal, as we had planned. Together, we went to Catarina of the Cross.

"The Sister's name is Amélia Rodrigues de Bragança," Luzia said to the Madre Superiora, glancing at me, and I nodded. "She has been on Porto Santo for possibly ten years or more. She has done her penance, surely. We are here to see if there is a possibility of her being returned to her home convent."

"I remember her," the Madre said. She rose and pulled a rope that hung by the door. A young Sister appeared, and they spoke quietly. The Madre came back to the desk, sat and folded her hands on it. She appeared to be waiting, and we did the same.

The Sister returned with a thick book, set it on the desk and stood to one side. The Madre opened it in the middle. She turned the pages with great slowness, and the Sister leaned forward. I realized that the old Madre Superiora was no longer able to read the tiny script, and the young Sister acted as her eyes.

At a small sound from the Sister, the Madre lifted her hand from the page. The Sister ran her finger down it. I strained to see what was written, but the book was upside down for me, and the writing faded.

The young nun tapped her finger against a line, then spoke into the Madre's ear, so low that again I couldn't hear.

The older woman nodded, and the Sister left. "Yes. Sister Amélia is indeed on Porto Santo. At Nossa Senhora da Piedade," she said.

I had to clamp my lips shut so I didn't utter a sound of impatience. Hadn't Luzia just told her that?

"There is no indication here," the Madre said, touching the open page, "that the penance could be ended. She will remain there."

I breathed in through my nose, deeply, and looked at Luzia.

"Madre," she said, leaning forward. "Perhaps on the mainland, the decisions of the Church are irreversible. But here, on the islands, surely the rules can be loosened."

The Madre Superiora frowned. "Rules are rules."

Luzia smiled. "Is there any . . . offering that can be made? Something that could benefit the convent?"

In the hot, still air of the room, I waited. Finally, the Madre Superiora spoke. "Occasionally, very occasionally, we can reverse a decision if it would benefit the holy sisterhood."

Luzia leaned back. Her face was slightly damp from the heat, as I knew mine was. "And is there something that would benefit your holy sisterhood?"

Another pause. The back of my dress was wet.

"We are always in need. We depend on the goodness of the parish to provide donations that allow us to make much-needed repairs to the convent. It is very old, one of the first on Madeira."

"I see." Luzia looked from the Madre to me, then back at the Madre. She raised her eyebrows slightly. "Perhaps Senhora Rivaldo and I could work together to provide a donation worthy of bringing Sister Amélia back to Funchal, and this holy place. Is this a possibility?"

The Madre laced her fingers together on the desk. "It would require an endowment worthy of such a breach of the rules. But should a wealthy patron provide us with a substantial donation, we might be able to consider your request." She stood.

Luzia and I did the same. "Thank you, Madre," she said, "for your time, and for your consideration."

Once outside, Luzia turned to me. "So. There is a way. I can ask Eduardo—"

"No," I said, putting my hand on her arm. "You've done enough."

"But surely you don't have—"

Again I interrupted her. "You've done enough, Luzia. Thank you. I will manage the rest."

"All right," she said. "If you're sure." We walked down the street. "Espirito seems much happier," she said unexpectedly. She stopped and looked at me. "You are different as well. Maybe, for the first time since I met you, you seem . . . happy with life. You smile a great deal now, a true smile, not one you think people want to see. Your whole face is alight."

I looked down in a sudden panic.

"Diamantina," she said, "look at me." I raised my head. "I love you as a daughter, and I love Espirito as a son." Her eyes were wet. "Sometimes, after great sadness, happiness pushes through in an unexpected way, like a flower between the stones of a city street. Some might say it doesn't belong, and will step on it. I am not one to say this. I say it might survive, and I step around it."

My face was burning, my chest rising and falling.

For Luzia, kindness was an instinct. "The happiness of those I love brings me comfort. Come, now. It's been a good day." She walked again, and I joined her, our footsteps ringing on the stones.

⁂

Candelária sang one of Binta's songs as I weeded and trimmed the flowers around my parents' gravestones. Her voice blended with the whir of the bees and the twittering of the birds as they caught the insects that emerged in abundance as the day cooled. She sat in the soft soil and drew with a small stick.

I hadn't been able to stop thinking of Luzia. She had made it clear she knew about me and Espirito, and yet she had not condemned us. She had found a way for me to bring Sister Amélia back to Funchal; I knew that I would do it as soon as harvest was over.

"Look at my pretty picture," Candelária said, and I brushed the dirt from my hands and went to her. As I stared down at her drawing, I felt as though the air had been taken from me.

It was a replica of one of the marks that had been repeated on my mother's torso: a curling fishtail with wavy lines over it. Candelária had drawn it over and over, creating a pattern. It was unlike any I had on my own back. Candelária had often traced my marks with her fingers as I sat in my shift, brushing my hair.

"Did you see this drawing somewhere?"

"No. Just inside my eyes," she said.

I smiled at her then, but knew it was time to teach her to hide her gift from Bonifacio.

CHAPTER SIXTY-NINE

It was the last day of the grape pressing on the quinta, and I arranged for our usual Festa do Vinho. I wore my best muslin gown, with its silver bodice and pewter-coloured skirt.

When Espirito stepped into the warm dust of the yard, Candelária ran to him and threw her arms around his legs, and he made the silly face that always made her laugh. I smiled, happy as always just to be in his presence, to have him near.

Eduardo and Luzia had not come; they were visiting friends in nearby Câmara de Lobos.

After the last pressing, the teams of men who had trod the grapes, their families and those of us from the quinta enjoyed our celebratory meal at long tables in the yard. I had helped Binta and Nini in the kitchen, preparing cuts of beef and pork and mounds of vegetables from the garden and fresh, savoury breads. Sitting together over dinner, Cristiano spoke English to Espirito, and Candelária switched back and forth between Portuguese and English as she chattered. Bonifacio was the only one unable to understand the conversation fully, and I suspected this was carefully orchestrated on Cristiano's part.

As the sun lowered and the shrieking of the cicadas intensified, the musicians strummed their *cítaras*. Cristiano and Tiago turned handstands, showing off for the girls who had come to watch their fathers and brothers work in the *lagar*. Candelária had attached herself to one of the visiting girls, and was sitting on her lap as the older girl wove flowers through her hair. I glanced at Espirito. He was watching the young people as well, but was clearly lost in thought.

Bonifacio, sitting beside me, accidentally knocked over a cup of burgundy wine, and it splattered my skirt, sticky and dark.

I jumped up, wiping it with a napkin. "I'll have to soak this so it doesn't stain," I said, and left for the cottage. Partway there, I heard footsteps behind me.

It was Espirito. "Bonifacio's gone to the pressing house with some of the men. I didn't know when I'd next get the chance to be alone with you. Let's go to the summer house."

"Espirito," I said, smiling, "you know we don't have time to—"

"Please. I have something I want to tell you."

My smile faded at his expression. "Is something wrong?"

"Come," he said, and I followed him to the summer house.

Standing on the step, we looked out at the harbour. The flowering shrubs surrounding the open structure were especially strong in the evening, and I breathed in deeply, almost tasting their sweetness on my tongue.

"The water is merging with the horizon," I said. "It must be raining heavily far out at sea." I turned to him.

Instead of putting his arms around me as I expected, he picked up my hand. "I wanted to tell you first," he said.

"Tell me . . ." I studied his face.

"I'm going to Brazil."

I looked away from him, to the harbour, seeing the tiny twinkling lights of the anchored ships like stars upon the water in the falling darkness. "To make new contacts for Kipling's? You'll be away for more than a year, then?" I asked, trying to imagine not seeing him for so long.

"No," he said, and I looked away from the distant lights, to his face.

"No to what?"

He hesitated. "I'm not coming back, Diamantina."

"Not coming back?" I echoed. I hated the sound of my voice, accusatory and yet somehow desperate.

"It's best if I start a new life." He took a deep breath and pulled a paper from inside his jacket. "Abílio Perez has written. He sold Kipling's to a Portuguese merchant in Oporto—Plácido Fernandez

Lajes. He'll take it over in the next few months." He held the letter out to me.

"He can't," I said after I'd read what Abílio had written. "Abílio can't do this to Dona Beatriz. The winery and the quinta are hers forever. It's written in the deed her father gave to her. Leandro will inherit everything. It can't be sold."

"Perez must have had her sign the deed over to him."

"She wouldn't do that. She wouldn't, Espirito." As I spoke, I realized I hadn't had a letter from Dona Beatriz for the last few months. How long had it been? I'd been so caught up with Espirito that I'd thought of little else.

He shook his head. "I don't know how Perez has done it, but it's obvious Lajes is under the impression he's bought everything. And this means life will change, Diamantina. Lajes will bring his own people into the winery. And . . . well, you can guess that Lajes won't keep you on either. It's because of Dona Beatriz—and Henry— that you were there. This man will never agree to a woman in his *adega*. The quinta is part of the sale . . ." He stopped. "I'll speak to Henry about this. Perhaps he can find work for Bonifacio and you in his business. But that's up to Henry—I can't promise anything."

My home. My work in the *adega*.

"I spoke to Henry only last week, while he was in Funchal. He's as shocked as I am. He says Perez told him that Lajes isn't interested in partnering with the altar wine operation. It will be over, and Henry's business will suffer."

"And so you . . . you're going to work for him? For Henry?"

"I'll start up a branch of his business in Rio de Janeiro."

"But why can't you stay here and work for him?"

"It's not just the work, Diamantina. I can't do this anymore. I can't be with you in this half-life, knowing we can never truly be together. You're my brother's wife. There's no future for us."

"But . . ." I stared into his face, willing him to say, *Come with me. Bring the children and come with me and we'll live together in Rio de Janeiro, where nobody knows us, or about Bonifacio.*

"You are married to my brother," is what he said. "That will never change." He looked over my head, towards the darkening sea.

My legs felt watery, and I sat on the nearest chair.

"The one good thing that will come out of this sale is that you will be done with Abílio Perez."

I waited a few seconds. "What do you mean?"

"Won't you be glad he's out of your life?"

My mouth was suddenly dry.

"Any time Abílio Perez is mentioned, your face turns to stone. I understand your distaste—perhaps that's too mild a word for it—for Perez." He took the letter from me and put it back into his jacket.

I swallowed. "You understand my . . . What are you talking about?"

"I see the joy Candelária has brought you, though, and have thought that perhaps it was an unexpected blessing."

"Candelária?" My voice faltered as I spoke my daughter's name. "Why are you talking about Candelária?"

Espirito finally sat down across from me. "I always knew that Bonifacio couldn't have fathered Candelária. That day when we came from Curral das Freiras, and I went out to look for him . . ." He stopped, raking back his hair with his fingers as if the memory still disturbed him. "When I found him . . . he told me why he was so ill. He told me what he'd done, and why he'd done it."

I looked down at my fingers, spread on my stained skirt.

"And then, when I saw Candelária for the first time after she was born, saw her toes, I knew. I'd seen Perez's feet at the harvest festival here before you came to Funchal. He was drunk and making a fool of himself in the *lagar*."

I couldn't look at him for a long time. Finally I raised my head. "Do you want to know how it happened?" I asked him, a challenge in my voice. "Do you want to know why I . . . why I did what I did?"

"At first I imagined that he'd forced himself on you. But the more I thought about it, I couldn't believe that."

I covered my eyes with my hand.

"Not a woman like you. If Perez had taken you against your will, you would have said something, done something. Told Bonifacio. He never would have worked for the pig had he known. And you wouldn't have wanted to stay on the quinta."

I dropped my hand. "I went to him of my own will. I did it to ensure Bonifacio got the position in the Counting House." My voice was too loud, too fast. I was humiliated that Espirito had all along known the truth. "Because I wanted this life. This life, Espirito," I said with a sweep of my arm. "I couldn't count on Bonifacio, and I didn't want to go back to Curral das Freiras. I wanted something more for myself. And so I took it, in the only way it was offered." The last few words seemed to ring in the air around us.

In contrast to my voice, Espirito's was soft. "Bonifacio knows that Candelária is Abílio's, then?"

I felt a ridiculous smile hovering on my lips. "I didn't tell him, because what you said was true: he wouldn't have worked for Abílio, knowing." I looked at the twinkling harbour lights again. Espirito had known all along. He knew what kind of woman I truly was.

"But he accepted her," he said, and I looked from the lights back to him. "In that way, he has been a good man."

"Is that how you see him?"

He didn't answer, but then said, "You know why I can't stay, Diamantina. It's not a life for either of us. It's not fair to Bonifacio, or to you or me. Nobody can win in this situation. Nobody."

I was crying now. I stared at him, willing myself not to drop to my knees, not to throw my arms around him and beg.

"And I can't . . . I won't see you alone again before I leave."

"What? Why?" My voice rose like a bird's, warbling in the still evening air.

"I've made my decision to go. To be with you any longer . . ." I reached for him, but he rose and stepped out of my reach. ". . . would only weaken my resolve. It's the only way I can do it. Try to understand. You have a life here, with Cristiano and Candelária. And a husband, such as he is. I have nothing here but my work."

"You have me here. You have me," I repeated.

"I don't have you, Diamantina. Not in the right way."

"There's nothing I can say that will convince you to stay?" My voice was little more than a whisper.

"Please. Try to see it from my point of view. Can you not understand?"

I could. Of course I could. But I couldn't move, or speak.

"I have to go back, in case Bonifacio returns and sees us both gone." He finally came to me, and I stood. He brushed my hair from my face, wiping my cheeks with his thumbs. I wanted him to hold me so badly that I pulled on his arms, trying to wrap them around me.

But he gently removed my hands, and went down the steps. He stopped at the bottom, turning to me. "I'll always remember you here, in the summer house. I'll think of you like this, with the breeze in your hair, and your scent— What is your scent, Diamantina?"

"Rosemary." My voice was strangled.

"Rosemary," he repeated, and then was gone.

I was numb, in shock, trying to imagine a life without him. All that time, he'd known Abílio was my daughter's father.

I wanted to go to the cottage and lie down and close my eyes and sleep and not think about any of it. But Candelária was in the yard; I couldn't leave her.

I slowly walked back to the celebrations and sat at the table. The young people were on the grass, and Candelária ran around them, trying to get their attention. Espirito and Bonifacio were walking from the pressing house together. As they drew nearer, I saw that Bonifacio held the letter Espirito had shown me.

Bonifacio sat beside me and Espirito across from me. Bonifacio looked at the drying stain on my skirt. "Senhor Perez writes that he's selling Kipling's, and it will change hands in another month. It appears doubtful I will retain my position. Even if he does allow me to continue working for him, Senhor Perez states, the new owner will object to us living here." I just looked at him, and let him think my silence was surprise, or dismay. "That arrangement was through Dona Beatriz, and there will be no further obligation to us." He handed the letter back to Espirito. "And what will you do?"

"I'll work for Duncan in Rio de Janeiro."

"You'll leave Madeira," Bonifacio stated. Did I hear anything in his voice? Satisfaction, relief? Or was it my imagination?

Cristiano's laughter echoed across the yard.

"Yes. I sail on the *Padre Eterno* next week."

"Next week?" My voice was sharp, and both men looked at me. "It's just . . . so soon."

"I've bought my passage. There's no point in lingering," Espirito said, and then he got up and walked over to the group of young people. Candelária was tugging on Cristiano's shirt sleeve. Espirito picked her up and put her on his shoulders, and she laughed, and put her hands into his thick hair so she wouldn't fall.

CHAPTER SEVENTY

In spite of Espirito telling me he wouldn't see me alone again, I couldn't take it as truth. I waited to receive word from him. Three days after I'd last seen him, I went to the *adega*. He wasn't there, nor was he in the blending room.

The next day, I went again, carrying a note I'd written and sealed and addressed to him, asking that he contact me. I left it on the table of the blending room. I went to the summer house every afternoon, on the chance that he was waiting for me.

I couldn't sleep or think properly. Tears were always close to the surface. On the fifth day, I snapped at Candelária, making her cry, and then held her, soothing her as Cristiano watched. That evening he came to my bedroom when Candelária was asleep.

I was sitting on my bed, a closed book in my lap.

"I know something's wrong," he said. "Is it . . . you're not having another baby, are you?"

I made a sound that could have been a laugh or a sob. "No, Cristiano. It's not that."

"What, then?"

"Espirito is going to Brazil. He's never coming back."

"I know."

"He told you?"

"On the night of the *festa*. I'm spending tomorrow with him."

"What are you doing?" I asked, too eagerly.

"I don't know. He just asked me to spend his last day with him."

I nodded. It was as it should be. Espirito should be spending time with Cristiano, and certainly Eduardo and Luzia, and his friends. We had had our last time together at the summer house. I understood. And yet it hurt.

❧

Espirito came to the cottage with Cristiano the next evening.

"I didn't expect to see you again," I said, feeling heat in my neck and face, thinking, for one absurd moment, that he'd come to say he'd changed his mind, and wasn't going.

"Did you think I wouldn't say goodbye to all of you?"

I stared at him, so stricken that he was actually leaving that it was difficult to breathe.

"Where is Candelária?" he asked.

"I just put her to bed. She's not asleep yet."

"May I go in and see her?" he asked, gesturing towards my bedroom, and I nodded.

When he came out, he said to Cristiano, "You have the address in Rio de Janeiro where I will be staying. I expect to hear from you."

Cristiano nodded solemnly.

"I think we should shake hands to say goodbye," Espirito said. "You are a young man now."

Cristiano held out his hand, his chin quivering. "*Adeus*, Espirito," he said, and then Espirito hugged him. I saw how tall Cristiano had become.

"Maybe in a few years you'll sail to Brazil to work with me," he said.

A few years. I couldn't even think of the next hours.

Espirito went next to Bonifacio, who hadn't risen from the settee. There was a heavy, awkward moment as Espirito stood in front of his brother and held out his hand.

Bonifacio reached up and shook it. "Goodbye, Espirito."

"This reminds me of another parting, so long ago. Except it was you going off to Brazil for the rest of your life," Espirito said. "Or so we all thought. This time it's me."

"We can never know the ways of the Lord." Bonifacio spoke slowly, as if emphasizing the phrase he used too often.

At the door, Espirito said, looking at me, "I'll write, once I'm safely there."

I went to him and put my hands on his shoulders and kissed him on both cheeks, so aware of Bonifacio watching. "Safe journey," I said, my voice thick, then followed him out to the step and watched him walk away from the cottage. When he disappeared, I stood for another moment, thinking I still saw his white shirt in the falling dusk.

"Diamantina," Bonifacio said, suddenly behind me.

I turned and stared at him.

"Come inside." He held the door open and, when I didn't move, repeated, firmly, "I said to come inside."

⁂

I was tilting, rising and falling with the rhythm of the ocean, although I was firmly rooted on land. I watched the sea, a silver plate, and on it the *Padre Eterno*, its tall sails billowing, full of the morning's wind. I stood on the top step of the summer house and watched Espirito sail away. I thought of my father sailing away, although I had never witnessed it. I had always thought I'd see him again.

That was back when I knew so much less than I knew now.

⁂

Over the next days, I pictured Espirito far out on the water, and wondered if he thought of me as I of him. I imagined a life with him, all of us together, he and I and Cristiano and Candelária.

I had my six diamonds. If my life became unbearable here, if Bonifacio made it intolerable to raise my daughter in his presence, I would use some of them to buy three passages to Brazil. I would go to Espirito, even if he hadn't asked me to come. More than once I took out the little diamonds and was comforted by their coolness in my hand. I arranged them in different patterns on the blue velvet as I pictured the happiness they could bring.

I knew I should go to visit Luzia, as she would be missing Espirito as well. I knew I should go to Catarina of the Cross and speak to the Madre Superiora about Sister Amélia. I knew I should write to Dona Beatriz and ask her what had happened, how Abílio had coerced her into selling Kipling's. And yet I seemed unable to accomplish anything. I hoped for the local women to come to me so that I might talk to them and dispense healing remedies, and I longed to stand in the *adega* and breathe in the richness emanating from the barrels. But no one came to the quinta, and I had no excuse to go to Kipling's. When the new owner took over, I might never again go into the heat of the *adega*, piled high with barrels of fermenting wine.

On the afternoon that marked two weeks since Espirito's departure, I told myself that I could not continue to wallow any longer. I took Candelária and went into Funchal. At the Convent of Catarina of the Cross, I was admitted to the office of the Madre Superiora.

She silently indicated a row of chairs. I sat on one of them, and patted the one beside it, telling Candelária to sit.

"I trust you remember our conversation about Sister Amélia." I said to her, opening my bag and setting one of the diamonds on the desk between us.

The diamond caught the light from the window behind the Madre, and cast a dancing prism on her hands, folded in front of her.

She looked at the gem, and smiled gently at me. "I'm afraid this isn't sufficient."

I cleared my throat and put another beside the first. When the woman made no comment, I added a third. At that, she stood. "I'm afraid that reversing an order is not so easily amended," she said.

"But you told us, Senhora da Silva and me, that—"

"It requires a great deal, senhora," she said. "A great deal."

I licked my lips. Then I took out the blue velvet and tipped the last three diamonds onto the desk. "It's all I have."

She looked at the six diamonds, then at me, and finally sat down again. She took a sheet of vellum from a drawer, and pulled the ink bottle towards her. She picked up a quill. Each of her movements was slow and methodical. She wrote, leaning back from the desk, her eyes narrowed so she could focus. Eventually she laid down the quill and sprinkled the page with pounce. When the ink had dried, she shook the paper to dispel any of the fine powder still left. She rolled the vellum, then melted wax and dripped it onto the seam to seal it. She touched a stamp to the warm wax, leaving the imprint of a tiny cross. I clenched my fists and concentrated on patience throughout this lengthy and painstaking process.

Candelária sat beside me without moving, watching intently.

"Sister Amélia has completed her penance on Porto Santo," the Madre said, "and will be welcomed home." She handed me the sealed scroll.

"Thank you, Madre," I said, and she bowed her head. Neither of us had looked at the diamonds again.

I put the scroll in my bag and took Candelária's hand, and we went out into the sunshine and walked to Francisco Square. I bought her a cup of sweet citron. As we sat at the table under the shade of a high palm, she talked about Raimundo's little granddaughter, Sabela, who sometimes came to the quinta to see her grandfather. Candelária liked to play with her.

"Sabela was sad yesterday, because she had to go home before she got to see the new kittens."

"She can see them the next time she comes."

She nodded and took a sip of her drink. "Why are you sad, Mama?"

I put my head to one side and tried to smile. "Do you think I'm sad?"

"Is it because of your friend?" she asked, and my attempted smile disappeared. Could she mean Espirito? But she would call him Tio, not my friend.

"Which friend, Candelária?"

"Your friend who wants to come home. The one with the birds in the pretty cage," she said, and on this bright and sunny day I felt as though a chilled breeze had swept down from the hillsides, or up from the sea. "Can we go to the waterfront and look at the ships?" she asked then, finishing her citron, her little mind skipping about in its usual rush.

"Yes. Let's go to the waterfront," I said.

We watched the unfurling sails of a caravel filling with the wind. I looked at the other ships anchored out on the water, wondering which of them would sail to Brazil.

I knew I would never be on one of them and, as I watched the restless sea, understood that today I had been given a test. Bonifacio so often spoke of tests. Today had been a test of my ability to sacrifice.

I had known Espírito's love, and until a few hours ago had imagined I could not live happily without it. Today, in the convent, I had lost my chance of knowing it again.

But it had been my choice. I had long understood the repercussions of choice.

⁂

I told Bonifacio that I planned to go to Porto Santo to bring Sister Amélia back to Funchal.

"When will you go?" he asked, too quickly. Was it eagerness? I waited for him to ask why I had made this decision, or how I had accomplished it. He did not.

"On Tuesday, and I'll return Thursday. Binta and Nini will care for Candelária, and Cristiano can stay with them as well. I'm also planning to go to Lisboa soon." I had made this decision on the walk back to the quinta.

Now he studied me. "Lisboa? Why?"

"I want to see Dona Beatriz."

"Why don't you write to her?"

"I must see for myself that she's all right. Dona Beatriz has a deed from her father. She owns everything. I can't imagine why or how she would have allowed Abílio to sell it. I don't trust him."

"You call him Abílio now?" After another heartbeat he asked, "Why don't you trust Senhor Perez?"

"I've heard too many stories about him. Surely you've heard them too, at Kipling's."

"I don't listen to stories."

"Bonifacio, aren't you concerned about our future?" My voice rose in exasperation. "Once Kipling's is sold to Senhor Lajes, you won't be employed in the Counting House. I won't work in the *adega*, and we won't have a home. Doesn't all of this disturb you in the least?"

The clock ticked, slower and slower; I had forgotten to wind it the night before.

"We will talk about all of this when you return from Porto Santo," he said.

I felt a warning beat in my chest. It wasn't just my distress over Espirito leaving, or my thoughts of returning to Porto Santo, or our uncertain future. There was something else, something I couldn't identify. For one mad instant I thought of burning wormwood, and looking for the answer in its smoke, as my mother had done. As I had done the night I made my decision to marry Bonifacio.

The clock gave one final tick, and stopped.

⌒⌒

Candelária was distraught when I told her that I was going to Porto Santo the next day. "It's only for three days and two nights, Candelária."

"Can I come with you tomorrow? Please, Mama. Don't leave me."

"No, *minha querida*. It will be a long day of sailing, then a day to do what I must, and then another long day to sail back. I'll take you another time."

"I don't want to stay here."

"You'll be with Binta and Nini. You like staying with them."

She wept then, and said, "I feel bad."

"Does your stomach hurt? Or your head?"

"No. Something else. Something scares me."

I talked reassuringly of the shortness of the voyage, the calmness of the weather, the strength of the ship, trying to calm whatever troubled her.

Candelária shook her head, her cheeks still wet. "It's not the ship, Mama," she said, but then said nothing more.

I dried her face and comforted her as much as I could, then stayed with her until she fell asleep.

I was relieved that she didn't cry as she said goodbye to me in the kitchen the next morning. Nini was distracting her by having her help with the bread, twisting dough into elaborate shapes.

CHAPTER SEVENTY-ONE

It was too late to go to Nossa Senhora da Piedade when I arrived at the long landing wharf in Vila Baleira.

I was counting on staying in the one small inn off Palm Square that had rooms to rent for the occasional visitor to the island. I walked up the jetty. Rooi's was still there, but looked much different than when I had left. There were flowers blooming in the window boxes, the shutters were freshly painted and the stones at the front door swept. A neatly lettered sign boasted a dining room. I was excited at the idea of seeing Rooi and finding out how life had treated him for the last six years. And wanted him to see how life had treated me.

I wore my best dress and shoes, and a hat in the latest style from Lisboa. A plump dark-skinned woman with her hair in an elaborate wrap of colourful fabric came through the back door as I entered through the front. She looked at me in an inquiring fashion. "Is Rooi here?" I asked, setting my bag on the floor and looking around.

The front and back doors were open to create a pleasant cross breeze, and the big room was decorated with matching tables and chairs. The tables had tidy embroidered cloths, and a small container of flowers sat on each one. It was gracious and pretty, nothing like the filthy, stinking inn where I had spent my younger years, playing dominoes and pretending to drink the wine.

She nodded. "He's in the back room. I'll go and get him," she said, in heavily accented Portuguese.

In a few moments, he followed her into the dining room. "When Palma told me there was a tall yellow-haired woman here," he said, coming towards me and taking my hands, "I could only hope. This is Palma, my wife, from the Canaries."

I tried not to show my surprise. Rooi, at his advanced age, finally marrying. Or maybe he'd long been married to Palma but had only brought her back to Porto Santo after I'd left.

"Look at you," he went on, squeezing my hands tightly before letting go. "My own Diamantina, grown into such a fine woman. What brings you back to Porto Santo after all these years?"

"I'm here to take Sister Amélia to her convent in Funchal. I've brought you something." I took three bottles from my bag.

He lifted each of them with an appreciative whistle. "Kipling's?"

"I'm . . . I was affiliated with them."

"You still do a little blending?" he asked, winking, and when I nodded, he said, "I can see you've made a good life. I'm not surprised. Nothing the Dutchman's daughter does should surprise me."

"I have a daughter now: Candelária. Coming close to five years old and quick as a fox. Like my father used to call me. *Klein vos*," I said, smiling.

"You must bring her here, so I can meet her," Rooi said. "Like you, my fortunes have changed." He put his hand on Palma's shoulder and with the other gestured at the dining room. "I collected on an old debt in the Canaries, and with Palma's influence—and her cooking—I have been able to enjoy a different life."

We ate dinner together, Rooi and Palma and I, a dinner Palma had prepared with unknown and wonderful spices. I told Rooi about my father, and a little about my life since I'd left Porto Santo. Rooi and Palma insisted I stay with them. Palma led me to the upstairs room Rooi had formerly used to store his pipes of wine, and where I had occasionally run to escape a drunken sailor, or simply to get away from the chaos of the inn for a few moments. Now it was quiet and clean, with a comfortable bed and a wide window that opened to the star-studded sky over the ocean.

The next day, I crossed the square and saw the same palm and dragon trees, the same benches with men sitting on them, what looked like the same dogs sleeping in the shade. The square was smaller than I remembered it. If anyone recognized me, they gave no indication.

I spoke to the young Father at the church, and gave him the sealed scroll. He read it, nodding gravely when I told him I would take Sister Amélia with me on the packet the next morning. I thought briefly that he would be annoyed at this news, knowing he would be forced to bring in local women to take over her duties, but he smiled. "Good," he said. "It's a lonely life for her here."

Sister Amélia dropped the small copper pan she was holding and put her hands to her cheeks when I stood in the kitchen doorway. "Is it really you, Diamantina?" she cried out after the clang of the pan hitting the stone floor receded. I went to her and hugged her, and she held me tightly.

As we stepped back and looked at each other, I heard familiar sounds. "They're still alive?" I asked, and she nodded. I thought of Candelária's vision.

"Since you left, they have brought me daily companionship and happiness," she said, and together we went into her tiny cell to look at Zarco and Blanca, their cage hanging in the open window. "They remind me, always, of you. It is good to have something to care for."

I smiled at the familiar little green lovebirds with their red heads, and then at her.

"I never imagined I would see you again," she said. "Your letters have brought me such joy."

"You received them?"

"The young priest is kind. Although it is against the rules, he gave me each as it arrived. I've kept them all, and I read them often. I saw your life in Funchal as you described it, and I remembered so much of my own life there. But the Father could not allow me to write back to you. If his indiscretion had ever been discovered, it would go badly for him. I was grateful you didn't give up, and kept writing."

I took Sister Amélia's hands. "I worried so much about you. I went to the Madre Superiora of Catarina of the Cross, and she

decided that you had served your penance. She's given written permission for you to leave, and—"

Sister Amélia cried out, dropping to her knees, still gripping my
hands.

"—and I've already passed it on to the Father. We will leave
tomorrow morning."

At that, she kissed my hands, tears streaming from her eyes,
while the birds sang of their love.

❧

After I left Sister Amélia, I carried my boots and walked down the
beach to Ponta da Calheta. Along the way I picked up a rusted belt
buckle as it washed against my bare foot, then a knobby whelk, and
finally a foreign coin encrusted with tiny barnacles. I took them
with me to the end of the beach, holding them as I sat on the rock I
knew so well, watching the waves. After a time I left the sea's offerings on the rock and walked back to Vila Baleira, never looking
behind me.

❧

It was difficult to say goodbye to Rooi the next morning, but I
promised to send him a sketch of Candelária.

At the back gate of the church, Sister Amélia waited for me with a
large basket and the birds in their cage. Her cheeks were flushed, and
as I took the basket of her few belongings and we walked out through
the gate, she gripped my arm, her bare feet suddenly faltering.

"What is it, Sister Amélia?" I asked. The colour had left her
cheeks, and her skin was now dough-coloured.

"Everything feels . . . it feels too big."

"The square?" I looked at the small area.

"Not just the square." She fought to catch her breath. "The sky.
The sea. Everything."

I led her to a bench, and we sat for a few moments. When she
could breathe normally again, she said, "I've dreamed of walking

more than my daily counted steps and seeing more than a tiny slice of sky the whole time I've been inside the church. And now . . ." She smiled. "I couldn't sleep last night. The idea of being with the other Sisters, and the beautiful gardens of the convent—of it being real, and not just my dreams . . . it feels as though I've been truly touched by God's hand."

We had a good following wind, and anchored in Funchal by late afternoon. I went with Sister Amélia to the gates of the convent. She set down the birdcage and reached for the bell cord, hesitating for just a moment, and then turned. "I won't be able to ever do this again," she said, as she put her arms around me and I returned her embrace.

She wiped her eyes and pulled the cord.

A nun slid back the grille on the heavy wooden door. "Is it really you, Sister Amélia?" she asked after a moment. "There have been a few whispers, but none of us knew if it was true."

"Yes, Sister Gabriella. I've returned."

The grille slid closed and the door opened. "Welcome back, Sister." The two women gazed at each other for a moment, their eyes showing their pleasure.

Sister Amélia said, "This is Diamantina. She brought me from Porto Santo."

As she picked up the birdcage, Sister Gabriella looked at the lovebirds and said, "They will enjoy living in the garden. And we will all enjoy them as well."

"You will come for the yearly visits?" Sister Amélia asked me. "We will only be able to speak through the grille—"

Sister Gabriella cleared her throat. "Monthly. We are allowed monthly visits now."

Sister Amélia shook her head as if this were another wonder.

"Of course I'll come," I said. "Every month. I can't wait for you to meet Candelária," I told her, and then watched as she went into the cloisters of Catarina of the Cross.

❧

As I walked up the hill to Quinta Isabella, I felt peaceful for the first time since Espirito had told me he was leaving.

I had loved Espirito, and he me. To have been loved and given love in return was more than many ever knew. I had been able to bring some measure of happiness to Sister Amélia. I had my own small sum of money from my work in the *adega*, more than enough to buy passage to Lisboa to see Dona Beatriz. I didn't know what I would find, but I was confident that once I spoke to her I might be able to put together a bright new life on Madeira. Maybe Henry Duncan would hire me—and Cristiano—to work for him.

As for Bonifacio . . . I would try to teach myself patience. With Espirito gone, perhaps he would be less suspicious of everything I did. As Candelária grew older, I would explain to her that the things Papa said were not to concern her.

More than anything, as I approached the quinta, I was looking forward to holding Candelária, feeling her little arms around my neck, smelling her sweet child's scent.

And so, yes, I told myself, I would forge happiness out of life, even without Espirito.

❧

Ah, life. What lessons you set before us, so that we will never forget to be humble.

CHAPTER SEVENTY-TWO

"You're back, Diamantina," Nini said, smiling. She and Binta and Raimundo were sitting in the kitchen, empty plates in front of them. "Cristiano has eaten, and he and Tiago have gone to town. Sit down, and I'll get you some dinner."

I looked around. "Where is Candelária?"

Binta and Nini stared at me. Raimundo shook his head.

"What is it? Where is she?" I slowly set my bag at my feet.

"But . . ." Binta looked at Nini and back at me. "Bonifacio said . . ."

"Said what?" My voice was sharp.

"He came to us only an hour after he took you to the waterfront. He told us you'd changed your mind and wanted to take Candelária with you. He said he had to go to Lisboa, but first he would take her to you on the ship," Binta said, blinking rapidly. "Candelária was so excited."

The kitchen was too hot. "You let her go with him?" I heard my voice, shrill. "Why? Why did you let her go?"

"He's her father. How could I stop him? And why would I?" Binta said.

A terrible fear came over me, and then whiteness.

"If she isn't with you"—Nini's voice came from far away, as though through water, and I was pushed down, onto a bench—"where is she?"

There was the hard smoothness of tin at my lips, and then water in my mouth. I swallowed. As the whiteness edged away, I said, "He took her."

"Bonifacio took her? He took her with him to Lisboa?" Raimundo asked.

A name was nudging at the back of my mind. I would remember it.

"To Lisboa?" Binta repeated.

"A convent. He took her to a convent." I stood, my legs shaky. I straightened and wiped my forehead with my palm. "Raimundo, take me to Funchal in a cart. I need to buy my passage to Lisboa right now. For tomorrow."

"It's too late. The ticketing is closed. When it opens in the morning—"

"The morning?" I cried, my voice loud. "I can't wait until morning." I walked around and around the kitchen, then stopped, suddenly remembering Candelária's anxiety about me leaving. *Something scares me. It's not the ship, Mama, not the ship.*

"I'll take you first thing, Diamantina," Raimundo told me.

At the kind, worried expression on his face, I grabbed my bag and ran out of the kitchen, through the yard and up the path to the cottage. I slammed the door, my back against it as if keeping out some danger, and dropped my bag with a thud. I went into my bedroom and opened the wardrobe. All her clothing was still there, the small dresses and shifts and stockings and her extra boots. Then I knelt at Candelária's wooden chest and pulled everything out, scattering the toys on the floor. I didn't know what I was searching for. I picked up a rag doll—her favourite doll—and pressed it against myself, looking around with jerky, panicked movements. A folded letter sat on my dresser. I scrambled to my feet and grabbed it, and unfolded the parchment with trembling fingers.

Diamantina,

    For close to five years I have raised my brother's child.

    Like you, she was born of immoral parents, and from birth there has been the threat that she will follow your crooked course as you followed your mother's. I have already seen the evidence, and it is my duty to prevent this further spread of evil. She must be shown God's light, and since you are incapable of knowing it, you are incapable of teaching it. Realizing that your mother's curse will be driven out

*of her, and that she will be shown how to walk the righteous
path, and live purely and in a state of grace, will be your reward
on this earth, for you can expect none in the next life.*

*I embark on a new journey, following the direction God—
not man—has set for me.*

It was unsigned. The black ink gleamed. I saw the thin loops of
each letter in Bonifacio's familiar crabbed style. I saw my hand,
with my wedding ring, holding the paper. I dropped it, and it fell
to the floor in a slow, delicate flutter. Before me I saw Candelária,
her pointed chin and arched brows. A little sylph, a slender, graceful child. I thought of how she looked at the world around her in
wonder, with my mother's eyes. I thought of Sister Amélia as we
crossed from Porto Santo to Madeira, and how her wimple pre-
vented her from seeing anything other than what was directly in
front of her.

The blood drained from my head as it had in the kitchen, and I
had to take long, deep breaths. I put my hands on the dresser and
looked at myself in the mirror over it. The woman who stared back
was not familiar. She was older, her face rigid. Frozen, like the ice
my father had described when I was a child.

Convento Teresa de Jesus. That was the name Bonifacio had once
spoken. "Convento Teresa de Jesus," I whispered to that stricken,
frozen face.

⁂

I was still in the travelling clothes I'd worn for my voyage to Porto
Santo when I stood before the clerk at the ticketing office the next
morning. I had lain on the bed fully dressed but hadn't slept, waiting for the light. I heard Cristiano come in shortly after dark but
couldn't bear to see him, couldn't bear to utter the terrible thing that
had happened.

I would tell him when I had the strength, tell him that instead
of taking him to Brazil, as he'd threatened, Bonifacio had taken
Candelária away.

"A ticket to Lisboa. Senhora Rivaldo," the clerk confirmed as he wrote, yawning, and then asked, "And who is your travelling companion?"

When I didn't answer, he peered at me. "Senhora? Whom do you travel with?"

"I go alone."

He shook his head. "I cannot sell passage to a woman travelling alone to Lisboa. It's against our policy. You can have anyone accompany you—servant, relative, it matters not—but you cannot go alone," he repeated. "You must go with another woman, or a male of at least twelve years."

"Fine. Fine," I said, taking more réis from my bag. "Give me the second passage."

"And the name?"

"Cristiano Rivaldo."

"A relation," he stated.

"Yes."

"Age?"

"Thirteen."

He painstakingly wrote. "Passage for two adults on the *Bom Jesus*, leaving in two days' time."

"You have nothing for today, or tomorrow?"

"Two days' time," the clerk repeated, and pushed the tickets across the counter.

PART IV

LISBOA, PORTUGAL

Boarding the square-sailed *Bom Jesus*, Cristiano straightened his shoulders. It was the first time he'd been on a ship since the long and terrible journey he'd taken with Bonifacio from Brazil.

As for me, hadn't I planned to do this: go to Lisboa to speak to Dona Beatriz about the sale of Kipling's? All was changed now. I didn't care about Kipling's, or Quinta Isabella, or where I would live, or how. What importance was any of that if I did not have my child?

What had Bonifacio told Candelária? How did he imagine she would be accepted into a convent at four and a half years old?

After only one chaotic, horrifying thought that he might take her all the way to Brazil with him, I didn't let myself think that again. I wouldn't be able to put one foot in front of the other if I allowed myself that image.

As we left Funchal, I leaned my head on my arms along the ship's railings, our travelling cases at our feet. Cristiano touched my arm.

"Does the sea make you ill, Diamantina?" he asked.

"It's not the sea, Cristiano. It's my fear for Candelária."

He put his arm around my shoulder. He was as tall as me now, his voice sometimes dipping and rising. As he had been a handsome little boy, he was now growing into a young man of striking looks, with his smooth, dusky skin and soft curls, his eyes glowing a dark greenish brown.

When Madeira was far behind us, its outline blurred on the horizon, the sun rested near the sea, warm and orange. I watched it, knowing I would have to find the strength to face whatever awaited me in Lisboa.

⁂

Cristiano and I spoke little on the week-long journey, as the *Bom Jesus* fought against the strong wind that swept towards the bottom of the earth. I watched the waves and the life they held through the day. At night the sky was a mantle of stars, and sleep was near to impossible. I grew more distraught the closer we came to Lisboa, and clung to the only comfort I had—the name of the convent Bonifacio had once spoken, Teresa de Jesus. If my daughter was not there, I would travel to every convent in Lisboa, and beyond, in all of Portugal. I would not stop looking until I found her.

Cristiano knew my fear and turmoil, and one stormy night came to my cabin to beg me to come outside to the deck. "You must come, Diamantina," he said over the creak and groan of the ship as it rose and then plunged downwards. He was dripping wet, his eyes alight.

"But it's a thunderstorm," I said, holding the door frame with both hands to keep from sliding into Cristiano.

"It's something wondrous. Please."

I wrapped myself in my cloak and followed him outside, struggling to stay on my feet with the rise and swell of each high wave. My stomach churned from the movement. Lightning filled the sky, each flash followed almost immediately by a thunderclap. I pressed closer to Cristiano on the tilting, slippery deck. The crew and other passengers clutched the railings and each other for support as they stood with heads tilted back, staring at the tops of the foremast and mainmast. From their points, a glowing ball of blue light streamed upwards into the tempest.

"What is it?" I shouted over the storm.

"Corpo Sancto," he yelled into my ear. "The sailors say it's a divine token, the presence of our guardian saint. It means that the worst is passed."

I jumped at a huge clap of thunder, and when it had died, I asked, "The worst of the storm is passed?" I held my wet hair back from my face as I looked into his.

"You may take it as you wish, they say. The worst of what haunts you."

We stood together in the pounding storm. In spite of Cristiano's assurance, I felt that everything around me was in flames—the sky with lightning, the water with luminous particles, and the very masts.

⌘

We sailed inland down the wide estuary to the Tagus River, buffeted by a strong current. The sunlight flickered on the water and, towering in the distance, the grand city stood proudly, as if held on the palm of God's hand. The ancient royal residence of Castelo de São Jorge dominated the vista on the tallest of the hills, while bell towers and church spires competed with each other above the rooftops of the houses below. I looked at Cristiano, and he at me, and we both felt the power of the magnificent city that lay before us, glowing in the early afternoon light.

In my dream that last night on board, I stood on the summer house steps, and all around was the blue of Madeira, hydrangeas at my feet and jacaranda trees above. There was the blue of ocean and sky, and when I looked at my hands, blue marks were on them as well, the symbol of the forked tail and wavy lines. And then, from the corner of my eye, came a flash of Candelária's dress, her favourite dress of pale blue, dyed from the leaves of woad. When I awoke and thought of the blue fire I had seen on the masts during the storm, I felt that this dream of blue was an omen, a good omen, and I needed one on this day.

I had brought three of her little dresses—including the pale blue one —for her to wear when I found her. When I found her. I would not say *if*. I had brought her rag doll.

At the dock, there was a confusion of fishing boats and caravels unloading their cargo, and gun salutes as ships arrived and departed, and bells ringing near and far. There were crates of noisy poultry, and cages of milling sheep and goats. Masters of the ships shouted and bullied the black men working in pairs, hauling loads on their heads and backs. What riches they carried: bales of cotton and indigo, animal hides, copper and timber, and too many wonders I had no names for. We alighted with our cases and made our way across the thronging quay, stopping as a procession of pilgrims passed in front of us with their litanies and tinkling bells.

"Convento Teresa de Jesus," I said to the driver as we climbed into one of the waiting carriages lining the square, after Cristiano had loaded in our bags. "Is it near?"

"It's in the parish of Alcántara. Not so far, west of the city," he said, and slapped the reins on the horses' backs.

⁂

The sights of Lisboa continued to astound us as the carriage slowly made its way through streets jammed with other carriages and coaches and chaises and wagons and litters. Near the waterfront were the cries of the street vendors with their grains and sugar, bananas and yams, pepper and tobacco and cacao. Cristiano touched my arm, pointing at a long tuberose root.

"Cassava," he said. "I remember women pounding it to make manioc flour. And the taste of the bread they made with it." It was the first memory he'd ever shared of his life in Brazil.

The waterfront rang with the sounds of sawyers and carpenters and stonemasons. I saw ship riggers and rope makers at work, and as we left the riverside and went farther into the city, we heard the blare of distant trumpets and muted drum rolls, a fanfare that surely announced some royal procession. Along leafy streets were the open windows of tanners and carpet weavers and clockmakers, and sitting outside, their backs against the walls, women worked on lace and embroidery.

"Why is rosemary burning everywhere?" I asked the driver.

"To ward off a recent plague," he said, and I sat back again, breathing in the unmistakable fragrance. My mother's scent, and Candelária's middle name. Another good sign.

"Here is the edge of the city, the parish of Santos," the driver eventually said, "and soon we will arrive in Alcántara."

A light rain had started by the time he stopped in front of high grey walls, with gardens and a small orchard and a mill behind a maze of connected buildings. I paid him the réis he named. "Please wait for me," I told him. My greatest hope was that I would emerge from the convent with Candelária. And we would go directly back to Lisboa, stay overnight at an inn, and board the next boat to Madeira. Home, to Quinta Isabella, for as long as it was home. To the blue of the sky and water, the trees and flowers, and my daughter in her blue dress.

The walls of the convent were damp and dreary. From behind them the nuns could be heard intoning their prayers. Their voices merged with the fall of the rain in a mournful dirge. I looked at Cristiano, and hoped for the gift of grace.

⁂

At the gate, I asked to see the Abbess. I was admitted and taken into a small, austere room with two benches. High, narrow windows revealed nothing but similar windows on an opposite wall. I waited an interminable length of time, listening to the same distant chanting I had heard outside. There was silence, then more chanting. At the very moment I began to despair I had been forgotten, the door opened. A Sister bowed her head, and I followed her along twisting hallways. I did not hear the voices of children, or any sound. It was painful to imagine Candelária in this place.

I was ushered into the office of the Abbess. "How may I help you?" she asked. She sat on a straight, high-backed chair, her fingers loosely moving along the beads of her rosary. "Please. Sit."

"I'm Senhora Rivaldo, Madre," I said, perching on the edge of the chair facing her. "I'm looking for my daughter, and believe she may have been brought here."

The Abbess shook her head. "No child with the surname of Rivaldo has been brought to Teresa de Jesus as a candidate for our order's novitiate."

A moan escaped me. "Candelária Rivaldo," I said. "You're certain?"

At that, her fingers stopped their movement. "There was a Candelária brought very recently for the orphanage. But she was Candelária Perez."

I stood, my small drawstring bag falling from my lap onto the floor. "The orphanage? Perez?"

"Yes. Candelária Perez," she repeated.

I swallowed, sitting down and picking up my bag. "There's been a mistake. Candelária should never have been brought here." *Why did Bonifacio give her name as Perez? He knows, then. How does he know?*

"So you're saying Candelária Perez, not Rivaldo, is your daughter?"

"Yes. And . . . please, Madre. I wish to take her home. I've said it was a mistake." I attempted a smile. "As you can see, she is not an orphan."

"Her father felt it better she remain in our orphanage until she can eventually enter the convent as a novice."

Again I tried to speak rationally. "I am her mother. She does not need to be in the orphanage."

The woman's expression was inscrutable. "Frankly, your presence is surprising. Your husband informed me that you were no longer in the child's life."

"Not in her life?"

"He informed us that you had left the child. For unsavoury reasons."

"Unsavoury?" I couldn't stop repeating her words.

"He said you had chosen another man over your marriage and child. After what she'd . . . experienced, he said, he felt this was the best place for her. He did not give the reason he felt incapable to raise her until she was ready to enter as a novice, and it was not my place to make this inquiry."

I shook my head. "No, no, Madre. This is a complete fiction. No," I said again. "I would never leave my daughter. He took her from me, Madre. He took her." Although I spoke calmly, my heart leapt at the tiniest movement of the woman's thick eyebrows.

"His was a most compelling case, senhora, and his sincerity touching. He wants the best for his child."

I tried to breathe evenly and speak very slowly and carefully, knowing how important what I said next would be. "May I speak frankly, Madre? My husband is . . . he is unwell. He imagines things which are illusions. I'm afraid he suffers a malady, a form of brain fever. Did you not witness anything irrational in his behaviour?"

"He was very lucid," she said. "Very convincing."

"No," I said firmly. "My husband has lost his way. I only ask that you consider that his words may have been affected by his inability to reason clearly."

She studied me, her expression never altering. "You can understand my doubt over the best way to approach this situation, senhora. The child's father came to me with one story and the child's mother now comes with another."

My blood thudded in my ears.

"As I have told you," she said, "your husband presented a compelling story about what he described as your unacceptable behaviour. Have you some way to refute that story?"

I stood again, this time clutching my bag. "I am here, Madre. I did not leave my child. Bonifacio did not speak the truth about me no longer being in my daughter's life."

"Bonifacio?"

"Yes. My husband. The child's father, Bonifacio."

She expelled a long breath. "I'm further confused, senhora." Her voice held the slightest edge of impatience. "The child was brought here by Senhor Abílio Perez, and the dowry paid by him."

"I beg your pardon, but it was not Abílio Perez who brought her. My husband Bonifacio is about my height, with thinning dark hair threaded with grey. Is this not the man you refer to?"

She shook her head. "No. This man was quite tall, with thick dark hair. No grey." She looked thoughtful. "He had a scar on his neck, just under his jaw."

I tried to lick my lips, but had no saliva.

"Senhora, perhaps you should sit down. May I offer you some water? I can see that you're very disturbed by all of this. Was the man who brought your child here her father, or not?" When I didn't answer, she said, "Senhora Rivaldo, surely you understand that with all this confusion I can't release the girl to you."

"Please, Madre. Tell me what to do, tell me . . ." As I heard my voice verging on hysteria, I stopped.

"I'm afraid I can only release her back to Senhor Perez. A father's pledge of his child is not easily revoked."

"But—"

She extended her hand towards the door. "That is all for today, Senhora Rivaldo. Perhaps the only thing for you to do now is speak to your husband."

"Yes," I said, fighting for composure. "I will bring her father back, and we can straighten this out. But first, Madre, please. Let me see my daughter."

"It would not be prudent. Seeing you would only distress her. We have already begun her spiritual training. I'm certain you do not wish to confuse her."

"But she has been taken from me."

"By her father," the Abbess said firmly.

I knew how she viewed me at this moment, and it was a time for caution. "I only want to assure myself that she is well. She must be frightened and bewildered, as she had no preparation for being removed from her home. Or from me. If I could talk to her for only a moment, Madre. Please."

"As I told you, I don't think it wise. But . . ." She glanced down, touching her rosary again, and that one word carried the strength to help me wait as she paused. "I do understand your concern," she finally said, rising, and went to the door, opened it and spoke quietly.

The Sister who had brought me to her appeared. "Take Senhora Rivaldo to the south garden, Sister Matilde. There she can view her child. She is not to speak to her, and the child is not to see her."

I stepped forward. "I'd only tell her—"

"I'm allowing you to see her," the Abbess said. Her tone held a warning.

"Thank you," I said then, knowing I must not do anything to tip the balance of this fragile moment.

CHAPTER SEVENTY-FOUR

Candelária sat on a small bench at the far side of the rectangular courtyard, open to the sky and shadowed by high walls on all four sides. The rain had stopped, but the stone walls were weeping with damp. Surely the bench she sat on was also damp. Although the Abbess had called it the south garden, there were no trees, no flowers. It was a courtyard of grey stone: stone walls, stone floor, cold and surely echoing, should there be any sound.

I watched Candelária through a grille. Her head was down. She wore brown boots and a brown tunic over a white blouse. I had never seen her so still, so melancholy. I had never dressed her in brown.

"Why is she all alone?" I asked. "Why isn't she with other girls?"

Sister Matilde put her finger to her lips. "Until she has been closely observed to make sure she will not influence the others negatively, she remains on her own for certain periods of each day. It is this way for all of the new girls. These intervals give her time to consider her spiritual learnings, as well as to grow used to silence."

"Negatively influence the others? She's not even five years old," I said angrily. I leaned forward to call Candelária's name, to have her come to the grille so that I could comfort her, and tell her that whatever lies her father—or Abílio Perez—had told her about me were not true. That I did not wish this for her, and that I was here to take her away. That I would never let her go.

Sister Matilde put her hand on my arm and shook her head.

"I only want to bring her comfort," I said. "To let her know her mother is here."

"You heard the Abbess. You are not to speak to her. You must believe that the child's Heavenly Father will bring her all the comfort she needs," she whispered, and then pulled on my arm with surprising strength. I was wrenched from the grille, and the sight of my child. "You can see she is well cared for. You may take solace from that," Sister Matilde said.

I stared at her in disbelief. Could she truly believe that any mother would be consoled at the sight of her child so alone and bereft? Then she led me back through the long, confusing passageways to the door. I emerged into a weak sun at the front of the convent.

Cristiano came to me. "She's not here?"

"Yes," I said, and he smiled with relief, saying, "Thanks to God."

"They won't let me take her yet. Not yet," I repeated, and we went towards the waiting carriage, the two white horses shaking their heads to dispel the flies that had returned with the sun.

Cristiano held my arm as I climbed in. "Where will we go now?"

"Take us to Santa Maria de Belém," I told the driver, giving him the name of the street I knew so well after corresponding with Beatriz these last five years. "And hurry," I urged him, as if the next hour might make a difference in Candelária's life.

⁂

As the horses trotted along the main *avenida* that ran beside the waterfront of Santa Maria de Belém, I wondered, over and over, what Abílio had to do with this. How had Candelária come into his life, and why had he taken her to the convent?

"Diamantina?" Cristiano said, and I turned to him. "You're whispering. What are you saying?"

I shook my head. "Everything is so confusing. I don't . . . I don't understand what has happened."

"To Candelária?"

"Everything. It's everything," I said.

The driver stopped at last outside a huge and elegant two-storey structure of white stone, gleaming in the sun. It was surrounded with formal gardens shaded by tall trees. There was a coach house on one side, and through its open doors I saw carriages, chaises and carts.

We climbed down and I started towards the pathway.

"Diamantina," Cristiano called. "You must pay the driver again."

I fumbled for more réis and put them into the driver's hand. Cristiano carried our cases as we walked along the pathway through flower beds and small fruit trees, now dropping their leaves in the autumn air. At the grand door I pulled the bell cord.

A black-skinned man in a fine set of rich brown velvet breeches and jacket, the wide ribbons of his white shirt tied in an elaborate bow at his neck, opened the door to us. He had a swollen eye and badly bruised cheekbone. I gave my name. He looked surprised, and then frowned. "Senhora Rivaldo?" he repeated, and I nodded.

"I am a good friend of Dona Beatriz," I said.

He glanced at Cristiano and the travel cases he carried, and then ushered us into a wide receiving hall with a two-storey ceiling. The walls were lined with silk hangings and huge canvases of countryside and nautical scenes. The servant indicated satin-covered chairs, but I was too agitated to sit, and Cristiano stood by my side, our bags at his feet.

The servant bowed his head and disappeared down a long hallway. In a moment there was the sound of a door slamming once, twice, and then Beatriz hurried into the receiving hall.

"Diamantina!" she said, delighted surprise on her face. "When Samuel gave your name, I couldn't believe it. Hello, Cristiano. You're so grown up! But Diamantina, why didn't you write that you were coming to Lisboa? And you didn't bring Candelária? She and Leandro could have— Diamantina? What is it?" she asked as I clutched her hands.

"You haven't seen Candelária?" I asked. "Or Bonifacio?"

Her smile faded. "What?"

"Abílio put Candelária into a convent. He has to get her out for me."

"Abílio? What are you talking about, Diamantina? You're trembling. Come with me." She looked at the servant, who had silently reappeared and now stood to one side. "Samuel, take Cristiano into the small receiving room and give him something to drink."

She led me into a huge, bright salon. I was vaguely aware of crowded excess, decorative pieces of porcelain and lacquer and ivory, chairs and chaises upholstered in damask and silk. Tall glass doors opened to sculpted greenery. "Sit down," she said, lightly pressing on my shoulders until I sat on one of the chairs.

She went to a high side table along one wall and poured two small glasses of ruby cordial. As she brought one to me, I pulled off my gloves. She sat down in a matching chair across from me. "Tell me what's happened."

"I was away from Funchal when Bonifacio took Candelária," I said, holding my glass. Bright droplets bloomed on my skirt; I couldn't hold the glass still, and set it on a small table beside me. "He took her, Dona Beatriz, to the orphanage of Convento Teresa de Jesus in Alcántara. I've seen her there. I wasn't allowed to speak to her. She doesn't know what's happened to her. He took her," I repeated.

Dona Beatriz put down her own glass. "Why did Bonifacio take her from you?"

"It's too long a story. He's . . . he's gone mad. I do believe he's mad. That's the only reason I can give right now. But it's Abílio I need." When she shook her head, frowning in consternation, I said, "Abílio took her to the convent. That's what the Abbess told me: that it was Abílio, not Bonifacio, who took her there and paid her dowry to be admitted. I don't know how it came to be, or why. And the Abbess will relinquish Candelária only to him. To Abílio."

"Nothing about this makes sense, Diamantina. When did this happen?"

"In the last two weeks—I can't be sure of the exact day."

"I've been in Estoril with my aunt for the summer. I waited until the weather here cooled to return. I came home only two days ago." She went to the door, calling for Samuel.

Although not young, Samuel was tall and had a straight bearing, with a gentle face and a shock of tightly curled white hair. "Samuel. Do you know anything about a child being here while I was away? A girl, a little younger than Leandro?"

He didn't speak, although his eyes widened just the slightest.

"Samuel. Answer me."

"Yes, Dona Beatriz," he finally said. "There was a little girl." He spoke slowly, his voice deep and refined. I stood.

"Why didn't you tell me?" Dona Beatriz demanded.

"Dom Abílio . . . he told me I wasn't to speak of it."

Dom Abílio. My lips tightened. So Abílio demanded that he be addressed as though born of nobility.

"I'm asking you to tell me what happened, Samuel," Dona Beatriz said.

He clasped his hands. "Father Bonifacio brought the girl here, and when—"

"Father Bonifacio?" I interrupted. "Father?" I repeated.

"Yes. He wore the Jesuit cassock and cincture. He told me he was Father Bonifacio Rivaldo when he came to the door."

"Samuel," Dona Beatriz said, "this can't be true. You disappoint me—"

"He's telling the truth," I said.

"What are you talking about?" Dona Beatriz asked.

"Bonifacio was once a Jesuit. He kept his robe—"

"He was a Jesuit?" Dona Beatriz's voice rose in disbelief.

"My daughter, Candelária—how did she appear, Samuel?"

"She was quiet, and she looked very tired. Neves—my wife—took her to the garden, and while she cared for the child, I stood at duty in the salon. Father Bonifacio spoke to Dom Abílio with great passion about the life of spiritual joy he wished for the girl. And his own wish to again spread God's word. He seemed a devout and pious man, Dona Beatriz. He asked Dom Abílio for money for the girl's dowry for entry into the convent. He said they demanded a great amount, and he didn't have enough to pay that as well as his passage to Brazil. He said he was going to Brazil the following day." Samuel was trembling now. "Father Bonifacio grew very upset when Dom Abílio didn't want to give him the money. Father Bonifacio said Dom Abílio owed it to him, because he had worked with honesty for him for many years."

"So he was leaving his position in the Counting House to go to Brazil, dressed as a Jesuit," Dona Beatriz stated, "and he came to collect money?"

"Dona Beatriz," I said, glancing at Samuel, who trembled even more now, "we were told that Abílio has sold Kipling's—the wine lodge and the quinta. We would no longer have positions with the new owner. But where is Abílio? I can't leave her in that convent one more—"

"Sold Kipling's? But . . . he can't." Beatriz's face had gone grey, and the twitch I had once seen jumped violently.

"Please, Dona Beatriz! Please, let us talk about this later. Samuel, why did Abílio go with Bonifacio to the convent? Was it to pay the dowry?"

Samuel wrung his hands, looking down, and I made a sound of impatience. "I don't have time for this. Dona Beatriz, please. Can you call Abílio?"

Dona Beatriz pressed her fingers against the ticking beside her mouth. "He's not here."

"No! Where is he?"

"Lisboa. He went this morning." She wrapped her arms around herself and rocked. "*Meu Deus*. But he can't do this. The deed . . . he can't—"

"Only Lisboa," I interrupted, relieved. "He'll be back tonight, then?"

She shook her head, reaching for the chair behind her and sitting down. "He always stays a few days, a week. Sometimes longer. He spends more time in Lisboa than here. I prefer not to think about his activities there, and don't know how to find him. It's as I once told you—we live separate lives. Whom did he say he sold the business to?"

I closed my eyes for a moment, thinking. "Lajes. His name is Lajes, and he's from Oporto."

"I don't know anyone by that name. But Henry Duncan might know something about this."

"Yes, yes. Is Henry at his home in Lisboa right now? Maybe he'll know where Abílio is."

"He was in England. I don't know if he's returned."

"Please. Give me his address."

She looked back at me, a vertical line between her eyebrows.

"Dona Beatriz, I need Henry's address. I need to find Abílio now. Today. I must get my daughter back," I said, and she rose and said, "Come with me," and I followed her.

CHAPTER SEVENTY-FIVE

Cristiano and I climbed into the carriage Beatriz had supplied, along with her driver. Samuel had given us a basket of food. I couldn't eat, but urged Cristiano to take what he needed.

It was much longer returning to Lisboa than it had been leaving it. Pilgrims were making their way into the city to attend Masses at the city's churches the following day, All Saints' Day.

"Lisboa is preparing for one of the biggest celebrations in the religious calendar," the driver told us. The roads were thronged with those travelling by carriage or by horse or donkey or on foot. "It will be late by the time we get there. We may have to stay in Lisboa overnight—the roads will be dangerous after dark. Highwaymen do their worst at these times. Dona Beatriz instructed me not to return if it was too late, and to arrange an inn for you."

I wished to jump out of the carriage and run; I had no patience with the milling throngs.

We finally drove into Lisboa, and slowly made our way through a warren of hilly, narrow cobbled streets. Eventually we came into a more aristocratic area, with elegant homes surrounded by walled gardens. The driver stopped in front of a set of high gates. There were three carriages lined up along the wall, their drivers standing together, talking. "This is the place," he said.

I hurried to the door. *Let Henry be here, let him be here.* If he wasn't, I had nowhere else to turn, no way to search for Abílio.

It was Henry himself who opened the door at my knock. I felt weak at the sight of his friendly, familiar face.

"Diamantina! What are you doing here? How did you find me? Come in, come in, this is such a—"

"Henry. I'm looking for Abílio. I must find him."

"I don't know where he is, Diamantina. Have you been to his home—"

"Yes, yes, I've just come from Santa Maria de Belém. Dona Beatriz gave me your address."

"Please come in. I'm having a small dinner party. You must join us." He glanced behind me, out to the street. "Is that Cristiano in the carriage?"

"Yes. But I can't stop. I have to find Abílio. Please, Henry. It's . . . it's about my Candelária."

"Your little girl?"

I nodded. "I need to find Abílio," I said again, gripping his arm, and he looked at my hand, then back to my face.

"I have no idea where he might be, but maybe Lajes can help you find him."

"In Oporto?" It came out a high, desperate wail. "No! Isn't it many leagues from here?"

"Plácido Fernandez Lajes has a home here as well. Maybe he would know Abílio's whereabouts," he said, trying to give me hope.

"All right," I said, "I'll go there."

"I'll come with you—"

"No. I can't take you from your guests. I have Cristiano, and the driver. If you can just tell me where he lives, I'll go there right now."

"I'll find the address. Please, step inside."

I did as he asked, standing in the entrance hall. There were decorative candelabras and thick tallow torches throwing warm yellow light on the walls. A burst of laughter came from somewhere inside the house, and I smelled tobacco and perfume and pomade.

Within moments, Henry returned with a slip of paper. "Let me know if you need my help," he said to me.

"Thank you," I said, taking the paper and running down the steps and back to the carriage. I told the driver the address.

"Alfama?" He shook his head. "I can't get the carriage through the streets there. It's all uphill steps, and very narrow."

"Just take me as close as possible, and we'll walk the rest of the way."

"But Dona Beatriz wanted me to make sure you were safe, and—"

"Take me there," I demanded. He opened his mouth, then closed it and slapped the reins on the horses' backs.

⁂

It was dark when Cristiano and I entered the narrow, twisting streets and steep cobbled lanes of old Alfama. It was a jumble of leaning houses with flower-laden balconies and red-tiled roofs, the alleys and tiny squares laid out in a puzzling manner, connected by winding stone steps. We frequently stopped to ask the way of men sitting in the squares, smoking their pipes and playing cards by lamplight.

When we finally found the address, I had to knock twice before the door was opened by a wide-eyed serving girl.

"I wish to speak to Senhor Plácido Fernandez Lajes," I said.

She looked at me, and then at Cristiano.

"Please. Fetch him for me," I said, wanting the authority in my voice to make him materialize.

When she nodded and disappeared, I took a deep breath. In a moment a middle-aged man in his shirt sleeves came to the door. A wide napkin, smeared with tomato sauce, was tucked into the top of his shirt.

"Yes?" he said, obviously displeased at having his dinner interrupted.

"I'm looking for Abílio Perez," I said.

He raised his chin, glancing at Cristiano. "Who are you, senhora, coming to my door after dark? And why do you think I would know where Perez is?"

"Senhor Lajes. I work for Kipling's on Madeira. I am a friend of Dona Beatriz. I've been with her at her home today. It's imperative that I speak to Senhor Perez as soon as possible. It was suggested you might be able to help me find him."

"What do you mean, you work for Kipling's?"

"Surely Senhor Perez has spoken of the overseer there, Espirito Rivaldo. The former overseer. I am his sister-in-law. Please. Do you know where I might find Senhor Perez?"

He pulled the napkin from his collar. "Is there some trouble at Kipling's?"

"No, it's more of a . . . it's a personal matter."

He glanced out at the quiet street, as if confirming we were alone. "Abílio was here earlier," he said, and I put my hand to my chest.

"And . . . where is he now?"

"He told me he had an event to attend, and then was going home."

"So he'll be back in Santa Maria de Belém tonight," I said, thinking about making the dark journey back along the same route we'd just taken. In spite of Dona Beatriz's instructions to the driver not to traverse the roads at night, I would insist he take us back.

"Santa Maria de Belém? No. Not the summer residence. His home here, in Príncipe Real. Didn't you say you were there, with his wife today?"

"I've just come from Santa Maria de Belém. That's where I saw her."

He shrugged. "I'm afraid there's some misunderstanding, senhora. I'll be going out to Santa Maria de Belém in the next few days, to see the house. I own it now—it's part of the sale of Kipling's. But tonight Abílio is with Dona Beatriz in Principe Real."

I stared at him. He had a fleck of dark spice caught on his top lip. "Can you tell me where in Principe Real?" I asked slowly.

He shook his head. "I don't know. We've always met at my homes, either here or in Oporto. But he's coming here tomorrow for lunch with Dona Beatriz, after Mass, to drink a bottle of Kipling's wine he's bringing to seal our transaction."

I put my hand against the door frame. "Dona Beatriz? You're saying she's coming as well?"

"Yes."

I felt as though I were back in the convent, speaking to the Abbess, full of confusion over Abílio again.

"I only met her recently, when she provided the signatures necessary for the sale," he said. "Charming lady."

He has another life in Lisboa, Beatriz had told me.

"Tomorrow after Mass," I repeated.

"Yes."

"Thank you, Senhor Lajes. I'm sorry for disturbing your dinner."

He nodded and closed the door.

❧

The driver was waiting for us at the base of Alfama. He had already arranged for us to stay the night at a small inn there.

"Would you like me to come for you early tomorrow morning, to take you to one of the grand cathedrals for Mass, Senhora Rivaldo?" he asked.

"No, thank you. I will need to get back to Santa Maria de Belém tomorrow, I'm sure, but I don't know what time. Just come here, to the inn, at noon, and wait for me." I had no idea what would happen when I went to Plácido Lajes's home the next day, and saw Abílio and the woman posing as Beatriz. I only knew I would force him to get Candelária back for me.

I would force him.

Cristiano and I climbed the stairs to our rooms across the hall from each other. We had left our bags at Santa Maria de Belém. All I'd brought was my small drawstring bag with a purse of coins. I had not thought of anything apart from finding Abílio.

"Good night, Cristiano," I told him. "And . . . thank you for accompanying me. I'm sorry for all I'm subjecting you to."

"Tomorrow is All Saints' Day," he said. "I know it will be a good day. Tomorrow we will get Candelária back."

❧

I was sleepless through much of the night. Before dawn I rose and went for a walk along the quiet streets. I passed a chapel and heard the low voices of monks or friars or priests intoning their prayers.

When the day broke with a serene sky and a gentle breeze, I went back to the inn, imagining Cristiano to still be asleep. But he was standing outside, his hair damp. He came towards me, relief on his face. "I was worried when I found your room empty," he said.

"I just went for a walk. We'll have to wait until after Mass, and then return to the home of the man we saw last night. I'm sure the inn serves breakfast. You must be hungry."

"Avó told me about a church with her name in Lisboa: Santa Luzia. I asked the innkeeper about it while I waited for you. It's here, in Alfama. We could go to it and light a candle for Espirito after breakfast. It's his birthday today." He gave me a half smile. He looked like a young man, but was still a boy. "Espirito, named as all boys born on this day of saints."

I knew Espirito's birthday was the first of November but hadn't thought of it today; all I could think about was Candelária. There were a number of empty hours before I once more stood at Plácido Lajes's door. Going to the church would fill some of them.

"As long as we are at Senhor Lajes's home by noon," I said, and we went back into the inn.

I watched Cristiano eat, still unable to think of putting food in my mouth and chewing and swallowing. And then we set off again, climbing the stone steps, which Cristiano, with his new knowledge from the innkeeper, told me led all the way to the highest point, where Castel de São Jorge sat above the city.

We trailed a row of pilgrims, and eventually arrived at Santa Luzia. Standing on the large open terrace outside the church, we surveyed the vista of Lisboa and the Tagus spread below us. Murmurs came through the open doors. "The Mass has begun," Cristiano said.

Just as I opened my mouth to respond, there came a noise like the hollow, distant rumbling of thunder. It grew louder and louder, terrible in its intensity. The great thudding seemed inside me, and I thought, for that instant, that my time had come: that this is what it was when the heart lurched and tore and then stopped.

And yet in the next instant, I realized I had no pain, and that it wasn't *my* heart but the heart of the earth that pounded and shook.

CHAPTER SEVENTY-SIX

The earth shuddered, jerking upwards, and I saw the church behind Cristiano sway. I grabbed him; everything trembled as if caught in a convulsive fit. Cristiano and I held on to each other, trying to stay upright as the rumbling and shaking grew fainter, and then stopped. But before we could speak, the terrible quaking beneath our feet began again, as if that first shock had been only a test, and the second one would carry the true horror.

We were thrown to one side and then the other, as if back on the *Bom Jesus* during a storm. Below us, the buildings of Lisboa swayed like saplings in the wind and, clutching Cristiano, I watched them crumbling in vast clouds of dust and debris.

Screams came from all around as people were crushed by falling walls, and I tore my gaze from the hell below to look at Santa Luzia. Some rushed from the church as it caved in, pushing, scrambling, screeching as the ground rocked. Through a gaping hole in its front wall I saw statues tumbling from their niches. The candle holders hanging from the ceiling, lit with hundreds of candles, swung wildly and then were wrenched loose and fell onto the heads and shoulders of those still trapped inside.

Cristiano and I were carried along in the frenzied crowd as the ground continued to shake. We rose and fell with the movement of the earth. I was pushed violently from behind and went down, trying to put my hand over my head as I was trampled.

And then, as suddenly as it had begun, the shaking stopped.

I don't know how long I lay where I had fallen, something heavy across my back and legs. But finally I lifted my cheek. A piece of shutter was in front of my face, and I looked through the broken slats. It was a vision only the worst nightmare could conjure.

Lying everywhere were bodies. Not just whole, bleeding bodies, but parts of bodies. Limbs. A torso. A hand clutching a rosary lay on a block of stone in front of the shutter. I knew from the fingernails that it was a female hand. I watched it as though waiting for the fingers to begin praying the decades of the rosary. With strange calmness I likened that hand to the one of Our Lady of the Grapes, broken and resting, pale and unmoving, on the chapel floor.

I felt as though I had cotton in my ears; the shrieks and wails of the injured and those calling for others in the thick dust from the fallen stone were strangely muted. I didn't know whether I was hurt or not: I felt nothing. After some time I moved my head enough to see that the weight on me was the sprawled body of a man. He was covered with broken stone, and part of his head was caved in. His body had protected me.

It took an interminable length of time to manoeuvre myself out from under him. I slowly got to my knees and then shakily to my feet. At that moment my hearing unblocked, and the world came back with a terrible, shocking clarity, so loudly I put my hands over my ears. The screams of the dead and dying were unlike anything I'd ever imagined. Others wept, praying, "Most Holy Mary, Virgin and Mother of God, save us, save us."

I added my voice to the cacophony, screaming Cristiano's name. I stumbled in a circle, stretching my hands in front of me as if I were blind, as if reaching for him, even though I couldn't see him.

And then I realized I was looking at him. He stood a short distance from me, so coated in dust I hadn't recognized him. It was as if he was in his old nightmare, unmoving, his eyes wide. Weeping, I climbed over stones and bodies. I grabbed him and said, "Are you hurt? Cristiano, are you hurt?" but he didn't answer me. And then a third rumble came, and now all around us was a different cry— *"Terremoto! Terremoto!"*—and we braced ourselves for the next quaking of the earth.

But the third shock was not as strong as the second. And when the earth was once more still, and Cristiano and I had not died, had not been crushed beneath the tumbling walls of stone as we crouched, covered in debris, in the open space of the small square, my only thought was of Candelária.

❧

Cristiano helped a man pull his limp wife from beneath a pile of stone, and I picked up a child with a bloodied head while its mother stood looking around her in shock, whimpering, "João, João," until I put the child into her arms. She looked at him as though she didn't know him, and continued to repeat his name.

"We have to go," I said to Cristiano. "Come. Down into the Terreiro do Paço, where we will be safe should there be another earthquake. Look," I told him, pointing over a broken wall. "Look at all those on the open quay, where nothing can fall on them. Let's go."

Others, thinking the same, were pushing ahead of us. The narrow lanes were blocked with stones and with bodies, with furniture and burning timber. We fell over and over, crying out as we pushed forward and were pushed from behind, stumbling downwards.

"Come this way," I panted, pulling Cristiano from the crowd towards a cracked-apart building. "Through here, away from the others."

As we clambered over a fallen wall, I straightened and looked below. The quay was filled with people rushing towards the water, many dragging others. Hundreds were crowding onto the ships docked there, wishing to be on the water should another quake occur, and to escape the fires that were burning everywhere. I was about to continue downwards when I saw something I couldn't understand. I stopped, staring in disbelief. Cristiano had continued ahead of me, and now I screamed to get his attention. "Cristiano, no! Stop! Don't go down. Come back up!" I kept shouting, until finally he heard me over the calls and cries and looked back at me.

"Come, come up here," I shouted, beckoning, and he climbed to join me, and then he saw what I had seen: the river disappearing, rolling back from the harbour as if it were a carpet peeled from a floor. Within minutes we could see the sandbars far out at the mouth of the Tagus. In front of the marble quay was the exposed riverbed, filled with half-submerged barrels and crates and all manner of objects caught in the sludge. Some people climbed down from the boats and off the quay into that mire, tugging at found treasures.

And as we watched this unbelievable emptying of the harbour and the river beyond, I was filled with the most terrible premonition. "Higher. Higher, Cristiano!" I turned and started back up the way we'd come, holding my skirt above my knees.

"Why are we going back up?" he called behind me, as we fought against the masses heading down.

"The water," I said over my shoulder. "The Tagus leads to the ocean. The ocean is taking it, but something is wrong. It can't be pulled away without coming back. It will have to come back."

Cristiano climbed beside me then, and we held each other's arms, and moved slowly past the burning rubble of Santa Luzia. When I couldn't go any farther, I stopped, panting, leaning against a section of ancient wall. I pressed my hand against my side, and Cristiano climbed onto the wall and looked out over the debris of the broken city and the departed river.

And then he breathed, "*Salva nos. Doce Jesus*, save us," and I climbed up beside him and saw a vast body of water, rising like a mountain, heaving and swelling and rolling towards Lisboa, towards the wharves and the ships, laden with people looking for salvation from the destruction of earth and fire. It came roaring and foaming, rushing at the quay, and although we were too far away to hear the screams, I saw the people running, running away from the quay as they'd run towards it, running back into the burning city. Those foraging on the bottom of the river struggled to climb out as the water returned with ferocious speed. The ships were ripped from their anchors, and tumbled and tossed, crashing into each other. Some turned keel upwards as if caught in the grip of a violent storm, and bodies were thrown from them and sank under the water. As Cristiano and I watched, the wave swept away the buildings on the riverbank, and then the entire quay and its people. All was swallowed up and disappeared, as if into the depths of a whirl-pool, and did not reappear.

࿇

We stayed where we were for some time, until I grew aware of the pain of my torn and bruised flesh. I saw, beneath the dust, all of Cristiano's cuts, some still trickling blood. The earth's tremors continued, but eventually the flooding water stilled.

I felt exhaustion unlike any I'd ever known, and thought I might not be able to move. But I had to find my daughter. Cristiano and I slowly, slowly started the descent through Alfama a second time. The danger lay not only in the sudden falling of buildings shaken off their foundations but also in the fires raging everywhere. Every cathedral and church and chapel had been ablaze for All Saints' Day. With the falling walls and columns, the candles had lit all the curtains and altar cloths and then spread to the woodwork.

"We must get to Alcántara," I told Cristiano. I couldn't bear to say her name, couldn't bear to think of my daughter as we passed the ruined, broken bodies of infants and children everywhere, some in their dead parent's arms, others alone in the rubble, limbs askew, like tossed-aside dolls.

Survivors were attempting either to save those who could be saved or to leave the city, moving away from the centre towards higher ground and open air. In all the narrow streets Cristiano and I stumbled through there were bodies, half buried and half burned, three, four, five or six in a heap, of those who had been crushed by the collapsing buildings as they tried to flee. The hardest to bear were those people still alive and crying out for help, the weight of the stone upon them too great for those trying to lift it off. People tore at timbers and stones with bleeding hands, crying *misericórdia, mercy, charity, the world is at an end, misericórdia*. We clambered over or went around fissures in the buckled stone streets, some wide enough for bodies to have been caught within. Coaches and carriages and carts lay atop dead horses and mules, and riders were crushed under their dead mounts.

We passed a cemetery with the graves heaved up, the smell of raw earth and the putrefaction from the broken caskets so powerful I had to cover my nose with my arm. Bones and skulls lay about, and, horror of horrors, already the looters were at work, their greed more powerful than the reek of death and decay. Their faces covered with strips of cloth against the stench, men calmly picked through the decomposing flesh and bones and wormy rags to remove the jewels of the dead, pulling off cold, rotting fingers and ears to more easily remove the rings and ear bobs.

In contrast, priests knelt, giving absolution to the dying. As we walked out of Lisboa with those limping and bleeding, those half naked, those carrying dead children in their arms, the flames burned all around us, moving in red waves before my eyes, and the very air felt bloodstained.

CHAPTER SEVENTY-SEVEN

The ground continued to shake in sudden small starts and fits, and at every tremor, cries of *"Terremoto!"* again filled the air. Cristiano was limping heavily. We passed a huge shaggy dog with blood on its fur, flies already gathering, bound to its master by a leather strap wrapped tightly around the dead man's arm. The animal struggled and whimpered, maddened by the smells of blood and death around him. Cristiano stopped and pulled the leather strap free, untying it from the animal's neck. The dog shook himself, sending droplets of blood flying, and then stood looking up at Cristiano. I touched his arm, and we started again, the dog following.

As we passed a marker along the road to Alcántara, I turned once to look back at Lisboa, and could see only a cloud of dust and smoke too vast to describe. A man came towards us. Everyone else was walking out of Lisboa, but he walked towards it. I grabbed his arm. "Convento Teresa de Jesus," I said. "Have you passed it? Does it still stand?"

One of the man's ears had been torn from his head. The wound was thickly scabbed. He looked at me, using a strip of rag to polish a silver button he held.

"Is it standing?" I asked again, but he kept polishing the button.

He held it in front of my face. "Have you seen a button like this?" he asked, and then said, "Teresa de Jesus? Rubble. Nothing but rubble. If you find my button, will you let me know?"

"Don't listen, Diamantina," Cristiano said, pulling on my arm as I stood, one hand over my mouth. "He's lost his mind. We have to keep going."

Outside the convent, filthy water littered with unspeakable debris swirled against the grey walls. Although parts of the main building still stood firm, there was obvious damage to the roof. A jumble of stone and tile was spilled along one entire side. I waded through the ankle-high water to the door, and put up my fist to pound on it, but at the first touch it swung open. I went inside and saw a novice, wandering the empty corridor.

"Where are the children?" I asked her. "The children from the orphanage."

The novice looked at me, blinking tearfully. She was perhaps a little older than Cristiano. Her head scarf was torn and marked with something oily, and there was a gash on the back of her hand. Her bottom lip trembled.

I grabbed her arm and shook it.

She looked down at my hand, streaked with ash, nails broken and rimmed with blood, and then up at me with something like surprise.

"Where is my child? Her name is Candelária. She is almost five, and in the orphanage." I shook her arm a second time, and then a third, and finally she flinched.

"We were all in the church, for the All Saints' Day Mass," the girl said, "but the smallest girls were in the chapter house beside it, because they—"

"Were they hurt?" I cried now, my voice hoarse with smoke and fear.

"I don't know . . . the Abbess . . . she's dead, and I don't know . . ." She stared at me as if waiting for me to tell her what to do. I knew she was suffering from shock, and I tried to speak more calmly.

"Can you take me to the youngest girls?" I asked, and she nodded.

She turned and started down the hallway, but then stopped and looked at me. "The Abbess is dead," she repeated. "Others are dead. None of us know what to do."

"It will be all right," I encouraged, trying to keep her moving.

She opened a door, and as I pushed her aside and went in, at first

I only saw little girls lying on the hard stone floor. I didn't know if they were alive or dead. A few sisters moved between them. Then I grew aware of sobbing and wailing, and the overpowering smell of urine and blood and vomit. Some of the children had parts of their heads or bodies wrapped in gauzy linen, and still blood seeped through. Others lay unmoving. The light was strangely bright, and I looked up at the pale, desolate sky through the hole in the roof.

I walked among the children. They all looked alike, in their filthy brown tunics and white blouses, all with dark hair. I stooped and looked into the faces of little girls, some with eyes wide and terrified and in pain, others with eyes closed and too still. One lay on her back, staring at that white sky with the unmistakable gaze of death, and I bent and closed her lids with my palm.

And then there she was, on her side with her back to the room. How could I have thought I wouldn't recognize her? Of course I knew my daughter's hair, her back, the way she liked to draw up her top leg and stretch out the bottom one. I spoke her name, and when she didn't move, I dropped to my knees and put my hand on her shoulder. It tensed, and I let out a long cry and she sat up, and turned, and the look on her face . . . I cannot describe it without weeping.

She flung herself against me and I held her, weeping into her soft hair while her small, busy fingers combed through my tangles, and she said, "Mama, Mama, it's all right, don't cry. I knew you were coming for me. I knew you would come," she kept saying, comforting me—her comforting me—until I could no longer kneel but stood and picked her up as I had when she was smaller. Now her long legs dangled against me. She had, in the last year, grown too tall to be carried easily, but on this day she was light in my arms as I carried her out of the rubble and away from the weeping and praying, out into the air, where Cristiano waited, the big dog sitting beside him.

❧

It was growing dark by the time we finally arrived on the outskirts of Santa Maria de Belém, because where else were we to go? I heard, as we walked, that the area had not been badly affected. All along the way there was debris from the waves, splintered timber from broken boats and occasionally a larger vessel grounded. Worse was what the water had carried from Lisboa, and I often pressed Candelária's face against my skirt or urged Cristiano to pick her up and hide her face against his shoulder as we passed corpses, some already being feasted upon by vultures and stray dogs. Carts bumped along the road, carrying the bodies of the dead or those who still breathed.

The open spaces around the parish were filled with crowds of people. Braziers and torches had been lit to show the way. Already priests and nuns were handing out bread and blankets. I turned again to look at Lisboa. The whole city was ablaze, the flames reflected in the eyes of those who watched in silent grief. The earth still trembled, and at each tremor there were muted, weary cries.

Candelária was too pale, and Cristiano's face was fixed in exhaustion as he slowly hobbled to a patch of grass with Candelária. The dog followed, then sat and licked one paw.

"We'll stay here tonight, and tomorrow we will go to Dona Beatriz." I couldn't remember how to get to her home, or how much farther it was; I only knew we couldn't go on. I left the children and got blankets and bread and flagons of water. We lay under the night sky, and within moments both Candelária and Cristiano slept. I was between them, Candelária held against one side and Cristiano's back curled against the other, and although my body was desperate for rest, my mind would not be stilled.

All around us, people cried and coughed and prayed. The night breeze brought the smell of charred flesh, and I inhaled the ash of those who only that morning had lived and breathed, who knew desires and dreams. The dog lay at my feet, and at one point I sat up and held on to his stinking, matted fur, as though he anchored me to the tilting earth.

And I did finally sleep, and dreamed of strangers whispering to me, their voices rising and falling in the heavy, death-filled air.

I opened my eyes to light streaming down, another bright, sunny day, as yesterday had begun. Candelária and Cristiano slept on, and I touched their faces, their hair, marvelling that we had all survived.

And then I stood and looked towards Lisboa. It still burned, its fires fanned by a strong northeast wind.

The dog had gone.

I was relieved to see that the buildings of Santa Maria de Belém were still standing. Some showed cracks, and glass littered the ground from broken windows, but on the whole the parish had survived the earthquake.

Unlike the frenzied chaos of Lisboa, here there was still order. We went slowly through the wide streets, Candelária beside me, clinging to my skirt. Cristiano leaned on a gnarled stick, and I remembered how he had once held my skirt in Curral das Freiras as my daughter did today. With the help of strangers, I found Dona Beatriz's home.

Samuel opened the door when I pulled on the cord. Before I could speak, his eyes widened and he tried to shut the door. I struck my palms against it and pushed back. "Wait," I said. "Samuel, wait. It's me, Senhora Rivaldo. Diamantina, and Cristiano. And Candelária," I said. "Look, it's Candelária."

The elderly man stood back, nervous and uncertain. "I'm sorry, Senhora Rivaldo. I'm not to allow anyone in."

"Please get Dona Beatriz," I demanded.

"She's at the chapel of Santa Ana, handing out bread to those in need."

"Is Senhor Perez here?"

He shook his head.

I gripped Candelária's hand tighter. "Samuel," I said, "please. Look at us. We've come all the way from Lisboa. You know I'm a friend."

He looked at Candelária for a moment longer, then stood aside to let us pass.

CHAPTER SEVENTY-EIGHT

Cristiano had been shown to one bedroom, and Candelária and I to another. Warm water was brought for us to bathe.

I dressed Candelária in her pale blue gown, and she held her rag doll as I brushed her clean, wet hair.

"Make sure you put on your boots," I told her. "You can't run about in bare feet. This is not the quinta—it's a fancy house." I turned her to face me. "Do you understand? You must always wear your boots while we're here."

⁂

Dona Beatriz got back in the early evening, dirty and tired. She greeted me with cries of happiness. "I was so, so afraid for you, Diamantina," she said, tears in her eyes, "for you and Cristiano. And Candelária? You got her back," she said, dropping to her knees in front of her.

I stood very still as she picked up Candelária's hands. "Hello, Candelária," she said. "You once played with Leandro, but you were too small to remember. Have you seen him today?"

Candelária nodded.

Both she and Leandro were tall and slender, but that was all they appeared to share. Would anyone suspect them of being brother and sister?

"Would you like to go to the nursery and play with him now?" Dona Beatriz asked.

Candelária shook her head. "I want to stay with Mama."

"I should put her to bed," I said. "She's been through so much."

"Of course," Dona Beatriz answered.

A short time later, as Candelária was falling asleep in the big bed I would share with her, Dona Beatriz came to the doorway. "Can I speak to you for a moment, Diamantina? I know you must need sleep terribly, but . . ."

I went to her, and we stepped into the hall. "The stories I've heard coming from Lisboa, Diamantina. Is it truly as terrible as they say?"

"It is more terrible than anyone can imagine. I can't speak of the things I saw." I wondered how long it would be before the images of the maimed and mutilated, the dying and the dead faded, or if they ever would. If the screams would ever stop ringing in my ears.

"The people who have come to the churches here looking for help . . . it's so awful. Every one of them has lost someone they love. We must never stop praying our thanks that our children were spared." She squeezed my hand. "Tomorrow I'll go back to the church to help. I plan to do what I can for as long as necessary." She let go of my hand. "Now I must let you go to bed. I mustn't keep you up with questions I have, about . . . about the rest of our lives. There will be time for that when the world is once again a familiar place."

The next morning, I went with Beatriz to the church. I left Candelária with Leandro and Neves, Samuel's wife. She was dark-skinned, like Samuel. She had blue markings on her face—a series of fine vertical stripes from under her bottom lip to the end of her chin—and I knew she had come from North Africa, like my mother.

Cristiano, limping only slightly now, came as well, and was immediately put to work building shelters and digging latrines.

Beatriz handed out food and prepared rolls of bandages. I sought out the rough canvas tent where surgeons moved between the rows of injured. I went to the nearest surgeon, his clothing soaked in blood and his face beaded in sweat.

"I can help however you need me," I told him. "I'm a *curandeira*, and also have worked as a midwife."

"Good, good," he said, hardly glancing at me. "Go and see to him," he said, pointing at a man lying on a bed of straw, moaning.

I spent the rest of the day with needle and thread and rolls of lint and linen. I also delivered two babies. By the time Beatriz and Cristiano and I returned to the house, I was so weary I fell into bed without dinner.

We worked in this way for the next four days. Many of the severely injured died, and others with limbs showing signs of rot had them cut off by the surgeons. At first they tossed the darkening feet, legs, hands and arms into piles, but it was quickly determined that the body parts must be deeply buried and covered with stones after they attracted roving bands of hungry dogs. Word came that the unidentified dead in Lisboa were being taken out to sea on barges and deposited into the water to stop the spread of disease.

After five days, the fires of Lisboa were finally out, and a few days after that, the roads cleared enough for the passage of carriages. The people who had come to Santa Maria de Belém for refuge began to make their slow journey back to the city, to move through the rubble of what they had once called home.

Dona Beatriz and I had not yet spoken of Abílio.

⸺⁂⸺

I thought of going home too.

"Soon I'll have to try and get us passage back to Madeira," I said to Cristiano in the salon that evening. I was bent over his palm with a needle, trying to dig out a long sliver of wood that had become deeply embedded under his skin as he had built the temporary shelters.

"A boat, Diamantina?" He sounded slightly incredulous. "Do you really suppose boats will be coming to or leaving Lisboa yet? Do you not remember what we saw at the harbour?"

He was right, of course, but all I could think about, now that I had Candelária, was getting away from here, and Abílio. What might he disclose about Candelária should he have survived and come back to Santa Maria de Belém to find me here with her?

"I've asked a lot of people about Funchal, but nobody knows," Cristiano said. "Do you think the earthquake destroyed it as well? Will we still have a home?"

I sat back on my heels and took a healing salve from the small medicine case I had brought with me. "I don't know," I said, thinking of Plácido Lajes, and the woman Abílio had pose as Dona Beatriz to sign the papers. I also thought of Bonifacio, on his way to Brazil, and of Espirito, also making his way across the sea, a month or more ahead of Bonifacio. "I don't know."

⌒⌒⌒

Cristiano had left the salon, and I was straightening the contents of my medicine case when the door slammed.

I went to Dona Beatriz, alarmed. Her face was the colour of chalk, the skin around her eyes blotchy. *Abílio,* I thought. *Abílio has died in the earthquake.*

"I'm surprised you had the nerve to come back here with her," she said, and I reached towards her.

"Dona Beatriz," I said, putting my hand on her arm. "What is it?"

"Remove your hand," she said with icy calm and control. "Well? When were you going to tell me? Did you really think I would never find out?" She stepped back from me and adjusted her lace collar.

I waited, my heart thudding, because I knew what had happened. Dona Beatriz pulled on her skirt to straighten it, then lightly brushed her hands together as if they were dusty.

"When was it?" she asked. "Was it when I lay in childbed? When you comforted me when my father died? When I left you in charge of my home because I trusted you?" She crossed her arms. "I just went to say good night to Leandro. On a whim, I stopped at your room, to say good night to Candelária as well. She was asleep on top of the coverlet. As I started to pull a blanket over her, I saw her foot." She nodded. "So? When exactly was it that you were fornicating with my husband?"

"Dona Beatriz," I said. "You don't understand how it happened."

She stared at me. "I don't care. There is no reason good enough. What kind of woman are you?"

I did know that my reason wasn't good enough. I did know what kind of woman I was—had always been.

"Do you think I care whom he beds? He hasn't come near me in years, and I'm glad, because his touch repulses me. He's always made a fool of me with other women, but I long ago stopped caring. I abide him because is my husband. But *you*, Diamantina? *You* made a fool of me?"

I stayed very still.

"Well? Are you going to deny it?"

"No," I said, without taking my eyes from hers.

"You slept with my husband, and conceived a child with him," she stated, as if to be completely certain.

"Yes. It wasn't . . . you need to understand, Dona Beatriz, it wasn't what I wanted. I . . . I felt I had no choice."

She raised her eyebrows. "You *felt* you had no choice? Do you mean you *had* no choice? Are you saying he violated you, against your will? Tell me this, and I will believe you, for I know my husband for the animal he is. I've seen him too many times with the servant girls, in spite of his women in Lisboa and Oporto. But you are a friend. You wouldn't betray me. Would you?"

I could tell her Abílio had raped me, I could tell her this right now, and she would believe me.

There was a quiet knock on the door, and Dona Beatriz looked towards it, her face hard, and then went and opened it.

"Both children are asleep, Dona Beatriz," Neves said. "May I retire for the night, or am I needed?"

"There's nothing else, Neves. Thank you." Dona Beatriz closed the door and came back and stood in front of me. "Well?" Her voice was harsh.

If I was to tell the truth, it must be now. I straightened my shoulders. Abílio had forced himself on me in the chapel when Candelária was conceived. That was true. As for the other times . . . "No," I said quietly. "I didn't wish it, but it was not entirely against my will."

She reached out and slapped me, the force making me stumble backwards. As I held my stinging cheek, shocked at the blow, Dona Beatriz looked unsteady, as if she were the one who had been struck. She gripped the back of a chair. "For all these years I was happy you were at Quinta Isabella. It actually pleased me that you could enjoy that life. Well, no longer. I don't know what has happened on Madeira now, but Quinta Isabella is no longer your home. You are not allowed on the property, and I will enforce that with the servants still there. And I want you out of here. Take whatever you brought with you, take Cristiano and your daughter, *Abílio's* daughter, and get out. Not tomorrow. Go now, tonight, into the darkness. Go and stay in one of the shelters at the church, and tomorrow walk back into Lisboa. Or walk into the sea. I no longer care where you go, or what you do."

CHAPTER SEVENTY-NINE

As I passed Dona Beatriz to leave the salon, she caught my wrist.

"Just tell me one thing. The day you came here looking for your daughter, you knew about Abílio's plan to take Kipling's from me. You know about the deed. Are you involved in this in any way? Are you helping Abílio?"

"Helping him? Helping Abílio?" Her grip on my wrist was iron. "How could you think that? No. He sent a letter to Espirito about the sale. It was Espirito who told me."

She dropped my wrist. "Does your husband know Abílio is her father? Is that why he took Candelária away from you?"

"No. He doesn't suspect she's Abílio's."

"And you've had no contact with Abílio over these last years? When he went back to Funchal two years ago—did you continue your relationship with him then?"

I shook my head. "He tried, Dona Beatriz. I threatened him. The scar on his neck?"

She nodded.

"I did that. I cut his neck with a knife and told him that if he ever tried to manipulate me again, the way he had manipulated me before, I would end his life."

She looked at me suspiciously. "He would have overpowered you."

"He didn't. Can you deny the fresh injury he had when he returned from Madeira?"

She didn't answer for a moment. "No."

"Then believe me. Abílio is as much my enemy as he is yours. You, more than anyone, know how he uses everyone to get what he wants. How he used you," I said, expecting she might slap me again.

A look of resignation came over her face. "I do know what he's capable of," she said. "Of course I know Abílio's true nature, and . . ." She sat down. "I so often thought that if I hadn't married Abílio, my father might be alive today."

I sat across from her and leaned close. "You suspected Abílio, Dona Beatriz?"

She frowned. "Suspected what? I knew I caused my father distress marrying Abílio against his wishes. Not only because my father knew Abílio wouldn't be a good husband to me, but because he didn't want to take him into the business. I put so much strain on him so soon after the deaths of my mother and sister. Surely that contributed to his untimely death."

"Ah," I said, sitting back.

"What do you mean about suspecting Abílio?"

I hesitated, deliberating whether to tell her the secret I'd carried, and then said, for what harm could it do now, "He poisoned your father with fleabane oil, the fleabane I used to help you after Leandro's birth."

She sat straighter. "What? Are you certain?"

"Yes. As soon as I heard of your father's symptoms, I accused Abílio. He didn't deny it, except to say he didn't wish to kill your father, only incapacitate him so that he had more control of the business."

"But . . . why didn't you come to me? Why didn't you speak of this before? I've known you for over five years. Why haven't you told me?" She was wringing her hands.

"Dona Beatriz, I had no real proof. It was only my word against Abílio's. I was a stranger to the quinta and all those on it—including you—at that time. I thought if I spoke of my suspicions, it might only bring you more pain, and . . . and then what? You might have completely disbelieved me, but I would have planted a seed of doubt in your mind that caused you consternation every time you looked at your husband, and thought of—"

"Enough!" she said loudly, and stared at me, her hands still now. "I want to hate you, Diamantina, but I can't." Her voice lowered. "We have both suffered because of Abílio's twisted desires." After a moment of silence she said, "All right. This plan of his to sell my business: tell me what you know."

"The buyer is the wine merchant Plácido Fernandez Lajes. I found him, through Henry, in Lisboa the night before the earthquake. He thinks he's bought the business and the quinta and this house. I believe it's done. He said the papers were signed, so he surely paid Abílio."

"What papers?"

"I don't know. Abílio must have created false documents, something that made it appear he was outright owner of all your father's holdings." I paused. "You still have the original deed?"

"Of course."

"There's something else. Senhor Lajes told me that a woman was present at the signing of the papers, putting her signature to them. Your signature. He called her Dona Beatriz, and thought she was Abílio's wife."

"Ah—Sofia." A sound, perhaps an attempt at a laugh, came from Dona Beatriz's throat. "Abílio will do anything to have his way, as we have discussed. Sofia is the other life in Lisboa. He bought her a house, and he lives with her when he's there. I've known about her for the last few years."

"I'm sorry, Dona Beatriz."

"At least they have no children. That would further complicate the already sordid situation. What will happen now, Diamantina?"

We sat in silence for a long moment. I took her hand and held it. "I will do whatever I can to help you, Dona Beatriz. Please accept my apology for what happened with Abílio." She didn't speak, but also didn't pull her hand from mine. "At first, when I knew I carried Abílio's child, I wanted rid of . . . of her." Loving Candelária from my soul, it was difficult to speak of that bleak time. "And yet you can see that she's what I live for, as Leandro is for you."

She shivered suddenly, as though a spirit had passed by, and took her hand from mine.

"It could be that neither Abílio nor Senhor Lajes survived the earthquake," I said. "All of Abílio's planning and scheming may not matter at all. You may not need my help with anything."

"And if Lajes lives?"

"If he meets you and sees you are Abílio's lawful wife, and you show him the deed, he could have it confirmed. I'm sure officials studying it would attest to its truth, and could also determine that the papers Abílio created—and the other woman's signature—were forgeries."

She frowned. "Maybe yes, and maybe no. And what of Abílio? What if he's still alive?"

"I doubt he'll show his face again. He has the money he wanted. Maybe that will be enough for him."

"Enough for him? Abílio never has enough. He has to be stopped once and for all, Diamantina. You said you would do whatever you could to help me. And so, if Abílio lives, what I am going to ask you to do *must* be done." She rose and paced in front of me before facing me again. "Should Abílio return, I want him to suffer the same fate as my father. I will leave it up to you to ensure that it happens. And when it does, I will put all else behind us. No matter what happens with the business and quinta, I will make sure your future is protected. Do you understand? Kill Abílio, and your life on Madeira will be one of security."

⁂

"When can we go home?" Candelária asked as we lay in bed together the next morning.

"Soon, *minha querida*. We must wait for the ships to sail again."

"Why did Papa bring me here? Where is he?" Her face was thinner, with a hardness not right in a child. "Leandro said maybe his papa died in the earthquake."

"Your papa was very unhappy. He decided that it was better that he didn't live at Quinta Isabella anymore. That it would be better if he went away."

"He didn't want to live with us?"

I stroked her hair. "He cared about you, Candelária. But he thought he should help other people who live far away."

"Where?" she asked.

"Brazil."

"Like Tio Espirito?"

"Yes."

"Will they live together?" She didn't wait for my answer. "I asked him over and over, on the ship, why he dressed like a Father, but he only said it was God's wish. That he had to do as God wanted him to do. When is he coming back from Brazil?"

I stopped stroking her hair. "I don't believe he will come back, Candelária."

She pulled away from me. "He didn't even say goodbye to me. Maybe Tio Abílio didn't let him. I heard him and Papa shouting."

"Papa was shouting?"

She nodded. "I was in the garden with Neves and I heard them. And then Tio Abílio came to get me. I said I wanted my Papa, but Tio was angry, and shouted at me as well, and told me I couldn't see Papa. I was afraid of him. He took me away, to the convent. I kept crying and calling out for Papa, because I knew he wouldn't let Tio Abílio put me there. But Papa didn't come." She pressed against me, and I felt her trembling ever so slightly. "I hated that day, and I hated the day of the *terremoto*. Except that was the day you came for me."

In spite of Bonifacio's unpredictable and zealous behaviour, I couldn't believe he would let Abílio take Candelária away without saying goodbye to her or without any final words of comfort.

"Papa didn't come to the convent with you and Tio Abílio?"

She shook her head.

"And you never saw Papa again, after you were in the garden with Neves?" I said into her hair.

"Never," she said, her voice muffled against my shoulder.

CHAPTER EIGHTY

Dona Beatriz and I sat in the salon. Cristiano read in his room, and Leandro and Candelária played in the garden. The door opened in a sudden rush of air.

It was Abílio. His face altered slightly when he saw me, but he immediately regained his confident expression. He walked across the room with the same swagger as always. "What are you doing here, Diamantina?"

He didn't even greet Dona Beatriz.

"I came for my daughter," I said. "And I have her."

"She's here?"

"Yes," I told him.

He smiled and looked at Dona Beatriz. I knew he was thinking of a way to fully savour having her and me together for the first time. "What do you think of Candelária, my dear?" He was clearly enjoying himself. "Charming little thing, isn't she?"

"I know the whole distasteful story," she said, and a flicker of annoyance crossed Abílio's face. "Do you think there's anything you could do that would shock me after these last seven years with you?" She looked at him, from his polished boots to his carefully groomed hair. "What good fortune you had not to be harmed in the earthquake." The last sentence held clear sarcasm.

"I was able to keep myself safe," he said.

"At least you can tell us what information you bring from Lisboa. What of the rest of Portugal?" she asked. "There is no official news, and we've heard only rumours. Do you know if Madeira was affected?"

Abílio waved his hand with an air of indifference. "I'm weary of all the talk of destruction and divine retribution." He went to the side table and poured himself a glass of wine. "I don't wish to discuss it."

Dona Beatriz stood, shaking her head in disbelief. "What have you come back for?"

He took a drink. "This is my home. I have every right to be here. Oh—that's not quite right. It's not my home any longer. Nor yours. We shall have to vacate, my dear. I've sold this house, as well as the wine lodge and quinta. But don't worry, I've secured a lovely home for us in Oporto. I'm going on ahead. You can pack up what you wish to bring, and come with Leandro when you're ready. It must be soon. The new owner is coming within the next few days to take possession."

Dona Beatriz still maintained her calm, although I could only imagine with what difficulty. "What are you talking about?"

"As I just said, I sold this house and bought us a new home in Oporto. Kipling's, Beatriz, is no more." He said the last sentence slowly, watching her closely. He was enjoying the game of trying to destroy her. It was another version of how his father had beaten down his mother.

She slowly sat again. "Why? Why did you sell everything my father worked so hard to create for his family? It was all to be Leandro's. He wanted it to be Leandro's."

"I'm starting my own business in Oporto. My *own* business," he repeated, "with my name on the signboard. And I will run it as I please, without your interference. You will have no say in anything I do, and I will tell you what money you can spend, not the other way around. In the last few days I've been able to confirm that, although there was also destruction in Oporto, it was not of the severity of Lisboa. The properties I've been accruing there were undamaged."

"At this apocalyptic time, with such death and terrible, terrible losses, you talk of gain," Dona Beatriz said, her face pale.

He drank. "There's no profit in speaking of loss." He looked around the room. "Just be thankful the house and everything in it was spared, so that Plácido Lajes won't be able to complain."

"Everything? Don't you mean *everyone*, Abílio? You haven't

even asked about your son. Hourly I thank God for His mercy in letting us all survive."

He drained his glass. "Sofia will come to Oporto later, when everything is in readiness. I have bought her a pleasing home there as well."

We watched Abílio pour another large glass of wine. He drank with a sound of appreciation, then poured a third glass and smiled benignly at his wife. He hadn't glanced at me after his first moment in the room, as if I were only a spectre, a grey mist beside the fireplace. I watched the scene unfolding as though I were in a theatre, and Abílio and Dona Beatriz upon the stage before me.

"I'm going to have Samuel start packing my belongings." He set down his empty glass. "I look forward to dining with you both tonight."

We sat in silence for the first moments after he left.

"So they both lived. Abílio and Senhor Lajes," Dona Beatriz finally said, staring at me. "It appears that it must be tonight, Diamantina. You will carry out my wishes tonight."

⌒

I went to my room with the bottle of wine Dona Beatriz had given me. Opening my medicine case, I untied the twist of paper containing four yew seeds, and put them onto a small marble dish. Using the end of my hairbrush, I crushed and ground them into a fine powder. I took the stopper from the bottle of wine, but then backed away and sat on the bed.

I hadn't known of yew on Porto Santo. It was Rafaela, the *curandeira* in Curral das Freiras, who had introduced it to my medicine bag. She had instructed me to use it with high caution, as all parts of the yew tree, apart from the fleshy crimson arils surrounding the seeds, were highly lethal. A few flakes of a seed were useful as a laxative, and in urging on a woman's courses, or as an ingredient in an abortive mixture. Hadn't I added a tiny pinch of it to the rue and tansy tea I had once drunk, trying to abort my daughter?

Even one whole seed, if ingested, would almost immediately, Rafaela had said, cause difficulty breathing, followed by muscle tremors and convulsions, culminating in the heart stopping. It would be a rapid, ugly and painful death.

I could tell myself it was Dona Beatriz I was helping, that she depended on me to ensure Abílio would never again be a threat to her in any way. But I also knew that with this help she would forgive me, and so I would be doing it for myself, for the security she promised.

Unbidden came the image of Abílio as a young man, his smile true and tender as he held out the ribbons he'd bought for my hair.

I shook my head to push away the old memories, then rose and went to the table, and added the ground seeds to the wine.

⁂

Cristiano and the younger children had already had their dinner when Abílio entered the dining room that evening with Samuel behind him. Dona Beatriz and I were waiting for him, seated across from each other at the table. It was decked with a damask tablecloth and glowing candelabra.

"This is a comfortable scene," he said. "It appears you two share many secrets." He sat as Samuel pulled out his chair. "Do you discuss me, and compare your experiences?" He leaned back as Samuel placed a heavy napkin on his lap.

"You may bring the first course, Samuel," Dona Beatriz said. Then she asked Abílio, "You said you leave for Oporto tomorrow?"

"Yes," he said, looking at the sideboard. "Why is there no wine?"

"Samuel will bring it. I plan to stay here for now," she said. "Until I can get passage to Funchal. I am thinking of moving back to Quinta Isabella with Leandro."

"Beatriz. Did you not understand what I told you earlier today?" He shook his head and glanced at me with a wry expression, as if we shared some measure of mirth at his wife's expense. "It's all gone, Beatriz. This house, the business, the quinta. I've been paid in full."

"It's not gone," Dona Beatriz said calmly.

"I think Plácido Lajes would disagree with you, my dear."

"You had all the papers drawn up?"

"Of course. I am owner of everything Martyn Kipling once owned.

We both have always known that was the reason I married you."

"And killed my father," Dona Beatriz said.

I counted two heartbeats, and then Abílio lifted his shoulders in a careless shrug. "And who would believe you about that long-ago event?" he asked. "Another secret disclosed, I see, Diamantina." He looked at me, then back to Dona Beatriz. "My dealings with Lajes were completed at exactly the right moment. The papers were all signed and the money in my hand the day before the earthquake. God was on my side. Who knows how the land is damaged on Madeira, and how long it will be before the vines are again fruitful?" He picked up the bell beside his plate and rang it. "Where is Samuel with the wine? Come now, Beatriz. You'll be able to make a good life in Oporto. All you need is your finery, and the church. That's all your life is about."

"And Leandro," she added. "My life is about my son. No, Abílio. I will not come to Oporto. I will return to the quinta, and run Kipling's."

Abílio put his head back and laughed as if delighted. "How do you propose to do that?"

"I have the deed."

Abílio stopped laughing. He blinked, and then frowned. "Deed?" he said, for the first time losing a modicum of his cockiness. His pupils grew in the candlelight, but he immediately covered his discomfort by standing and ringing the bell loudly. He set it down and looked at Beatriz. "Use caution, Beatriz. The wife of a man with power should not become hungry for power of her own. Are you truly imagining you can intimidate me with such a lie?"

"It isn't a lie. My father had the deed drawn up long ago, foreseeing this circumstance. I hold the deed to Kipling's. To the quinta and this house, which belonged to my mother's family. My father's deed states that no one has the right to sell any of it. It will all go to Leandro."

"You expect me to believe this? Produce this deed, and let me see it." His face darkened.

"Do you really think I would put it in your possession? I'm keeping it to show Senhor Lajes."

"You'll give it to me now," Abílio said, his tone threatening. I glanced at the row of knives laid out to the right of my plate.

Samuel entered with a gleaming tray. Abílio sat down. Samuel lowered the tray onto a side table, and then set a covered dish in front of each of us.

He stood behind Dona Beatriz and removed her silver cover with a slight flourish. "As you requested, Dona Beatriz. Waterfowl stewed with quinces, as well as pastries filled with marrow, to start. Fish will be the main course." He uncovered my plate, and then Abílio's.

"The wine, Samuel," Abílio demanded. "Why have you kept me waiting?"

As Samuel reached for the opened bottle on the tray, my heart thudded. *No,* I thought. *No.*

Dona Beatriz stood and took the bottle from him. "That's all for now, Samuel. I will pour my husband's wine." She wanted to do this herself. She did not have the capability to poison the wine, but she would pour it, and watch Abílio drink it.

As Samuel left, Abílio looked up at her. "This behaviour is not becoming, Beatriz. All these lies about a phantom deed are making you even more unravelled than usual."

I saw that her hands trembled, and I tensed. Dona Beatriz tipped the bottle forward and poured, but the ruby liquid ran over the side of the glass and onto the white tablecloth.

"Give it to me," Abílio said crossly, and reached for the bottle.

In that instant, I knew what I must do. I rose and wrenched the bottle from Dona Beatriz's hand before Abílio could take it. I stepped backwards, lifting the bottle, and I smashed it against the edge of the marble side table. Dona Beatriz cried out as Abílio jumped up, looking at the rich burgundy liquid running down my skirt and pooling on the floor at my feet, and then at the jagged neck of the bottle I still held.

There was a moment of silence. "One of Kipling's better blends," Abílio said then, but his voice held the smallest note of alarm. "What a waste."

"You're not worth it," I said.

Dona Beatriz's mouth was open, shock and puzzlement on her face.

"Do you suppose I can't call for another bottle?" Abílio said. "This is simply a disgusting display of your true character, Diamantina."

I aimed the sharp edge of the broken bottle at the scar on his neck. "Just get out. Go to Oporto."

He shook his head, disbelieving. "You? Ordering me out of my own home?" He laughed, a strange, coarse sound. "You love to threaten, don't you, Diamantina? More proof of your low beginnings." He threw his napkin onto his plate. "I will leave the table, but not because of your ridiculous attempt at intimidation. I've lost my appetite. And so I bid you both good evening, ladies," he said, with an exaggerated bow first at me, then at Beatriz. "I will go to Oporto in the morning, and you will follow, as I told you, Beatriz."

"I'm not coming to Oporto, Abílio," Dona Beatriz said, her whole body shaking. "I'm going to Madeira."

"Fine. But you have nothing there."

When the door closed behind him, Dona Beatriz turned to me. "Why did you break the bottle?" she cried. "If you'd let me pour him the wine, he would have been out of my life—our lives—forever, Diamantina. We agreed. We want him dead. With all the good people who lost their lives in the *terremoto*, he should not have been spared." She sat down, staring at me. "You said you would help me. You said you would do as I asked."

I set the jagged bottle top on the table. I couldn't speak for a moment, and then I managed to say, "What you say about Abílio is true. But as you started to pour the wine, I thought of your father, and how Abílio had so easily ended his life with no thought but to further his own. And I . . . I don't want to think of myself as being of the same calibre. I would like to think I am a better person than Abílio."

The door swung open, and we both jumped. "There's just one more thing, Beatriz," Abílio said. "I really don't care what *you* do, but I will be coming back for my son. You won't know when it will happen, but I will take him." Then he came towards me, and leaned close. "And my daughter. I may decide to take my daughter as well."

When he had left again, I picked up a sharp knife from the table. "Take Leandro to your bedroom," I said. "I'll bring Candelária there, and we'll spend the night together." I put the knife to my waist, only to realize, as I did, that my silk frock did not have a waistband, but a delicate lilac ribbon.

CHAPTER EIGHTY-ONE

The night was long and restless. Even with Dona Beatriz's bedroom door firmly bolted, we both sat up at each small noise.

Candelária and I shared layers of feather-filled comforters on the thick carpet, and Leandro slept under a heavy satin cover beside his mother on the large and elegant bed. A golden rosary was draped on the headboard, and Dona Beatriz's embroidered silk slippers sat on the step that assisted in climbing onto the tall bed.

With weary relief, I watched the first weak light come through the long windows, festooned with curtains of crimson damask trimmed with rich lace. As I rose on one elbow, Candelária stirred, and Dona Beatriz roused Leandro.

When we all went downstairs, Samuel told us that Abílio had driven off earlier with two carriages piled with cases, and Dona Beatriz closed her eyes for a moment. She had Neves take the children to give them breakfast.

"Thank God he left without any more threats," she said to me when they were gone. "But you won't leave me yet, will you, Diamantina? I'd like you here when I face Plácido Lajes. And knowing Abílio may return at any time and try to take Leandro . . . I don't know how we'll stop him if he does, but . . ."

"I'll stay with you," I told her.

"My life . . ." she said, looking to one side. "I thought about it all night. Today it feels . . . as though it's over, in a way. I will never allow Abílio back into my life, but I will be tied to him forever.

Married but alone. I will be alone for the rest of my life, save Leandro, if I can protect him from being taken."

Was my situation not exactly the same? But it was not my time to speak of this.

The smell of the foliage outside the open windows wafted in, reminding me of the scents of the flowers surrounding the summer house. "There are things we can't know with complete certainty. There is sometimes the unexpected," I said.

⌒⌒⌒

Two days later, when the afternoon shadows were deepening across the garden, I sat with Neves and watched Candelária and Leandro play while Dona Beatriz rested in her room. Cristiano sat in a patch of sunshine and read.

I heard the ringing of the bell at the entrance, and went back into the house. Samuel was admitting Senhor Plácido Fernandez Lajes.

"Please ask Dona Beatriz to come downstairs. Tell her Senhor Lajes has arrived," I told Samuel.

As he left, Senhor Lajes looked at me in surprise. "You came to my house, the night before the earthquake," he stated. He had a deep, raw gash on one cheek, and his hands were wrapped in gauze.

"Yes. I told you I was a friend to Dona Beatriz."

"I now own this house, and I came to view it as soon as I could get away from Lisboa."

I nodded. "You were hurt in the earthquake?" I asked, gesturing at his bandaged hands.

"As many able-bodied men as possible were called upon to help find bodies and . . ." He stopped. "My injuries are from digging through the burning rubble. There's no telling how many are still buried beneath the ruins. And the looting has become rampant." I remembered the grisly grave robbers I'd passed. "The Marquês de Pombal has erected gallows, and is having looters hung as a deterrent to others."

"And those who survived?" I asked.

"They're carrying on with great difficulty. But every day more is being done. The Marquês de Pombal is very capable, and has already done so much to organize the city to assist the destitute and the injured. King José is lucky to have him as his Secretary of the Kingdom."

"So little news comes to us. What of the rest of Portugal?"

"Much of the western coast was damaged, and south, along the Algarve, the coastal towns and villages were flooded. The earthquake didn't affect only Portugal—it was felt across many countries. Parts of Spain and North Africa saw thousands dead."

"What of Madeira?" I held my breath, waiting for his answer.

"I've heard there was some damage from the shocks in villages closest to the ocean, and a bit of trouble in Funchal Town from high water, but on the whole it survived well. I'm relieved to know that Kipling's wasn't affected."

He looked over my shoulder, and I turned to see Dona Beatriz coming towards us. She held the scroll I remembered.

As she stopped beside me, I said, "Senhor Lajes. Allow me to introduce Dona Beatriz Duarte Kipling Perez."

Senhor Lajes half smiled at me, then at Dona Beatriz, as if he imagined himself the victim of a hoax. Then he stopped smiling and looked back at me.

"She is Abílio Perez's wife," I told him. "The woman you met was not."

"I don't understand."

"Please, Senhor Lajes," Dona Beatriz said, "let us go to the salon."

Once there, she extended her hand towards a settee. "I'm afraid I have bad news about Abílio. Sit, please. May I offer you something to drink?"

He shook his head. "No, thank you. I saw Abílio in Lisboa only a few days ago. He's been hurt since then?"

"Abílio is not injured. It's about your business transaction with him. As I said, please have a seat, Senhor Lajes."

He sat on the settee, and she sat across from him. I stood behind her. "This is the official deed to all of the Kipling holdings," she said, holding out the scroll. "It is signed and dated by my father,

Martyn Kipling, and authenticated by the legal counsel in Funchal. Abílio had no lawful right to sell anything. I'm afraid, Senhor Lajes, that my husband has played you for a fool."

The only sounds were the children's voices from the garden. Senhor Lajes's face first paled and then flushed. He took the scroll and unrolled it and read. When he had finished, he sat with the paper held loosely in one hand, and looked at her.

"The documents Abílio had you sign were forged, by him and by the woman he called his wife. The wine lodge and quinta and this house are still mine. Of course, you will wish to consult legal counsel. I'll be happy to be available for any discussion, and bring my own advisers as well."

Apart from the clenching of his jaw, Plácido Lajes hadn't stirred from the time he'd started to read the deed. Now he gave a small nod.

"Abílio came here a few days ago," Dona Beatriz said. "I told him about the deed—he was unaware of its existence—and I don't know whether he believed me or not. I refused to let him see it for fear he would destroy it. He informed me he was going to Oporto with his mistress, who is the woman you thought to be me. At least, that's where he originally intended to go. But he may stay in hiding for a while, fearing that I spoke the truth about the deed. I don't imagine he would want to face you." She put both hands on her cheeks to stop the twitching.

Senhor Lajes stood and handed the deed back to Beatriz. His chest rose and fell, and the flush had grown darker, extending down his neck. "If you think Abílio Perez will not be found, you are wrong. I have a great deal of power and influence, and have many men working for me. He will be found, and he will pay back what he's stolen from me. And more. His life may not be worth living when I'm done with him."

⌛

"It appears Senhor Lajes has accepted the truth," Dona Beatriz said once we were alone in the salon again. "Legal counsel will confirm the authenticity of the deed. I feel he will not fight me on anything. His fight will be with Abílio."

"I agree."

"And so all will be as before. I expect you to continue at Kipling's, and to live at the cottage."

"Even though I didn't do as you asked?"

She took a deep breath. "You were right to act as you did. The past is the past. I wish both our lives to move forward, and will deal with Abílio if and when I am forced to. I'll keep Leandro safe. And I don't believe Abílio is interested in Candelária. It was just a bluff."

I nodded.

"So you will continue to work with Espirito at the *adega*?" she asked.

"Espirito has left."

"He left? When?"

"Close to two months ago. Because Henry thought Kipling's sold, he hired Espirito to— Oh, there's so much you don't know yet, Dona Beatriz."

She shook her head. "Everything is in disarray. Espirito or Henry may have written while I was in Estoril, but I hadn't had a chance to attend to the months of correspondence here before the earthquake. I'm worried about Henry. You said you saw him in Lisboa the night before the earthquake. I can only hope . . ."

"I know," I said. "Soon we will be able to go into Lisboa and make inquiries."

We sat in silence for a few moments.

"If Espirito is gone, then you must take on the role of overseer at Kipling's," she said, "and hire on whoever you like to assist."

I sat straighter. "You would give me this responsibility?"

She tilted her head. "Why wouldn't I believe you could do it? I would do it myself if I felt more adept in the intricacies of wine-making. I think my father had long hoped I would one day step in to run the operation. And maybe I would have, had I not married. How different everything might have been if Abílio Perez hadn't come into my life."

"Or mine," I said, and we looked at each other, but then Leandro ran into the salon chasing Candelária, their playful shrieks filling the room.

"Yes. How different our lives might have been," Dona Beatriz said, and now we smiled as we watched our children. Neves followed, shushing them and trying to shoo them back outside.

"They can play here, Neves," Dona Beatriz said, and Neves nodded and stood by the door, her hands folded in front of her.

"Don't look, Mama," Leandro said, and Candelária echoed, "Yes, Mama, don't look. We're going to hide."

Dona Beatriz and I dutifully covered our eyes with our hands. There was rustling from the curtains, and tiny whispers and giggles.

"Look now!" Leandro called, and Dona Beatriz and I rose and exclaimed loudly as we searched the room for them.

Candelária's voice rose from behind a long, heavy satin curtain. "No! It's mine!" she shouted, and then scrambled out, swishing the curtain angrily.

I went to her. "Candelária, we are guests here. You must behave."

"I should have it," she insisted. "It's my papa's, not his."

Leandro hid something in his hands.

"May I see what you have, Leandro?" I asked as Dona Beatriz came over to us.

"I found it," he said, "so I should keep it." He opened his hands. Bonifacio's heavy pendant with a cross, bearing the sign of the Jesuit, lay on his palms.

"Papa wore it on the ship," Candelária said.

"He must have left it here," Dona Beatriz said.

I took it from Leandro's hand. "The leather thong is ripped. I suppose it could have dropped without him noticing."

Samuel entered and announced dinner. "Samuel—" I said, turning to him, dangling the emblem from my fingers, but stopped as his skin turned ashy.

He backed away, shaking his head. Neves stepped up to him and put her hand on his arm.

"What's wrong? What is it, Samuel?" Dona Beatriz asked.

"It's Father Bonifacio's. But I didn't see it," he said. "I didn't see it."

"What do you mean, Samuel?" she said, a little more sharply.

His chest heaved.

"Samuel," Neves said under her breath.

"Neves, take the children to the nursery and bathe them before dinner," Dona Beatriz said.

Neves looked at Samuel, concern on her face.

"Neves? Please take the children as I've asked," Dona Beatriz said.

"Leandro won't get to keep it, will he?" Candelária asked.

"That's enough, Candelária," I told her. "Go with Neves."

Once Neves and the children left, Dona Beatriz said, "Sit down, Samuel. You look ill."

The elderly man lowered himself onto the chair. "I knew it would be discovered. A sin such as this can never be hidden," he said, crossing himself.

"Tell us what happened," Dona Beatriz demanded.

CHAPTER EIGHTY-TWO

"**F**ather Bonifacio was here with the little girl, Senhorita Candelária," Samuel said.

"When he asked for the money," I said.

Samuel's lips were dry. "Yes. And Dom Abílio said to him, 'I don't owe you anything more than I owe any of those who work for me. You will be paid at the final sale of the company, not before.' But Father Bonifacio said, 'No, I need it now,' and again Dom Abílio refused. The Father said, 'I will go then, to Estoril, and tell your wife what you're doing.' They had talked about you, Dona Beatriz, when Father Bonifacio asked where you were and Dom Abílio told him you visited your aunt."

"Go on," Dona Beatriz said.

"Father Bonifacio spoke of a paper, a paper that said Dom Abílio would never be allowed to sell Kipling's. That it belonged to you, Dona Beatriz, and that the paper would stop Dom Abílio. Father Bonifacio then spoke of you, Senhora Rivaldo, of his wife Diamantina, and I didn't understand how a Father could have a wife. But he said that you told him about this paper.

"At this, Dom Abílio laughed, and said to the Father, 'You would believe anything your wife tells you?' And then he said . . ." Samuel stopped, looking at me. "I'm sorry, Senhora Rivaldo. I cannot repeat what Dom Abílio said about you. It made the Father very angry, and he denied the accusations about you. And then . . . I don't understand this part, Dona Beatriz. Dom Abílio took off his boots, and his stockings. I thought it must be because of his misery with the gout, but for him to remove his boots in the presence of a guest . . . a Father especially." Samuel raised his eyebrows. "And he didn't tell me to bring him the footbath. Instead, he showed his feet to Father Bonifacio."

Dona Beatriz was staring at Samuel, her face pale and fixed except for the twitch at the side of her mouth.

"What happened then, Samuel?" I asked.

"Dom Abílio said to the Father, 'Look at my feet and tell me you don't think your wife is . . .'" Again he stopped. "Once more he spoke harsh words about you, Senhora Rivaldo, and then he said to the Father, 'So now you know the truth.'

"Father Bonifacio grew even angrier. 'I thought she was my brother's child,' he kept saying. 'I accused my brother, and lost all those years with him,' the Father said. Then he again asked Dom Abílio for money, and when he was again refused, he said he would nevertheless go to you, Dona Beatriz, and tell you what Dom Abílio was doing."

Samuel ran his hand over his face. "And then the Father turned to leave." Samuel looked at a side table holding bottles and heavy crystal decanters. "Dom Abílio told him that he wouldn't allow him to go to you, Dona Beatriz, but the Father kept going towards the door, and Dom Abílio . . . struck him." Samuel swallowed and gestured at the decanters, filled with ruby and amber and mahogany spirits. "He struck him down," Samuel repeated, looking from Dona Beatriz to me. "A Jesuit Father," he finally said, in almost a whisper.

We sat in silence. And then Dona Beatriz said, "You must tell us what happened after that, Samuel."

Samuel's next sentences came out in a rush. "Father Bonifacio was on the floor, lying in the wine. He looked up at me, confused by the blow. He lifted one hand. 'Help me,' he said, and I went to him. But Dom Abílio shouted, 'No, leave him.'" Samuel took a white scrap of cloth from his pocket and touched his forehead, his upper lip, his neck. "And then . . . it becomes worse, Dona Beatriz, Senhora Rivaldo. I don't know how to tell you."

"It's all right," Dona Beatriz said softly.

Samuel clenched his fists and beat them lightly upon his thighs. "Dom Abílio went to Father Bonifacio, and . . . and pressed his bare foot onto his throat. Father Bonifacio put his hands around Dom Abílio's leg and tried to push him away, but he was already weak. There was so much blood spreading from under his head. I tried to pull Dom Abílio away. He still held the decanter, and he swung it at me, hitting me in the face."

I remembered meeting Samuel the first day I arrived. His swollen eye and bruised cheekbone.

"I fell. As I struggled to rise, Dom Abílio pressed, harder and harder, on Father Bonifacio's throat. I finally was able to stand, but Father Bonifacio's face was growing dark as he choked, and his tongue . . . The blood was still coming from the back of his head, making a puddle with the wine under him, and then . . . he lay still." Samuel's eyes were wet, and he continued to pound his own thighs as if trying to drive away the image in his head.

I saw it too, and heard Bonifacio, choking and gasping as he died, with Candelária outside in the garden.

And then there was a rustle of silk, and Dona Beatriz was at the window, her back straight as she stared at the greenery.

"Dom Abílio said he had to get rid of the little girl quickly, and would take her to the convent." Samuel wiped his eyes with the scrap of cloth. "The blood was there," he said, pointing at the carpet. "I cleaned it, but I know it's still there. I'll always know it's there. I stayed with Father . . . with the body of Father Bonifacio, until Dom Abílio returned from the convent. We left the salon, and he locked the door from the outside so none of the servants would come in, and when it was dark, and the other servants asleep, he came to get me. We wrapped Father Bonifacio in a blanket and together carried him out to the carriage house and put him in the small carriage. Dom Abílio told me to take the body to the Tagus and throw it in. I put a horse in the traces and wrapped burlap around its feet, so as not to make any noise as I left the carriage house. Then I went, slowly and quietly, to the river." He rubbed his face with trembling fingers.

"But I couldn't do it. I couldn't throw him into the water. If I were to do that, I would be part of this crime of taking the life of not only a man, but a priest. And I am a servant of Christ," he said, crossing himself. "And so I took him to the side steps of the Mosteiro dos Jerónimos, and left him there, so that he would have a burial proper for a Jesuit Father. I couldn't bear to think of this man—a man of God—with no proper resting place. I knew the good Fathers at Mosteiro dos Jerónimos would care for him properly when they saw by his robe that he was a Jesuit."

Dona Beatriz still hadn't turned from the window.

"I worked all my life for your mother's family, Dona Beatriz, and then I tried to carry out my duties for Dom Abílio. But I couldn't do what he asked that night."

Finally, Dona Beatriz turned and faced him. "Samuel. You did what you could. You tried to stop Abílio. And it was right to take Bonifacio to the church."

Samuel looked at me. "I'm sorry, Senhora Rivaldo," he said, lowering his head.

Dona Beatriz came to me. "Diamantina," she said. Her face, in spite of its jerking dance, was soft with sympathy. "I'm sorry as well, truly sorry for what Abílio did to Bonifacio. I'm so, so sorry that because of Abílio, Bonifacio died alone, in such a terrible way, far from his home." She put her arms around me then. "We have both lost our husbands."

⁂

I left Dona Beatriz in the salon and went to Cristiano's bedroom. I sat beside him and said that Bonifacio had unexpectedly met tragedy before he could leave for Brazil.

"Tragedy?" he repeated, and when I nodded, he said, "He's dead?"

I looked into his face. "Yes." How much to tell him—and to what end? In spite of his harsh feelings for Bonifacio, I didn't want Cristiano to think of Bonifacio dying in such a horrible manner. But Cristiano didn't ask me what happened. "Can we still live at Quinta Isabella?" he asked.

"I think so," I told him. "Don't worry about that now."

We sat in silence for a while, and then I went to Candelária, playing with her doll on the bed. I put Bonifacio's pendant into her hands. "Candelária," I said. "Papa went to God."

She stared at me. "Not to Brazil?"

"He's with God, in Heaven," I said, then held my breath, waiting for her, as I had waited with Cristiano, to ask what had happened to him. But they had both seen so much death now.

She traced the starry sun with her fingertips. "Is Papa happy?" she whispered.

"I'm sure he's happy."

She nodded. "He always wanted to be with God. And he was good, so he will be in God's Kingdom," she stated, and wiped her nose with the back of her hand.

"Yes," I said. "He only wanted to be with God, and now he is."

⁂

The next morning was bright, the wind off the Tagus brisk, when Dona Beatriz, Cristiano, Candelária and I went to Mosteiro dos Jerónimos.

I left Candelária with Cristiano in the nave, and sought out the Monsignor. I spoke to him about the body of a Jesuit being left on the steps in the weeks preceding the earthquake.

"Yes. We did discover the body of a Jesuit Father on our steps. You are his family?" the man asked.

"Yes," I said. "He was Father Bonifacio Rivaldo, a former missionary in Brazil. We have only now heard of his death, and that he was left here by . . . a friend."

"I offer my deepest sympathy," the Monsignor said. "There was no way to identify him, apart from his Jesuit robe. Because of his order, we arranged to have him taken to Igreja de São Roque, in Lisboa, to be interred. He was treated with great respect," he added.

"São Roque is very lovely. It's the oldest Jesuit church in Portugal," Dona Beatriz said, squeezing my hand.

"I'm sorry to say that I haven't yet heard if the church withstood the earthquake," the Monsignor said. "I could dedicate a funeral Mass to Father Bonifacio here, if that would be of comfort."

When I nodded, he said, "I will arrange it."

As the four of us walked out of the church, we passed the mural at the front of the monastery. As a former sailors' church, there were many engravings of sea life—sailing ships and anchors, patterns of knotted ropes, fish and sirens.

Candelária stopped in front of a *sereia* with long flowing hair and swishing tail, lips curved up in a smile. "This is a picture of Avó Shada," she said, tracing the mermaid's outline with her fingertips. I realized it was the depiction Candelária had repeatedly drawn in the earth when I put up the headstone for my mother, the image my mother had drawn on her own body: the forked tail and waves.

Was this my mother's story, then, her myth? That she had become a mermaid when thrown from the Algerian ship, and washed up on the shores of Porto Santo, losing her tail to earthly legs? That she hadn't wanted to go back into the water before she was ready to return to the depths whence she had come?

Candelária looked up at me with her shining dark eyes. "It looks like Avó Shada swimming in the water. She likes it there," she added, and then kissed her fingertips and touched them to the long-haired siren, and we walked from the church, into the crisp, fresh-smelling November air.

EPILOGUE

Porto Santo
Ten Years Later
1765

The sweet smell of laurel and tamarisk filled the air as Candelária
added more branches to the fire.

My daughter was past fourteen, and a woman now. We had come
alone to Porto Santo, although Espirito had offered to sail with us
from Funchal.

As dusk fell, we walked down the beach to Ponta da Calheta,
where my hut had once stood. Later we would return to Vila Baleira
and spend the night with Rooi and Palma. Rooi was losing his sight
and becoming forgetful, but when we stepped into the inn earlier
in the day, he spread his arms in welcome and reminded all that I am
the Dutchman's daughter. He charmed Candelária with stories of
his long-ago life in Nederland, tales of snow and ice and skating on
the canals, as my father had once charmed me.

Now the bonfire was high and bright. Barefoot, Candelária and I
walked around it three times. I had always told her that when the
time was right, I would bring her back to the place I grew up to
mark her, as she had long begged, as my mother had marked me. I
consented to three small images, and brought a small pot of powdered antimony and another of indigo, and a fine, sharp needle.

"I want the mermaid symbol for your mother, and the vines for
you," she said.

"And what mark do you choose for yourself, Candelária?"

"This," she said, and with a stick, drew what looked to be a
feather surrounded by stars into the sand. I didn't ask her what it
meant; it was hers to know. "Look at the moon," she said now,

pointing at the rising orb above the water's horizon. "It seems even brighter here than from the quinta."

I watched the moon, knowing that its light shone through the cottage bedroom window onto Espirito and our son—Arie Vitorino Rivaldo—the little boy born to us as though a miracle only a few years ago.

I thought of the moon shining into one of the small servant homes at Quinta Isabella, where Cristiano and his new wife lived. I saw it glow into the gracious rooms of Eduardo and Luzia, who were Avô and Avó to our son as they were to Candelária.

When word had come, six years ago, that Abílio Perez had died in Oporto, ravaged by syphilis, Dona Beatriz and Henry married, and formally merged their families and their businesses into Kipling and Duncan. Now they spent their time between Lisboa and Quinta Isabella, with Leandro, at fifteen, working alongside Henry in preparation for one day carrying on the Madeira enterprise.

At the time of the merger of the wine lodges, Espirito and I had gone to Dona Beatriz and Henry and offered to buy the second Kipling *adega*. "We will pay what we can now," I'd said, "and work to pay off the rest."

Dona Beatriz and Henry accepted the offer, and Henry added, with a laugh, "With you and Espirito and Cristiano all working there now, you may as well rename it Rivaldo's Wine Merchants."

We did.

A wave washed over my feet, and I looked away from the moon and at my daughter. "This is where my mother found my father."

"Right here?"

"At first she thought him a dead pirate."

"Could he have been a pirate?" Candelária's voice rose in excitement. "Maybe he— "

"No, you know he was a sailor," I said, smiling, "thrown from his ship and miraculously surviving. But I've never told you that when he opened his eyes and saw my mother, he thought he had died, and she was an angel." Another wave broke over our ankles, wetting our skirts. "I always liked that part of the story." The moon was reflecting in my daughter's eyes, and I felt my mother's presence. "And you know how she came to this beach, weaving through the water to the shore like a mermaid."

She smiled back at me. "That's my favourite part of the story."

I took her hand. "My parents were both gifts from the sea."

She nodded. "Make my marks now, Mama. It's long past my time," she said, pulling on my hand, and together we walked back to the fire, the flames pulsing into the warm night air as they whispered the memories of my mother's past, and the secrets of my daughter's future.

ACKNOWLEDGEMENTS

Part of the challenge—and excitement—in writing fiction inspired by history is bringing the place and time alive in the pages so readers become immersed. Many people provided insight and guidance in furthering my understanding of life in Portugal and the Madeira Archipelago over two hundred and fifty years ago. Any errors are mine.

My thanks to the people of Porto Santo for your welcome and your openmindedness concerning the characters I created who might have lived on your island. On Madeira, thank you to the city of Funchal, with your fascinating chronicles of sea exploration and wine production. The knowledgeable guides at the Blandy Wine Lodge helped me envision the scenes for Kipling's wine lodge. On mainland Portugal, thank you to Rui Carvalho at Vinihold in Vila Nova de Gaia for sharing your expertise on winemaking.

And thank you Lisbon, glorious Lisbon, for your passionate history and for nights of *fado*. Uncovering the stories of Lisbon's 1755 earthquake and tsunami furthered my desire to write about this era.

My gratitude also goes to Albino Silva of Toronto for the use of your home in Ferragudo in the Algarve of Portugal. The first startling images for Diamantina's story came into my mind as I stood on the windswept, most southwestern point of land at Cabo de San Vincente near Sagres.

Both inspiration and special insights came from *Madeira, the Island Vineyard* by Noel Cossart; *The Blandys of Madeira* by Marcus Binney; *Madeira: Of Islands and Women* by Susanna Hoe; Jose

Saramago's *Baltasar and Blimunda*; *The Madness of Queen Maria* by Jennifer Roberts; *Letters of a Portuguese Nun* by Myriam Cyr; and *Chica da Silva: A Brazilian Slave of the Eighteenth Century* by Júnia Ferreira Furtado. I was enlightened by travelogues and old photos found in bookstores and museums in Lisbon and Belém, as well as in the Christopher Columbus Museum in Vila Baleira on Porto Santo. On Madeira, the Madeira Ethnographic Museum in Ribeira Brava and the Madeira Story Centre in Funchal were huge sources of information that helped me understand and visualize life in Funchal and in the island's villages and quintas in the eighteenth century.

Thank you to my agent, Sarah Heller, for your support and encouragement. Thanks also to Camilla Ferrier and Jemma McDonagh at the Marsh Agency in London for ushering my work into the wider world.

I owe a huge debt of gratitude to Anne Collins, for her generosity and meticulous attention to detail in gently guiding this story onto the right paths. My appreciation also goes to the book's copy editor, John Sweet; its brilliant designer, Terri Nimmo; its managing editor, Deirdre Molina; Michelle Roper, whose help chasing images was invaluable; my publicist, Shona Cook; and the rest of the team at Random House Canada, for their many and varied contributions.

As always, a huge thank you to my dear extended family and my understanding friends, for bearing with me during the writing times, tolerating and forgiving my silences and absences.

Special loving thanks to Marty for accompanying me to Portugal and the Madeira Archipelago on my two research trips, and for always encouraging me to go one step further when I think I've reached my limit. Your unflagging belief in me and your own inspiring knowledge and wisdom in the world of creation and imagination during our daily "story time" provided endless motivation and moral support over the writing of this book.

And, of course, I thank my children with all my heart. Zalie, Brenna and Kitt, you provide me with unwavering encouragement not only in my writing life but in all aspects of my world, and you continue to amaze and inspire me with your own richly challenging and diverse lives.

LINDA HOLEMAN is the author of *The Lost Souls of Angelkov*, as well as the internationally bestselling historical novels *The Linnet Bird*, *The Moonlit Cage*, *In a Far Country* and *The Saffron Gate*, and eight other works of fiction and short fiction. Her books have been translated into eighteen languages. A world traveller, she grew up in Winnipeg, and now lives in Toronto and Santa Monica, California.